OFF BROADWAY

Garbhan Downey

First published in June 2005

Guildhall Press, Unit 15, Ráth Mór Centre,
Bligh's Lane, Derry BT48 0LZ
T: (028) 7136 4413 F: (028) 7137 2949
info@ghpress.com www.ghpress.com

Cover image courtesy of John McCloskey

ISBN 0 946451 86 9

A CIP record of this book is available from the British Library

We gratefully acknowledge the financial support of the Arts Council of
Northern Ireland under its Multi-Annual Lottery Programme.

This project is supported by the European Union, administered by the Local
Strategy Partnership for the Derry City Council Area.

EU Programme
for Peace and Reconciliation
in Northern Ireland and the Border Regions of Ireland

LOCAL STRATEGY PARTNERSHIP
DERRY CITY COUNCIL AREA

arts
council
of Northern Ireland
LOTTERY FUNDED

Contents

To Fiachra and Brónagh

About the Author

Garbhan Downey cut his journalistic teeth editing University College Galway's student magazine in the late 1980s. He followed this with stints as a columnist for the *Derry Journal* and as a staff reporter with the *Londonderry Sentinel*, before moving to the *Irish News* to become the paper's Derry correspondent. His offbeat reports of the 1994 World Cup for the *IN* were subsequently published in the book *Just One Big Party*.

Downey then spent several years with the BBC in Derry and Belfast, and co-wrote the local history book *Creggan: More Than a History* with Michael McGuinness, before completing a three-year stint as editor of the *Derry News* in 2004. Since then, he has written two works of fiction, *Private Diary of a Suspended MLA* and *Off Broadway*, and is currently completing a novel.

Downey is married to Una, has two children and still kids himself he could pursue an alternative career in indoor football.

Previous Books by the Author

Just One Big Party: A Fan's-Eye View of the 1994 World Cup, Forum Books, 1994

Creggan: More Than A History (With Michael McGuinness), Guildhall Press, 2000

Private Diary of a Suspended MLA, Stormount Books, 2004

Foreword

Let's start with the title. In the ten years or so I spent visiting and revisiting these stories, *Off Broadway* was always the front-runner. Mostly.

You'll realise pretty early on that the American humorist Damon Runyon was a hefty influence. Yes indeed and more than somewhat. So, given that Runyon's 1930s book about New York wiseguys, crooks and other assorted characters who talk out of the side of their mouths was entitled *On Broadway*, I figured the twenty-first-century Derry reprise should preserve the link. And, as a couple of the stories are set just off Creggan Broadway, it would have been churlish of me not to tip my hat.

Then about a year ago, I took the complete head-staggers and changed the title to *The Cure for Bad Breath*. It's catchy, I thought. Quite clever, even. I could see it on the Best-Sellers list. So this is how I presented it to the publisher – who immediately threw me, and it, out point blank. Everyone, and I quote, will think it's an expleting 'How To' manual. Except he did not say expleting. So, I was eventually re-affirmed in my original opinion, and *Off Broadway* it remains. Though anyone who truly loves Runyon should stop reading now, as at this point all similarities bite the carpet.

So my particular gratitude to Paul Hippsley of Guildhall Press for his meticulous steerage of this book and his brutal honesty about what is and is not a good idea. Many thanks also to editors Declan Carlin, Gerry Downey and Michael O'Hanlon for attempting to put grammatical, stylistic and sequential order on this decade-long venture, and to John McCloskey for another outstanding cover. Not forgetting, of course, designer Joe McAllister, who is about to discover that there is no greater privilege in life than being married to a Monaghan woman. A special mention also to my mother Aine, who at crucial stages rescued me and my sanity from barking children and hungry dogs.

Finally, can I just dedicate this book to Fiachra and Brónagh, with the advice that, if you ever meet anyone who remotely resembles any of the characters in this book – run a mile. It's too late for Una and me.

A CHRISTMAS CAROL

A rich man's joke is always funny – even if Sparkly does tell it at every Christmas party since the Three Wise Men are dumb and ignorant.

"These two polar bears," he says, "a Daddy one and a baby, are standing at the North Pole, when the little one asks, 'Hey, Pop, am I really a polar bear?'

"'Course you are,' says Pop.

"'Are you sure?' says Junior.

"'Sure I'm sure,' says Pop – though he has lingering doubts about Offspring's purity of lineage, given that Mrs Bear has more callers than a taxi on a wet night.

"'Are you absolutely, positively sure?' persists Junior.

"'Absolutely and positively – and even definitely,' says Pop, 'but why do you keep asking?'

"'Well, it's like this, Pop,' says Junior. 'I'm feckin' freezing.'"

*****

We all laugh – Shakes, myself and Sparkly.

Dessie 'Sparkly' Barkley, our host, makes some of his many crusts selling bottom-of-the-range cigarette lighters and what is passed off as Ladies' Toilet Water to the hawkers who operate under Derry's Walls.

Once a year, to show what type of guy he is, Sparkly throws a no-expense-spared bash for his clients. Two complimentary glasses of sparkling wine, free crisps, sausage rolls, Battenburg – you name it, Sparkly lays it on. And today, we are at Sparkly's own up-market American theme bar, The Jack Kennedy Inn, which he has given over no expense spared for the occasion.

I am here as guest of Charlie 'Shakes' Coyle, former street drunk and passer-by frightener extraordinaire who is, for two years now, dried out and selling lighters three for a pound under Castle Gate. Shakes, in keeping with the festivities, is decked out in the traders' seasonal uniform – red Santa suit, cotton-wool beard and Noddy cap.

The reason for Shakes's conversion to One Day At A Time, you will recall, is that Mrs Shakes ups and dumps him for a runaway priest she meets at an Al-Anon meeting. Indeed, Mrs S stops only long enough to leave their eight-year-old daughter, Dear Little Kylie, in Barkley's Off-Licence, the one place she is sure Shakes will find her.

Dear Little Kylie is the apple of Shakes's blurred eye. And he knows that if he continues in his present career, she will be stuck in a shelter run by single men in their fifties, about whom we will say no more as cases are still pending. So Shakes forswears the bottle on the spot. And six weeks of One Day At A Timing later, he returns to Barkley's Off-Licence to ask Sparkly to set him up as managing director of his own market stall.

Sparkly, of course, is only too happy to help out an old friend and, no expense spared, gives Shakes a start-up loan. Sparkly doesn't even look for a guarantor, though when your closest pal is Harry 'the Hurler' Hurley, Chief Executive of the Civil Defenders, collection is rarely an issue.

Shakes takes to the lighter-selling business like a man reborn. He works night and day, day and night, only ever leaving his patch to go home to Dear Little Kylie. Business is so good that within a year, Shakes pays off the twelfth and final £500 instalment on his three-grand loan.

Surprisingly, Shakes's brain remains remarkably unpickled by the years of heavy drinking and he works out all sorts of dodges to stay one step ahead of the lighter-selling pack. By keeping an eye on the tabloid press, Shakes discerns whichever stars are flavour of the month and then gets his cousin to stencil their images onto his wares. This costs him five pence a time but lets him hike his prices by fifty.

Dear Little Kylie helps out on the stall at the weekend and, as she says herself, is proving a chip off the old blocked. For Kylie, it must be said, has a patter that can sell lighters to lung surgeons.

Moreover, despite her tender years, Kylie is not a lady upon whom very many flies will land, as those of you who do business with her know well. One day, it is reported, two young hoods decide to rob her while Shakes is on a break. They put their hands in their pockets like they have guns and demand all the takings. But quick as you can blink, Kylie tosses a cup of lighter fluid over them and then offers them a three-second start before she tests some new flame adjusters.

"Indeed," says Shakes when Sparkly shoots off to fetch another round of cocktail sausages, "things are starting to look up for myself and Dear Little Kylie. We are going to open up our own specialised shop in the new year. There's a guy up in Belfast who can sell me lighters at half what Sparkly does. He's the guy that Sparkly buys off – but he tells me he's all for free trade. So I buy five grand of stock off him yesterday – to arrive later today.

"Then this morning, I put down a two-G deposit on a little shop and storeroom at the top of Waterloo Street. It's all my savings but I'll make it back in a couple of months. It'll be a little competition for Sparkly, but as a fellow businessman, I'm sure he'll understand."

I am not so sure – though do not say so. Sparkly, for all his free sausage rolls, is a thief in a suit with a heart like a rotten apple.

Out of the crowd, another Santa suit veers towards us. And who is underneath it but Shakes's old pal and fellow stall-holder Lily 'Rusty' Gillespie. In a previous life, it is alleged that Rusty earns her living as a singer with a jazz band, before too many early-morning gin parties take their toll. But now, like Shakes, she is taking each day at a time.

Rusty herself, even Saved and sober, is unaware of the damage the gin does to her pipes. Indeed, between ourselves, she gets her name not from her dark red hair as she will tell you, but because it is commonly advised that her singing is deadlier than a rusty nail. Indeed, I personally know of several slaughterhouses which are more tuneful.

Nowadays, she generally confines her performances to her earrings' and joss-sticks' stall. If the weather's right, you'll hear a version of *Summertime*, which will bring tears to the eyes of any music lover. And in the winter, her version of *Have Yourself a Merry Little Christmas* has to be heard to be believed.

No singing today, however, as Rusty, unlike her old supping-buddy Shakes, is in bad old form. It seems that Danny Boy Gillespie, her number one son and heir, is this morning awarded a two-year sabbatical at St Mildred's Shelter and Young Offenders Centre after he is photographed close to a Civil Defenders' protest rally with a bottle in his hand. Danny Boy, who's seventeen and still a bit wet, argues it's Coca Cola. But six police witnesses and a resident magistrate agree that it identically resembles a lighted petrol bomb.

"I'm a good mother, I warn him all the time," weeps Rusty, wiping her nose on the piping on her sleeve.

"Yes, yes, there, there," says Shakes, patting her shoulder. But she only becomes more distressed.

"I warn him all the time," she cries, her shoulders starting to go.

"Terrible, terrible," murmurs Shakes sympathetically and puts a protective arm around her. But it is no use.

"I warn him all the time," she sobs wildly. "Always wear your bloody mask, you stupid fool!"

Shakes, who for a one-time passer-by-frightener is a very gentle soul, eventually settles Rusty with a chorus of 'Don't worrys' and 'He'll soon be homes'. And before long, she is smiling up at him and giving it the My Knight In Shining Armour eyes.

Thinking this is a convenient moment to hit the circuit, I drift over for a natter with Getemup Gormley. Getemup, I learn, is leaving behind the business of waving replica guns in bank clerks' faces to the altogether more profitable dodge of flogging them to youngsters on Union Hall Street.

Within minutes, however, our chat is interrupted by some loud yelling from the direction of Shakes and Rusty who, strangely, seem to be loudly questioning Sparkly Barkley's parentage. Then, all of a sudden, two Barkleyguard security men are banging Shakes's head off the corner of the door on his way out of the building.

Rusty tries to intervene, and succeeds in landing Sparkly a particularly fine blow just below the money belt, before she too is dumped out into the back lane with yesterday's rubbish.

*****

It is one year and one week later before I see Shakes again. It is a freezing Christmas Eve morning and he is sleeping in a doorway on Waterloo Place, legs showered with snow and an empty Buckfast bottle in his hand. He is in poor fettle. He has no coat, and his ragged jacket and trousers are splattered in blood and grime. The drink-sweat on his blistered brow is frosting over, and his nose is the colour of a melted Union Jack.

I manage to rouse him and pull him up onto an iron bench, which is quickly vacated. He tells me that I am his best friend in all the world, and that he wants me to take him on the bus to see Dear Little Kylie. Kylie, as you know, is in St Mildred's Shelter in Belfast for ten months now after the gendarmes spot Shakes back scaring city-centre pedestrians.

Like yourself, I hear bits and pieces about Shakes's fall from grace – how he loses the shop deal, his Belfast connection and even his trader's licence, and then goes back to hitting the syrup harder than ever before.

So I agree to listen to the full story, if he will only let me oxter him back to his flat in Sackville Court and hose him down a little.

"It all dates back to that party last year," he tells me, in between me ducking his head under the cold tap.

"That motherless dog Sparkly Barkley knows all along I intend to branch out and is just waiting to put a pin in me. When I tell him at the party that I am setting up shop, he just laughs and laughs at me like I am an idiot child. 'You big dummy, you big dummy,' he keeps saying.

"When he finally settles himself, he says that both the dealer in Belfast that I give five grand to for supplies and the guy I buy the shop from are his stooges. And that I am now seven Gs lighter than when I walk in the door.

"I tell him that's against the law. But he just laughs again and says, 'The magistrate might take a dim view of Dear Little Kylie if he hears she is selling fancy Ladies' Toilet Water which Knuckles Doherty is nicking to order for her.' He then declares that his good wife is terribly distressed to learn the Chanel Numero Cinq she purchases from Dear Little Kylie is stolen goods. And Mrs B, it seems, is now actively considering doing her civic duty by revealing this to the peelers – good job she keeps the bottle."

"What is Kylie doing with lowlifes like Knuckles?" I interrupt. "And anyway, isn't he supposed to be out of commission? Word is the Civil Defenders are after busting his fingers in the Advice Centre door for filching three kegs from The Jack Kennedy."

"Children grow up so fast these days," explains Shakes, tutting indulgently. "You can't watch them all the time. So Sparkly leaves me a choice: either I lose the business or I lose Dear Little Kylie. But I, being smart, lose both."

Shakes then starts to sniff and before long he is off again, crying like Knuckles when he hears he's for the Advice Centre door.

After a while, I quieten him down by reminding him that we're going to see Dear Little Kylie. Shakes even agrees to hoke out a fresh shirt, but this proves to be an unreasonable demand, the only clean vestments in the flat being a red Santa suit, a cotton-wool beard and a Noddy hat.

No-one comments much on Shakes's attire when we finally get on the Belfast Flier at Foyle Street, but only because there is already another passenger on the bus similarly bedecked. And most likely, people think there is a last-minute Santa convention being held in the Big Smoke. The other Father Christmas on board, it transpires, is none other than Rusty Gillespie, also en route to St Mildred's to visit her son, Danny Boy, who's still in the

Secure Wing. Rusty, you'll remember, is allowed to hold on to her stall, despite her bopping of Sparkly – and only has to pay him compensation totalling twenty per cent of her gross profits for the next five years.

Our seventy-five-mile journey passes off peacefully, apart from a minor incident at Castledawson when a departing passenger of no apparent scruples entices Rusty to sing a few bars of *Little Drummer Boy*. But happily, we manage to persuade her to save her voice as a treat for Danny Boy before the driver makes good his threat to turn the bus round and go back to Derry.

We get to Belfast and I hail a Black Hack to take the three of us to Mildred's. At the Centre, I wait outside, chewing the fat with the driver, while Shakes and Rusty shuffle inside to pay their seasonal respects.

About an hour later they reappear together. And judging by Shakes's straight back and broad smiles, he is a lot happier than when he goes in.

"Dear Little Kylie is so excited to see me that she nearly knocks me over," laughs Shakes. "She tells me that the home isn't so bad and the nuns are very good to her – even if they do shut down her bedroom stall after an Elvis lighter explodes in Father Carlin's trouser pocket. Though he is likely to make a full recovery and need only minor surgery.

"Kylie also says she is very glad to be getting my weekly letters telling her how well I'm doing. And while I immediately suspect that someone else must be penning these – given that I am barely able to shake out an X on my Giro these days – I play along."

Rusty blushes a little, but Shakes just smiles.

"Anyway," he says, "I am just about to leave when I realise I have no present for her. 'Whatever you want in the world,' I promise her, 'I will bring it for you on my next visit.' But she just smiles and tells me she is so proud that I am off the syrup for three months now. And all she asks is that I stay off it for good and take her back home."

I cough, a little embarrassed at this surprise revelation, and Rusty's face lights up like a Sacred Heart Lamp. But Shakes is unbothered.

"So," he continues, "I have a word with Sister Assumpta on the way out, and she tells me that as soon as I can produce a valid One Day At A Time certificate, I can have Dear Little Kylie back."

Sister A, you'll gather, knows well that Shakes is not with the programme just yet. For despite my best efforts and those of Mr and Mrs Minty-Mouth Mouthwash, there is still an unmistakable odour of twelve months' street drinking off his general environs. But she is a kind old doll and wants to give some Christmas hope to Dear Little Kylie – who is blind to the hum.

We pile back into the Black Hack – Rusty and Shakes on the back seat and me in the front – and get back to the station at Glengall Street. There, Shakes hits on the idea of celebrating our day out with a few cigars. And he buys a pack of King Edwards out of the ten-spot Sister A slips into his pocket.

The inspector, however, tells us we are not allowed to smoke in the bus, not even celebration cigars, so we save them for when we dismount in Derry. And as soon as we arrive at Foyle Street, we stop a passer-by and ask him for a light.

But who is it only Sparkly Barkley, as drunk as three houses. Moreover, he is so juiced up that he has no idea who we are, though this is not altogether surprising given that two of us are Father Christmas.

"Shure you can have a light," he laughs, the gold from his rings and bracelets shining in the flame he holds to Shakes's cigar.

"In fact, you can keep the lighter – no expenshe shpared for a good pal like you, Shanta. I have more of them than I know what to do with, thanks to a shtupid old wino who's gonna be a big shot. I think he's dead now. If not he should be – way he lets down his little girl."

Sparkly then laughs so hard at his own wit and goes so red in the face that I think he is going to have a stroke. But God is a rich man who looks after his own. And Sparkly recovers to stagger along happily to the Guildhall, leaving a trail of broken hearts in his wake for the second Christmas in succession.

*****

Now, given that this is real life and not a storybook, I do not expect it to be too long before I am picking my old chum Shakes out of doorways again. Though remarkably, this is not the case. Indeed, he drops off the radar altogether – and whatever other occupations Shakes is pursuing, he is not presently passer-by frightening.

Then, one full year after I leave him crying his sad heart out on Rusty's shoulder at the bus station, Shakes calls into The Jack Kennedy on Christmas Eve to wish me season's greetings.

I have rarely seen a guy so changed. His stride is the stride of a guy with a big pile of folding money. And his suit alone would break the back of five hundred clams.

He sits down on the empty stool next to me, so allowing me to order another drink. But he shakes his head no when I ask him will he join me.

"Do not worry," he laughs, "I will not be preachy. And I will not try and save you too, even though by your demeanour and attire I see you are a man who should consider a little One Day At A Timing.

"Myself, I am now not drinking exactly one year, ever since the day we meet up round the corner in Waterloo Place. I am tempted now and again, of course. But now I have my dear little wife and daughter to think about. And, of course, my new stepson. I am also so busy with the business that I have no time to waste shooting the breeze with deadbeats in gin palaces, present company excepted."

"Good job you're not being preachy," I counter, a little miffed at my attire being one-lined by a guy who is wearing a cotton-wool beard the last time I see him.

"I am sorry," he says. "But it is hard sometimes not to spread the Good News. Ever since our last meeting, God in his grace is smiling down on me. Though I must admit that much of my good fortune is due to a dramatic conversion by another sinner who sees the light. But that is also God's influence, and I don't doubt it."

Shakes then tells me a tale which I would not believe if it is served up to me on the front page of the *Derry Standard* with a marker from both bishops.

It appears, says Shakes, that the very Christmas night after we meet him at the bus station, Sparkly is badly smashed up in a car crash. And while he is lying in a coma, he sees this vision, who tells him what a bad guy he is being to Shakes and that he must not die with this on his conscience. So immediately after Sparkly comes round, he summons Shakes to his private hospital room at Ballykelly.

When Shakes arrives, Sparkly takes his hand with tears in his eyes and says to him, "Charles" – for that is Shakes's real name – "I am truly sorry for all the pain I cause you and Dear Little Kylie. Please accept my sincerest apologies, and if there is anything I can ever do for you, anybody giving you bother, you can call me, any time."

He then hands Shakes a little packet. "I now realise, thanks to my near-death experience, the error of my bad old ways," he says, "and I wish to make amends with you. This parcel contains the seven Gs I liberate from you, along with ten more for good faith.

"I am instructing my supplier in Belfast to sell you his stuff at the same rate he gives it to me. You can also take the two thousand lighters I have in the store behind The Jack Kennedy. But avoid the Elvis ones, as some dollar-an-hour flunky in the Taiwan plant hates him and they tend to go bang in the pocket for no reason."

Well, of course, Shakes is overcome. The two men hug one another, cry a lot and praise the Lord for their good fortune.

"This is the turning point in my life," Shakes tells me. "Not only do I get my fortune back, but more importantly, I now know there is hope for us all when a thoroughly rotten sinner like Sparkly Barkley can see the light. And from that night to this, every day is better and better.

"Within three months, Dear Little Kylie is out of St Mildred's. We immediately get a new shop on Waterloo Street. And in July, Rusty Gillespie consents to become my bride. Rusty's son, Danny Boy, even gets out of Mildred's Secure Wing a couple of days early for the event. And Sparkly, God be ever good to him, fixes Danny up with a job here in The Jack Kennedy, which so far keeps him out of trouble.

"It is exactly as if Sparkly is visited by the Christmas spirits and resolves to change his entire life for the good."

And with that, Shakes, who is a busy man and has no time to waste shooting the breeze with deadbeats in gin palaces, excuses himself and heads back to his shop for closing hour.

*****

I sit alone for a while on my high stool, mulling over whether I should have another stout on my own or also enlist on the programme. But when I look up, as if by magic I see a full glass sitting on the counter in front of me. And who is standing grinning behind it but the new bar-hand, Danny Boy Gillespie.

"Praise the Lord," he says, winking the wink of a total rapscallion.

"Season's blessings to you too," I grin, tipping the glass Thank You in his direction. "So are you enjoying your first Christmas at large for quite a while?"

"Well, yes," he replies, a little coyly. "But it's not entirely my first at large for quite a while."

"But last year, you are in Mildred's Secure Wing," I remind him.

"Not entirely," he answers, still holding back.

"Do enlighten me," I say.

"Strictly between ourselves," he whispers, looking over his shoulder for dramatic effect, "when Old Ma Rusty visits me last Christmas Eve, I become terribly homesick and sentimental. Particularly when she sings *The Town I Loved So Well*. For there is no-one who can sing a sad song with more feeling than Old Ma.

"So after she leaves, I am feeling very low indeed. And on Christmas Day, I decide that I must go home to Derry to see all the Christmas lights and decorations and nippers playing on their new bikes. And when Father Carlin, who's looking after the Secure Wing, is sleeping off his Crème de Menthe, I take his keys, let myself out and borrow his Merc . . ."

"Isn't that place like Fort Knox?" I interrupt.

"No, no," says Danny, "there are so many comings and goings that no-one knows who is who. People skip out all the time. It is as easy as falling in love with the wrong girl.

"Anyhow, I get into the Merc and don't stop until I reach the new garage outside Dungiven, where I pull in for some smokes. As I'm about to get back into the car, this guy on the forecourt takes one look at me, sees what I'm driving and says, 'Son, while I am not a man to give advice, I feel it might benefit you to know that the gendarmes are hosting road blocks a couple of miles out of here on the main Derry road. And again, while I am not a man to jump to conclusions, I feel that they could extend your journey home by several months.'

"I thank the guy politely and agree that under the circumstances it might be best to go into the city via the Claudy back road. So I take the next turn left.

"But here is the point," says Danny, lowering his voice. "And you must not reveal this to anyone – particularly my mother and new father.

"I am about five miles along the back road and am thinking that I am getting lost when, all of a sudden, I hit this patch of ice and start to career all over the place. I skid for about fifty feet, before ramming smack bang into a little sports car which is parked tight into a home-made lay-by.

"My initial reaction, as you'll gather, is to engage in a quick spot of cross-country running. But then I hear these desperate shouts coming from the other car. And despite my better instincts, my conscience kicks in. So I go up to the window for a look. And who is stretching across the front seats in considerable pain and discomfort but Sparkly Barkley.

"And sitting in his lap, and also in some distress, is a lady. And take it from me, this lady is not Sparkly's better half. More strangely still, she bears an uncanny resemblance to Red Light Lorna, ever-loving wife of Harry the Hurler – the Chief Executive of the Civil Defenders."

Danny and I guffaw at this; first at Sparkly's comeuppance and then at the deal which Danny Boy strikes for his help – and his silence.

"The best part," chuckles Danny, "is that both Rusty and Shakes are convinced the conversion is all down to the Christmas spirits. They are Praising the Lord and Blessing their Souls ever since."

We both kee-hee at the irony and at the fact that a guy like Danny Boy can all of a sudden own a guy like Sparkly Barkley.

"But I must confess," says Danny, straightfaced, "that even a man like me – who is sceptical about this religious hocus-pocus – thinks it is more than coincidental that I should bump into Sparkly in the middle of nowhere on Christmas Day like that. Especially, as we are both supposed to be in other places.

"In fact, I would say the chances of it happening are as remote as those of getting found again with a lighted bottle of Coca Cola in my hand. Without wearing my mask."

THE CURE FOR BAD BREATH

"'Bout five years ago, before the last truce, myself and Harry the Hurler go down to Dublin for the Grand Convention of all the Civil Defence Units in Ireland. Central Office pay for us to stay in the Shelbourne Hotel – nothing but the best for the Derry leadership.

"Anyhow, one morning we are standing at the reception when Harry goes up to this little old fella in the foyer and says, 'I know you, you're from Derry – you're from Creggan, aren't you?' Well, the old guy protests his innocence, in what sounds to me like an American accent. But Harry persists and says, 'No, no, you're lying. You are definitely from Derry – I know you.'

"This goes on for maybe five minutes before Harry gets tired and comes back over to join me. With that, the desk clerk comes up and asks him, 'So what exactly were you talking about to Mister Sinatra?'"

*****

We all laugh at the story, despite the fact that it appears about once a week in the London papers. The press like to use it to prove that Harry the Hurler, Chief Executive of Derry's Civil Defenders, doesn't have the brains to put his finger up his nose. And it is now being rehashed by the former leading revolutionary, Bad Breath Bradley.

Bad Breath – a Belfast blow-in who, sadly, never considers blowing back – is currently in dispute with Harry the Hurler. But his past record suggests it is still a good idea for us to smile at his jokes.

We are sitting, as ever of a Thursday night, in Swanky Frankie's Curry

Parlour and Grill Room on William Street, eating chips covered in Tikka sauce. And tonight Bad Breath is honouring us with his presence, after his early evening companions decide to shake him off at the pass.

"I just pop into the jacks and when I come out the bar is emptier than the Pope's dance-card," he grins. "Those guys are always winding me up."

Bad Breath is not, of course, Bad Breath's chosen name. He himself insists on the term 'Plunkett', which was given to him by his father, Bad Breath Senior, in honour of the martyr Joseph Plunkett. Unfortunately for Breath, however, nicknames tend to stick to families as reliably as halitosis.

Normal times, our company – Dumpy Doherty, Getemup Gormley and myself – would all vote not to be seen dead in Breath's company. Breath's standing in polite society ranks up there with swearing in court or drinking gin in chapel. But even in impolite society, his stock is diminishing. Word is that only this very week he is relieved of his command as manager of the Four Green Fields Bar on Waterloo Street, in rather controversial circumstances.

But there are few ways of losing Breath's company without risking offence, and we may as well hear his story while he is here. So we ask him what happens with his bar.

"It is true," he explains, "as you know, that I am asked to stand down after ten years at the helm. Off the record, this is due to my opposition to the softly-softly politics being peddled by the Boys' new management. It is my contention that old hands like myself are being pushed aside by Johnny-come-latelies on the sniff of a big peace payday. But when I mention this to Harry, he gets all protective of his new buddies and drops me quicker than a ticking box."

Pausing for dramatic effect, Breath casually takes Dumpy Doherty's fork from his hand. Dumpy is so shocked that he lets it go without a struggle. But the shock is to become outrage when Breath spears three Tikka-covered chips from Dumpy's plate and shucks them back. Into *that* mouth, as Dumpy points out later.

"The problem with Harry," continues Breath, oblivious, "goes back to the early seventies, when I am hosting training schools out in the Poisoned Glen. You'll remember them, Getemup. Anyway, Harry the Hurler and his cousin Jimmy Big Mouth each get a big Barrett rifle and are told to fire them at a target on a quarry wall three hundred yards away. Jimmy hits the centre of the target five times out of five. His hand is as steady as a glued-on wig. But when Harry fires one round, the kickback hurts his shoulder so badly, he starts to cry. And he vows he'll never lift another weapon as long as he lives.

"Of course, Harry now gets somewhat embarrassed when I remind him of the good old days."

With that, Breath spears another chip, then hands the fork back to Dumpy, who looks about as happy as an open sore. He coolly refuses the fork and tells Breath, "No thanks. You finish them."

"After I retire from the boot camp," continues Breath, "the Boys install me in the Four Green Fields as a reward. Good job it is too, three C notes a week and more fresh tart than Milanda Bakery. Course, first thing I must do is clear out the lowlifes and thieves who are subbing the place dry. And before long, the bar is quite a classy joint indeed with big acts like The Flying Fenians and The Brimmer Boys queuing up to play every week.

"But in time, Harry gets jealous and decides he wants the bar for himself. He gets the Executive of the Civil Defenders to put it to the vote and all of a sudden, I am as welcome as an electric fire in a metal bath. What Harry doesn't know, however, is that I am now in for a licence of my own. The owner of the Cellar Bar is getting terrible gyp from the Concerned Residents Against Pushers group – which, incidentally, is chaired by my good wife. It seems there are lots of druggies using the place. So I feel he may just respond to the right bid."

The Cellar Bar, for my money, houses about as many druggies as the Christian Brothers' Choir. And the thought of Breath in charge of it is too ghastly for comment. So we keep schtum. This is also possibly the only way to get rid of Breath without risking offence.

Sure enough, after several minutes of us making yawning noises, Breath announces he has to go and meet some fresh tart who, he assures us, contains more sizzle than spit on a griddle. And he departs.

*****

After Breath leaves, Dumpy shouts up to the counter for a new plate of Tikka-covered chips. Now most people, Breath included, are not aware that Dumpy is married to a full cousin of Harry the Hurler. Dumpy never discusses family business, except when he has a few in him and is quite upset. Like when someone violates his chips.

"From what I'm hearing," says Dumpy, "the story Breath is telling, about him falling out with the Boys because he opposes the truce, is very self-serving. In fact, I have it on very good authority that when he is manager of the Fields, Breath is skimming fifteen per cent off everything but the toilet walls.

"Harry the Hurler, never mind what Breath will tell you, is quicker than a three-card trick – particularly when it comes to money. And he is not best pleased that his old friend is fleecing him closer than a bald head. Between you and me, Breath has more chance of finding a new dentist than he does of forcing Leo the Limp out of the Cellar. Indeed, I wouldn't be at all surprised if Breath should shortly decide to quit the bar trade altogether."

*****

A month passes with no further mention of the Green Fields controversy. Then one Thursday evening, we are sitting in Swanky Frankie's, eating Tikka-covered chips again, when who pokes his head round the door but Bad Breath. And, as he would say himself, he appears to have some fresh tart in tow.

"I'd love to join you losers, but some of us have pressing business to attend to," he harr-harrs before buying his companion a packet of Regal King Size. No doubt to calm her nerves.

As Breath disappears back to his second-hand Jag, Dumpy goes to the payphone at the back of the restaurant and makes a quick call. When Dumpy sits down again, we ask him for the update on Breath's standing both in polite society and elsewhere. He is a bit reluctant to open up at first, but we needle him by reminding him how Breath violates his chips the last night. And eventually, he gives us the story.

"Strictly off the record," says Dumpy, "the reason that nothing more happens up until now is that the Boys can't prove that Breath is stealing.

"Shortly before Breath is stood down, the Boys get an independent auditor – that's an expert in spotting how you are being ripped off – to check out the bar. The guy they appoint is the best in the business, the ex-lawyer, Chiselling Phil Stevenson. Phil's philosophy is that there are only two types of people in this world – those who are stealing from you, and those who are still working up the nerve.

"Now, when Chiselling Phil reports back to the Boys, all he can tell them is that they are being short-changed to the tune of about fifteen cents in the dollar. But he has to confess that he is completely baffled as to how the scam is being pulled."

Phil and his team of scouts are very thorough. His first check is to make sure that every drink is charged into the tills. This he ascertains by having his men watch the cash registers for several nights. And they are quite surprised to learn that every cent that comes over the counter goes into the boxes. Indeed, the workers at the Green Fields are not allowed to carry any money at all into the bar with them – thus spoiling their chances of even making the minimum wage. So there is virtually no petty theft.

The next check Chiselling Phil performs is on the spirits. A favourite dodge of manys an enterprising barman is to transpose Ukranian vodka, at two quid a gallon, into empty bottles of the upmarket brands which retail at a tenner a pint. Other scurrilous charge hands are known to fill gin and whiskey bottles with water and cold tea, which they then pass on to drunks. But all tests on the Fields' spirits at the Boys' science lab in Belfast show they are the genuine article.

The one scam it is generally very difficult to prevent is bringing in your own hooch. So a barman may install his own bottle of off-sale whiskey in an optic and sell it off at bar prices, pocketing his profit at the end of the night. But the Civil Defenders are no dozers in this department either. And for some years now, all their bottles are computer coded. So this option is also ruled out.

Chiselling Phil does have a couple of minor breakthroughs. He discovers that someone in the Fields is lifting up to thirty quid a week from the vending machine in the Gents'. The last time the machine works is when Bobby Charlton still has his perm, but there is no Out-of-Order sign, and the Waterloo Street locals are mostly too bashful to complain. Likewise, Phil reckons that the poker machine is re-rigged to pay out even lower than the thirty pence in the pound which the Boys allow the mugs who play it.

But such losses are small beer and can be written off under sundries in the balance sheet. So Phil is not in the least bit excited. In the end, Phil is so desperate for a result that he even checks the spillage ratio. Out of ninety-six pints in a keg, good bar workers will waste no more than four. But the Fields' staff are so careful that they even sell off the first pint of the day and most of the slops – so averaging ninety-four pints a barrel.

"Chiselling Phil is not a happy man," says Dumpy. "He is certain that the Fields Bar is clearing about a sixth less than it should be – given its crowds and prices. But his report – which is more detailed than any investigation he ever does before – is inconclusive.

"More importantly, however, the Boys cannot encourage Breath to see the error of his ways, until they work out how he is conning them."

Our contemplations are briefly interrupted by the sirens and flashing blue lights of an ambulance racing by outside. But Dumpy doesn't seem to notice.

"So that's the situation as it stands earlier this week," he grins. "But all things come to those who wait.

"Last Monday, Chiselling Phil is in the neighbourhood, checking out a bent bookie's clerk, when he pays a courtesy call to Harry the H. The two get chatting and Phil says he is still unhappy how Bad Breath gets the better of him. 'The whole operation is so meticulous,' he tells Harry. 'I even post men to watch each of the Fields' six cash registers every night for a week.'

"'Say that again – but slower,' says Harry. So Phil repeats himself, slow as a prayer.

"'Aha!' laughs Harry, clapping his hands in delight. 'We have him at last. The Four Green Fields, my friend, is only supposed to have *five* tills. Though there is no way you can know this. It is my strong opinion that a certain cheap thief installs this sixth register himself, to beef up his take-home pay. And it is my stronger opinion still that this cheap thief and Plunkett 'Bad Breath' Bradley are one and the same.'"

Dumpy smirks again and looks back over his shoulder out the grill-room window. He is enjoying playing to the audience, so we do not stop him.

"I am not a gambling man," he continues, lowering his voice, "but I would bet that the meat wagon which just zooms past here is heading for a second-hand Jaguar parked in a dark lay-by on Lowry's Lane. Bad Breath's fresh tart, it seems, is anxious to take him there so she can sizzle like spit on the griddle. The pair are actually supposed to team up last night, but the fresh tart, who incidentally is no tart at all but my wife's youngest sister, gets cold feet."

"So is that what your phone call is about?" Getemup asks.

"Well," Dumpy replies, "Harry the Hurler knows I like to dine here on a Thursday. So he asks me if I will ring him when his little cousin calls in – just to let him know her date is going okay. Harry is a good sort and tends to worry about people, especially when they are jammed alone in a car with a guy like Bad Breath. Though after tonight, I don't think that Breath will be presenting much of a danger to fresh tart for quite a while.

"You see, from what I understand, the senior officers of the Boys' Chastisement Committee are hoping to give Bad Breath a sharp reminder of his obligations to the Civil Defenders – and also a quick refresher course in the basics of boy-girl etiquette. And they intend to do this by introducing him to their old friends Mr Baseball Bat and Ms Stiletto Heel – the latter to be applied, incidentally, by Little Sis.

"And while, like all civilised people, I disapprove entirely of this Chastisement Committee, it will be a cold day in hell before Bad Breath Bradley shows his head in here again to violate my chips and Tikka sauce."

HORSE SENSE

"Most of the guys I do business with, I wouldn't leave alone with a mid-dling-to-well-dressed corpse," says Barry the Bookie. "But horsey people are the worst of them all. As my old man always says: 'Never trust a jock-ey with brown eyes – nor indeed any other colour eyes.'

"Give you an example. Myself and 'Hate the World' Herbie are out at a flapping track near Long Island, one day not so long ago. It is a very bad meeting indeed, with a very poor standard of horses. In fact, the last time I see so little talent in one place is when I go to see my son Firstborn's Christmas play.

"Anyhow, Hate has word that a certain big-shot owner from Astoria is going to give his new Arab thoroughbred a hush-hush run-out against the local donkeys – just to see how it'll fare under a bit of pressure. Personally, I figure that the owner won't want the mount to win, as it'll cut its odds whenever it hits the serious tracks. But after we spot the horse on the card, Hate decides to risk a score at five-to-one.

"We go over to the far side of the track, at about the three-quarter way point, to watch the race. There's only a small crowd at the meeting, and there's no-one within about two hundred yards of us. So the race gets underway, and Hate's horse leads from the outset. It is good. So good, in fact, that I make very careful note of its size and shape in case it's run out under a different name at any track where I am working. By the time the horse reaches halfway, it has time to sit down for a coffee and send post cards back to the also-rans. And I am cursing Hate up and down for having the foresight to invest a few dollars.

"Then, just as the Arab gallops past our part of the track, with the finishing line in sight, the jockey looks over his shoulder, sees no-one near him, and no crowd but us two . . . and throws himself off the horse.

"I must confess that I find this very amusing altogether. But Hate the World is quite upset. Indeed, he is only restrained from shooting holes in the jockey's knees by the rapid intervention of the horse's owner and his hundred bucks . . ."

*****

Barry the Bookie is a rare event among his profession in that he is never backward in bringing the drinks home to his friends. And it is this role which he is performing for us now in The Michael Collins Tavern at the corner of 196th and Irish Boulevard in the Bronx. For those of you who don't know him, Barry is also quite a gent. He pays up on his dockets to the cent, and you will never hear him utter so much as a soft oath at a prodigal client. Not that he needs to, with Hate the World around.

Today's visit from Barry is sadly brief, however. "I am under starters' orders," he explains, draining his beer. "I have to go back to the mill and try to recoup some of Firstborn's legal fees. Hate the World will stay in the chair if anyone fancies another snifter. And do not be put off by his ungenerous reputation."

But Scoop Scallan, who, like me, is currently forsaking the watering holes of Waterloo Street to watch the World Cup here in New York, shoots me an eye to warn that the party is now over. Unless, of course, we start buying our own.

*****

Through his work as a newspaper hack, Scoop Scallan gets to meet all sorts. He knows Hate from the old days when Hate works as a special advisor to Harry the Hurler back in Derry. Though Scoop is far too astute to bring this up, at least until Hate retires to the restroom. At which stage I am brought up to speed.

According to Scoop, Hate – whose Old Ma back in Derry still calls Herbie, after his long-gone GI father – strikes up with Barry on the boat to New York about three years ago. Both men are after suffering business setbacks in the Old World and fancy a change of scenery.

Not surprisingly, Hate is widely shunned by respectable citizens like you and me. But Barry's son, Firstborn, who's then about sixteen, takes a real shine to him. Likewise, Hate – whose only friends are normally either primed or loaded – breaks with tradition and lets the lad hang around the boat with him for company. When they aren't playing deck tennis, they are making little catapults and winging the English waiters with folded-up paperclips. And before long, the pair are as close as two teeth.

Anyhow, as happens, Hate soon gets to know Barry senior. And Barry, being a bookie, immediately recognises a great opportunity.

Barry knows that the most important element in profitable turf accountancy is the enforcement of judgements against debtors. And he rightly suspects that this is a subject in which Hate could graduate with first-class honours. So instead of offering Hate money to stay away from Firstborn, as you or I might do, Barry the Bookie asks Hate to become his business partner as soon as he sets out his stall Stateside.

*****

"Why ever does Barry leave Derry in the first place?" I inquire when Hate sits down again.

"It's not a story that I normally divulge," replies Hate. "Indeed, a guy less tolerant than me might consider it impolite to ask. But perhaps if I have the privilege of seeing one of you two walk to the bar and making with the Three Beer sign, we can chat some more."

Scoop loses the toss and gets to buy the drinks. The stout is a bit high, so Hate shucks off the head before taking a big deep breath in.

"For a long time," he begins, "Barry the Bookie has a perfect life in Derry. Well, almost perfect. Business is booming, he's smart enough to lay off anything he can't handle, and he has a lovely house with a lovely wife he adores.

"The only fly in the custard is Firstborn. Not to put too fine a point on it, the boy is dim. Dim as fog. Don't get me wrong, I like the lad, but the only reason you can't see in one ear and out the other is because of the big wooden peg pinning his head to his shoulders.

"Anyhow, Barry knows his son and heir is never going to make it at school, so as soon as Firstborn turns fourteen, he lets him become an apprentice in the business. First indications are that he isn't that bad. He's a very tough kid – not afraid to stand up to the clients. He can compute the bets using a calculator – he's been watching Barry senior doing it all his life. And he knows enough not to accept any slips once the bell goes. Besides, there are strict instructions never to leave Firstborn alone in a shop or to let him pay out more than a hundred pounds without checking the bet.

"All goes well for about six months, after an initial hiccup when one joker convinces him that an each-way bet means he has to pay out if the horse wins or if it doesn't. Then one day, Forty Faces Friel comes into the shop . . ."

Scoop and I are already well-acquainted with the late Forty Faces. Suffice it to say, not only has he a moustache and shifty eyes, he also wears white socks and polyester ties. Forty Faces will tell you that he gets his alias back when he runs with the Boys and is a master of disguise. Though you and I both know it is because he is the biggest lying hypocrite in all of Derry.

"Faces is as crooked a gambler that ever stole a breath," explains Hate. "And he knows Firstborn is running on a low wattage. So this day, while he is standing in the shop, he hatches the simplest of plans. He looks up on the board and spies a twenty-to-one winner from a race run an hour ago. He then writes the name on a docket, marks it five hundred quid to win, tears off the punter's half and puts it in his pocket. He then scrumples up the bookie's half a little and sidles up to the stalls. Firstborn is the only one working the booths – the manager's in the back.

"At the stall, just inside the screen, is the docket box, where the bookie stores his half of the ticket after he stamps them. Forty Faces asks Firstborn to turn up the radio till he hears the next race. And when Firstborn turns his back, he slips the scrumpled bookie's half of the ticket into the box.

"Then, when Firstborn turns around again, Faces says, 'Oh, by the way, you owe me ten and a half thousand pounds on the bet I made an hour ago,' and hands him his docket. 'But it's not stamped,' protests Firstborn. 'And anyhow, I don't remember you putting on any bet today.'

"'You are always forgetting to stamp the dockets – check your box,' replies Faces. And sure enough, sitting in the box is the other half of the ticket.

"Well, after a day-long stewards' inquiry, during which there are consultations with the Boys, the Turf Accountants' Professional Society and even the cops, Barry the Bookie finds himself with no option but to pay the bet. Even though all agree Faces is as dirty as a wet dog.

"I am pally with Harry at that time and, off the record, I can tell you that the Boys are so displeased with Faces that they snatch two big ones back from him and tell Barry that the money will cover his Voluntary Donations for the next year."

"So what happens Firstborn?" I ask.

"Strange thing," says Hate the World, "Barry does not hold Firstborn accountable at all and tells him so. But the youngster is a very sensitive child and is racked with guilt at losing so much of Pop's rent. He's also very embarrassed at being caught out on such a simple dodge. And Faces, of course, as soon as he gets his money, immediately starts to dine out on the story of how he is after conning Barry the Bookie out of a lottery win.

"Desperate situations make for desperate men. And a couple of weeks later, Firstborn goes into the National Bank on Shipquay Street and asks for ten grand on a long-term loan. In fact, he asks if he can keep the money outright on the strength of the imitation Luger he is holding in his right hand. And although they give him the ten G he requests, he doesn't even make it to the bottom of the hill before several burly gentlemen with non-imitation Lugers demand it back, and haul him off to St Mildred's Centre for Young Offenders."

"So does Barry the Bookie then lose heart and decide to emigrate to the Bronx?" I ask.

"Not immediately," says Hate. "First, he has to get his money back. Word travels fast and Barry knows that there is not a punter on earth who wouldn't get to hear if he lets a client stick him for a full pension. After all, it is a matter of honour to fleece a bookie who is down on his luck."

Hate drains his glass and holds it upside down in case we fail to notice its condition. This time, I am forced to travel to the bar.

"Getting even takes Barry a long time indeed," continues Hate, when normal service is resumed. "First of all, he bans Forty Faces from his bookie shops for life. And all the other bookies in the neighbourhood say they'll follow suit for at least a year.

"Now about this time, there is a Derry jockey, Shorty Doherty, working in England who begins sending back the occasional wire. His information is very good. Indeed, in the space of about six months, Shorty sends home eight winners on the trot, some of them with long prices. Eventually, Derry being such a village, Forty Faces soon gets to hear of it. And never being a man to resist getting his fist in the pie, he decides to place a tidy bundle on Shorty's next big wire.

"By now, Faces is mostly rehabilitated into polite bookmaking society though Barry's ban still applies. So when Shorty's next wire comes through for a horse called Ballybay Darling, Faces goes into Duffy's Bookies on Foyle Street and attempts to stake a cool twenty grand at two-to-one.

"'Close the door on the way out behind you,' he is told by the manager, who immediately warns every one of his shops within a thousand-mile radius not to take a cent on this horse, which is running the next day.

"Faces then spends the rest of the afternoon moving from bookie shop to bookie shop trying to get them to take his bet," says Hate. "But he would have a better chance getting a decade of the Rosary said in an Orange Hall.

"Then he hits on an idea. He will disguise himself and lay down the money in one of Barry's outlets. So he dons an old Afro wig, a pair of beer-bottle glasses, and a fake beard he once wears at the Easter Ceremonies and marches into Barry's shop on William Street. But who is it behind the counter only Firstborn, out on parole.

"Faces sweats a little at first, but Firstborn barely glances at him. He looks at the docket and the bundle of money, and goes out back to check with the manager. But a minute later he is back, nods okay to Faces and hands him back a stamped docket."

Hate pauses for dramatic effect and to examine his pint which is still of a reasonable depth. "Now, you are probably thinking that not even Firstborn is dim enough to take a twenty-thousand-pound bet from a complete stranger in beer-bottle glasses and a dodgy wig," he says. "And you would be right. Faces is the man responsible for all Firstborn's woes, and he sees through the disguise immediately. But Firstborn and his father out back have no intention of letting go of Faces's twenty Gs.

"So that same night, Barry the Bookie rings Shorty Doherty the jockey direct and warns him of the penalties for insider dealing. He puts it to Shorty that if Ballybay Darling comes any higher than second, not only will Shorty be disbarred from racing for life, but his family and all his friends – including several leading Boys – will be investigated by the Fraud Squad.

"To cut a long story short, the next day, Shorty pulls out all the stops and manages to drag Ballybay Darling, a complete flier if there ever is one, back into second place. This is despite the efforts of the eventual winner, who is heavily backed to come second and does everything but pull up the handbrake and wave Shorty through to overtake."

"I take it that Forty Faces is not happy with this," I interrupt, "and is unhappy to let go of his twenty K without a fight?"

"You take it correctly," replies Hate, "particularly seeing as the twenty K belongs to the Boys' Emergency Fund and is invested without their permission.

"Shortly after the race, Faces bursts into Barry's shop, marches up to the booth and loudly accuses Firstborn of stealing his money. Firstborn, who as I say does not scare easily, just laughs and proposes that the two of them go outside in the laneway to discuss the matter the old-fashioned way.

"The rest, as they say, is history. An old score is settled, and several days later Barry and family discreetly leave for America. At the moment, the cops back home are trying to extradite Firstborn for what he does to Faces, as it appears Faces winds up dead. But they'll never make it stick – not with Barry's lawyers.

"The Boys aren't too happy at first, though eventually they manage to reclaim two-thirds of their losses from the Turf Accountants' Professional Society. Nor are they too pleased about one of their former lieutenants going for his tea like that, regardless of how rotten he is. But after negotiations they announce that as Firstborn is only a kid, they will forego due process and allow him instead to spend some time in exile."

*****

We laugh heartily at the happy ending. Indeed, even Hate the World gives what might amount to a little chuckle. The entertainment over, Hate tips his pint to his head, tut-tuts at his watch and heads out into the dark Bronx night.

As he's disappearing round the door, Scoop Scallan, who is being very quiet all evening, flaps his hands at me to stay sitting for a moment. "That is not quite the end of the story," he says in off-the-record tones.

"What Hate omits to tell you is that the day Forty Faces loses the bet, Hate himself is sent to escort Faces to a special meeting about the missing twenty K. So he trails him to the bookies and then into the alleyway, where he sees Firstborn knocking the tar out of Faces. Hate ducks into a doorway to watch. He's in no hurry and he owes Faces no favours. But then, all of a sudden, Faces pulls a gun.

"First of all, he pistol-whips Firstborn. Then he orders him to kneel down and asks him does he wish to say a last prayer. But with that, Hate, who is still standing in the doorway, steps forward quickly and shoots Forty Faces in the back of the ear.

"Firstborn is very grateful and vows never to tell anyone of what happens – which is no little relief to Hate. And at the emergency inquiry that night, Firstborn even tells the Boys that it is he himself who is responsible for leaving Faces toes-up. The Boys, however, begin asking some questions about why Hate doesn't do a better job of protecting Faces, seeing that he is in the neighbourhood. And while no-one claims that Hate could be in any way responsible for Faces's demise, Hate figures a change of scenery might be a smart idea. So given that he is officially an American citizen, he decides to go the States where he will continue to act as New York advisor to the Executive."

"How do you know all this?" I ask Scoop, perplexed.

"Well, Barry the Bookie is, coincidentally, my mother's one and only little brother. And strictly between ourselves, he witnesses all the alleyway negotiations from the upstairs window of his shop. Right down to Hate saving his son's life.

"So when the pair later hook up on the boat, Barry is only too happy to recruit his son's guardian angel on a twenty per cent retainer. And Hate the World is only too happy to work for Barry, safe in the knowledge that no-one else will ever hear what happens in the laneway.

"It is quite a perfect arrangement for two men with perfect horse sense."

Double Indemnity

"Not so long ago, I decide to give up glasses and start wearing contact lenses," explains Mike 'Binlid' Mahon, former Derryman and current patron of The 33rd County Bar in South Boston.

"It is about the same time that I am erroneously indicted over that exploding coffin at Logan Airport. And my lawyer advises me to lose the bottle glasses and invent a more dashing, all-American image. Pricey jobs they are too, with a little blue tint for that special Paul Newman look.

"Well, the day after I get the lenses, Hate the World rings up from New York and invites me to come down and join him and Barry the Bookie at the track over in Jersey. They are privy to sensitive information about a certain colt who is being so modest with his talents that he will start the betting as far out as Kate Logue. But Hate, who has excellent business sense on these matters, reckons that the horse is quick enough to sell you a second-hand car on the home straight and still win the race.

"So I head off for Jersey as there is little advantage in sitting by and watching. The colt, sure enough, crosses the line before the track book-ies even get a chance to bless themselves. And those of us who are in on the surprise make sure to collect our twelve hundred dollars each before the bookies start squealing to the stewards.

"Anyhow, to celebrate our result, we head back to Jameson's on Seventy-Third and Second for a feed of poundies and bacon, and to suck the poison out of a couple of bottles of stout. If only a man could stop at the couple of bottles . . . Next thing you know, it's closing time, and I'm folding Hate the World into a cab, on our way back to Barry the Bookie's where we can crash for the night.

"I win the toss and get the couch, while Hate has to pull two arm-chairs together. As you'll expect, he is complaining like someone steals his First Communion money. But he is too fuzzy round the edges to start a row. Then I remember I have to take out my new lenses, so I get two pint glasses out of a press and half-fill them with water. I then drop one lens in each and leave them on the mantelpiece.

"Well, I wake in the morning and immediately reach for the glasses – as everything looks like the Shroud of Turin without the lenses. But the glasses are gone. So I feel my way out into the kitchen, where Barry and Hate are sitting sipping Alka Seltzer, and I make out these two empty glasses on the drainer.

"'Oh God,' says I, 'tell me the water in those glasses isn't down the sink.'

"'Not at all, Binlid,' says Hate with a rare smile. 'In fact, I can't thank you enough for being so thoughtful.'

"'What do you mean?' I ask him.

"'Well,' says he, 'when I open my eyes this morning, the first thing I see is the pint glass of water you leave out for me last night. Though I must confess I have such a drewth on me that I end up drinking the one you put out for yourself as well.'"

Hate, admits Binlid, is not all bad and offers to look out for the lenses – but he can no longer guarantee the blue tint.

Though this is perhaps more than we need to know.

*****

Binlid Mahon gets his name from his previous occupation as a teen entrepreneur in Creggan, where he is a dab hand at trapping rubber bullets with the inside of a steel lid. He then sells the bullets off to journalists as souvenirs, though ever the patriot, he charges the English press double. A lad of shrewd judgement, Binlid always stays just far enough from the firing line to ensure that when the bullet smacks his lid, it does not rebound and wing the ear off one of his colleagues – as sometimes occurs with less-skilled operators such as Ear-Winger Brady.

Binlid is also very careful not to let go of any cash he makes. And over the years, his business acumen becomes so well-thought-of that, for the two years preceding his departure from Derry, he is appointed the Boys' Chief Treasurer. The title is largely an honorary one, as his role mostly entails fundraising – soliciting private donations from banks, building societies, local businesses and the like. Unlucky for Binlid, however, one morning he is collecting a contribution from a local post office, when he accidentally drops his gun and is gripped in a neck lock by an overzealous security guard.

The security guard, however, when he realises whose neck he is after locking, develops post-traumatic stress disorder, so rendering himself unable to testify. And before long, Binlid is pronounced as free as a mother's love.

The judge at Belfast High Court, however, takes the unusual step of instructing the press that, despite his acquittal, Binlid is as guilty as Nixon – and we will get him the next time. So Binlid and the Boys figure that a change of scenery might be in order.

By chance, the Boys have some foreign-aid dollars they are looking to invest, so they give Binlid a loan to set up a foothold in South Boston. Southie, of course, being the second biggest Irish municipality in the world. So two weeks later, Binlid and a small suitcase full of cash touch down at Logan Airport and get straight to work.

For a one-suit Derryman just off the boat, Binlid is able to buy a stake in a very popular emporium, The 33rd County Bar, quite easily. And while, initially, the owner is reluctant to turn over a share in the most profitable business since the three-card trick, he is quick to grasp that half a pub is better than no pub at all. And before long, Binlid, with his head for money, has a stake in about a dozen establishments across Southie and Forest Green.

On the face of things, Binlid seems quite prosperous. But he knows he's only the good-looking guy at the front of the shop for the Boys back home in Derry. So he decides to establish a sideline all for himself. And one day, as he is looking out the window of The 33rd County, he asks Time-Gents, his head barman, what is the huge building out there in the distance.

"That is the Prudential Insurance building," replies Time-Gents, "the tallest building in Boston."

"Well, that's settled," says Binlid decisively. "I'll go into insurance." And he does.

*****

When Binlid hears from Barry the Bookie that Scoop Scallan and myself are on a trip to New York for the World Cup, nothing will do but he must send a car down from Beantown to bring us up to visit him. The prospect, I confess, leaves me worried as a sheep. For since the explosives find at Logan, Binlid is a guy that law-abiding people like you and me do not want to be seen with. But the Cadillac is at the door, and the 300lb driver says get in the back, so who are we to argue, being only 260lbs between us – even when soaking wet.

We stop at New Haven for the chauffeur to stretch his legs. And Scoop takes the chance to get me up to speed on the Binlid CV.

"Lid starts off small, in health insurance," explains Scoop. "In fact, it all kicks off very quickly. About a week after Binlid decides to diversify, Time-Gents is taking a shortcut along an alleyway to the bank with the weekly takings when a Puerto Rican steps out of a garage doorway and suggests he might lighten the load.

"Well, the Puerto Rican robber, who incidentally is holding an eight-inch blade, is so pleased with his day's work that he decides to attempt the same trick the following week. But this time, Binlid's two new body-guards appear from behind another garage doorway and persuade him to desist. And, as a reminder to him not to do it again, they then shoot him once behind each knee.

"The Puerto Rican naturally takes the hint and volunteers to save his elbows from similar disruption by returning the previous week's takings. But later, the Massachusetts Public Insurance Board awards the Puerto Rican a hundred K to compensate him for the two holes in the back of his legs. And when Binlid gets to hear of this, he reclaims half to cover his administrative overheads.

"So nowadays, every time any hood between Philly and Boston gets clipped on the back of the leg, you can be assured that Binlid is getting fifty per cent of the compo."

I often hear rumours that similar arrangements exist back in Derry. Though it is not the sort of thing a guy would ask too many questions about, in case he is given the opportunity to investigate them first hand.

"Binlid eventually sets up his own attorney to handle all his insurance cases," continues Scoop Scallan. "And he rapidly becomes a specialist in personal-injury compensation.

"He then hits on the idea of sending cars to all the GAA matches taking place in Boston, Cambridge and Brighton. So when a player gets injured on the pitch, he is rushed to the car, dressed back into his civilian clothes and driven to one of a thousand badly cracked pavements which are the responsibility of Boston Municipality. And for thirty per cent of the compo, Binlid provides two witnesses who will swear in court that they see the guy trip on the broken sidewalk.

"This area of work is very successful, even if some courts begin to ask why there is this sudden rash of red-headed Irish guys tripping up – and always on Sunday afternoons. So again, to stay one step ahead of the chasing pack, Binlid launches another initiative, though this time he reworks an old scheme from home.

"This particular enterprise is worth a small fortune. It entails about a dozen of Binlid's men buying old beat-up cars in another State, registering them in Mass, and insuring them to the hilt. They then wrap the cars round trees, out on the back roads round Worcester, and claim huge amounts of damage insurance and personal injury.

"Binlid is absolutely cleaning up," explains Scoop, "until, that is, a twenty-year-old Chevy, driven by his personal chauffeur, Willie 'the Wheels' Ferguson, blows up like a pipe bomb on impact.

"After this, there are suggestions that Binlid's judgement is on the wane. And worse again, there are even allegations that his contributions to his friends in Derry are coming up short of what is originally agreed."

*****

About two hours later, we team up with Binlid at The Littlest Bar in Boston just off Beacon Hill, a surprising choice given he has no stake in it and will thus have to buy a round. But we are just as happy to be in an area where no-one might recognise our host. And likewise, we don't object when he proposes that we go for a bite to La Famiglia Giorgio's in North End, far from Southie.

The poundies and bacon is unfortunately off, so the three of us settle for spaghetti amatriciana – on condition that Giorgio runs over to O'Flaherty's Gin Palace across the street for a few bottles of stout.

"I'm thinking of taking early retirement from the insurance business," says Binlid as we start shucking back our pasta. "You may perhaps be aware of the Willie the Wheels incident. Well, things are getting even more complicated. The insurance company, for some unknown reason, is refusing to honour his policies.

"What with sudden-death cover, his missus is expecting anywhere up to a hundred K. But apparently there is a hitch, and they are threatening to slap her in the chokey if she submits a claim. Unfortunately, the mad old bat believes I am in some way responsible and is now looking for me to make good her chit. She even kicks me out of Willie's wake."

All this conversation, Binlid stresses, is off the record – and, between ourselves, a little more than either Scoop or myself ever want to know. But as we are Binlid's new best friends, he further reveals to us that his latest venture, the three-coach crash, is also running into problems.

The pile-up is another old dodge from Derry, which is first pulled off to spectacular effect on Massachusetts Avenue last Patrick's Day – and then again, in a very convincing fashion, at Columbus on the Fourth of July. But they go and overstretch themselves by trying it on Tremont Street on Christmas Eve.

The deal, you'll recall, is that for $200 up front and fifty per cent of the compo, you can buy a ticket for a seat in a major crash-to-be. And generally, you can be sure that the coach drivers are so skilled that there will be very few serious injuries.

"But nobody is to know about the black ice at the corner of Essex and Tremont," says Binlid. "And besides, all volunteers take part at their own risk, as I later explain to the families of the five victims.

"But it is always a good idea to stay one step ahead of bad luck. So I feel that it is now exactly the time to branch into something new. And Scoop, you might be just the guy to help me. I have been talking to your uncle, Barry the Bookie, about selling me the New England franchise for his business and want you to put in a word for me."

I slurp back some pasta strings as loudly as I can to let them know I am not listening.

"I'll do what I can," says Scoop, albeit a bit nervously. And we all tweak open another bottle of stout.

*****

After our tiramisu, we repair to the Purple Shamrock, near Quincy Market, for a couple of pints of digestif. But Binlid is very edgy and will only sit with his back to the corner and facing the door.

After the first pint of fine stout is successfully negotiated, Scoop excuses himself to phone Barry the Bookie in New York to let him know we'll be staying the night. And after a couple more, we agree to move onto the Kells Bar across the river in Brighton. But outside the Purple Shamrock, just as I am about to follow Binlid into the Cadillac, Scoop shouts at me to watch out and pulls me to one side.

With that, two completely unfamiliar chaps, whom I could not identify again if my life is at stake, push past us and bundle their way into the car, which then tears off. Several other eyewitnesses later give the gendarmes a description of one of the guys which closely matches a file picture they have of Hate the World. But he, of course, is back in New York playing poker with Barry the Bookie and five other sworn affidavits.

"I think we'll take the night train back to Manhattan," says Scoop, "and perhaps not mention this whole affair to anyone at all."

.

*****

The midnight express is quiet, and we have no problem getting a carriage to ourselves. So Scoop tweaks open another couple of bottles of the Purple Shamrock's takeaway stout. And as soon as we are sitting comfortably, he begins.

"Ever since the Boys sort out Binlid's difficulties with the exploding coffin, they are keeping him on a very close leash," says Scoop.

"The cops are also, of course, watching him night and day. His acquittal on illegal arms supplying causes a bit of a shock for the judge and the district attorney – and indeed the American TV-viewing public. Particularly as they have video of Binlid purchasing the explosives, packing it all into a coffin and driving the hearse to the Dublin plane.

"But, as you may recall, the night the jurors retire to consider their verdict, all their photographs, names and addresses appear on memoriam cards which are pinned up in every Irish bar in New England and New York. And some people say that this has a bearing on the jury's decision.

"But this makes Binlid begin to think he can get away with anything. And while the Boys are happy enough with the money the bars are making – and the occasional coffin that lasts the distance – Binlid's private-insurance business is starting to reflect badly on them. Things finally reach a head when Mrs Willie the Wheels rings Hate the World in New York and tells him that Binlid is refusing to pay up on her late husband's policy."

"Why won't the insurance company pay it?" I ask Scoop.

"Well," says Scoop, "it seems they immediately become suspicious when they find that Willie the Wheels works as a driver to Binlid. And they become unhappier still when the forensic reports reveal that both Wheels and his unidentifiable passenger are wearing crash helmets and body armour. For while the roads around Worcester are pretty dangerous, there is a feeling that these guys are wrapped up a little too well – and that maybe there is some form of fraudulent behaviour afoot.

"Binlid refuses to discuss the issue and is no longer seen about Southie. So Barry is asked to smoke him out with the promise of a bit of business. And when I ring Barry and tell him how much we are enjoying ourselves at the Shamrock Bar tonight, he figures he'll have a couple of old friends from home drop in for a chat."

"So Binlid's for a long walk off a short bridge?" I suggest.

"No, not at all," laughs Scoop, as if I am a fool. "He is far too important an earner and way too good at running the bars. But, as he himself says to us earlier this evening, he needs to retire from the insurance game. And the only compensation cheque he'll be collecting from now on is the hundred K he'll get from the Massachusetts Public Insurance Board to make up for the two holes in the back of his knees, which incidentally will be developing about now.

"But all of this money will, of course, go directly to Mrs Willie the Wheels."

Stammering Stan
Gets His Stripes

When new reporters start at the *Derry Standard*, Mary Slevin, the editor, likes to call them into her lurid red office to give them the benefit of her thirty years in the game.

"There are two basic rules in journalism," she declares. "The first is trust no-one. And the second is: in the case of an emergency, always refer to rule one.

"Also, you must always remember that the two most important attributes any journalist can possess are honesty and integrity. Once you can fake them, you've it made."

With 'Stammering' Stan Stevenson, however, she just wishes him luck.

*****

I first come across Mary Slevin when she is a tidy-looking court reporter, many more years back than either of us would care to admit. On that occasion she agrees, after no little persuading, to lose the notes of a drunk-driving case against Harry the Hurler's young cousin Drillbit Devlin.

I get to know her pretty well over the years, though we never exactly swap spit. My mother, a woman of immense judgement, warns me at a very early age that no-one should ever become too pally with any member of the Fourth Estate or entrust them with anything more confidential than your views on the weather. And Mary, in particular, has more angles than a Chinese puzzle.

Anyhow, this lovely September evening, Mary spies me on the Rock

Road. And before I can go hide in a garden, she invites me to join her in Cole's Bar for a gin, no protests. Mary is late for her meeting with the football-star-turned-city-councilman Seamus 'the Saint' Timoney. So I figure she wants to bring an alibi in the door with her, in the form of me.

"You're in big trouble," she tells the Saint as she shucks back an inch of her first gin.

The Saint, who clearly has been waiting a while, chugs back a mouthful of what I later understand is his fourth and looks pained.

"Our Diary column," explains Mary with a grin, "is being asked to raffle off some videotapes I receive in the post. And while they are not the normal calibre of videos we get for competitions, they could make someone a very interesting prize.

"You see, the star of these movies is none other than a very good-looking, and immediately recognisable, man in his late thirties, who we both know well. And in the film, he can be observed reciting shrieks, pants and snatches of assorted prayers with a not-very-dressed young lady who does not appear to be his wife – unless she's just turned seventeen again and started speaking Spanish."

The Saint's face, as Mary maliciously recalls later, lights up like a brake lamp. He opens his mouth to argue but catches her sharpening eye and instead just nods he understands.

"We, of course, will not touch the tapes," continues Mary. "We have our journalistic ethics, and besides, the entire newsroom reckons there's very little there we can show in a family paper. But it is not us you have to worry about. The Northern Broadcasting Company have them as well. Your only hope is that Ivan the Terrible will set Stammering Stan on the story."

The Saint nods again, fighting off a sudden urge to dash to the Gents'.

"Why is that?" he asks.

"It's a long story," says Mary, "but the bottom line is that Stan's as decent as he's dim, and he might help us save your hairy hide. But Timoney, if I pull you out of this, we're even forever. In fact, you will owe me forever."

"Who is this Stan man?" presses the Saint, apparently ignorant of one of our latter-day civic icons.

"Stan is singly the most empty-headed reporter working in this city," sighs Mary. "And take it from me, that is some achievement. It's not that he's stupid – though, in fairness, he has fewer qualifications than it takes to walk a dog. It is more that the light-switch inside his head is never quite in the On position.

"He can actually be very smart and quite funny in an innocent sort of way. But ultimately, he is the guy you send to the market with your cattle and who comes back with magic beans. And yes, I myself must shoulder a large share of the responsibility for unleashing him on the journalistic world, as it is me who gives him his first start as a junior with the *Standard*. But given that he bears a spitting resemblance to our financial director and chief shareholder, his Uncle Hugo, I figure I have little option."

Mary, however, is a believer in making the best of a bad situation. So she adopts Stan as her own pet project and begins knocking some rough edges off him. It is no easy task.

"For his first two years as a reporter," says Mary, "Stan doesn't know the difference between 'literally' and 'figuratively'. So it's not unusual to read in his columns how a defendant 'literally' throws himself on the mercy of the court, how a footballer 'literally' runs a mile offside, or how an irate politician – such as yourself a minute ago, perhaps – is 'literally' beside himself with rage."

The Saint, who's curiously bright for a local councillor literally caught with his trousers down, chuckles at the irony.

"Next, we have the joy of teaching Stan the difference between 'condone' and 'condemn'," explains Mary, warming to her subject. "Of course, we only realise there's a problem after he publishes a statement from a magistrate 'utterly condoning' the brutal murder of a mother and daughter. That costs us five thousand pounds. To this day, I don't think Stan understands the difference – and if you listen to his interviews on NBC now, you'll notice he never uses either.

"After we sort that one out, we then have to deal with Stan's unwitting double entendres. On one advertising feature about the huge expense of organising a wedding, he puts the headline: 'Newly weds being taken for a big ride' – which somehow escapes my eye and makes the paper. You'll no doubt remember that one – everyone else in the town does.

"But thankfully we do spot his caption on an ad for Bradley's Butchers just at the last minute. I really don't think the people of Derry need to know that 'Nothing fills that hole like Bradley's Giant Pork Sausage'."

I have a sneaky feeling that Mary is making up this last part to put the Saint back at his ease. Bradley is a big pal of his and Mary is cute enough to figure that the two will be able to dine out for years on the story.

"But worst of all," she says, "is his interviewing technique. Not even I can do anything about that. He just can't think under pressure. He stutters, stammers and is liable to say the first thing that comes into his head.

"You remember the big recruitment drive for new priests the Church launches about two, three years ago? Well, at the press conference to announce it, Stan decides it's his time to become a real professional. So he puts on a serious reporting voice and asks the Bishop of Derry if preference will be given to candidates who were women or members of religious minorities. Bishop McLaughlin knows Stan, of course, and just tells him that he'll consider all applications on their merits.

"The problem even seems to get worse with time. Only three weeks ago on live radio, he asks the widow of a shot cop: 'Is a policeman's job particularly dangerous compared to other professions?' It is a real talent.

"Stan's saving grace, however, is that because he is so innocent, people never feel threatened by him and tend to tell him their life stories as soon as they meet him. And that, of course, is very useful in this line of work."

*****

Stan's departure to the Northern Broadcasting Company is also Mary's fault in that she is so convinced they will never hire him, she gives him the best reference she ever writes. Two other *Standard* reporters are also in for the job and Mary gives them decent enough testimonials. But she is one hundred per cent certain that NBC will spot Stan immediately at the interview and throw him back.

Mary, however, is too clever by far. And typical NBC, it all boils down to the paperwork; so Stan gets the job.

What Mary fails to mention, however, is that when Stan tells her the news, she ushers him out of the room before he can even sit down. For underneath it all, Mary – who thoroughly deserves her reputation as a crabbed old bat – is very fond of Stan. And she doesn't want him to see the tear in her eye.

*****

The Saint, as I'm sure you already know, is a member of the Voice of Ireland Party, aka the VIPs, which the *Derry Standard* currently supports. Hence Mary's warning to him about the tapes. The Northern Broadcasting Company, however, have no such loyalties. And worse again, the NBC's Station Editor, Ivan 'the Terrible' Coltroun, hates the Saint with a passion.

This is not always the case, however. Back when Ivan works for the BBC in Derry, both he and his then News Editor, Mary Slevin, were pretty pally with the Saint. In fact, in those days, Ivan is a not-at-all terrible guy, with a lively wit – on those occasions that he is sober.

Then one afternoon, about ten years ago, the BBC top brass catch him Broadcasting Under the Influence, and he is run out the door. While I don't recall the show myself, apparently Ivan is giving an obituary of a bishop who had a great sense of humour. And it seems he attempts to say that His Lordship's 'shafts of wit' will be greatly missed but commits such a Spoonerism that the programme should only be aired after the nine o'clock watershed.

Despite his habits, Ivan is a damn fine journalist, and NBC quickly step in to offer him a new start. As part of the package, however, he must give up the gargle. But it seems that the pressure is so great that Ivan also disowns his friends, pronounces himself Saved and joins the Ulster Planters – the VIPs' deadly rivals.

*****

For some unknown reason, Ivan seems to blame his former drinking buddy, the Saint, for his sacking by the BBC. And from that day on, every opportunity he gets, he hits the Saint a slap. For instance, the day before the Saint becomes mayor, Ivan reveals to the world how Timoney Timbers, the Saint's family business, owes £250,000 and is just about to go to the wall.

Then, one week before last year's council elections, Ivan puts on general release an old photograph of the Saint at a NBC party, in which he needs all four legs to make it to the taxi home. The picture, as you'll remember, appears on the front page of every paper in the North – except, of course, the *Standard*.

*****

When not making the Saint's life a misery, Ivan's other favourite target is his new junior reporter, Stammering Stan. Bad enough that Stan is recruited when Ivan is on annual leave, but he is also a *Standard* old boy. And Stan, unfortunately, is proving just as jinxed on air as he is in print. His news reading is so bad that the pirate station, Cityside FM, runs a special Stanley's Stoppage slot in its *Review of the Week* programme.

Likewise, Stan's live two-way interviews are quite remarkable. When the Miss Derry finalists decide to organise a special pageant for the US presidential visit, Stan informs the lunchtime listeners that a 'bevy of local beauties are lining up to service Mr Clinton's entertainment needs'.

Though, eventually, even the station editor is forced to concede that this is not libellous whatsoever.

Indeed, between you and me, and the cops listening in on the phone, Stan is on his last legs at the NBC. His probation period, which is supposed to be only three months, has now lasted twenty-four. And Ivan the Terrible, who would be shot of Stan long ago but for the Fair Employment laws, vows that one more foul-up and he'll be dumped quicker than a smoking gun.

So when the Timoney tapes come in, Ivan sees a way of killing his two pet hates with the one story. He will not only expose the Saint in all his hairy-backed glory but Stan will never be forgiven for killing off such a local hero and the VIPs will not rest until Stan is drummed out of the media.

*****

It is some time later before I meet any of the parties concerned again. And I figure, because of the lack of excitement in the press, that the Saint is on top of the situation, so to speak. Like everybody else, I am keen to find out what is happening. So when I next bump into Mary Slevin on the Strand Road, I let her haul me off to Charlie McCafferty's Gin Emporium for a late-afternooner with very little argument whatsoever.

"The very day after I tell the Saint about the tapes," she declares, "Ivan the Terrible instructs Stan to leave the office and not to come back without the Saint's notice-to-quit in his pocket.

"But Stan, for all his faults, is bright enough to know that he is punching way above his weight. The way he reads it, if he sinks the Saint, he's finished. And if he doesn't, he's finished. So as always in a crisis, he comes to see me."

Mary, of course, like any journalist, is tickled pink to be in the middle of the mêlée.

"Now, the Saint's long enough around to realise that seventeen-year-old Spanish students come here for English lessons and not French ones," sniffs Mary. "But even a guy who walks around as many corners as him could not expect Juanita and her pal to be running a private competition between themselves, the results of which can only be verified with a hidden camera.

"From what I can glean, there are seven or eight other oddly-shaped Derrymen on the tape – though the Saint's the only one who can be identified. Typical politician – sits back and gets someone else to do the work, then gets his face, and some other bits and pieces, in the picture."

I immediately experience a slight chill as I wonder who the other victims are. But as I am certainly not one of them, the feeling quickly passes.

"Stanley thinks his only option if he wants to save his job is to sink the Saint," continues Mary. "But I tell him to bide his time. 'Look,' I say, 'he's not breaking the law – even if his understanding of how the Student Exchange Scheme works is a bit primitive. If this breaks, the scandal will kill him, figuratively speaking. And then his wife will kick him to death, literally.'

"So I advise Stan to go and talk to Harry the Hurler and the Boys. They, of course, know everything that goes on in this town – even what's happening in home videos. And I tell Stan that they may provide him with a way out of his situation."

*****

According to Mary, Harry and the Boys have a soft spot for Stan, ever since he and his uncle make sure that the Bad Breath Bradley affair never sees the presses. As a rule, Stan tends to be less high-handed in his coverage of the Boys than the rest of the pack. So when he calls at the Boys' smoked-out offices on Rossville Street, he is greeted like an almost important guest. In fact, Harry the Hurler even has one of his party's Senior Advisors go wash out a mug so Stan can have some tea.

"Normally, I'd not interfere in a matter like this," tuts Harry. "But I reckon that Timoney will be a whole lot friendlier to us in the future if we help him. And perhaps he'll quit all this sniping about these Chastisement Committees that we have nothing to do with. Particularly if we hold on to our own copy of the tape.

"Your problem, Stanley, is that you haven't watched the tape from end to end, if you forgive the phrase. Our information, which as you know is always correct, is that a leading member of the Ulster Planters – who's a close buddy of your boss – can also be identified on the video, thanks to an egg-shaped mole on his back.

"You can take it for granted that Ivan the Terrible will shoot down the story when he learns this."

*****

"Stan then goes home and watches the video, eight, maybe nine times," says Mary. "Though, even using Slo-Mo and Freeze-Frame, he can't spot the guy with the mole. But when he goes back into the NBC newsroom, he decides to tell a little fib. And he announces that there is a guy on the tape with an egg-shaped mole on his back. He tells Ivan that it isn't he who spots it, but Harry the Hurler, who also has his own copy of the tape and who clues him in about it on the street.

"From what Stan tells me, it's like watching a man implode. Ivan lets out a frightened yelp, the colour vanishes from his face, and the tape he's holding jumps out of his hands. He tells Stan that he is completely mistaken and that claims like that could ruin the station.

"He then insists that the whole story is inappropriate for a serious organisation like the NBC and that, moreover, there is absolutely no proof that the video is genuine. And he pleads with Stan to drop the entire story. Eventually, he hints to Stan that if he forgets about the whole thing, his probation will be over and he'll be a full staff member. Stan, of course, has no idea what is happening. But he is not enough of a fool to pass up the opportunity and asks when he gets his full-time contract.

"Ivan tells him it'll be on his desk by the end of the day," continues Mary. "Stan then comes over to give me the good news and leaves Ivan to phone his One Day At A Time counsellor."

"So what am I missing about this mole business that it can make Ivan the Terrible tremble at the knees?" I ask Mary.

"Well, Harry only tells Stan what I tell him to say," replies Mary. "You see, the information carries a lot more weight if Ivan thinks it's coming from the Boys . . ."

"But even so," I interrupt, "it's hardly a silver bullet, is it?"

She shucks back another large inch of Charlie's gin then chews her lip as if she's figuring how much to say.

"About ten years ago," she begins at last, "when Ivan and I are both at the BBC, the entire newsroom will often go out after the lunchtime programme on Fridays and sink a glass or two. One Friday, just before Christmas, about fifteen of us head to Cole's and push the boat out a little further than normal. We then descend en masse to the station again, where Ivan leads an assault on the manager's drinks' cabinet.

"To cut a long story short, later that night, two members of staff, a girl and a boy, are spotted by a security camera in the bushes outside performing a popular winter sport all of their own – though they are not at all dressed for the weather.

"Neither of their faces appears on the camera. But the tape is widely appreciated nonetheless by the scores of BBC staff throughout the world who get to watch it on the in-house circuit."

"So what's the problem if no-one can be identified?" I ask.

"Good question," she responds, pursing her lips. "Unfortunately, some God-botherer in Belfast sees it, gets a fit of the Heavens-to-Betsys and orders an investigation into who's responsible. And at the end of the hunt, a senior journalist – and a married one at that – is sacked, betrayed by a large egg-shaped mole on his back. The girl, who can't be identified, gets off scot-free.

"To spare everyone's blushes, the BBC put it about that the guy's fired for conduct unbecoming on air – on a late-night programme that no-one ever hears. And to this day, that's what everyone believes, until Stan marches into Ivan's office two weeks ago and asks how the mole on his back is . . ."

"So Juanita's home video contains literally no moles whatsoever?" I suggest.

"Not a one," says Mary. "Though Ivan knows that it might as well. And given that it is now ten years since he leaves the BBC, and Mrs Ivan is still none the wiser as to the real reason, Ivan feels there is now little point in re-airing old laundry – or trawling through old videos."

"But that still doesn't explain why Ivan hates the Saint so much," I point out.

Mary hesitates for a minute and chews her lip again.

"Well, rumour has it that the Saint is also at that same Christmas party," she concedes. "And word is that he accidentally surprises the two outdoor gymnasts while answering a call of nature. And from what I hear, Ivan holds a grudge against the Saint ever since for not giving away the girl, leaving him to take the fall all on his own."

"Aha!" I say. "Good job for the girl that the Saint is an honourable man."

"Good job indeed," nods Mary impassively.

"So who is the girl?" I ask her casually.

"I have no idea at all," she comments. Equally casually.

Though from where I am sitting, you would swear that Mary's face is starting to light up like a brake lamp.

Boys And Dolls

The wedding is still going full tilt, and I'm just making my goodbyes to barman Danny Boy Gillespie when Harry the Hurler slopes up from behind and wraps the two of us in another bear hug.

"The first time Danny Boy is up for throwing stones without a mask, we all tag along to Bishop Street to support him," says Harry, beaming proudly. "I even agree to defend him myself. So we're sitting in the court when the magistrate asks me if there is anyone in the audience who can vouch for his good character. 'Yes, Your Worship,' I tell him, 'Chief Inspector Murphy of the RUC there.'

"Quick as a flash, Murphy jumps to his feet and shouts, 'But I don't even know the boy.'

"'Per-zackly!' says I. 'Danny Boy is living in this town for fifteen years and the Super wouldn't know him if he hits him with a pipe. Surely that is reference enough?'"

We all laugh, as Harry's jokes are always funny.

"Totally untrue, of course," declares Danny Boy when we draw breath. "But you know that anyway, because the only way Harry ever visits court is at the point of a subpoena . . ."

*****

Generally, I am not a man for weddings, preferring to leave them to those who see them as occasions for joy. But one day I am sitting in my kitchen working my way through my morning cornflakes and Alka Seltzer, when an envelope falls through a rarely-used slit in the door and lands on the mat. And inside the envelope is a summons to Harry the Hurler's kid brother's wedding in a fortnight's time.

And while this will certainly be a joyous event, the prospect of a day spent with the Hurley clan and the entire cast of The Secret Army immediately renders the seltzer null and void. Now, don't get me wrong, Gerry the Hurler is a young fellow of almost unquestionable character, whose tearful account of *Boolavogue* is held in very high esteem in diddle-dee-dee circles. But given that every second cop in Occupied Derry will be outside The Jack Kennedy Inn filming his nuptials, a guy would really want to be on top of his parking fines before taking part in such a rally.

And unfortunately the RSVP is to Harry, who's hosting the bash. For it would take a braver man than me to poke Big H in the eye with a sharp stick. Moreover, as Harry erroneously believes that I am in someway responsible for attaching the two lovebirds, it may be considered rude of me not to appear. So rude, in fact, that Harry writes at the bottom of the card that if I don't appear he will give me 'the sack'. This is a little joke, of course, which no doubt reminds you of the time Pizza Phelan forgets to go to Harry's Granda's funeral and wakes up drifting down the Foyle in a potato sack. Though thankfully for Pizza, the cable ties come off his hands and feet before he goes down for the third time.

*****

The reason for my invite to such a grand occasion is a little complicated. About six weeks ago, I am sitting in The Jack Kennedy on a quiet spring afternoon, picking at a crossword and watching barman Danny Boy Gillespie spitting peanuts into his mop bucket, when in walks Harry the Hurler – head honcho of all the Boys in Derry – and sits down beside me.

I swiftly look round to see who else is in the bar. For, as you know, there are many people in this city who like to keep track of all Harry's known associates. These would include gendarmes, magistrates and other less-recognisable guys who dispense with due process a little too rapidly for my liking. But as there's no-one else about, I risk a quick nod, then engross myself in Six Across.

"You are obviously a smart guy to be doing a crossword in a newspaper like that," says Harry conversationally, shrugging off his tweed jacket and making a Two Pints sign to Danny Boy. "And I am looking to find such a smart guy who could perhaps give me some advice."

"But I am sure there is very little I could advise a man such as you about," I answer carefully.

"Do not worry yourself," he laughs, "this is not a matter of politics, where there are more than enough people ready to give me counsel. It is about women – a matter about which I know nothing, being married now this long time."

Now, given that my shirt hasn't seen an iron since Ireland is last free, and the cheeks of my trousers are as shiny as two bullets, you would think that Harry the Hurler might work out that women are not my strong point. So I look round for Danny Boy to join in. But he is a much smarter sort of guy than me and is practising so intently for the nightly peanut-spitting contest that he doesn't even see us.

"Gerry," continues Harry, gripping my shoulder earnestly, "that's my little brother, is after falling out with his bride-to-be. And unless he reaches a peace agreement very quickly, there'll be no June wedding. Gerry is totally distraught, and our dear Old Ma – who is looking forward to the wedding more than anything – is sicker than a kitten in a flush pipe."

Harry releases my shoulder to grip his pint with equal determination and sighs the sigh of a troubled man.

"The problem," explains Harry, "is that he loves her ever since he first clocks eyes on her."

"Eyes on who?" I ask before I can stop myself.

"You are right," nods Harry. "I better give you the whole SP from the start."

So I tell Harry that I am most interested in hearing the full story, if he can hold on a tick till I visit the jacks. But it is no use, as Danny Boy is one step ahead and is after padlocking the back door.

*****

Harry and Gerry, it seems, are sitting in Swanky Frankie's Fine Curry Parlour and Grill Room on William Street late one night about two years ago, eating chips and Tikka sauce, when all of a sudden, this vision in her summer finest passes by their table.

She is as classy a doll as you'll ever see – drunk or sober: short, black hair in a spiky Pixie cut, narrow little eyes as dark as coal, and teeth so straight and white you could play Chopsticks on them.

But it's her legs that win the star prize. They're long and sleek, and give her this mischievous little spring in her step as she walks by. Gerry, who doesn't normally notice much, can't take his eyes off her.

"She, naturally, spots Gerry straight away – he's a good-looking boy like his brother," grins Harry. "But she ignores him, cool as a judge. She just stands in front of us for ten minutes twirling around, looking at the four-line menu – making sure he gets a damn good recce of the target from all sides. Little short dress she's wearing, you could barely blow your nose in it.

"Anyhow, after ten minutes oohing and aahing and shifting from her good side to the back view, she and her pals sit down at the table so far away from us she's going to need room service.

"Well, for the next half-hour or so, I cannot get a word of sense out of Gerry, as he's too busy moon-eyeing the far corner. Then, all of a sudden, the girl gets up and bounces up to our table, her eyes grinning like a Chinese bookie's.

"Excuse me," she says to Gerry in this soft but challenging sort of voice, "would you have a match?

"Well, Gerry, who's so excited he's barely fit to bite his thumb, starts stuttering like Stammering Stan the Radio Man and tells her he doesn't smoke. And he then points out that smoking is a filthy habit anyway. Wrong answer. And the vision is as ticked off as a cat in a cold bath. So she turns on her heels and stomps back to the corner, those lovely legs bouncing gently all the while.

"Now even Gerry is smart enough to realise this doll is offended," says Harry, "so he leaps up to make amends. He gets to her table about five seconds after her. But it's too late for her to hide the packet of matches sitting in front of her. Gerry, naturally, spies the box, grins at her, lights a match and holds it to her cigarette.

"The girl, who is called Alice – or, more often, 'Alice Springs' on account of her bouncy walk – flashes the laughing eyes at him again and then breaks the cig in half. 'I'm quitting,' she tells him. And before you can say Love In A Bucket, the two are making plans to hold hands in the back row tomorrow night. For the next two years, they're tighter than a photo-finish, and a few weeks ago, they go and order up the double-decker cake."

Harry then holds his empty glass up to the light a bit obviously, so I give Danny Boy the Two Pint sign, motioning for him to start me a slate. Danny is part responsible for my predicament and signals Just This Once.

"What is the problem then?" I ask my new friend Harry. "Everything looks as rosy as a poem."

"Even rosier," he agrees. "Until three weeks ago, when Alice hears Gerry is playing kissy-face with another doll."

"Aha!" I reply.

"Aha is right," says Harry.

"So . . . is he?" I suggest.

"Technically, yes," says Harry. "But I can assure you he doesn't want to do it – neither does she. It is a necessary evil."

"This is a new excuse on me," I reply, "and one which I think would hold little weight with any jury. Or at least one which contains any women."

"You are spot on there," sighs Harry. "When Alice Springs hears the news, she kicks Gerry so hard in the lower belt area that he returns a full portion of Tikka-covered chips onto her stilettos. She then takes off the engagement ring he buys her – four grand worth, wholesale – and flings it into our living-room fire. She then smiles over at Ma, who's watching all this in horror, says: 'Goodnight, Mrs Hurley, God bless,' and bounces out the door.

"Lucky, however, Ma has only a letting-on gasfire, so we are able to retrieve the ring. But poor old Gerry is devastated. And he's getting no sympathy from anywhere, as the whole town believes he's a two-timing rat. Ma, God be good to her, thinks Love will sort it all out – she's still convinced there'll be a wedding. Gerry spends his day banging on my door and ringing on my mobile, looking for advice. And Alice Springs, the bad article, is putting it about that she's moving on with her life and seeing someone else.

"I don't need this, I've a business to run."

Harry is clearly finished his story, so looks up slowly at me, waiting for inspiration. Now, I know as much about the fairer sex as I do about singing in tune. Though I realise this mightn't be the time to share this with Harry, so I say nothing, but make like I'm in deep thought.

"I'm thinking of getting Gerry to leave town for a coupla weeks till everything calms down," says Harry eventually. "What do you reckon?"

"Hmm," I reply, wondering how to retire from this advice-giving business.

Personally, I figure it can't do any harm to keep Gerry away from this other woman with whom he is playing kissy-face regularly – even if only on a technical basis. But my mother is a clever lady and does not raise her children to offer wrong advice to guys such as Harry the Hurler.

So in spite of my better judgement, I confess to Harry that I actually know Alice Springs since she is a nipper and will go and find out what is going on with her – all totally off the record.

And this, I suspect, is why Harry sits down beside me in the first place.

Danny Boy Gillespie, like all good barmen, hears every word of our discussion. And the tail of Harry's tweed jacket isn't out the door when my fair-weather pal hustles over beside me and sets me up a medicinal brandy.

"So what's the score with Gerry and this other girl?" I inquire casually. "She must be off the Richter scale altogether to get him to play away from home."

"Not at all," grins Danny Boy. "In fact, she is as ugly as a trout and tiny enough to hang on your key ring."

"Then she must have a bigger bankroll than Sparkly Barkley?"

"Not at all," chortles Dan. "In fact, Bridget the Midget owes money to every bookie in the town."

"In which case," I reply, working it out, "she works for the Boys, is now stuck in the Secure Wing at Maghaberry, and Gerry has to go up once a fortnight to pass polythene-wrapped messages to her mouth-to-mouth. And he can't tell Alice about it, because there's some internal business afoot – like a surprise vacation for her block, perhaps."

"Per-zackly!" laughs Dan. "And a certain no-good prison warder, who's in Derry a few weeks ago for the march, spills the kissy-face business to one of Alice's business associates."

Now, the only sensible action for someone retiring from the advice-giving business is to avoid The Jack Kennedy for the next few weeks. So despite my natural homing instinct, I manage to find other nooks to nestle in.

Then, at the end of one long evening, I remember I have no seltzer for the morning, so I decide to go to Swanky Frankie's for some pre-emptive stomach lining. And who is sitting in the corner, all on her own and moping into a bowl of stew, but Alice Springs. She beckons me down sadly, her face as long as a four-day wake.

Now, I know Alice Springs from back when she is just plain Alice, an innocent-looking youngster, who makes pocket money fleecing Americans on the city Walls. Though this is long before she moves up in society and starts dating young Hurley. Among her many skills back then are an ability to repackage polyester ties as *Dior Exclusifs*, siphoning North African gin into iffy bottles marked Chanel Eau de Toilette, and selling off gold-plated cigarette lighters, two for a pound. On one memorable occasion, as you may recall, she sidles up to a visiting stag party and promises, for a fee, to take them to see gyrating young girls in exotic costumes. Then, as soon as the bundle is in the bag, she leads them into the Guildhall for the Irish Dancing Championships.

This, of course, is many moons ago. And today, Alice is a respectable member of the community who has a franchise in Foyleview Superstore, offering genuine Chanel perfume, mostly-real silk Dior ties and gold-plated lighters at £20 a throw.

*****

"Of course, I don't believe for one minute that Gerry the Hurler is doing a line with Bridget the Midget," she begins, before I have even speared my first chip covered in Tikka sauce.

"Hmm," I reply.

"Whatever else my ex-fiancé is, he is not some empty-headed Johnny-Kiss-All-The-Girls," she explains.

"Hmm," I tell her.

"And besides," she continues, "Bridget the Midget is as ugly as a trout and owes money to every cheap bookie in the town.

"No, what I think's happening is that Gerry is letting his big brother use him to pass in poly-wrapped messages mouth-to-mouth – probably to organise some home leave. And he can't tell me about it because I'm some high-class lady who knows nothing about such things. Gerry, of course, is still unaware of my own twelve-month sabbatical in Maghaberry Secure Wing for repeated breaches of the Trade Descriptions Act – as I tend to omit this from my CV. And he has no idea that in my day, I myself swallow more poly-wrapped messages than he does Tikka-covered chips.

"Maybe it's time for me to come clean with the Hurley clan, though God knows how Old Ma will feel at having a common criminal in the family. What do you think?"

"I think I am going to stop eating supper here," I grin.

*****

Now, I have to confess that when the envelope lands on my mat, I am not altogether shocked – given that Gerry and Alice are as lost as two lambs without each other. And as there is no ducking this particular wedding, I buy the obligatory new shirt, rent out a tux and set off for the festivities.

Like most weddings, it is not nearly as bad as the anticipation. The coppers outside The Jack Kennedy even refrain from taking photos of the guests, after the Boys' Internal Security team agree not to give out their home addresses on the PA.

Everyone who's everyone, or indeed anyone, is inside; from Councilman Seamus 'the Saint' Timoney – who steers clear of the wedding video crew – to Barry the Bookie and his son Firstborn on their first trip home from the States since the charges are dropped. Bridget the Midget and her ten colleagues from Block IV are unfortunately unable to attend, as since taking their surprise vacation a fortnight ago, they are still somewhat reluctant to travel openly in this jurisdiction.

After an hour or two of passing myself, I am just working out how I can exit the stage discreetly, when Harry the Hurler lumbers up to me at the bar and wraps me in a bear hug.

"I can't thank you enough for your help," he says, his eyes glistening with emotion and drink. "After your talk with Alice that night in Swanky Frankie's, she realises how much she misses Gerry and agrees to kiss and make up.

"Old Ma is smiling like a Mormon choir ever since. And Sparkly Barkley's even agreed to give us a late licence tonight. Couldn't do enough for me, that man."

Harry then gives me another tearful handshake and goes off to bear-hug someone else.

I recommence inching my way to the side door, when the new Mrs Gerry the Hurler suddenly spies me and hauls me over to a quiet corner.

"I'll never be able to thank you for your help," she whispers, giving me her Chinese grin. "After our talk that night, I realise it's time to come clean with Gerry and confess my earlier CV. Even Mrs Hurley agrees it could happen to a bishop. And it's all back to Love In A Bucket again."

Alice then bounces off to change into her honeymoon outfit, which, she assures me, contains so much sizzle that it'll make every guy in the place want to kick a hole in a reinforced door.

At last the exit is clear, and I am just about to duck under the security cordon, when Danny Boy Gillespie flags me down with a medicinal brandy for the road, which he slips into my hand.

"So they all live happily ever after," I say to him.

"Hmm," he says and laughs. "Just between you and me, things aren't quite as simple as Alice and Harry will have you believe."

"They never are," I agree. "And isn't it curious that no-one has yet mentioned the sudden disappearance of eleven unarmed women from a wing so secure even the mice have their own keys."

"You're on the right track," laughs Danny Boy. "Though I will only tell you the story in full on the understanding that it remains strictly in this room. If not, Gerry the Hurler will demonstrate to you how he can hit a golf ball over three hundred yards with his hurl. Except he will not use a ball."

This is no idle threat, as Gerry is quite a golf champion since he gives up the hurling. So I nod okay.

"After you leave Alice in Frankie's that night, she comes to see me," says Danny Boy. "She asks me to do a bit of research in the library and hoke out the newspaper report of her unfortunate conviction for selling inaccurately-labelled merchandise. And she tells me to send this report to Gerry – anonymously, of course – which I do.

"Gerry quickly realises that he is badly misjudging his Honey Bunny's ability to find her way about, so he tracks down and confronts Alice, who admits, tearfully, how she knows all about the message-passing game. But she also admits something to him that very few people in the world know – even the likes of you, who remember Alice from back when she is ripping off the Yankee peacemakers.

"You see, about half-way through Alice's own sabbatical at Maghaberry, four young offenders take a surprise vacation from the Secure Wing one night. And their travel arrangements, believe it or not, are devised by none other than the new Mrs Gerry the Hurler. Then two months later, another six take extended leave, again courtesy of Alice Tours. In fact, the only reason Alice doesn't jump the wall herself is that she's making too much money as a holiday consultant. And by the time she comes out, she has enough bread to buy a little perfume franchise in Foyleview Superstore, which is all she really wants out of life in the first place.

"So when Gerry hears all this, Alice is drafted in as a travel agent for Bridget the Midget and her gang – who, as we speak, are as free as cold rain."

We look round and see that Alice is bouncing back into the hall. And sure enough, she is wearing a tight little mini-dress which has every guy in the room wondering who Gerry the Hurler kills in a previous life – and indeed this one – to get so lucky.

But it is time for the scratcher. So I admire her briefly from the door, drain my brandy, and head for the night air.

"One more thing," calls Danny Boy over to me as I head for the taxi. "It's not her walk."

"What do you mean?"

"How Alice Springs gets her name," replies Danny.

"I'm way ahead of you," I grin. "The Hurleys aren't the only wiseguys in this town . . ."

First Communion

We are sitting in the Merc waiting for Donna-Bop to find the matching white purse when Curly-Bop asks her Granda if he knows any stories. Now Dominic 'the Hurler' Hurley, patriarch of all the Hurley clan, knows many stories, some of which are even repeatable in front of seven-year-old children. Not that you'd believe it if you ever read his witness statements, as these invariably start with No Comment, end with I Want My Lawyer and are emptier than his conscience in between.

"Make it a holy story, seeing as how I'm making my First Communion today," pleads Curly-Bop.

This, however, poses Dominic the Hurler a problem. For Dom is a man whose knowledge of matters spiritual is generally limited to sending Remember Me notices attached to wreaths.

So he hmms and he hawws, furrows his forehead and scratches his neck. Then, after a minute, someone switches on the light in his head and he announces that he remembers a religious story.

"This is a true story," he begins, winking over to me. "The Pope on his last visit to America gets a call to give the last rites to a cardinal in New York. His Holiness is only up in Boston, so they figure it'll be just as handy to drive down in the Popemobile.

"They're travelling through Connecticut and the Pope asks his driver if there's any chance he can get a wee turn at the wheel. Now, the driver's a bit cagey at first but, after the Pope pulls rank, agrees to give him a quick spin and hops in the back.

"Well, His Holiness gets behind the wheel and takes off like a Pope out of Hell. He's cruising along the freeway at one hundred and twenty miles an hour when two state troopers snare him in a radar trap and, after a harum-scarum race, slow him down. The cop goes up to the Popemobile window to check the licence but returns quickly to his buddy.

"'We're in deep, deep trouble,' he says, 'I'm just after pulling over someone extremely big.'

"'What, it's not a Congressman, is it?' asks his buddy.

"'Bigger than a Congressman,' replies the cop.

"'A Senator then, perhaps?' asks the guy in the squad car.

"'Bigger than a Senator,' says the cop.

"'God almighty, it's not the President, is it?'

"'Worse again,' says the cop.

"'Well, who is it then?' demands his buddy.

"'I'm not rightly sure,' says the cop, 'but he has the Pope for a chauffeur.'"

*****

Darling Curly-Bop, of course, doesn't understand the moral in this parable, but smiles appreciatively anyway, as mean old Gramps is still holding onto her First Communion money.

Curly is supposed to make her First Communion in April last with the rest of her class, but her mother Donna-Bop refuses to let her for fear Curly's father, Sergeant John Gilmore – known locally as Jack the Black – might turn up. And instead, Donna-Bop promises the child she can have her big day on a secret date in July. Though naturally, she's not counting then on the road closures and the bridge blockades.

Curly is her mother's double – a vision of wavy blonde locks, little dimpled cheeks and eyes as blue as a hot summer night. And today she's all decked out like an angel in a white lace dress for her big occasion.

The reason I am in the car with Curly, Donna and Dom is a little complicated – so much so that I'm not sure I understand it myself.

As you may know, Harry the Hurler, Donna's eldest brother, is Curly's godfather, despite Father Carlin trying to rule it out. He says it's like putting a pyromaniac in charge of the matches. But over the years, Harry performs his duties very honourably, showering his godchild with gifts and taking her on surprise outings to hurling matches and the dog track. Unfortunately, however, Harry the Hurler is currently unable to visit Curly's home in Claudy – about ten miles east of Derry – as some of the locals there are not so keen on the Boys and would lynch him from the lamppost.

64

And Harry also has serious difficulties with Donna's soon to be ex-husband, Jack the Black – largely because of Jack's past attempts to consign him and many of his associates to ten-year sabbaticals.

In fairness, Jack the Black is not a bad sort, for a cop, and he even agrees to kick with a new foot when he marries Donna-Bop. He is generally sympathetic to his clients and is never a man to distribute Drinking After Hours tickets – except for the night he discovers nine of us in the Ladies' toilets in The Jack Kennedy at 4.00am. Jack points out, in his defence, though, that the magistrate might not believe that all of us are in there looking for our mothers.

So Harry won't be travelling to Claudy – not this year anyway – and will instead wait for Curly at the church. And one evening last week, he tracks me down in The Jack Kennedy and nominates me to represent him on the journey into town. Though only because Danny Boy Gillespie discloses that I am probably in the last cubicle in the Gents'.

*****

"The first time I ever clap eyes on Jack the Black is on duty outside our house on Creggan Broadway," recalls Donna-Bop as Dom pulls the Merc out onto the Derry road. "The rest of his squad are inside pulling up our floorboards while he's out minding the gate. My mother's so upset at the wreckage they're causing to the kitchen that I take her out to the garden for a bit of air. But she becomes hysterical and collapses on the ground, sobbing.

"Well, out comes this brash young inspector, bends over Ma, pokes his face down into hers and starts roaring at her to get up you Dirty Old Bag or you'll really have something to cry about. But then, all of a sudden, a half-brick shoots over the hedge; there's an almighty thump and the inspector slumps over like a bag of fish.

"Now, I look out on the street, and the only person I can see is this good-looking cop about twenty feet away. 'Where are all those stones coming from?' he shouts. He then winks in at me, wipes the dust off his gloves and whispers, 'If I ever become a rioter, the cops'll never stand a chance.'"

*****

The first serious problem we encounter is at Burntollet Bridge, when Dominic the Hurler refuses to hand over his licence to the Planter with the matching Union Jack windcheater and neck tattoos. The Planter, like tens of thousands of his colleagues, is upset that new parade restrictions are spoiling his democratic right to spend the summer winding up Home Rulers.

Now, given that Dominic is the father of the Chief Executive of all the Boys in Derry, it is probably a good idea for him to keep his licence in the pocket, not least because he is driving a forty-thousand-note Mercedes. And nothing would give these particular Planters greater pleasure than to consign the Merc – passengers included – over the railings and into the ready-made car wash below.

The picket know they've got Home Rulers in the car because of the little girl in the First Communion dress in the back. So they pull us into a lay-by while Neck Tattoo checks out the number plate – via a police-issue walkie-talkie. This may take a while.

"How long since your last confession?" Dominic jokes to me.

"Last night – my first time," interrupts Curly-Bop from the back.

"So what does the priest say when he hears about you throwing stones at the Planters' school bus?" asks Gramps, pulling the hard line.

"He doesn't say anything," replies Curly-Bop with a sniff. "In fact, he tells me he once does it himself when he is my age – though he says he never splits anybody."

"Well, I'd say he's very annoyed when he hears what you call that soldier who tries to look inside your schoolbag?" continues Dom.

"Nope, in fact he tells me he once uses that word himself at a soldier who asks to check out his Bible," says Curly-Bop.

"So does this priest find any difficulty with you at all?" demands Gramps.

"Well, yes," says Curly-Bop coyly. "He gives me ten Hail Marys for letting Andy Cameron kiss me on the cheek when we're playing Mummies and Daddies."

"So Father Carlin never plays Mummies and Daddies when he is a nipper?" laughs Dom.

"He does, of course," chips in Donna-Bop from the back. "In fact, I remember him to be a Johnny-Kiss-All-The-Girls. But never with the ones from the Planters' School . . ."

"Aha!" says Dominic.

There is a knock at the window, and it's Neck Tattoo again. Neck, it seems, is not the leader of this pack because of looks alone, and he's back to try a new tack. He leans in the driver's window and smiles at Curly-Bop.

"That's a beautiful white dress," he says. "Who would buy you such a thing?"

"My mommy," replies Curly-Bop proudly.

"And what's your mommy's name?" responds Neck Tattoo patiently.

"Donna Gilmore – and my Daddy's the police sergeant, Jack the Black," replies Curly-Bop, exactly as we tell her.

"Indeed," says Neck, his face lighting up like a neon sign. He turns to Dom: "Please drive on, sir, and enjoy the rest of your day. Sorry about the delay."

Dom glares out angrily as if he's considering staying put. So Neck thinks for a moment, reaches in his pocket and then adds, "And here's a fiver for the little girl."

Dom laughs, slips the Merc into gear, the fiver into his top pocket and makes tracks for Derry.

*****

After a brief but unforgettable run-in with a Planter roadblock at Drumahoe, three miles outside the city, we finally reach Craigavon Bridge and can see the spire of St Eugene's Cathedral in the near distance.

Unfortunately, however, this bridge is also blocked by Planters. And they are led by none other than the city's former mayor, Elizabeth Biggard – or Betty Bigot, as she's better known in the *Derry Standard*.

Betty's eyes light up as she spots the Communion dress, and she immediately waves the car into the side lane with all the other suspected Home Rulers. The gendarmes, who are out in force to keep order on the bridge, stand back and do nothing.

"That's a very pretty dress," she says to Curly-Bop, when Dominic eventually winds down the window. "Aren't you a bit young to be getting married – even for your sort?"

"No, it's a Communion dress, silly," replies Curly-Bop with an exasperated tut.

"It's a pity no-one's going to see it, though," snaps Betty nastily. So nastily, in fact that Curly starts working off her own script.

"My mommy," she pipes up, "says you're as black as a coalman's armpit. But my Granda says you're orange through and through. You look white enough to me. Though you're just as fat as they say."

"What else does mommy say?" asks Betty Bigot, eyes narrowing.

"Well, mommy says that people like you who block roads should be hosed down with cowshit and turfed into the Foyle," answers Curly-Bop.

"And what about Granda there, what does he say?" inquires Betty, clearly on a roll.

"He thinks drowning's far too good for you and that they should feck you from a great height onto iron spikes," replies Curly-Bop, quoting Dom word for word.

"And what about this other guy in the front?" says Betty, pointing at me.

"Well," hmms Curly-Bop, "he is very quiet since Granda Dom drives over that stupid Planter's foot at Drumahoe. I don't know this other guy very well at all. Mommy says he's only here as a representative of Uncle Harry the Hurler, who doesn't like travelling to the Waterside."

"Is that a fact?" whistles Betty Bigot, grinning the grin of a big fat wolf.

*****

After about an hour in the stationary lane, Curly-Bop announces that she wants to go wee-wee, so Betty Bigot agrees to take her over into Dukes Bar as she doesn't want Donna out of the car.

"Why don't the police step in?" grunts Donna as Curly disappears through the pub door.

"You should know better than me," says Dom with a sharp look in his eye. "After all, you're still married to one of them – and a mostly decent one at that. In fact, maybe you'll care to explain his absence today, now that Curly-Bop is otherwise engaged."

"They just can't accept our culture, Daddy," snuffles Donna, playing to the gallery. "You know what they're like yourself. Look out the window."

"I think you'll need to do better than that," responds Dom kindly. "Jack the Black, I hear, is taking it very bad altogether and drinking like a man with hollow legs."

"Okay," sighs Donna, "but you're not to get angry. About six months ago, Harry tells me that it's about time Curly-Bop enrols in some music and culture classes. As the child's guardian, he reckons she's not getting enough extra-curricular fulfilment."

"So what's the problem in that?" asks Dom.

"Nothing at all," says Donna, "until Jack the Black sees Curly's picture on some CCTV footage, posing as a drum majorette at the front of the Fighting Fenians' Junior Flute Band."

"Aha!" nods Dom slowly. "So I imagine Jack wants to put a stop to it?"

"Wouldn't you?" says Donna. "And to be honest, so do I. But Curly-Bop loves her green, white and gold dress, with the little crossed-rifles on the badge. And she also loves all the attention she gets as star of the show. So I don't want to ask her to leave.

"And when Jack the Black says either the band uniform goes or he does, I dig in my heels and tell him I'll miss him."

And with that, Donna starts weeping quite hard – like she really does miss him.

*****

We are sitting making There-There noises to Donna, when Curly-Bop hops back into the car with a smarty-pants grin all over her face. Personally, I can't see what she has to be so happy about, given that the Planters are promising that we are going to spend the rest of our lives on the bridge – and even that mightn't be so long. But as Betty waddles back to her battalion, Curly leans over to her Granda and whispers that Uncle Harry will be here in two minutes.

"How do you know that?" Dom whispers back.

"Well, a long time ago, Harry gets me to learn his mobile number in case of emergencies," explains Curly-Bop.

"And lucky, there's a phone outside the little girls' room. So while Betty's in the lounge getting a wee Bush and Ginger for the heartburn, I make a reverse charges call to Harry.

"They're all at the chapel for the past two hours – and want to know what's keeping us. So I tell him about Betty Bigot and the bridge and the Planters – and how you all reckon Uncle Harry is nothing but a cowardly wastrel, who should get down here right away to protect his little goddaughter."

"But no-one's saying anything like that," replies Donna.

"Yes," sniffs Curly, "but you're not the one sitting in the little white dress with nowhere to go."

*****

Two minutes later, almost to the second, a group of around one hundred men appear at the mouth of Abercorn Road, with Harry the Hurler and Father Drownem Doherty at the head. And they start marching towards the lines on the bridge. Father Drownem, as you'll no doubt recall, gets his name thanks to his great enthusiasm for baptising children. He believes that once you're christened by him, you stay that way for life. He's an old wizened guy, with more wrinkles than my shirt – but equally hard wearing.

"We are going to perform the Communion ceremony on the bridge here," he instructs Betty Bigot, through gritted teeth.

Now, you and I both know that First Communion services are supposed to take place in chapels and not on bridges. But, of course, politics is all about public relations. And Harry the Hurler and Father Drownem are not about to let Betty Bigot walk away from a catastrophe all of her own making.

So someone produces a little felt card table from the boot of a car and Father D sets it up as his altar.

"No need," says Betty, sensing disaster, "we'll let you through."

"Do not try and stop us," continues Drownem, ignoring her, "or we'll have Curly-Bop cry for all the cameramen behind me – and I assure you, you will not be able to put your big fat hide outside the door in this city ever again."

But you cannot start a First Communion service without a hymn. And this leaves Father Drownem at a considerable disadvantage. Harry the Hurler, his assorted Boys and the posse of thirty cameramen are not worth one chorus of *Be Not Afraid* between them.

"Tell you what," says Father D. "Seeing as it's just Curly here on her own, you can all sing *You'll Never Walk Alone*."

So the entire assembly – apart, of course, from the Planters and a few Man United fans – let loose with a fair-to-middling chorus of *Walk Ons*. Meanwhile, a young red-haired cop comes up to Father D and confesses that he once is an altar boy before he disgraces himself and turns his back on his own sort. So he is recruited to hold the plate – a job he does with great aplomb, despite the hisses of the picket.

The ceremony gets underway and Drownem keeps it short, aware that the film crews will be wanting to turn it around for six o'clock. Even the Planters get in on the act, with Betty Bigot and a bunch of Methodists chiming in with a version of *Be Thou My Vision* as Curly comes back from the altar. But as Harry says, this is only to take the bare look off them for when the TV footage goes out at teatime.

As proceedings come to an end, I look up from the bag I am breathing into and notice that Donna-Bop is having a word with Harry. And this word is not Please or Thank You. In fact, Donna-Bop is grabbing Harry by the arm, staring straight into his eye and making a pointing sign right into his face. And from what I can see, Harry is swallowing hard – not at all accustomed to this end of the discussion – and eventually nods Yes.

*****

About a month later, I am sitting in The Jack Kennedy, still mulling over my heroic escape, when who comes in but Sergeant Jack the Black.

"Do not panic," he smiles as I move towards the door. "Your drinking-on fine is no longer on the books after what you do for my little girl. You must learn not to dwell too much on these things and stop worrying. Indeed, I hear Mr and Mrs Alka Seltzer have to take on extra staff to cope with the demand. Curly tells me her First Communion day is the best a girl could ever wish for. I'm only sorry not to be part of such a religious experience myself."

I don't know, in truth, if it is precise to describe Curly-Bop's Communion as a religious experience. Though I will concede that it brings me a whole lot nearer to God than I ever intend to be. For some years yet.

"I also want to thank you for taking care of my beautiful wife," says Jack, "though it is perhaps not so gentlemanly to leave your lunch in her shoes when Old Dom drives over that Planter's foot at Drumahoe. And by the way, the guy is not now going to sue Dom. His lawyer, it seems, is about to lodge the papers when he gets word that his client is in the running for seven Public Order offences and that the judge will fine him exactly double whatever compo he gets from Dom."

Jack is sounding so cheerful you could choke him. But the last time I hear, he is for hooking up the hosepipe and switching on the engine. So despite my natural reluctance to speak to policemen in public places, I ask him what prompts this return to hale and hearty form.

"Well," laughs Jack, who has a good sense of irony for a cop, "I suppose it is okay to tell you – given that Harry now regards you as family and all. Later on the evening of Curly's big day, I happen to be on point duty on Burntollet Bridge. So I'm standing trying to dissuade this drunken Planter with a neck tattoo from self-servicing a Home Ruler's petrol tank, when all of a sudden, I see Dominic the Hurler's Merc come down the hill.

"Naturally, I flag it down as it appears to my trained eye that it is carrying a most undesirable criminal type in the front seat, namely Harry the Hurler – who, incidentally, is patron of the Fighting Fenians' Junior Flute Band. And as you can imagine, I am waiting for this day for the past three months.

"But I haven't even got my book out of my pocket when Harry leans across from his seat and says to me, 'I have some news which may sadden your daughter, so perhaps I will tell you that you can break it to her.' He then gets out of the car and signals me over to the side of the jeep where he'll be safe from missiles.

"'Curly's flute band is being wound up, as their grants are all of a sudden being withdrawn,' says Harry. 'I hope this won't inconvenience her too much, but she is welcome to become a cheerleader at the hurling club, if that would be acceptable.'

"'Very much so,' I tell him. And the two of us shake hands on it."

"So what happens next?" I ask Jack.

"I look into the back of the car," he explains, "and what do I see there but two visions in blond curls – my wife and my daughter. So I grab the guy with the neck tattoo, throw him into the back of the jeep, and radio the base to advise them that I'm taking some time owed – starting immediately. I then tell Curly-Bop and Donna-Bop to bunch over in the back seat, as we're all going home together."

"So Harry comes along?" I inquire.

"Yes," grins Jack, "we all have a damn fine evening, with fantastic food, buckets of wine and marvellous music.

"And at the end of the night, Harry turns to me and says that if the company's good enough for his father, his sister and his goddaughter, well, it's good enough for him too.

"Though, of course, he insists that I never breathe a word of this to anyone."

"Of course," I laugh. "After all, a man has his standards to keep."

SWITCHBLADE VIC GOES TO COURT

The columnist Charlie Camberwell, as you will already know if you read the newspapers or are involved in any wing of politics, is a rotten little scumbag.

He is more often and accurately referred to as Cheapshot Charlie, on account of the sneaky gossip and catty one-liners he likes to pass off as humour in his *Londonderry Leader* Diary pieces. And while he is no particular friend of mine, I will always say hello to him in The Jack Kennedy Inn – but that is more out of fear than anything else. For Cheapshot Charlie is the type of guy upon whose right side it is very important to stay put.

This is something that even the very powerful, like Councilman Seamus 'the Saint' Timoney should bear in mind, as the Saint himself discovers after he remarks on radio that Cheapshot's column is about as funny as a fatal heart attack.

The following Thursday, the headline story in the *Leader* Diary exposes how the Saint is conducting rigorous "one-on-one negotiations" with a junior party colleague over the need for a more "hands-on" management style. The article reveals that the party colleague is a recent Miss Foyle Banker, whose legs are so long that Father Drownem eventually asks her to wear trousers to Mass, so that he can remain the main event. And just in case anyone is still missing the point, Cheapshot further discloses that the Saint's secret meetings are taking place in a private bedroom upstairs in Mulligan's Pub. This bar, incidentally, is so disreputable that it needs all the Saint's support to keep its licence.

Mrs Seamus Timoney, as you can imagine, is so enraged by these aspersions that she instructs the Saint to haul foot into court and protect his good name. But their solicitor, Tommy Bowtie, advises them that a statesman like the Saint should avoid the courts at all costs, as they can become very messy and expensive.

Tommy Bowtie is also shrewd enough to know that the one great defence against libel is the truth. And he is privately of the opinion that the Saint is to marriage vows what Al Capone is to Valentine's Day. Though naturally, he doesn't say this to Mrs T.

*****

For many years, Cheapshot leads a charmed life. His proudest boast is that after twenty years in the business, he never even gets one writ. Many bluster, though none see it through.

You'll no doubt remember that Bad Breath Bradley promises all sorts of legal repercussions after Cheapshot reveals the full SP on his recent split-up with the Boys. But Chas Camberwell does not stay king of the dung heap for so long without having a few tricks up his sleeves. And he is smart enough to tape Breath's telephone threats to him – which include a detailed account of how Cheapshot is to be stripped naked and hog-tied, while Rufus, the Bradley family rottweiler, plays Find the Hot Dog.

The lawsuit, needless to say, is dropped. Though Breath is still as sore as a busted spot.

*****

The years of neat gin and ugly threats are beginning to take their toll, however, and Cheapshot's pen is becoming more and more outrageous. And so there is no surprise in the chattering circles when it emerges that the leading Planter, Victor 'Switchblade Vic' McCormack is issuing proceedings against Charles Camberwell and the *Leader*.

Cheapshot's column, it seems, alleges that Switchblade Vic is responsible for discharging several dozen live rounds into a car belonging to Father Drownem Doherty, taking little or no account of the fact that Father D is still sitting in the driver's seat. Miraculously, the curate escapes without a single mark, although his nerves are as shot to pieces as his Merc.

Now, of course, Cheapshot does not come out directly and state that Switchblade Vic – a man widely renowned for his peremptory method of dispute settling – is behind the attack. Cheapshot is nowhere near that stupid. In fact, he doesn't even name Vic. But the paper does suggest that a leading Planter is "getting his knife into the clergy" – a reference which Switchblade Vic reckons personally identifies him, given his working alias.

And seeing that Switchblade Vic is a respected publican, who has no previous convictions that are relevant, he is outraged to see his good name and reputation being sullied in this manner.

Generally, from what my good friend Scoop Scallan tells me, newspapers prefer to settle libel cases out of court. Juries, he says, are very unpredictable and tend to sympathise with the accuser in even the most spurious of cases. Judges, likewise, often favour little David against the newspaper Goliath.

But this case is obviously different. Switchblade Vic does not get his moniker from his love of fluffy animals. Indeed, many would argue that Vic is as deadly as a public toilet. So the *Leader* decides to take its chances and give Mr McCormack his day in court.

There is one slight problem, however. Money. *The Leader's* insurance will cover any libel award against it up to the tune of ten thou, which, as you and I know, is about ten thousand times more than Switchblade Vic's character is worth. But the insurance company will not pay for legal representation, and the *Leader*, with their small circulation and low turnover, can't afford to hire lawyers of their own.

They say that a man who represents himself in court has a fool for a client. But given he has no other option, the paper's editor, Prozac Jack Irwin, appoints himself the paper's senior counsel. Prozac Jack, who acquires his name from his easy-going attitude – particularly towards Cheapshot's column – finds the whole thing very amusing. So amusing that he gets Cheapshot Charlie to act as second chair.

When Switchblade Vic hears about this arrangement, he announces that – to level the playing field – he will follow suit and dismiss his very expensive legal team. Though most neutral observers say that this is only because Vic has to pay all his costs himself, as there is no state aid for libel.

*****

High Court cases, such as libel, are normally held in Belfast. But the two sides submit separate motions for a change of venue to Derry in a bid to keep expenses down.

Both teams also reckon that a jury would only be fixed by their opponents and would add to the expense so they agree to abide by the decision of the judge, as long as it's Louise Johnston. And after a bit of to-ing and fro-ing in the court offices, their requests are agreed.

You and I perhaps remember Louise better as 'Letemout Lou' from the days when she is Derry's most capable young defence solicitor. Indeed, Letemout wriggles so many lowlifes off the hook that she is considered a complete danger to society and appointed a magistrate at the age of twenty-eight, and a High Court judge a year after that.

Back in the good old days, however, as you'll expect, she has the dubious honour of defending both Switchblade Vic and Cheapshot Charlie. And both are impressed with her complete integrity and her ability to keep her mouth shut.

Even after she is called to the bench in Belfast, Lou still retains her rebel streak. And I will bet there are very few other High Court judges in Europe with a diamond stud in their belly-button – not to mention a little butterfly tattoo where no-one gets to find it. Though this can work to her advantage. Indeed, it is not uncommon for the most hard-bitten of defendants to become smitten with Lou's beautiful sallow face and sleek black hair – so much so that they will even thank her profusely when she is tossing the key away. But they – as indeed all those who come before her – would do well to remember that Letemout has the courtroom manners of a hungry wolf.

Mind you, she likes to maintain a good relationship with the press. And Stammering Stan the Radio Man, in particular, is always giving her quite flattering reviews before she becomes a wig. So she is more than a little pleased when she returns to the Bishop Street courtroom to see that Stanley's fresh face is beaming up at her out of the reporters' dock.

*****

Harry the Hurler, the Chief Executive and most feared of all the Boys in Derry, is to be called as part of Cheapshot Charlie's defence. Harry knows Vic from their schooldays when they peg rocks at one another over the Fountain peace line, before going on to take up their leadership positions with their respective outfits. So I figure he is to perform as a character witness in reverse.

But Harry is somewhat nervous of courts, given his thirty-four previous experiences. In fact, this could be the first time he is virtually guaranteed to come out the same door as he goes in. So he pops his head into The Jack Kennedy on the way past for a sharpener and asks me if I would care to join him for some moral support.

Now, as you will know, being seen in public with Harry at the best of times is a risky business. But holding his hand in a courthouse swamped with prosecutors, magistrates and gendarmes, has about as much going for it as playing leapfrog with a lemming.

But Harry finds me anyway, in the last cubicle in the Gents'.

*****

The court is already choc-a-bloc by the time we get there, with the public seats at the back full to capacity. Though it's mostly lawyers coming in to bitch about how much of a shambles the whole thing is without them. The cops, naturally, frisk us down as we come through the door, but it is okay, as the bulge under Harry's coat is only his mobile phone.

Because the lawyers are filling the gallery, Harry ushers us into benches normally reserved for solicitors near the front, so we have a good view of the fun.

Things get off to a good start with both counsel and most witnesses remembering to stand up when Letemout comes in. Letemout then spends about two hours explaining the ground rules, which all and sundry roundly sleep through. After that, as the sailor says, the only place to go is down.

"Okay, Mr McCormack," says Letemout to Switchblade Vic. "Let's have the opening statements. You're first. And keep it brief. But I warn you, if you try to pass any eyewash in this court, I'll throw you in jail. Don't forget, I know from personal experience that you are a dirty, lying toe-rag – so mess with me and I will throw the book at you."

Now, Vic might have fewer brains than a hard hat, but he is way too shrewd to challenge Letemout Lou at this early juncture. Particularly as she still recalls where his bodies are buried. Literally.

"If it pleases Your Majesty," he begins with a solemn nod, "I am bringing this case to clear my good name. Cheapshot Charlie is claiming in his column that I am now in the business of whacking clerics. And I believe that this is seriously injurious to my professional standing. Like all captains of industry, I abide by a code of honour, Your Highness, and stiffing reverends is a definite no-no."

He goes on like this for about half an hour, concluding: "In all, I will be seeking fifty K in damages for myself – and for Cheapshot to be tried before a criminal court for perjury and character molestation."

A few of Vic's henchmen at the side of the court start to clap – as do one or two of the court cops. But Her Highness quickly glares at them and they stop. She then nods to Prozac Jack to trot out his opener.

"Switchblade Vic, Your Honour," grins Prozac Jack, "is clearly watching too many late-night movies.

"Number one, the only thing seriously injurious in here is Switchblade Vic for what he does to Father Drownem. And number two, the *Leader* wouldn't have fifty K to spare even if myself and Cheapshot sell our houses – which, incidentally, both belong to our wives.

"Moreover, we are arguing that Vic is not identified anywhere in our article and that if he thinks he is, it is down to his guilty conscience and nothing more. Charles Camberwell is an honourable and scrupulous man who never would malign anyone or do anyone a day's harm."

"Does that include the piece he writes calling for me to be struck off and thrown in jail after I get the Semtex Seven off?" interrupts Her Honour.

"Objection!" protests Prozac Jack.

"Overruled!" thunders Vic.

"Agreed!" snaps Letemout, bopping the gavel off her desk.

*****

The opening statements over, Lou points over at Vic and tells him to call his first witness. And who is it only Cheapshot Charlie, looking shifty as a dog on a damp rug.

Vic is in no mood to stand on ceremony. "Question one, you little turd," he says after Cheapshot is sworn in. "In that story about Father Drownem, isn't it true that you are putting the finger on me?"

"Why ever would you think that?" sneers Cheapshot. "Are you having trouble sleeping at night?"

Vic ignores the sarcasm and presses on. "I put it to you, Cheapshot," he says, "that the comments about a leading Planter having his knife into the clergy are a direct dig at me."

Vic then turns to Letemout grandly and says, "It is my contention that I am the target of the published words. What do you reckon, Your Excellency?"

"Can't say for sure," replies Letemout. "It is what is known as a moot point and one which a jury would normally decide. But seeing as you gentlemen are too low-budget to pay for twelve honest men, why don't we just put it to the hands-up in here?"

Both senior counsel nod okay. And myself and Harry are appointed tellers. Not that we are needed, as the verdict is virtually unanimous, with even Letemout voting that Switchblade Vic is certainly the intended victim of Cheapshot's cheap shot.

"Okay, Vic," says Letemout, "round one to you. You are undoubtedly the target of the published words. So next it's up to the *Leader* to prove that their story's true. We'll start on that tomorrow, but for now we'll break for dinner. This is what is known as an adjournment."

Lou then turns to the reporters' box and grins at Stammering Stan. "Now," she says pleasantly, "as you're the only one in here without an axe to grind, you can buy me drinks in the Northern Counties.

"Oh, and by the way, Stan, when you're writing it up, remember it's 'Ms', and I'm only twenty-eight."

"The only people who use 'Ms' are women of thirty who don't want to admit they're still single," retorts Stan, though only when Letemout is safely back in her chambers.

*****

Cheapshot's first line of defence is now well and truly breached. So the next day, Prozac Jack has to show how he knows the allegations are true. To do this, he puts Cheapshot back in the stand and, for an hour or so, attempts to create a profile of the columnist as a responsible and caring pillar of the Fourth Estate, whose only goal is the quest for truth. But after many derisory wisecracks from the sidelines, and indeed quite a few from the bench, he senses it might be best to try another tack.

"Where do you hear that it is Switchblade Vic who does the job on Father Drownem?" he eventually asks his number two.

"I hate to give away a source, but I hear it from Danny Boy the barman at The Jack Kennedy," explains Cheapshot. "He sees Switchblade Vic at the corner of Harry the Hurler's street only minutes before the attack. And Danny is certain the bulge under Vic's Armani jacket is rather too large to be a mobile phone. In fact, he believes it is exactly the shape of an Uzi machine pistol."

It surprises me to hear that Danny Boy Gillespie talks so freely to such a well-known lowlife as Cheapshot. But when I turn to Harry the Hurler to inquire about this, he just taps his nose to remind me that it is absolutely none of my business.

"So why exactly does Switchblade Vic shoot at Father Drownem, then?" continues Prozac Jack.

"Well," says Cheapshot a little furtively, "Vic doesn't know that Harry has a new car, and Father Drownem is now driving his old Merc. Father

Drownem is just unfortunate to be in Harry's neighbourhood at the time when out steps Vic and starts rat-a-tat-tatting. Indeed, it is only a miracle that Father D is not now saying his Hail Marys person-to-person."

"So your thesis, Mr Camberwell," says Prozac Jack, "is that Switchblade Vic is actually trying to stiff Harry the Hurler – and gets the wrong car. The old one instead of the new one."

"Per-zackly!" announces Cheapshot triumphantly.

There is much sucking in of air in the courtroom and everyone nods Aha – except for Switchblade Vic who, curiously, isn't a bit perturbed.

"I must object to this testimony, Your Lordship," says Vic soberly. "You see, I know for this long time that Harry has a new car and that Father Drownem buys the old Merc."

"How is that?" asks Lou.

"Like Mr Cheapshot, there," says Vic, "I, too, have my sources. Though unlike him, I will refrain from ratting them out. Suffice it to say that there is nothing cops love more than a drink on the house – except perhaps dishing the dirt on Harry the Hurler. And to be honest, they are queuing up at the counter to tell me the make, model and engine number of his new motor."

For a second time there is much sucking in of air and nodding Aha. Except perhaps for Letemout Lou, who reckons all along that Switchblade Vic will hear all about Harry's new car before it even leaves the showroom.

The atmosphere in the court is now highly charged. So Lou figures that it is a good time to adjourn for lunch, saying that Prozac Jack can finish the defence case this afternoon. With that, she turns to Stammering Stan the Radio Man, who is assembling his notes in the reporters' dock.

"For the benefit of the court reporters," she sniffs, "I'd like to point out that I prefer to be called dynamic rather than legendary. Legends are generally very old or dead, whereas I am still in my mid-twenties – and certainly not that number you tell everyone this morning."

Stan, despite his reputation for being a late learner, is not one to lie down under heavy traffic. "With respect, Your Worship," he grins, "my arms are still sore from carrying your books to school when we are in the one class. And if I'm able to admit to thirty-one, you'll do well not to complain when I allow you to be twenty-nine."

Letemout shoots Stan a frosty glare and briefly considers locking him up for contempt – but then pronounces that he'll have to buy her lunch instead.

"One more thing," she asks as they leave for the Northern Counties. "You still can't tell the difference between literally and figuratively – can you?"

"Oh yes I can," asserts Stan.

"Then why is this morning's news bulletin reporting that the opposing sides are literally eating out of my lap?" demands Letemout.

"Ah yes," says Stan. "I do that now and again to entertain the teachers. They reckon they're the only ones who notice these things."

*****

The first indication I get that things are set to go a bit through-other is at lunch, when Harry the Hurler confides over a bowl of Kennedy's stew that he is "one hundred per cent certain" that Switchblade Vic is innocent.

This is a very grandiose statement indeed, coming from a man who will check three different newspapers before telling you he is one hundred per cent certain of the date. But when I press Harry to unburden himself, he clams up tighter than a coffin lid.

*****

Back at the court, Prozac Jack tells Harry the Hurler it's his turn to get up on the stand. Jack is certain he's about to play his trump card and is as excited as a puppy on a warm leg.

"Tell me, Mr Hurley," he starts, giving Harry his full title. "I wonder if you could please tell the court the name of your lifelong enemy – the man who hates you more than anyone else in all the world, and who would whack you even today at the drop of a hat?"

Harry begins to answer, but before he can get two words out of his mouth, Letemout Lou barges in to remonstrate with Prozac Jack about leading the witness.

"Okay," says Jack. "Can you name one person who hates you more than Switchblade Vic and is also in the vicinity of your old car, with an Uzi machine pistol, the night Father Drownem nearly buys the farm?"

"No," says Harry quietly. Though for my money, Harry looks a little shame-faced.

"No further questions," says Prozac Jack.

"I have a question, Your Reverence," interrupts Switchblade Vic. And he jumps up from his desk to look Harry straight in the eye.

"Mr Hurley," he says, "do you think I am responsible for attempting to stiff you?"

"No, I don't," says Harry, "well, at least not on that particular night."

"What about Father D?" continues Vic. "Do you believe I am guilty of installing the home-made air conditioning in his new car?"

"No. I have to say I don't," says Harry slowly.

"Objection," shouts Prozac Jack. "This is all speculation. Harry is simply showing Vic some honour among cut-throats."

"You see, Your Honour," persists Harry, ignoring Jack, "the bullets we fish out of Father D's car are from an M60 sub-machine gun – not from an Uzi pistol. And not even Switchblade Vic is a big enough fool to try and stash an M60 under his jacket."

"But what is he doing there with an Uzi pistol?" demands Jack. "Could he perhaps be the back-up party?"

"That is only conjecture," says Switchblade Vic. "And anyway, it's not the issue. I think what Harry is saying is that I certainly am not the guy who shoots up Father D's car."

Jack has no further questions and no further witnesses – Father Drownem being exempt on account of his nerves. So it's Switchblade Vic's turn to put the prosecution's case. And who does he call but Bad Breath Bradley.

There is considerable surprise at this development, because Breath, as you'll know, makes very few public outings since his split with the Boys. But a subpoena is a subpoena, and Letemout Lou sends round two cop jeeps to Breath's house that morning, to be sure, to be sure.

"Bad Breath is the one guy who can establish my innocence, Your Holiness, even if he's somewhat reluctant," explains Vic as Breath takes the stand.

Breath, however, immediately proves to be what is known in the trade as a hostile witness. And when Vic asks him to identify himself, he replies, "Your Honour, I refuse to answer any questions on the basis that I do not wish to discriminate myself."

"But, Breath," says Vic, "just tell the court you know I have nothing to do with the Father D business, that's all you have to do. You don't even have to say how you know it."

"I plead the Fifth," growls Breath with a smirk.

Lou pauses a minute to let the full weight of this sink in.

"Strike one, Bad Breath," says Lou. "Try again."

"I plead the Fifth," repeats Breath, still smirking.

"There is no Fifth here," says Lou, "and only one more strike."

"Dumb doll," grins Breath.

Letemout Lou's face reddens, and everyone in the court, with the possible exception of Breath, knows he's for a long walk off the short pier. So she smiles back at Breath, bangs her gavel on the bench and declares, "That's contempt, Mr Bradley. Six months in the jug. Haul him off."

Well, Breath couldn't be more surprised if you jab him in the eye with a sharp stick.

"I object, Your Worship," he shouts.

"Very well. We'll make it a full year," responds Lou. She then glares at the gallery where every hand in the place shoots up instantly. And Breath is hauled off down the steps to a spontaneous round of applause.

Switchblade Vic, however, still looks like someone lets the air out of him.

"Never mind, Mr McCormack," says Letemout Lou. "Harry the Hurler's statement means we know you're not the trigger man. And that punches enough of a hole in the *Leader*'s case to cast reasonable doubt. We'll put it to the hands-up, to be doubly certain."

Harry and myself are once again appointed tellers. And sure enough, while the tally is much closer than the last one, Lou's casting vote means that the *Leader*'s story is adjudged a big fat lie.

"So when do I get my fifty K?" asks Vic after the vote is announced. And he directs a big gloating grin at Prozac Jack.

"Well, this is the crux – that's the key point to you," replies Letemout Lou. "Even if a story is false, it doesn't mean a guy's reputation is damaged."

"I don't understand," says Vic. "He either libels me or he doesn't?"

"It is not that straightforward," explains Lou. "It all comes down to how much your character is defamed.

"Take, for example, the time Scoop Scallan writes that Stammering Stan is so dimly lit, he's the only guy in Derry who pays for his Chinese meal then runs out without eating it. Well, we all know that this isn't the case at all. Indeed, my own experience is that Stan is so near with his change that when he takes a doll out, he asks her if there's anything she likes on the Children's Menu.

"But the point Scoop is making is that Stanley runs on a lower than average wattage, which you and I know to be true."

Switchblade Vic is becoming uneasy . . . and begins tapping his feet.

"So what are you saying, Your Eminence?" he snaps nervously.

"Well," replies Letemout, "it all hinges on fair comment. Maybe you really are innocent of attempting to whack Father D. But let's face it, Vic, if we look at the whole game, you are as dirty as two rabbits in a mud bath. So taking all this into account, I can only award you twenty-five pence – and no costs."

Vic jumps to his feet in protest but Lou just bangs her gavel and points at the steps to the cells in warning.

"Just one thing, Your Eminence," persists Vic, mystified. "Why twenty-five pence?"

"Well," says Lou, "it is exactly the price of a packet of paper handkerchiefs. Now, go off home, Vic, and dry your eyes."

And with that, Lou stands up and announces the court is over. But she advises Cheapshot Charlie and Prozac Jack that's she's not finished with them yet and that they are both to stay behind and speak to teacher.

*****

Harry is not that keen to join all the legal eagles in the Northern Counties, so he suggests that we head directly down to WG's on Society Street for a quick reviver. We're first in, so I grab the snug while Harry orders two balls of malt.

"A fair result?" I ask him carefully.

"Absolutely," laughs Harry. "Letemout Lou is playing a blinder, right down to jamming Bad Breath Bradley in the chokey for twelve months."

"How's that?" I ask him.

"Well," says Harry, shucking back his Powers. "This is not really for public consumption. But I will let you in on it, on condition that you never repeat it in my lifetime. And if you do, I will personally feed you to Rufus, the Bradley family rottweiler. Understand?"

There is little to argue with here, so I nod okay.

"We know all along that Switchblade Vic is not the shooter," explains Harry. "You see, Vic is in my house that very night – discussing what we refer to as a bilateral ceasefire. That is, they'll stop whacking us if we stop whacking them. And these negotiations are being chaired by our old friend Father Drownem."

"Aha!" I nod.

"So Vic leaves the house first," continues Harry, "where he meets Danny Boy. Naturally, Vic is carrying some hefty health insurance under his coat, him being so far from home and all. But after he says Night-Night to Danny, he gets straight into his car and drives back to the Waterside.

"Two minutes later, Father Drownem leaves the street in my old car. And he's just rounding the corner, when no less a rogue than Bad Breath

Bradley himself appears at the mouth of the laneway and starts ratta-tat-tatting with the M60. He thinks he's getting me. Danny Boy, who incidentally is on point duty outside my house, sees the whole thing happen."

Harry gives me a smarty-pants grin and turns his glass upside down to indicate its condition. So I make with two replacements and sit down, still a bit unconvinced.

"Then why don't you tell the court all this?" I ask Harry.

"Things are still a bit too delicate," says H. "But Letemout Lou is quicker than a three-card trick. And she spots that the only reason Switchblade Vic calls Breath is that Breath is the dirt in the engine. So in the interests of fairness, she chucks him in the chokey."

We are sitting chuckling at this when who comes in the door but Stammering Stan and Letemout Lou.

"Anything to report?" I say to Stan, while Letemout is getting the drinks in, out of earshot.

"Nothing astounding," replies Stammering Stan, "just the contempt finding."

"So what about Cheapshot Charlie?" I ask.

"I'm talking about Cheapshot," continues Stan. "He is also starting a twelve-month sabbatical for contempt. Letemout is still sore about the piece Cheapshot writes when she gets the Semtex Seven off. So when Cheapshot doesn't stand up fast enough at the end of the court, Letemout sticks him with the full weight of the law. Actually, she tries to give him three years, but Prozac Jack beats her down to one. And coincidentally, you'll never guess who he'll be sharing a cell with?"

"His new best pal Bad Breath Bradley?" I venture.

"One and the same," says Stan. "Though it's just temporary – it'll probably only take Letemout a couple of months to sort out the paper-work."

Over at the other end of the bar, Letemout is beckoning Stan to come away from the riffraff and join her for a gin. "Could you hand me over my briefs," she calls across to him, gesturing at her files.

Stan gives Harry and me a big wink on Lou's blind side and whispers to us, "Okay, but I'll have to go into the Gents' first to take them off."

And I, for one, am starting to believe that Stanley is nowhere near as dimly lit as Letemout Lou imagines.

ROMANCING ORANGE JILLY

"Hey, Jilly," says head barman Danny Boy Gillespie, "I've one for you. When does a liberal-minded Protestant become a bitter Orange bandit?"

"When he leaves the room," replies Jill, coolly. "That's so funny, I remember wetting my nappy the first time I hear it.

"I'll give you one now – and you get a fiver if you get it right. There's three guys in a brand new Ford Mondeo. One's from Creggan, one from the Bog and the other from the Brandywell. Who's driving?"

"An RUC man," smirks Danny. "And don't worry about the fiver – I'll dock it from your wages, thanks."

*****

Like all conversations that take place in public houses after nine o'clock, the story I am disclosing is only told here on the understanding that number one, you never get it from me; number two, I forget many of the facts; and number three, what I do recall is completely deniable. Oh, and number four, I don't know you from Adam anyway.

Anyhow, here goes. Danny Boy Gillespie, as you're aware, earns his crust at The Jack Kennedy Inn ever since his early release. But to Danny, the bar work – which mostly involves wiping down tables during Sparkly Barkley's flying visits and organising the nightly peanut-spitting contest – is secondary. His real mission in life is to tell every woman he meets how he is a retired hero of the revolution.

A good-looking lad, with dark, disbelieving eyes and a broad, cynical grin, Danny is every inch the loveable rapscallion. And there are plenty of women around who still believe in the nobility of tossing Coke bottles at armoured cars. So Danny scores more direct hits than he ever does on police jeeps in his old life.

But those of you who know Danny realise that, like all heroes, he has a tragic flaw. He is forever falling in love with the wrong girl. Indeed, he falls flat on his face so often, that it is a good job he is not a horse or Harry the Hurler would be forced to shoot him. Some people would like to shoot him anyway – regulars of The Jack Kennedy, for instance, who find that Danny's tragedies often get in the way of a peaceful drink and an undisturbed stab at the crossword. For Danny, you see, is yet to master the art of suffering in silence.

Most patrons, as you'll know, prefer to pour their heart out to the barman and cry into their beer themselves, rather than paying the guy behind the counter to do it for them. And now, to the horror of every client ever to ping a peanut, Danny Boy is starting to make puppy eyes at the new barmaid, 'Orange' Jill Wattling. And sure as shooting, disaster is lurking.

*****

Orange Jill, who hails from some well-appointed hole-in-the-hedge south of Belfast, is only working in The Jack Kennedy this last couple of weeks. A sassy young woman, she gets the job by marching into Sparkly Barkley's office one day and telling him that she has a good work ethic and will make at least a small dent in his Fair Employment figures. Which, she adds, are almost as lopsided as the cops'.

Sparkly looks up from his spreadsheet, sees a pair of legs that would make a priest kick a hole in a confessional door, and signs her up immediately. And before you can say Roll Over On Your Bellies Boys And Beg, all the cheap wine drinkers in The Jack Kennedy are ordering the best brandy in a bid to impress her.

Jill, we learn, comes to Derry about two years ago to do a course in War Trauma Studies. It seems she hears from her school friends that this attracts a high number of revolutionaries from all sides. And while she herself is about as revolutionary as the Stranocum Ladies' Choir, she feels unchallenged by her social set. Or, as her mother puts it, she is partial to a bit of rough.

And given the big doe-eyes she is currently shooting back at The Jack Kennedy's head barman, that bit of rough could just be Danny Boy Gillespie.

*****

This particular day, I am sitting at the counter in The Jack Kennedy, sipping a quick Chilean Chianti while Orange Jill is out back serving in the off-licence. The crossword is a bit rough today, and Seven Across is giving me terrible trouble – *True love's around. Illegal gang could lead a mutiny (6).* So I look round the room for inspiration.

Unluckily, however, at this exact same moment, Danny Boy Gillespie is scouring the vicinity for a sympathetic ear. And spotting me on my own, he sidles over, under the guise of wiping the counter. He then pretends to be interested in my crossword – another part of his ritual – and to my consternation announces 'PIRATE' as the right answer.

"Okay, so I see it earlier in the paper Dr Death leaves behind him," laughs Danny. The local pathologist, Dr Death McGoldrick, figures that getting soaked in cheap alcohol shouldn't just be the preserve of dead patients. He is one of The Jack Kennedy's most dedicated clients and a good man to have in your corner on a tight crossword.

So I fill in PIRATE then stare up at Danny Boy, waiting. He cups his head in his hands, strikes a pathetic face.

"I want to die," he sighs.

"Do tell," I say, hoping he'll catch the irony.

He doesn't.

"You know the way, in all your life you only get one true soul mate?" he goes on. "Well, mine is no more. Unless the gods of Love intervene quickly, I will be forced to sacrifice my angel sent from heaven and left to live a life that is emptier than a peanut shell. For the last two months, my life is like a never-ending picnic. But today, the hungry wolves of Fate are about to devour it all."

"Hmm," I reply, wondering how to wean Danny off the romance novels.

"Off the record," he says – always a bad sign – "I am madly in love with Orange Jilly and we are having a furtive love affair."

Now, I can honestly say that this is not an entire shock, as Danny and Jill are currently in the habit of taking their fifteen-minute tea-breaks together and coming back with their hair still all damp from the upstairs shower. But I bid him to continue regardless.

"It all kicks off about a week after she starts here," explains Danny Boy. "Myself and Jill are alone together doing the clean-up. Someone's left a few songs on the jukebox, so before long, we're bopping about to Abba as we sweep the floor and wipe the tables. As you do. Then, Van the Man comes on with his nice slow number. So I look over at Orange Jill, catch her glancing at me, and ask her would Modom care for a boogie. As you do.

"Well, for a bit of crack, she pretends to have this girl with her and says to me: 'What about my friend? I can't leave her. Can she come too?' So I tell her, 'God no, your mate's far too ugly. Sure she can dance round her handbag. And anyway, there's only room for one on the handlebars of my bike . . .'

"So Jilly just turns round to me, dead sultry, and whispers, 'Okay – but only if I can ring your bell.' And that, as the man says, is a done deal."

"So why the long face?" I ask.

"Well," he explains, "a few days ago, I buy Jilly this diamond ring that Sparkly Barkley gets for me wholesale. And after we pledge our undying and eternal love to each other, and decide to order the double-decker cake, Jill tells me that I'll have to meet her father. And who is he, only Willie Wattling, the Independent Planter MP for Drumcree South."

This is not good news for Danny, as I'm sure you're aware. Wattling – who is known to all as Whistlin' Willie on account of the piercing sound he makes through his dentures when he talks – hates Home Rulers with a passion. And he will eat a guy like Danny for dinner and spit him out through the gap in his bottom teeth.

Indeed, Willie is only after being expelled from the Planters' General Council for joking that if every Roman Catholic in Ireland is laid end-to-end across the Atlantic Ocean, it'll be a good start. Though maybe next time he'll wait until the cardinal leaves the room first.

"Jill assures me that her Da is mellowing as he gets older," says Danny, "though I am not so certain."

"Ah," I reply, "and you, of course, are worried that he may hear about your revolutionary youth, and in particular your sabbatical for carrying a lighted bottle of Coke – with no mask."

"Per-zackly!" says Danny Boy. "Though, of course, he may never hear of that, given that I am a juvenile at the time and that it is now expunged from my CV.

"The problem I can't get around is this . . ." And with that, he pulls up his sleeve and unravels a bandage he is wearing for the past month on his forearm. And underneath that bandage he reveals a five-inch tattoo of a tricolour flag swaying in the breeze, with the proud teenage legend Death To All Planters inked out underneath.

I frown at Danny Boy and he frowns back at me; we both shake our heads and suck in some air.

"Jilly thinks it is a football injury," says Danny. "One of the first things she ever tells me is that when old Wattling's interviewing someone for a job at his factory, he makes them roll up their shirts to make sure they've no trappings. So I am thinking it's more discreet to wrap my arm up well before I start laying on the charm."

"Hmm," I advise him. "I wouldn't be ordering the double-decker cake just yet."

*****

Now, about this very time, Whistlin' Willie is in the news quite a bit because of his activities blockading roads and otherwise pulling the pigtails of Home Rulers who don't want him marching on their lawns.

Indeed, he is even on TV one night accepting a seventeenth-century antique pistol from the Londonderry Defenders in recognition of his good work. The musket is last fired at the Siege of Derry and is one of only two remaining in the entire world. Its pair, somewhat ironically, belongs to that other well-known collector of military paraphernalia, Harry the Hurler, one time Chief Executive of all the Boys in Derry.

"And I'll tell you something," says Big H one night in The Jack Kennedy, "I love my musket more than anything else in this world. And that big fat dinosaur will be marching over my dead body before he completes his set."

"We can always arrange that," quips Orange Jilly from behind the bar.

"I don't care who you are," laughs Harry. "But your milkman must certainly be a Home Ruler – the way you pour such a lovely pint."

*****

Orange Jilly is as yet unaware of Danny Boy's predicament and trots about the bar, showing her engagement ring to all and sundry. The ring, truth be told, is quite an elaborate affair and provokes some envy in certain circles. Gerry the Hurler's wife, Alice Springs, is quite catty indeed, and suggests to Jilly: Never mind, maybe it'll grow if you water it. So Jilly retorts that it least it won't grow moss like the one Alice has on – and is it true that Ma Hurley is still wondering where the hell all her gold fillings are gone?

Yes, Jilly is as happy as a spring lamb. Unfortunately, however, we all need Easter dinner, and the butcher's van is at the gate. It is Dr Death who gets to break the news of the tattoo to her, as we all reckon he has the most experience of dealing with grief. Although even he is a bit surprised at how hard she takes it. And we start to wonder if perhaps, she is afflicted with this hearts and flowers business as badly as Danny Boy.

By the end of the day, her little eyes are puffy with constant crying and her nose is red and raw. In fact, as Sparkly Barkley says, the entire tragedy is doing her so much damage that Maiden City Tours could even strike her off their new Inner-City-Babe-Watch route.

"Don't you maybe know anyone who could cut off the tattoo?" Orange Jill asks Dr Death, tears streaming down her face.

"I only know one guy in the tattoo-removal business," says Doc Death. "He's a plastic surgeon who now has a clinic in Letterkenny. He is very good indeed – indeed possibly the best in the country. But Danny Boy would have to cut off his other arm to pay this guy's bill."

"Maybe Sparkly Barkley would pay for it," says Jill.

"God no," retorts the Doc, "Danny Boy would be sacked on the spot if Sparkly even knew he had a tattoo. Look, I'll ring the guy and find out the price – though I don't think it'll be any good."

*****

Well, no-one ever hears just exactly what Danny Boy says to Sparkly that night or what wedge he uses to get the price of the operation.

But between ourselves, I would suspect the barman once again invokes the night that he finds Mrs Harry the Hurler, wife of the most feared of all the Boys in Derry, lying in Sparkly's lap. Nonetheless, it takes him three hours of hard bargaining. Barkley is well known as a guy who can tell you the dates on all his small change.

Now, while everyone predicts that Danny and Orange Jill won't even survive the six weeks until the tattoo is removed, they are all proved wrong. Indeed, the pair are so in love that The Jack Kennedy's brandy sales are at an all-time low. There is no longer any point.

The operation itself is quite painful. And, as Dr Death explains beforehand, it leaves Danny with a series of little white scar-lines on his forearm. What Danny doesn't account for is that it also leaves him with a similar series of little white scar-lines on his gluteus maximus and means he has to sleep on his chest for a fortnight.

"Sure it'll keep you on your best behaviour till the wedding," says Doc, "and you'll always have a little curio to show the boys in the shower room.

"Anyway, to know true love you must first know what pain is."

Danny Boy, who as you know is not a man for irony, nods in agreement.

"Thank you, Doc," he says, "my life is once more stretching before me like a never-ending picnic. We are finally off to meet Jill's father at the weekend. And all being well, I am going to ask to become his first and only son-in-law."

*****

Even without the tattoo, I am not sure I fancy Danny Boy's chances. And sure enough, when we see him the following Monday, he is about as happy as a man with next week's lottery numbers in his pocket and only forty-eight hours to live.

"It's a disaster from start to finish," he sighs. "When Willie meets us at the door, he wraps her in a bear hug and lifts her off the ground. But when I put out my hand, he completely ignores it. He is cooler than a grave.

"He then stomps off down the big huge hallway and says he'll be in the study if any of us want to talk to him. At this stage, I'm for going home, but then Jilly tells me that she'll make it worth my while – and don't I know Planter girls have no morals.

"This focuses the mind a little, so I trundle off after Willie and find him sitting by a fire in his library. I tell him that I want to talk to him in private. So he asks me to take a seat while he sweeps the room for bugs.

"He then asks me if I would like a drink – nothing alcoholic, mind, as I won't be staying and will be driving back to Londonderry tonight. Well, at this point, I figure there is no mileage in going through the niceties, so I close my eyes and inform him straight out that I want to marry his daughter."

"So how does that go down?" asks the Doc.

"Surprisingly well, " says Danny Boy. "He catches me on the hop completely and offers me his hand. I naturally grab it eagerly. But it is a trap. And right away, with his other hand, Willie grabs my sleeve and rolls it up. He then gestures at me to pull up the other one – which I do.

"He stares for a minute at the little white scars, then opens a drawer in his desk. And he pulls out this slip of paper – looks like a court sheet – and reads out: 'Daniel Bosco Gillespie. Two years incarceration for propelling potentially explosive projectiles at an armed jeep. Open brackets – Young fool has no mask – close brackets.' Well, I try to explain how the record is now expunged and that it is only Coke in the bottles – but it cuts no mustard."

"'Put yourself in my shoes,' says Willie. 'Would you want a petrol bomber for a son? I'd sooner be caught dead wearing your tie.' And he then banishes me from Wattling Towers immediately, before he feels the urge to test out his Siege of Derry musket."

*****

Every July, I depart Derry for my Castel Gandolfo at Fahan, so it is almost a month later before I run into any of these parties again. But lo, when I return *chez moi*, amid the little stack of bills and other assorted hate mail is an invitation to a wedding. And curiouser still, it is to the nuptial feast of one Daniel Gillespie and a certain Gillian Wattling.

It seems that there is considerable activity in my absence. And from what I hear now, Danny Boy and Whistlin' Willie are as close as two teeth – though just exactly how this comes about, however, remains a mystery. Willie, indeed, is said to enjoy nothing better than a quiet night at the fire pinging peanuts into the coal bucket with his son-in-law-to-be. And the old guy even agrees to host the wedding bash at The Jack Kennedy.

I myself am not a man for nuptials – as there is only a certain amount of warmth and sincerity a man can fake. But this is an occasion not to be missed. So come the hour, I don the statutory new shirt and head for the Cathedral. It is a gala affair. The Planters are all piped into the service in their kilts and tartans, while the Home Rulers trip in to the sound of the harp. And Orange Jilly, as you'll expect, is as pretty as a summer day.

The reception also passes off with virtually no serious incident whatsoever. Though it is perhaps a bit remiss of Harry the Hurler to try and cut in on Willie Wattling when he is enjoying his first dance with the new Mrs Danny Gillespie.

"No surrender," Willie tells him deadpan.

"What about my right to waltz?" Harry counters.

"Just this once, but you'd better stick to the specified route," replies Willie, releasing his daughter.

And we all breathe out again.

*****

At around midnight, I am fit only for the scratcher, so I go up to say my goodbyes to the very happy couple.

"So what's your secret?" I ask Danny Boy as Jill, God bless her, heads up to the bar to get me a brandy for the road.

"Not for public consumption?" demands Dan. I nod.

"Well," he explains, "the day after you leave for Fahan, there is a major crisis in the bar. Orange Jilly is serving Harry the Hurler a pint. And you know the way he's always winding her up about her Da? This time, because of all our trouble – and the wedding plans being off – Jilly's not up to the banter. So she collapses in a fit of tears.

"Now, Harry finds this very embarrassing, as you do. And the entire bar is giving him these Are You Happy Now You're A Big Shot looks. So he exits stage left immediately. But worse again for Harry, Old Ma Hurley gets to hear about what happens. And she starts blaming Harry for causing the entire mess in the first place by recruiting me to throw Coke bottles.

"Old Ma, of course, writes the Master's course in Applied Guilt, and pretty soon Harry is walking around the town, hanging his head like a rag doll. Both Harry and Old Ma know that there is only one way he can get back in the good books. So after about a week, he rings me up and tells me to come and collect his damn Siege of Derry musket and give it to Whistlin' Willie as a peace offering."

I put it to Danny that things should go a lot better for him the next time he visits Wattling Towers.

"A lot better entirely," he agrees. "Whistlin' Willie cannot believe his luck. He is so thrilled to get this old gun his hands are shaking. Indeed, it is hard to believe Willie is the same guy. Though I suspect that Jilly must be working on him very hard behind the scenes as well.

"So he sits me down in the library and pours me a Bushmills Whiskey – untouched by Fenian hand. He then tells me that while the likes of him and Harry the Hurler will always have their needle, he accepts there's hope for me and Jilly.

"He also says that any man who can work out where Sparkly Barkley buries his bodies and can persuade Harry the Hurler to hand over his favourite gun will have a great future in business. So he is quite sure we will not be relying on him for money."

"But what about the tattoo?" I ask.

"This is the best part," says Danny. "As I'm about to leave the room, all of a sudden, Willie peels back his two shirt sleeves and presents his bare arms to me. And even in the dim light, I can spot that there are little white patches on both forearms.

"'Anyone can make an honest mistake,' he says, 'but it's the guys who don't try to make good their mistakes – or keep making the same ones – that I've no time for. Marry my daughter, Danny Boy, and make her happy.'"

With that, Jill trots up with my brandy, probably the last that The Jack Kennedy will sell for a long time, and kisses Danny Boy on the neck.

"Hey, Hubby," she grins, "how many Fenians does it take to change a light bulb?"

"How many?" responds her husband.

"None," she grins "They think the State should do it for them."

"You're right," he laughs. "That way the Planters end up paying for it. But how many Planters does it take to change a light bulb?"

"How many, Sweetie Pie?" replies Jill.

"Two," says Danny. "One to phone the Fenian tradesman and the other to count the silver afterwards."

I groan, drain the brandy, and leave them at it.

HURLEY VERSUS HURLEY

It is accepted far and wide that it is not Red Light Lorna's brains which first bring her to the attention of her husband Harry the Hurler. Indeed, Harry himself will tell you that Lorna is dimmer than a switch. But thankfully, nature is kind to her in other areas. Tall and slim, with flaming auburn hair, she looks just like Marilyn Monroe, though without the hooked nose and bad teeth. Indeed, she is known as Red Light in the first place because she only has to put on her summer mini-dress to bring all of Strand Road to a standstill.

Anyhow, one particular Sunday, the sun is out, the sky is blue and all is mostly right with war-torn Derry, so Harry and Red Light set off on a run to the amusement arcades in Buncrana. This is back in the bad old days, when the bars in the North are not open on the Sabbath, so Harry decides to have a few swift sharpeners at the Drift Inn on the Free State side on the way home.

This is not necessarily Harry's brightest idea, given that Her Majesty's constabulary across the frontier are so keen to talk to him that each and every one of them carries around his picture in their wallets. But restricted and all as Big H may be in the matter of grey cells, Lorna has fewer brains than a two-ounce burger.

So when Harry is pulled in by the Northern cops at a border checkpoint, he instructs Red Light – under no uncertain terms – to keep her mouth shut.

"Out for a drive, Mr Hurley?" says the cop after Harry rolls down the window the statutory inch and a half.

Harry just ignores him and hands over his licence, carefully breathing out the passenger side of his mouth.

"You must be Mrs Hurley," says the sneaky gendarme, looking across at Red Light. "Enjoying your day out?"

"We're just coming back from Buncrana," says Lorna, forgetting the script. "Issha lovely day – perfect for playing the machines."

"And a coupla wee drinks?" laughs the cop.

"Who are you telling?" says Lorna. "Shure they're all shut this half of the border."

"I only take one wee brandy when I'm driving," interrupts Harry quickly. But it's no use.

"Apart from today, when it's four," giggles Lorna before her husband can get his hand over her mouth.

*****

Okay, so maybe it doesn't happen exactly like that. But there is no disguising the glee in Fort George Barracks the day Harry gets his twelve-month disqualification for failing the bag test. Indeed, the cop who nabs him gets made sergeant. But while most of you already know all about Harry's ban – what you won't know is how it nearly leads to a permanent rift between Mr and Mrs Harry the H.

The first I hear of a problem is when Harry spies me one day at the Diamond, where he is running a Touts Out protest. The picket is demanding the permanent exile of Jimmy Big Mouth, and one or two other guys who are said to be feeding dirty stories about the Boys to plain-clothes gendarmes. Now, like yourself, when I see such demonstrations I tend to skip lightly by. But Harry is quick off the mark and descends his hand onto my shoulder just before I get in the door of Bookworm. And he suggests how about a quick straightener in WG's Bar across the street.

So despite some grumbling from Harry's lieutenants about him playing hookie on the demo, we slip over to the bar and organise ourselves in the back snug while the barman lets the stout settle.

Harry then closes the door of the snug and looks over his shoulder furtively.

"I am going to divorce Red Light Lorna, and I want you to assist me," he whispers.

"Isn't that a bit drastic?" I suggest, not at all keen at the prospect of this assisting business. "I know Lorna's a bit scatty sometimes. But if scattiness alone is grounds for divorce, then all of Derry will be lodging papers."

"No, no," protests Harry, "Lorna is cheating on me, and I want you to find the proof."

The pints arrive and I motion to the barman for a couple of little short ones to level out the thinking.

"It is a very sad situation indeed," continues Harry. "Despite our occasional tiffs, I love my little princess more than anything in this universe. And I am very loath to believe she would wrong me. But when I am able to read in the *Derry Standard* that Red Light is playing away from home, I realise it is time to act."

"What exactly are they saying?" I ask him, baffled as to how such a libel-conscious paper as the *Derry Standard* would blow the whistle on Harry's wife.

"That's just it," says Harry. "It is all a bit subtle. From what I hear, this good-looking blondey-headed dame goes into the *Standard* office last week, smiles a big smile at Stammering Stan the reporter, and asks him will he put in a small write-up for new dance classes that are starting.

"The article states that Lorna Hurley would like to invite all comers to participate in an In-Out Hokey-Cokey spectacular at Quigley's Point on Friday evenings at nine thirty. Dress optional."

"No harm in that," I venture.

"Aha!" says Harry knowingly. "But you see, Red Light Lorna never dances a step in her life. And when she swears to me that she is not guilty of placing the article, I believe her. So I ring Stammering Stan and ask him to investigate but he gets nowhere. He says he doesn't recognise the filly who gives him the write-up but that it definitely isn't Lorna."

"So what's the problem?" I ask Harry.

"Well," he explains, "the popular theory is that this other lady, who gives Stan the write-up, is travelling in the vicinity of Quigley's Point one night. And she recognises my car, which, of course, I no longer can drive, parked at a picnic spot, right next door to her husband's. And after a little more up-close surveillance, she becomes convinced that her other half is sneaking off to the Point every Friday night to indulge in some one-on-one hokey-cokey with Lorna. Hence the advertisement in the *Standard*."

"Aha!" I comment.

"Aha! indeed," replies Harry. "And even though I never wish to leave my darling princess, a man in my position has little choice but to get a divorce if I am to retain my stature among serious men."

*****

Now, if you and I are to remain absolutely honest with one another, it does not require an advertisement in the *Derry Standard* to inform us that Red Light Lorna likes to do a little more than window-shop. There are unconfirmed reports for many years now that Lorna is shining up the back seats with the city's best-known mostly legitimate businessman, Sparkly Barkley, who, incidentally, is one of Harry's dearest friends. Though, of course, these reports are never mentioned in front of Harry.

Moreover, I will give you better than even money that the good-looking blondey-headed dame who places the ad is none other than Susie Short-Shorts, aka Mrs Sparkly Barkley. So wearing my new hat of marital assistant to Mr Hurley, I phone Stammering Stan at the *Standard* to see what gives.

"I hear your eyesight is going," I tell him. "So much so that you are unable to recognise the girl who places the dance ad as Susie Barkley."

"You know yourself," laughs Stan, "I have a terrible memory for faces and a worse one for names."

Stan, despite his rep, has a laudable sense of self-preservation.

"I pity the poor guy who is going to have to tell Harry the Hurler that it is his dear pal Sparkly who is the rat in the ointment," he says.

"That poor guy would be me," I reply.

"Oh dear," chuckles Stan. "But do not be put off by suggestions that Harry likes to shoot the messenger. In fact, he only does it that one time . . ."

*****

Stan is right, of course. Telling Harry that Sparkly is eating off his kitty-tray is only part of the problem. The real danger is knowing about it in the first place, as you can bet your eye teeth Harry will do everything he can to stop this information going out on the evening news.

But while I am sitting in The Jack Kennedy, dulling the panic with some Guinness, who comes in the door but Louise 'Letemout Lou' Johnston, who is taking a sabbatical from the bench to make herself some real money as a working lawyer.

"Stanley, the little smarty-pants, tells me that your tail is caught in the wringer over this Hurley divorce," announces Letemout cheerfully, motioning to Danny Boy the barman for two pints of stout. "But stop worrying; I have a cunning plan."

"Be still, my heart," I tell her.

"First of all, be sure to get Harry to employ me as his brief," adds Lou.

"That shouldn't be too hard, given that I handle all his political affairs anyway. I will then instruct him that – in the event of us not finding out just exactly who is the third wheel on this bike – we need to get ourselves a fall guy."

"I'm not sure I follow you," I reply.

"Well," says Lou, "given that you are never going to tell Harry that it is his best friend who is sniffing at his back porch, we are going to have to invent a decoy – or to give him his correct title, a co-respondent. This will let Harry get his divorce and at the same time avoid any unpleasant Hurley family laundry being aired in public. Big H, of course, will have to be in on the scheme otherwise we would have serious trouble getting a volunteer. Not that it's going to be easy anyway."

"So who do you fancy for this co-respondent bit?" I ask Letemout.

"Somebody good-looking enough to convince a judge he could turn the head of Harry the Hurler's wife but whipped enough to convince the public that he would never dare," replies Lou.

"Hard enough to find," I grin, the light slowly brightening in my head. "Someone like an honest, upstanding reporter, perhaps?"

"Per-zackly!" laughs Lou. And the two of us clink glasses and chuckle heartily.

*****

I do not know what Letemout Lou promises Stan to make him join the game. But I would suspect she plays to his greatest weakness which, strictly *entre nous*, is this sassy little red dress and six-inch black velvet pumps. And sure enough, the next time I see him, Stan is chief witness for the prosecution, looking as happy as a frog on the wrong end of a straw.

Matrimonial courts are normally closed hearings in Derry but Lou smuggles me in as her second chair, on the grounds that Harry needs as many friendly faces as possible. Shakes Coyle and Rusty Gillespie are also there as sworn witnesses to Lorna and Stan's secret tryst. But no-one is expecting much debate so as to save the blushes of both Harry and Sparkly. And there is a general consensus that the petition will go through on the nod.

So after the introductions, Stan gets up on the stand. And after some prompting from Letemout Lou, he admits how he is performing the Quigley's Point two-step with Red Light Lorna every Friday night for the past couple of years.

Next, Shakes and Lily Lungs get up and confess how they always give

Red Light an alibi by claiming to Harry that she is taking part in their One Day At A Time meetings, while all the time she is shining up the back seats with Stan.

But then, just as all looks to be as rosy as a poem and heading for the right result, Susie Short-Shorts Barkley stands up in the gallery and starts shouting at the judge that it's all a pack of lies.

"I can prove it too, Your Honour," she insists as everyone wonders what the hell she is doing in the court.

"Red Light Lorna has nothing to do with Stan. Indeed, it is I myself who is after spending every Friday night with him for the last six months. He and I are working on a new series of articles for the *Derry Standard*, Lifestyles of the Idle Rich. It's the only night my husband goes out, so I get a chance to pursue a bit of creative writing. And Stanley is my guide and mentor. No, there is no way that he is with Red Light Lorna during that time – it is obviously some other guy."

"Aha!" says the magistrate, wondering what the damn is going on. And there is much sucking in of air in the courtroom.

Letemout Lou, of course, is quick onto her feet and asks for two minutes to confer with her team. She thinks she knows why Susie Short-Shorts is picking at the seams. She figures Susie is annoyed that her husband Sparkly is being allowed to palm off his rightful place as co-respondent to Stan. So she is messing up Stan's alibi.

But Susie, in turn, can't rat Sparkly out to the court, because Harry the Hurler will feed him to the fish and confiscate his assets. And Susie feels that she is due a large spoonful of Sparkly's nest egg for her quite legitimate grievance.

Letemout Lou, who has been directing this production flawlessly up till now, is starting to sweat. She also knows that Susie is being a big fat liar because, strictly between ourselves, Lou and Stanley spend most Friday nights locked in their own private version of Judges and Jailbirds.

In fact, Lou has no idea how she is going to untangle this particular web. But that's not counting on Red Light Lorna, who leaps to her feet without warning.

"It is all my fault," she announces. "I confess all, and I throw myself on the mercy of the court. But most of all, I want to throw myself on the mercy of my husband Harry. I still love my darling prince with all my heart and would do anything to get him back."

Well, tears begin to stream down her beautiful face, and we have all the makings of a very embarrassing scene. But thankfully, Harry is quickly over with her giving it the There Theres.

"I forgive you, Princess," he whispers quietly, "I forgive you."

Lorna looks up, flashes Harry her most tender smile, and everyone's heart melts.

"I think my client wishes to withdraw his petition for divorce," announces Letemout, reading the spin of things.

"Just as well for your witnesses," replies the judge, who is a wise old bird. "You are lucky that I am not banging each and every one of them in the cold-room on account of the eyewash they are serving up to this court.

"Personally, I reckon that not even Stammering Stan's stupid enough to run around with Harry the Hurler's wife – and then come in here and admit it. Someone is putting him up to it – and if I ever find out who's doing such a thing, she'll be struck off."

*****

Thankfully, it is some time before I bump into Harry again. But one day about three months later, he pops into The Jack Kennedy for a hot whiskey on the way back from the late Jimmy Big Mouth's funeral and spots me in the corner.

"Thank you for assisting me in my recent difficulty," he says. "And you are right, of course. You cannot divorce a wife for being scatty."

"What about your stature among serious men?" I ask him.

"That is not a problem either," he replies. "Even the most serious of men can have foolish wives."

I am beginning to wonder whether Red Light ever admits the full SP to Harry. Though this is not a question I would ever ask him – or indeed anyone else.

Harry, however, is a mind reader – and gives me one for free.

"No," he says, "Lorna never tells me who she was visiting at Quigley's Point in my Merc. And I would never ask her. These things are behind us now. Though isn't it interesting that Susie Short-Shorts is up quicker than a greyhound out of a trap to tell the court that Stammering Stan isn't the man?"

"Mmmm," I reply, mindful of how little I know.

"You would almost think that she has an interest in this, wouldn't you?"

"Mmmm," I tell him.

"And coincidentally," he continues, "my dear old pal, Sparkly Barkley, is never nicer to me than over the past couple of months. He even offers to cover all the costs of the court case seeing as how his Susie spoils everything."

Harry stops to pluck half a clove from his teeth and grins again. "You are no doubt curious as to why I am not taking action against my dearest pal Mr Barkley," he goes on.

"I'm curious about lots of things," I grin.

"Well," says Harry, with a slightly sheepish look, "I actually discover the full SP for myself some time ago. You see, one Friday night, by chance, I am in a car in a remote area of Quigley's Point when I notice my own Merc parked in a quiet lay-by beside Sparkly's Beamer. Unfortunately, just then, I am not in a position to do anything about it. And I must admit, there's not a lot I can do about it since."

"How is that?" I inquire, a little puzzled.

"You see," says Harry, "and this is strictly off the record, I do not want to embarrass the driver of the car that I am in that night."

"And who might that be exactly?" I ask.

"I can't tell you that," he responds. "But suffice it to say, Sparkly may not be the only person in the Barkley household who knows how to eat off the wrong kitty-tray."

"Aha!" I reply.

"Aha is right," chuckles Harry the Hurler.

And he chins his whiskey, winks a goodbye and disappears out the door.

A Mother's Blessing

If saying your prayers ever becomes an Olympic sport, then there is little doubt but that Old Widda Johnston will bring home the gold medal for Ireland – unless, of course, she is disqualified under the No Professionals rule.

There are more pictures of the Sacred Heart in her home than there are of her three children and Michael Collins put together. And while the Widda is a very hospitable woman, famous throughout Derry for her strong tea and fresh scones, those in the know will advise you very strongly never to darken her door between the hours of seven and half-past. Or, depending on the list of special intentions, you will be called upon to sit through anywhere between five and fifteen decades of the Rosary. And Old Widda Johnston says her lines slower than a seven-year-old altar boy.

The Widda, however, is modest about her talent and disapproves heartily of those who beat their breasts in the marketplace. Once indeed, so the story goes, she is standing at a statue of Our Lady of Knock at the back of St Eugene's Cathedral, praying away quietly, when another elderly penitent comes along and starts making with the Hail Holy Queens so loudly that the Widda is forced to stop and look around.

But the other biddy – who would probably be worth at least a Highly Recommended in the Hallelujah Championships – resiliently ignores the Widda's cutting stares and bangs on with her beseechments, noisy as a choir.

Eventually, the Widda can take no more and bears down on the opposition.

"Be quiet," she hisses at her, "and please, show some respect for the House of God."

Well, the other woman is duly chastened and turns down her supplications to a mere mumble.

With that, Old Widda then turns back to the statue and continues in louder than normal tones: "As I'm saying, Our Lady, before that rude hoor starts butting in . . ."

*****

Now, you and I both know that the Widda would never use that type of language in a House of God and that the real credit here should go to the late, great Maggie McCay. But the Widda's daughter Louise likes to wheel the yarn out every Christmas, when the back table in The Jack Kennedy host their annual My Mother Is A Religious Maniac competition.

Indeed, Louise Johnston – better known to you and me as the judge, Letemout Lou – is remarkably well adjusted, all things considered. Stammering Stan the Radio Man reckons that he only ever hears Lou praying once. But that is when she is four horses up on a five-horse accumulator. And, as Stan rightly remarks, in a situation like that you take whatever help you can get.

"Any time I am up at Letemout's house," explains Stan one evening in Kennedy's, "the Widda works on me and works on me to try and bring Lou back into the One True Faith. She'll never get over the fact that Letemout goes Godless back when she's a student at Trinity."

"So what happens to Lou back then?" I ask.

"Well, according to the Widda," says Stan, "who, by the way, is one very smart lady, this is what too much education does to you. Though I wouldn't know, as I don't really suffer from this particular affliction myself.

"Anyhow, from what the Widda tells me, Lou's time at Trinity is a very unhappy one. I know Lou from when she is the fat little smarty-pants in the front row of Mrs Spellman's class, and I am the six-year-old in the corner with the pointed hat. But even though we're still as tight as skin on a stick, she never talks to me at all about her time in Dublin.

"She is actually put on transfer to Queen's at the end of her first year at Trinity after a particularly high-profile spat with the authorities. And apparently, she also has a big fall-out with the Boys at around the same time – though that is long since resolved."

This sounds very unlike the solid pillar of the community who now spends her days sending lowlifes and scumbags to the chokey. So I ask Stammering Stan just what is it that sends Lou off the rails.

"Officially," he says, "I don't know the full SP. But in recent months, Old Widda develops a bit a shine to me ever since I get Don O'Doherty to sing *Happy Birthday* to her on the radio. So one night, when Lou is called out to a special court hearing at Bishop Street, I stay on to keep Old Widda company and she clues me in . . . Though I warn you, if this story should ever become scuttlebutt in Kennedy's, Letemout may just pronounce her first ever death sentence and carry it out personally. On me."

"I'll take it with me to the grave," I tell him, giving it the scouts' honour sign.

"Letemout Lou," says Stan, "as you possibly don't know, has two brothers – Mickey Bangers and Light Heel Larry."

"I know of Mickey Bangers. Is he an engineer?" I reply. "The other guy doesn't ring a bell."

Everyone knows of Mickey Bangers, agrees Stan. And yes, he is an engineer. But Mickey's prominence in Derry society derives from a completely different type of work altogether. Mickey, you see, for a long time has a parallel career as a demolition expert. But, unlike many of his fellow professionals over the water or across the frontier, Mickey rarely gives the people whose building he is demolishing more than thirty minutes' notice.

During the economic war, Harry the Hurler, who is then Chief Executive of all the Boys in Derry, employs Mickey's services regularly. And before long, young Johnston is a very much sought-after guy. Indeed, he is so sought after that the local gendarmerie offer ten thousand clams for any information leading to his capture, and Mickey is forced to give up his day job as a technician for Derry Council.

Now, Old Widda Johnston predictably starts to hear of her son's other job and disapproves sharply – particularly as young Lou and Larry idolise their older brother. So the Widda works on Mickey Bangers, day and daily, warning him of the damage he is doing to his immortal soul. She puts holy medals in his pockets, sews scapulars into his jackets, and says three extra decades of the Rosary for him every morning and every night. She is relentless. And in the end, Mickey Bangers can't take any more of being prayed at and agrees to retire.

The Widda is as happy as three quick gins. And Mickey, who is a skilled engineer, is quickly snapped up by a chemical company just across the border in Buncrana. After a few months, the cops accept that Mickey Bangers' retirement is genuine and allow him to return to his Creggan home. And this means he can travel in and out to Buncrana every day in his old wreck of a Vauxhall Viva.

At this time, Letemout Lou is a first-year student at Trinity College, Dublin, where, following her brother's example, she becomes Secretary of the local branch of the Pádraig Pearse Society which acts as a political outlet for the Boys.

Light Heel Larry, meanwhile, the youngest of the Johnstons, is much more of a stay-at-home. Despite the fact that he's not much of a man for getting up early, he works as a baker at Bap-U-Like on William Street. Light Heel – who's a champion Irish Dancer – is also, of course, his mother's favourite.

"Apart from the very early start," says Stammering Stan, "baking is an eminently suitable trade for Light Heel because, between you and me, he is several baps short of a baker's dozen. He's a complete innocent – the type of guy who would sell the family silver to buy the Brooklyn Bridge. Indeed, the Widda often says that when God is passing out the brains to her children, Letemout and Mickey grab Larry's share as well."

Anyhow, one particular day, shortly after his retirement, Mickey Bangers is about to sit down to his breakfast when Old Widda Johnston comes into the kitchen and informs him that two of his old good-for-nothing cronies are looking for him. Mickey leaves his toast untouched and heads for the door. He quickly shouts back to the Widda that he won't be back from work until after six and is gone before she has a chance to have a go at him with the Holy Water.

"Old Widda," says Stan, "is as edgy as a bag of cats. She has a nose for disaster. And sure enough, this time, she's right."

At about ten past eleven there is an almighty explosion from the town, which sends every picture, holy or otherwise, tumbling from her wall. Old Widda remarks later that she feels a sharp chill down her spine. So she immediately falls to her knees, blesses herself and begins with the Rosary.

But it is no use. Less than thirty minutes later, Harry the Hurler and his kid brother Gerry are up at the Widda's door, their faces as long as their excuses.

"Mrs Johnston," says Harry, "I am truly very upset to say this, but Mickey Bangers is dead. That is his car which just explodes a short time ago. It seems that the alarm clock on the bomb rings an hour prematurely.

"The three of them are killed instantly – there's no suffering. Mickey is a brave Son of Ireland, and we are very proud of him."

Well, Old Widda clenches her fist, draws back her arm and bats Harry so hard across the mouth that he and Gerry vote to leg it before she gets a chance to get in a second blow. She then collapses on the step, crying and sobbing, shaking and trembling, until her next-door neighbour dashes round and ushers her inside.

The next couple of hours are all a blur for the Widda. She rings Letemout Lou at the Students' Union in Dublin and tells her to get the next bus home. And she then tries to get Light Heel Larry to go and ID the body. But the manager at the bakery says he's finished for the day – though she might try the bookies.

There is nothing left for it but Widda has to do the identification herself so Father Drownem agrees to come along to the mortuary. Sure enough, Old Widda recognises the corpses of Mickey's two colleagues lying on trolleys in the aisle.

"The third man," says the doctor gently, "is so badly disfigured that he is not really suitable for viewing. But he has the name Michael Johnston sewn on the inside of the jacket."

"It's only three days ago since he asks me to do that," the Widda tells him sadly.

After she gets back from Altnagelvin, the Widda rings the undertakers, who assure her they'll have the body ready for her by teatime. Father Drownem then rings Harry the Hurler to instruct him that the family do not want any trappings.

By the stage the casket arrives that evening, the house is full of mourners and Letemout Lou is back from Dublin. The Widda spends all the time alone in her bedroom, praying for it not to be true until Lou goes up to take her downstairs.

"It is the betrayal that's the worst," says the Widda. "Time and time again, Mickey says he is turning over a new leaf. And then this."

The closed coffin is set up in the front room, no flag, and shortly after six, Father Drownem begins a Rosary over the body. But he is hardly through his second Hail Mary when a commotion breaks out at the door.

"What are all those cars doing outside?" shouts a voice. "And what are all these people doing in my house?"

Every head in the place turns round, not believing. Mickey Bangers is at the front door and he is very much alive.

Old Widda bursts out of the front room and throws her arms around her eldest child. "I am praying for this moment all day," she says, laughing and crying at the same time. "You are my prodigal son given back to me."

Straight away, with great relief and some guilt, the Widda instructs Father Drownem to hurry the coffin back to the undertakers.

It then occurs to her to ask the obvious question as to how Mickey's car and two ex-colleagues are blown to kingdom come while he is still in the realm of the living. So Mickey confesses that, after much persuasion, he loans the car to his pals and takes the bus to work in Buncrana.

Mickey and the Widda stand back out of the way, arms around each other's waist, as the casket is carried from the front room.

"And what about the jacket with your name on it?" remembers Widda.

"Oh," laughs Mickey, "you'll have to change the name on it to Light Heel Larry. He's borrowing it all the time now."

And the Widda, who is a page ahead, collapses on her doorstep for the second time this day.

*****

Light Heel, God rest him, and this is true vows Stan, never learns to set an alarm clock because his mother always gets up at half-three in the morning to call him for work.

"To this day," says Stan, "Old Widda believes that she prays so hard she brings Mickey Bangers back from the dead. But in turn, God then has to take her favourite."

"So I take it Trinity College are quite keen to get rid of Letemout Lou when they discover that her brother blows himself up?" I ask Stan.

"No," says Stan, "though the reason for Lou's sudden departure is definitely linked."

About a week after Light Heel's funeral, Old Widda goes to visit Harry the Hurler at his offices on Rossville Street. Harry gracefully accepts Widda's punching him in the mouth as part of the job and is actually quite glad to see her.

"You're very good to allow us our little ceremonies after all," Harry tells her.

"Well," says Widda sadly, "if Larry is fool enough to die for you, it is the least you can do for him. But it is the last of your funerals that will ever leave my house."

"What do you mean?" asks Harry.

"I have two other children," says Widda carefully. "And I know they will live and die for you. But I want you to cut them loose forever – tell them that you'll have nothing more to do with them."

"I can't do that," declares Harry the Hurler.

"Listen, Harry," says Widda very firmly, "you will tell my surviving son and daughter that the best way they can serve Ireland is by becoming the smartest damn engineers and lawyers in the country. You already have one foot soldier from this family. That is enough. And, Son, if I ever find out that they are back doing your bidding, you will wake up some morning to see my tearful face looking out of every newspaper in the country, telling how you now intend to steal my entire family from me."

There is not a lot Harry can do, says Stan, when it is put to him like that. So a little later, he calls together Letemout Lou and Mickey Bangers for a private conference. Mickey sees the wisdom in what Harry tells him. He spots his mother's hand in the deal. But Letemout Lou is furious. She accuses Harry of insulting her brother's memory, tells him she'll never spit on the Boys again and storms off.

The following day, Lou heads back to Dublin, still in a massive huff. So when she gets off the bus at Connolly Street, she heads straight to her local, the Shakespeare Bar on Parnell Street, to drink the bit out. But she has hardly wet her lips when this awful racket starts up in the corner. A scruffy-looking drunk with an English accent is attempting to sing rebel songs.

Lou, who has enough of the revolution to do her a lifetime, yells down at him to shut up before she personally dispatches another martyr for old Ireland. The English guy, however, shouts back that there is nothing worse than an Irish woman who doesn't love her own country. This really ticks Lou off, so she goes down to the corner to give the English chap a piece of her mind. She tells him how the Boys are nothing but cowardly scumbags and that the country will be better off without them.

But the Englishman, unusually, is quite tuned in. And he begins engaging Lou in a debate on the justness of the Boys' cause – a cause which he clearly supports. Worse again, he is very clever, has a good knowledge of Irish and British history and law. And before long, he is tearing Lou, who considers herself an expert in these matters, into little pieces.

Indeed, eyewitnesses say that Lou is left like a fish sucking in air. So there is nothing for her to do but clench her fist, draw back her arm and bat him severely on the eye, before immediately leaving the bar.

"Not a very pleasant thing to do," I concede.

"No, indeed," says Stan. "But it gets worse. The following week, Letemout has to enrol in a new course at Trinity in Constitutional Law. So she goes into the classroom and is sitting on her own down the back, when who walks in the door but the scruffy young English guy she bops the week before – his eye still looking like a busted plum."

"I'd say that must be a great surprise," I comment to Stanley.

"Indeed and it is," says Stan, "but not half as surprising as when he puts his books down on the desk at the front and says: 'Good evening, ladies and gentlemen, my name is Professor Richard Smith, and I'm here to instruct you in Constitutional Law . . .'"

SPEECHLESS

If brains could burn, says Harry the Hurler, you can be certain that Switchblade Vic McCormack will never have to carry a fire blanket.

Harry, as the former Chief Executive of all the Boys in Derry, is no fan of Vic's. But as you and I both know, you do not get to be as rich as Vic without possessing a few grey cells. And running bars, particularly in this city, requires a real aptitude for doing business at the cutting edge. Indeed, it is precisely because Victor is so good at doing business at the cutting edge that he acquires the moniker Switchblade Vic in the first place.

The newspaperman Prozac Jack, who is well-clued up on these matters, will tell you that Vic first learns his business onions as a young gopher in a draper's shop on Spencer Road many years ago.

"This one day," says Jack, "a rich-looking guy comes into the shop and asks for a good hat. So Vic scurries out the back and returns with the best trilby in the shop. The guy tries it on, and it's a perfect fit.

"'How much?' says the guy.

"'Five pounds to you,' replies Vic.

"'Naw,' says the guy, 'I want something with real quality.'

"'I know just the thing, sir,' says Vic, and he scurries out the back again – only to return with the same hat. 'This fine chapeau,' says Vic, 'is of much superior quality, handcrafted from the best French felt in Vienna – but it'll cost you ten pounds.'

"'It's a deal!' cries the guy. And he goes away happy."

I laugh politely at this little con, though I have often heard similar yarns before. But Jack isn't finished his story yet.

"Unfortunately," continues Jack, "Vic's boss witnesses the transaction and isn't happy at all. The owner – despite the fact that he's in business – is quite a religious man. 'You are wronging that poor customer,' he tells Vic. 'And I think you should give him back that extra five-spot, which, incidentally, I see you are now stashing in your sock.' But the owner is also a fair man and tells Vic that if he can find anything in the Bible which justifies his actions, then he can keep the money.

"Needless to say, Vic is up all night, poring over the Good Book. And when he comes in the next morning, his boss says to him, 'Well, are you going to give the money back?'

"'Certainly not,' says Vic with a big grin. 'In fact, the Bible says my actions are spot on.'

"'How is that?' asks the boss.

"'Well,' says Jack, 'According to this chap called St Paul: If you see a stranger – you must take him in.'"

*****

Personally, I think Prozac Jack isn't entirely on the level with this yarn – largely because Vic is far too tough a guy ever to work in a business where he would have to take another man's inside leg measurements. But Jack is making a very serious point: Vic may look like an ox, and he may indeed have the vocabulary of an ox, but only a fool would ever make the mistake of thinking that he is as dumb as one.

Anyhow, the reason I am giving you this briefing on Vic is as follows. One fine spring day, I have to go to Belfast to visit the nieces and nephews at St Mildred's Home for Assorted Strays and Young Offenders. Generally, I travel up on the bus, which is cheap and quick. But this particular day, I read by chance in the *Derry Standard* that the train is by far the safest form of transport – down to all the hijackings and road blocks, no doubt. So for a change, I opt to go by rail.

But no sooner am I sitting in my empty carriage, when, as if to remind me never to believe anything I read, who slides open the door but Switchblade Vic McCormack. For as you are no doubt aware, Vic is on every hit list from here to Palermo.

"I know you," he announces cheerfully as he parks himself opposite me, "you're a pal of Harry the Hurler. I remember you from the court."

This sudden revelation leaves me cold – for my entirely involuntary friendship with Harry is something I almost always omit from my CV. So I am just about to protest my complete innocence and remember a sudden appointment with my bedridden Maw, when Vic motions his hand for me to stay where I am.

"It's okay, it's okay," he laughs. "Harry and I – while we're not exactly swapping spit in the back seat of the car – we're no longer sending one another bullets in the post. At least for the time being. So sit where you are. It'll be good company for the run up to Belfast. We can talk about old times."

Vic's other job, as you may or may not be aware, is as chief negotiator for the Planters' Independence Group, also known as the Pigs, who are currently in high-level political discussions with assorted Home Rulers at Stormont. These negotiations, from what I hear, hope to put an end to the current hostilities and to persuade both sides to hand in their pea-shooters. Though, as you and I both know, it is not peas which are being fired.

Anyhow, to steer the conversation away from me and my pal Harry, and figuring that Vic's heading for Stormont Castle, I ask him how the debates are progressing.

"Actually," says Vic, "I am not going to the talks today – I am on my way to a very sad funeral. You remember Joey Donnelly who runs against me last year for the chairmanship of the Pigs? Well, tragically, he is in a traffic accident at the weekend and turns up his toes."

I am, of course, already aware of this, as it is headline news in the papers for the past couple of days. The late Mr Donnelly – better known as Joey Handbag on account of the girly twang in his voice – is a considerable celebrity in Belfast. Though his sudden demise will cause considerable relief in large parts of the west of the city where Joey and his bandits are responsible for more sudden death than the Ulster Fry. It is no coincidence that he is the only man ever to get pegged out of the cops for unnecessary cruelty.

Joey's departure will, however, also cause considerable heartache in large parts of South Belfast and North Down, as it is here that he pursues his second career as a wholesale supplier of recreational medicines.

Now, I have no wish to start asking questions about the late Joey H for fear that a guy could be thought of as curious. But not wishing to seem impolite and drop out of the conversation completely, I put it to Vic that their election race for chair of the Pigs is very close.

"That's right," replies Vic, "in the end, I have only one vote to spare. But it is no doubt a good thing that I beat him otherwise we would all still be at war. Joey Handbag wouldn't be satisfied until every Home Ruler is as dead as old bones. And if required, he himself will arrange this personally."

You and I, of course, already know this is no idle boast. When Father Drownem visits the Handbag household to help negotiate the truce, Joey boasts that the priest is the first Home Ruler ever to cross the threshold. "The first one who's still breathing, that is, Father," adds Joey, quickly correcting himself.

"So what is the deciding factor for the voters between you and Joey?" I inquire of Vic as the train moves off.

"Well, that is a long story," says Vic. "Though most of it is after leaking out already. So I will fill you in – on condition that you're discreet. Though you may perhaps mention it to Harry the Hurler the next time he starts making fun of my better-than-average intellect. Indeed, he is always wisecracking about how I always burn my ear if the phone goes when I'm ironing. That only ever happens once."

*****

Unlike the rather dramatic methods the Pigs often use to deselect their old leaders, it seems that when they are picking a new chairman, they are very above board and democratic about it all together.

The Pigs have about a thousand fully paid-up members in all, divided between thirty-one different branches – three of which are in Scotland. And during the election for overall chairman, the candidates must attend a hustings at each and every regional branch in the United Territories. Then, at the end of each hustings, a vote is taken and the winner is accredited the entire support of that branch.

But when Joey Handbag and Switchblade Vic are vying for the top job, there is hardly a hair's breadth between them. Vic wins one hustings, Joey gets the next. And with the scores standing at fifteen lodges to thirteen in Vic's favour, the pair have to fly off to Glasgow for the final three debates.

Joey Handbag, because of his harder political line, is, however, expected to win the three Scottish hustings comfortably and snatch the chairmanship at the death. And unbeknownst to his party colleagues, he's also planning to smuggle home enough unlicensed medicine to fly half of Belfast to the moon.

"Joey, Lord rest him," explains Vic, "is an arrogant little sod. Even when the pair of us are flying out together from Aldergrove, he doesn't bother to take off his jewellery going through the security check. Naturally, the alarm goes off and the guy has to frisk him.

"To make matters worse, Joey then tells the seven-foot searcher to get your hands off me, you peasant. And it is all I can do to prevent a fist-fight. I, myself, take off my Star of David medallion and gold bracelet and sail through the check with no problem."

Vic pauses for a second as the train pulls in at Coleraine. An unwashed student with an end-of-term backpack makes to come into the carriage, but Vic assures him that it's privately booked. Initially, the scholar reckons that this is not possible and starts to argue. Then, all of a sudden, his eyes light up and he quickly runs along, dragging his backpack with a renewed energy. And indeed not for the first time, I remark what a marvellous thing an education can be.

The interruption over, Vic continues his story.

"As soon as the pair of us land in Glasgow, we get a taxi straight to our first debate at the Walker Memorial Club on Lower Sauchiehall Street, where around fifty of the faithful are waiting," recalls Vic.

"Joey Handbag gets to speak first on the grounds of alphabetical order. And just before he stands up, a respectable-looking guy in a three-piece suit hands him a sealed A4 envelope. And the envelope," explains Vic, looking over his shoulder for dramatic effect, "only contains the finest oration since Mrs Martin Luther King asks her husband how is he sleeping this weather.

"It talks about the honour of negotiations, the responsibility to reconcile, the duty of office, the need to learn from experience – and all this other palaver that Joey wouldn't know if it's tattooed on his arms. One minute it's Gandhi, the next it's JFK – full of classical allusions, poetry, and quotes from distinguished old Orange leaders. And the crowd think it's all from the heart and are mesmerised. I am on a complete hiding to nothing. There are people up standing on the tables and stomping their feet. They love it.

"My own speech afterwards – which basically boils down to how the Home Rulers are all bad guys and we are the good guys – goes down like a pair of cement shoes. And I lose the vote by about five to one. Though, I suppose, at least no-one throws any bottles at me."

Quitters never win and, despite his pounding, Switchblade Vic resolves to soldier on to the second hustings. The next debate is the following night in the Ibrox Arms. And once again it is a complete disaster for Switchblade Vic, if not a little worse. Joey speaks first, gives the same oration, and brings the house down – while Vic is asked to stop halfway through so that the karaoke man can set up his gear.

Joey Handbag wins the Ibrox match by about seven to one.

"I have to confess that things are looking very black," says Vic. "But later, in my hotel room, when I begin replaying the whole shooting-match in my head, I keep thinking of Joey's speech, and how he talks about the need to learn from experience. And it's at that stage that the light bulb in my head suddenly switches itself on.

"So when we arrive the next night at the Campsie Club on Princes Square for the final debate, I'm ready. Remember, the hustings are now tied at fifteen all and whoever wins this one becomes leader.

"The president of the Campsie Club is an old comrade of my father and knows I'm up against it. So when I beg a small favour off him, he reckons he can oblige, as long as I don't ask him to fix the vote."

This time, however, the two candidates draw straws as to who gets to speak first. And for a change, it's Switchblade Vic's honour.

"You have to put away your chances in this game," says Vic, "so I get up, look at the crowd, look Joey directly in the eye and say, 'Good evening, ladies and gentlemen.' I then proceed to rhyme off Joey Handbag's entire speech word for word.

"I give it the whole bit about the honour of negotiations, the responsibility to reconcile, the duty of office, the need to learn from experience. Verbatim. I use all the classical allusions, poetry and quotes, and do the whole JFK and Gandhi bit. In short, I mesmerise them. And when I finish, sure enough the crowd are up on their tables, stamping and clapping like wild men – well, all but Joey Handbag and the MI5 guy in the three-piece who's minding him."

"Joey, I take it, is quite surprised," I suggest.

"He is indeed," says Vic. "It's as if I'm after reciting a decade of the Rosary."

Joey, says Vic, then gets up and tries to talk off the top of his head. First up, he accuses Vic of stealing his speech and of not playing by the rules. But the mob laughs him down. And at the end of the night, even friends of Joey, who know well that Vic steals the speech, vote for Vic on the grounds of his great initiative. And Vic is duly elected supreme chairman of the Pigs by sixteen branches to fifteen.

"So you ask your Da's old pal to let you speak first?" I laugh.

"Indeed," replies Vic, "and he also gets me a photocopy of the speech. And this proves very useful."

The two of us laugh, and not a bit sympathetically, at the late Joey Handbag's hard luck. But Vic isn't finished his story yet.

Later that same night, Vic and Joey Handbag kiss and make up. And they agree to travel back to Belfast together the following day.

"Joey even gives me the envelope with his speech in it as a souvenir," laughs Vic. "Anyhow, all goes well with the flight home, until we come back into Aldergrove and have to go through the security check. Well, Joey spots the same security guard who stops him on the way out and immediately gets up on his high horse. He refuses to take off his jewellery and, of course, the machine lights up like a prison yard.

"So the guard pulls him into a little cubicle and begins searching him and sifting through his bag. He even squeezes half of Joey's toothpaste onto a clear plastic dish. Though, thankfully, he draws the line at snapping on the rubber gloves.

"I, naturally, am considerably nervous – given Joey's fondness for recreational medicine. More to the point, I have it on good authority that Joey intends to come home with a shipment big enough to feed a private army. But the guard searches and searches and doesn't even come up with a cigarette butt. So eventually he waves him on."

Vic, as before, does the sensible thing and divests himself of his medallion, bracelet and newly acquired Ulster Will Fight belt buckle before sailing through the machine.

"Outside the airport," says Vic, "myself and Joey get on the bus for Belfast. And I am blazing mad at him for his antics. 'What are you playing at?' I ask him. 'Are you looking to get banged up?' But he just smirks and taps his nose like there's some secret.

"'I know you are bringing stuff back,' I tell him. 'I know you are. Though for the life of me, I can't figure out where you have it stashed.' Well, Joey just smirks again. And this time he reaches over into the inside pocket of my jacket, where I have the envelope he gives me earlier. He opens it very carefully and removes his speech. And there, still inside, are about thirty sheets of very fine blotting paper.

"And every one of these sheets is divided into around two thousand tiny squares. Each of which, says Joey, represents one tablet of LSD – a very sought-after type of recreational medicine indeed. 'How much is that worth?' I ask him. 'Ten-to-fifteen years,' he laughs, and jams the blotting paper in his bag. 'Thanks for looking after it for me.'"

I suck in air and shake my head in disbelief. But Vic just nods sombrely. "Personally," he says, "I'm not sure whether to laugh or cry. But Joey just gives me this big what-the-hell grin, and there is no point in getting mad at this stage, so I grin back.

"You'll understand, of course, that I disapprove very strongly of such behaviour. An incident like this could do my reputation as a man of high integrity no little harm. But given that I am after stealing the speech in the first place, there's very little moral high ground around for me to stand on. Joey then turns to me and jokes, 'It is now your turn to be speechless.' And by the time we get into Belfast, the two of us are laughing it all off."

*****

The Derry train pulls into York Street in North Belfast, and even though this is not my stop, I reckon it will be better all round if I don't leave the train on Vic's arm. So I grab my bag and head for the corridor.

"As a matter of interest," I ask Vic as I shake his hand goodbye, "the reports about Joey's traffic accident are all a little vague. Why is that?"

"Well," explains Vic sadly, "we want to spare the family's feelings by keeping it under a lid. Truth is, Joey has a fondness for his own blotting paper. And it appears that his death comes about when he attempts to fly off the top of a motorway bridge. His maiden voyage ends quite prematurely when he collides mid-air with a forty-foot articulated truck. Poor Joey Handbag is squished flatter than a ripe tomato."

"A tragedy," I reply.

"I agree entirely," sighs Vic. "But who would think that Joey could eat an entire sheet of this blotting paper at the one sitting? Personally, I would only ever do such a thing at the point of a gun . . ."

No Flowers For Knuckles

Strictly between ourselves, there are those who still believe that Harry the Hurler, one time head of all the Boys in Derry, is still involved in the non-political end of things. Indeed, the editor of the *Londonderry Leader*, Prozac Jack Irwin, will tell you that to this day, Harry insists on having the final shout on all personnel matters – and, in particular, recruitment.

"You remember the time Harry appears in public with all that bruising to his face?" Jack says to me one evening in The Jack Kennedy. "Everyone assumes he falls out with Red Light Lorna again? Well, I can exclusively reveal that the injuries Harry suffers are not down to her – but are actually the result of some internal business.

"From what I hear, the Boys decide to give some new recruits a practical exam to establish their mettle. So they ask the apprentices to go into a darkened room and discharge several clips of ammunition into a hooded man they say is an informer. Course the gun is only loaded with blanks, though the new guys don't know that.

"Come the day of the test, the Boys can't find anyone game enough to be the tout. All the tough guys are a bit nervous about being nutted by rounds, blank or otherwise. So eventually, Harry the Hurler, who is actually still the chief enrolment officer, agrees to play the victim.

"Well, the first recruit goes into the room, lines up the gun and tells the hooded man to say his last prayers. But when it comes to the crunch, the rookie crumples and can't pull the trigger. Same goes for the second recruit – but he's so upset he runs out of the room crying.

"But the final character goes in, and Lord, is he eager. He storms into the room shouting how he's personally going to cut out this guy's liver and eat it as soon as he's dead. He cocks his gun and is about to loose off his first round when suddenly, he changes his mind. Instead, he leaps over the table, pushes Harry to the ground and roars at him: 'Shooting's too good for you, you dirty Judas.' And he then begins pistol-whipping him around his head and kicking him in the kidneys.

"Good job Jimmy Fidget manages to bust the door down or poor Harry will be beaten to death."

*****

The old ones are always the best. But there are three reasons I know the tale to be untrue.

First, Harry's lady wife Red Light Lorna has a punch like a Russian docker. Secondly, I get to witness this punch for myself in the Four Green Fields Bar one night after Lorna catches Harry sharing a seat with a barmaid in a locked cubicle in the Ladies'. And thirdly, if Harry is indeed still involved in the youth training programme, then there is no way a twisted little thief like Knuckles Doherty would ever be admitted to the ranks.

*****

Despite the fact that he is dead and so, technically, above all criticism, even now you would be hard-pressed to find someone who could say a kind word about Knuckles. His own mother will tell you that she would never leave him alone in a room with anything more valuable than a pair of locked handcuffs. For this is a man who would steal the hair from your beard and come back for the stubble.

Knuckles, as you'll gather, isn't his real name, but one which he acquires as a juvenile delinquent in Belfast, where he hails from. The name on his birth cert is actually Cathal, after the Civil War martyr, but he is known as Knuckles for many years now, ever since the Boys first step in and break his thieving fingers on behalf of the community. Though this deterrent, sadly, proves altogether unsuccessful – even when re-applied.

Then one day, about five years ago, Harry the Hurler's little brother Gerry is in Andersonstown on a spot of business when he catches a guy trying to nick his car. And who is the thief only Knuckles. But instead of securing Knuckles's fingers to the doorframe and bouncing the door off them, as you or I might do, Gerry decides to indulge in a little social experiment.

You see, unlike you or me, Gerry is an educated man. And he figures it would be much more intelligent to have Knuckles stealing *for* him than stealing *from* him. So he decides to invite Knuckles to Derry and offer him a job procuring cars and other materials for the Boys.

The Old Guard, as you'd expect, reckon you'd be better off getting the Sisters of Mercy in to run a knocking-shop, but Gerry the Hurler cannot be told.

*****

From what I hear on the q.t. from Harry the Hurler, Knuckles's rise to prominence is as rapid as it is ruthless.

"One night, soon after Knuckles comes on board, there is a crisis," Harry explains. "My sister-in-law, Moustache Sally, who is married to your pal Getemup Gormley, is out collecting the Boys' Support Fund contributions from the bars. But just as she's crossing the Great James Street car park on her way back to the offices on Edward Street, she is held up and robbed by a guy in a black mask, carrying a sharp knife."

Not only is this considered quite a heinous crime, but it is also a hugely daring one. No-one in full possession of their onions would hold up the Support Fund – and in particular Moustache Sally, who is built like a heavyweight boxer only not as pretty. So the list of suspects for the robbery is very short indeed. In fact, there are no names on it whatsoever.

After some discussions, however, the Boys decide that it may just pay them to set a thief to catch a thief. So, following a narrow vote, they temporarily promote Knuckles from poacher to gamekeeper.

Knuckles senses his big chance and moves quickly. And before the week is out, he hunts down four known lowlifes who are recent arrivals from rural Donegal and have no alibis for the night of the hold-up. Try as he might, he is unable to filter down the numbers any. But there is no way he is going to let anyone away with robbing his new trustees. So instead of remanding the defendants for further questioning, as is customary in such cases, Knuckles borrows a pistol from Gerry the Hurler and shoots each of the four gentlemen once behind each knee.

The word goes out quickly. Within hours, the stolen Support Fund money is left anonymously in a box outside the *Derry Standard* offices. And Knuckles's temporary promotion into the gamekeeping business is made permanent.

*****

Knuckles takes to his new job like he's to the manor born. He is gifted with a devious mind that is perfect for spotting a liar from the first double blink. Indeed, many people comment that he is so lowdown and conniving he could make an excellent cop.

He has very little sympathy for those who appear before him, and is as merciless in his judgements as you'd expect from a man whose own fingers are broken more often than a Confirmation pledge. So before long, he is appointed head of Internal Investigations.

His first masterstroke is catching the Hurley's own cousin, Jimmy Big Mouth Junior, with his fist in the pie. Knuckles's suspicions are aroused when he spots Jimmy standing in the foyer of McAleese's Travel Shop. There are very few families on the dole who are able to book two weeks R and R on the Italian Riviera, and although Jimmy Big Mouth is one of Gerry's favourite blood relatives, the Boys decide to pull him in. It is no help at all that Jimmy has five unexplainable fifties hiding in the back of his wallet. And Gerry refuses to accept that the notes arrive in an unmarked brown envelope earlier that day.

The fact that Jimmy is Gerry's cousin seals his fate, as the Boys can ill-afford to be seen to be going soft on their own. Knuckles himself insists on dispatching the first bullet into Jimmy, who hits the carpet, protesting his innocence.

Knuckles is also the man who snares Raymond 'Woof Woof' Barker, the Rosemount Supply Chief. Woof Woof, it seems, is in the habit of ringing up the gendarmes half an hour before kick-off to tell them that his team's on their way. After three heavy defeats without a single score, Knuckles gets his man in the telephone company to check all outgoing calls from each of the Rosemount unit's home phones. And lo and behold, when he dials one particular number, which features regularly on Woof Woof's bill, it proves to be a direct line to Victoria Market CID.

The Boys are certain that Woof Woof is dirtier than a public toilet, but he denies all the charges, and they can prove nothing. So eventually, after a lengthy stewards' inquiry, Harry intercedes with a conditional pardon, and Woof Woof gets to spend the next twenty years in hiding in England.

*****

Without question, however, Knuckles's crowning glory is the Frankie One Shot affair.

During one seriously bad spell for the Boys, four rifle dumps are discovered in the space of a month. Tensions are running high, as the only parties who know where all the goods are planted are Harry the Hurler and his brother Gerry. Gerry the Hurler is the head of the Boys' storage business and is baffled. So he decides to create a new hide – but without telling anybody, and waits to see what happens.

Three days later, and the Creggan Roundabout is dug up by six units of gendarmes. And the two new AK47s are unearthed exactly where Gerry buries them.

Certain he must be being tailed, Gerry gets his brothers Harry and Jimmy Fidget to shadow him the next time he's burying a new set of gear. So they provide full cover, using field glasses and sound-mike headphones, but spot nothing. Yet again the dump is raided. So in despair, the Hurlers call in Knuckles.

Even the master is stumped at first. And two more dumps – one quite a packed affair – are rumbled in the next couple of weeks. Then one night, after a training session on Grianan Hill, Frankie One Shot spends a little too long oiling down a rifle for Knuckles's liking.

Frankie, as the Boys' senior long-range craftsman, examines all new machinery coming into town before it is planted. And he is also responsible for checking out all materials after practice. But at the end of this particular session, Knuckles remarks that Frankie seems to be paying too much attention to a new Barrett and demands to see it. Frankie, however, resents taking orders from a jumped-up thief and refuses to budge – with the result that Knuckles pulls out a pistol and shoots him, dead as a nail.

Gerry the Hurler, who is also in the changing room, figures it's his turn next and scrambles for the door. But Knuckles throws down his gun and coaxes him back. Knuckles then picks up the Barrett that Frankie is, until very recently, oiling and breaks it open. And there, sticking in the breech, is a little magnetic disc, no bigger than a silver pimple.

"A homing device!" whistles Gerry the Hurler.

"Either that," laughs Knuckles, "or Frankie may have grounds for appeal."

*****

After Frankie One Shot's unscheduled demise, the Boys reckon it's time to streamline the organisation. So Knuckles is drafted in as Gerry the Hurler's right-hand man. And for some time, everything trucks along merrily – although admittedly the Boys go a little security-mad and aren't up for half as many fixtures as before.

But the problems plaguing Gerry's storage business seem to be behind him. And he even devises a new dumping scheme, which proves very popular indeed. Every time a friend or relative of the Boys shuffles off his mortal coil, Gerry the Hurler asks the family if they would like a little help with the funeral. Perhaps a special casket, or what have you. And Gerry's state-of-the-art coffins are hard to resist. Hand-carved blasted oak, with big bronze handles, they must weigh about a hundred pounds more than traditional boxes. Though that could also be down to the four rifles and eight belts of ammo stashed tightly below each false bottom.

Resurrection is generally effected late at night, within a three-month period, if at all humanly possible. Though Gerry and Knuckles believe it's best not to involve the families in this stage of the proceedings, as by now the deceased tend to be well past their best-before date.

Replanting the rifles, however, is not an issue, as, thankfully, people are dying all the time. And the Gerry-the-Hurler Deluxe Casket is now proving so popular that ordinary civilians are queuing up to buy them.

"The only problem they have," explains Harry the Hurler, "is that although the dumps are now safe, everyone is still too afraid to go out to play in case the gendarmes are still getting our game plans. Not that I know anything about these matters, mind you – being on the political end of things this long time."

*****

Then, one night, disaster. Gerry the Hurler and Knuckles are in the process of resurrecting Getemup Gormley's Great-Aunt Maeve, when they are surprised by a blacked-up company of rozzers sporting very heavy-duty machinery. Gerry is shot in the Adam's apple and is floored – though luckily not terminally. Knuckles, however, escapes by weaving his way across through the cemetery, ducking behind tombstones as bullets scatter here, there and everywhere.

He absconds over the wall and makes his way to a safe house before crossing the frontier via a back road. Then, two days later, he pops up at a press conference in Donegal Town, where he gives a carefully tailored version of events and blames the dastardly gendarmes for firing without warning.

After that, no-one hears anything at all of Mr Knuckles Doherty until about three weeks later when his photo appears on the front page of the *Derry Standard*. The picture, to be honest, does him little justice, and he seems to be wearing quite a glazed expression on his face. Though this could be because his hands and feet are bound together with cable ties and his bullet-ridden body is after spending nine days in a ditch.

*****

There are only two of us at the funeral besides Father Drownem and Knuckles's Old Ma, who travels down to Derry for the service. And I'm only here because Harry the Hurler shouts through my letter box that he knows I am in.

There are no flowers for Knuckles. And Father Drownem skips the sermon. There's little he can add to the usual condemnations in this morning's *Derry Standard*.

"So how does this all square up?" I ask Harry in the Merc on the way to the cemetery.

"Gerry just might get out on the entrapment rule," says H. "But I won't hold my breath."

"Entrapment?" I repeat.

"Yes," replies Harry. "It's very embarrassing. The gendarmes are running Knuckles for years. Though it's all Gerry's own fault. Ever since he gets that curse-of-God degree in War and Peace Studies, you can't tell him anything."

"So how much damage is done?" I ask Harry.

"Quite a bit," he says. "Basically, Special Branch are using Knuckles as their internal hit-man. They get him to pick off their personal favourites.

"Take for instance our cousin Jimmy Big Mouth. They put him in the frame by sending him bunches of fifties in the post and then get Knuckles to out him as a tout.

"Likewise Frankie One Shot. By this stage we're positive that he has nothing to do with rigging the guns. Though we figure he has suspicions that the weapons are being bugged – which is why Knuckles whacks him. And we are now virtually certain that it is the gendarmes themselves who are responsible for adding their own telephone number onto Woof Woof Barker's phone bill."

"So how do you finally rumble Knuckles?" I ask.

"Oh, I don't rumble anyone," grins Harry the Hurler, "I am on the political end of things this long time. But a man cannot escape his character. And Knuckles, unfortunately, can't shake the habits of a lifetime.

"From what I hear, no-one has any suspicions about him at all until he appears at the press conference after the cemetery shoot-out, carrying Fat Marty Doyle's cigarette case. As you'll recall, Fat Marty dies about six months ago from smoking a hundred butts a day. And as a concession to his number one pleasure, his wife thinks it'll be nice to bury his silver case along with him.

"So she is naturally very upset to see the little box reappearing with Knuckles on national television. And the Boys, who are already in the doghouse after their coffin-lining business is exposed, are concerned that a grave-robbing scandal will finish them off altogether. So they discreetly inquire off Knuckles where he gets the case."

A chill goes through my bones as we disembark from Harry's Merc to follow the coffin through the Killowen Gardens gate of the cemetery.

"Surely Knuckles is going to deny everything?" I ask him.

"And of course, he does," replies Harry. "He even tries to tell us that Gerry, who is by now out of commission, lifts it by mistake and gives it to him. But Gerry is the greatest fresh-air fanatic ever born. He is a fascist – he even puts Old Ma out in the back yard of his house if she wants a smoke."

"But it could be just an accident?" I suggest for sake of argument.

"Could be," says Harry. "But it puts the Boys' guard up. Anybody who robs the dead is capable of anything.

"Then, on the day of Gerry's arraignment for possession with intent, the Crown lawyer reads out a list of what they find in Great-Aunt Maeve's grave – four assorted semi-automatic rifles and six hundred and forty rounds of ammo.

"Gerry's lawyer, Tommy Bowtie, asks the Crown if the rifles are loaded. Because as you may or may not know, a loaded weapon carries twice the sentence of an empty one."

Surprisingly, says Harry, the Crown, albeit reluctantly, admits that the rifles are all empty – and hands Tommy Bowtie the full inventory sheet. Now, this sheet contains the make and model of each rifle from the coffin but on the paper, beside the details of two of the weapons, is a little asterisk. So Tommy asks the prosecutor what they mean.

"First of all the DPP says he doesn't know anything about the asterisks," explains Harry. "But then, when Tommy asks him if he's sure, he clams up entirely, saying it's a security matter. Tommy Bowtie, however, is thinking on his feet and suggests to the DPP that the reason for the asterisks is to indicate that these particular weapons are bugged. And he further suggests that the cops know all along where the rifles are stashed and are only waiting for a chance to punch Gerry full of holes.

"The judge, however, immediately steps in to rule out any further questions from Tommy in this area. And he bans the court reporters from publishing any of the details. But there is no doubt they are caught out."

"And Knuckles, I take it, is the only other person who ever handles the guns?" I venture.

"Exactly," says Harry, "though it requires several days of discreet questioning before we can establish this for a fact."

Some of the local newspapers allege that this discreet questioning involves three cold baths and six or seven encounters with an electric cattle prodder. But now is probably not the best time to press Harry the Hurler too closely about this. So instead, we stand there at Knuckles's graveside, baffing our hands together as Father Drownem begins the last prayers.

The little ceremony over, Father D hands Harry the Hurler the shovel, and he spoons some clay onto the coffin. No blasted oak for Knuckles, just cheap knotty pine.

We shake hands with the priest and Mrs Doherty, then head slowly for the gate.

"So what makes Knuckles swap sides in the first place?" I ask Harry eventually.

"Personally," says Harry, "I reckon there are only two reasons any of us do anything – out of fear, or for the money. And in Knuckles's case, the cops have him over a barrel.

"From what I hear, when Knuckles starts out, Gerry is only paying him a pittance. So Knuckles decides to do a homer or two to top up his income. And one of these is captured on the new closed-circuit TV cameras outside Victoria Barracks."

"So the cops threaten to slap him in the chokey if he doesn't tout?" I ask.

"No, no," tuts Harry. "They threaten to send the videotape to Getemup Gormley."

"And why is that?"

"Well," says Harry, "they figure it might be a bit tricky for Knuckles to explain how he can be filmed on the Strand Road removing a mask, just thirty seconds after Getemup's wife, Moustache Sally, is robbed of the Support Fund around the corner."

"Aha," I reply.

"So he signs on the line pretty soon after that," says Harry. "And by the time poor Jimmy Big Mouth is whacked, Knuckles is so compromised that the Branch even stop paying him and can run him for fun.

"People say, in the end what comes around goes around, and Knuckles gets just what he deserves. But I don't agree. Knuckles is no angel but you would need to be a lot more lowdown and conniving than him to be up to the boys who are pulling his strings, God rest him."

TWO LITTLE BOYS

For my brother Rónán 'Give Everyone A Middle Name' Downey

There is little doubt but that Chiselling Phil, loving younger brother of Stammering Stan the Radio Man, is one of the smartest guys in this collection of parishes. Though this can come as a surprise to those meeting Phil for the first time, as Stammering Stan hasn't the brains to empty wax from his ear.

Chiselling Phil, for the uninitiated, is a former lawyer who now runs his own pub on Waterloo Street. But this is only part of the story. Thanks to his years of handling a series of most delicate and confidential matters for a series of most publicity-shy individuals, Phil is in high demand across the city as a private consultant and negotiator.

Phil, for instance, is the guy drafted in by the Boys whenever they figure they have a rat in the ranks. A gifted interrogator, after two minutes of Phil's questioning, all but the very innocent fall apart like a cheap suit. Though again, you will not find this on his business card.

Likewise, Phil is the city's number one expert in spotting those who are skimming ten per cent off the top. He is the first port of call for Derry's richest man, Sparkly Barkley, whenever he suspects the help are trying to clean him out again. And he is the man that Harry the Hurler sends in to snare Bad Breath Bradley that time he is stealing everything but the light sockets from the Four Green Fields Bar.

But his talents are also respected by the Planters' Defence Groups – who regularly use him as a go-between when they have to mediate with the Boys across the water. Indeed, strictly between ourselves, the fact that Phil is on a retainer from both Harry the Hurler and Switchblade Vic helps bring about the first bilateral truce between the Boys and the Planters.

Phil's academic record speaks for itself, but those who deal with him also admire his strong pragmatic streak. Like yourself, they no doubt remember how the last guy to test Philip's non-academic credentials spends three weeks in St Francis's Nursing Home recovering from a chis-el-ectomy to the upper thigh. Indeed, this is the principal reason the Law Society asks Phil to give up the legal profession in the first place.

For all that, Phil is a gentle giant, a chap you will always want at your weddings on account of how he will fuss over your grandmothers and dance with your baby nieces. And if, God forbid, your relations have too much sparkling wine and become punchy, Phil, with his quiet authority, will go and sort them out quickly. This, needless, to say goes for your uncles as well as your aunts.

Stammering Stan is naturally very proud of his little sibling – to the extent that, nowadays, when he begins to drop his name over teatime pints and free Don't Go Home cocktail sausages in The Jack Kennedy, the company invariably make yawning noises and check their watches. Though I would hasten to add for the record that Phil is a very fine fellow altogether and that it is, of course, Stan we are yawning at.

*****

"Philip isn't always as smart as he is now," concedes Stan one Friday afternoon over stout and sausages.

"In fact, when he is a child, there are concerns that he might be a bit of a late learner. So much so that our father appoints me Philip's school-yard guardian. And let me tell you, this is quite a task. Day and daily I am called upon to pull him out of all sorts of scrapes that his big mouth gets him into. Ultimately, it takes none other than Letemout Lou to set him on the road to righteousness."

Letemout Lou Johnston, besides batting her eyes at Stan over Lamb Pasanda on a Friday night, is also Derry's newest High Court judge. But I don't remember Chiselling Phil ever appearing before her. And I mention this to Stan.

"No, no, it's nothing to do with the law," he explains. "Lou marks Phil's card long, long ago, back when we are still only two little boys. Though for reasons that will rapidly become apparent, we never discuss it any more.

"I know Lou about twenty-five years now, ever since she starts fol-lowing myself and Philip down to Bogside Infants. Back then, Lou is as fat as a barrel. And boy, does she invite comment about it. I, of course, am careful about such comment, thanks to my Pop. He is very astute for a man who never has any folding money. And he instructs me at a very early age that a guy should never make public statements about a doll's weight – even if she herself appears to be jolly about such teasing. Because you can bet your thumb nails that not only may she look like an elephant, but she will also have the memory of one. Unfortunately for Philip, however, he misses that lecture."

Letemout Lou is nowadays so skinny you could poke her through a buttonhole, so it is very hard to picture her as a ten-bellies. Though then again, it is just as hard to picture Phil ever commenting on it.

"Anyhow," continues Stan, "this particular day, we are on our way to school and Lou is in an especially sour mood. So she begins picking on little Phil. She starts to barb on at him that when he's a baby, he's so ugly that the doctor takes one look at him and slaps his mother.

"Well, Phil, who, as you'd expect, is a very good-looking child, is about as happy as a cat with his tail in the door. But he's a year or two younger than Lou – and about forty pounds off her fighting weight, so he's not really in a position to bop her in the eye. So I call him aside and whisper a little advice in his ear.

"About a minute later, he marches back over to Lou and taps her on the shoulder. 'I hear that when you're born,' he tells her, 'you're so fat that the doctor has to tickle you in the middle to see which end smiles.'"

"An old one, but nasty," I say to Stan.

"It gets worse," he sighs. "Lou moves in to give Phil a duffing, but I manage to face her down – bravely threatening to tell Teacher. So instead, she gives him this killer look and tells him: 'And you're so ugly, the doctor tells your mother to go down to the petting zoo and maybe they'll let her do a swap.'

"Well, this is easy meat for Phil, who bats it back on his own. 'And you're so fat,' he replies, 'that the doctor turns to the nurse and says, Quick, quick, run up and close the canteen – in case this one escapes.'"

I suck in air again.

"Lou is now white with rage," says Stan. "So she bears down on Phil and yells into his face: 'And when you're born, you're so ugly that the doctor takes one look at you and goes looking for the afterbirth.'

"Now, neither myself nor Phil really understand this though we believe it's pretty mean indeed. And I think he's about to cry. So I call him aside again for another confab. And, after about thirty seconds of consultations, Phil breaks loose from our huddle and strides up to Letemout. 'Louise,' he tells her, 'I am truly and deeply sorry for insulting you.' And he offers her his hand, which she takes. 'Particularly,' he continues, 'since I hear that when you're born, the doctor gets an x-ray of your belly to see if you're after eating the other two triplets.'"

By the time Stan manages to drag Letemout Lou off, Phil's face is puffed up like a beach ball and his nose is bleeding like a pump. Thankfully, however, there are no permanent scars, except for the little two-tooth gap in Phil's bottom set.

"Indeed," says Stan, "it is a good job I am there to intervene, as not only do I save Philip's life, but I probably also save Lou's chances of a career in law. But you can learn a lot from a beaten docket. And ever since, Philip always knows to quit when he's ahead."

*****

Phil also learns another very important lesson from this episode, but one which bypasses his brother completely. There is a time to talk, a time to listen, and a time to disregard everything you hear on the grounds that it's only going to get you into trouble. Many people reckon it is about time that Stammering Stan discovers this for himself. And none more so than the leading Planter, Switchblade Vic McCormack.

Switchblade Vic, as you'll recall, besides owning a chain of pubs, is the Chairman of the Planters' Independent Group ever since he retires from the sharper end of things. And up till very recently, he and Stan have a very good working relationship. Then, one night when Stan is returning from a press conference in the Waterside, he decides to call into The Sash and Drum to pay his respects. But as always, one quick belt leads to another, and Stan and Vic head off together on the mother of all sessions. And in the fog of early morning, Vic drops his guard and begins speaking a little too freely about some internal business matters which Stan needs to know nothing about.

*****

The Planters' non-political wing in the Waterside is divided into two units: the Fundraisers, who are based in Drumahoe, and the Hellraisers, who come from Caw. But despite the fact both groups answer to Vic, or so it is alleged in open court fourteen times, they enjoy a very strong and often bitter rivalry.

The Hellraisers' commander is a tough young doll name of Sue Clabby – better known to me and you as Runaround Sue on account of the difficulty that the gendarmes have in tracking her down. Stan will admit to you privately that Sue is quite a tidy little package, before her appetite for bottled stout starts to spoil the line of her tight jumpers. Though it will take a braver man than Stan to advise her of this, as Sue has fists like a docker and a temper to match.

She is also very quick to take offence. So when one day Stan shuffles into The Jack Kennedy sporting a big pair of panda eyes and announces Sue is responsible, no-one is too surprised.

Danny Boy the barman quickly runs to dispense the medicine while I attempt to help Stan into his chair. But he pushes me away and laughs that he's okay.

"You should see the other guy," he grins, displaying several missing teeth.

Stan is unusually chipper for a man in his condition, so I beg him to enlighten us.

"Truth is," he says, "I really should be dead. Strictly *entre nous*, I am on a Planter D-list up until about an hour ago."

"Which group?" I ask him. "Caw or Drumahoe?"

"The two of them," he replies soberly. "It appears that they're both after holding separate inquiries into a report in the *Derry Standard* which carries my byline and which they do not like at all. The result of which, interestingly, is that both groups independently are proposing to shoot me full of holes."

"That seems rather drastic," I say to Stan. "But this is what happens when you write lies about people."

"No, no," protests Stan, "lies are rarely a difficulty. It is when you start writing the truth about people that you run into problems."

"So which truth in particular is it that they are taking exception to?" I inquire.

"Well," grins Stan, "that is quite a story – and one which will require another dose of pain reliever. Indeed, I think I'll need a double measure this time."

*****

Most Planters with any academic or military merit, says Stan, tend to join the police or become real soldiers. And this leaves only the scrapings off the plate for the likes of the Drumahoe and Caw mobs. They are both, Stan assures me, very volatile bunches.

Switchblade is the unofficial overboss of both contingents, though since going political, he mostly restricts his input to arbitrating internal disputes and tut-tutting his head when his charges nut the wrong guy. As a former Caw Hellraiser, Vic tends to favour his old gang slightly on those many cases when he is called to intercede. Though the Drumahoe Fundraisers still regard themselves as by far the senior of the two outfits because of their financial input.

Problems start one afternoon when the Caw Hellraisers decide to do a little fundraising off their own bat. Runaround Sue puts on her prettiest pair of Pretty Polly tights and calls in at the Spencer Road Post Office, where she manages to solicit a generous donation of five K in old notes and thirty pounds in stamps. Though to improve her chances, she is, of course, wearing the tights over her head and holding a Colt 45.

The Drumahoe unit, when they hear they're being gazumped, are fit to be tied. And their head honcho, Billy Blue Nose, immediately marches up to Runaround Sue's office and demands back half the proceeds. Sue, as is her wont, gives this proposal short shrift, though as a concession, she will hand back just enough to buy Blue Nose a new saucepan – in which he can go and boil his head.

Blue Nose, however, is a guy who doesn't like being short-changed. So he invokes Switchblade Vic as a court of appeal.

"It is at this point," explains Stan, "that I get wind of what's happening and write a piece for the *Standard*. I give it the whole nine yards explaining how Sue is putting it up to Billy and gaining the upper hand in their turf war. And I flesh it out with details about their past disputes which is, of course, hugely embarrassing to both camps.

"My article, incidentally, isn't supposed to have my name on it given the sensitivity of the topic. But some donkey of a sub-editor, who thinks he's doing me a favour, decides to dress up the story. And believe me, the story is hardly dry on the paper when the mush hits the fan."

At 9.00am on publication day, Billy Blue Nose lands down at the *Standard* office, his face as red as a traffic light. He bursts straight through the reporters' door and starts promising all manner of violent retribution on Stan, who is currently out in the production room promising the same to the sub-editor.

Nose's main concern is to find out where the story hails from. The way he figures it, someone in his unit is getting mouthy. Or worse still, maybe they have a Home Rule spy in their midst, seeing as a rag like the *Standard* is first to get the story. So he drags Stan by the collar into the editor's office, fecks him into a chair and starts giving him the third degree.

Well, Blue Nose screams and he roars, he threatens and he pleads. But surprisingly, Stan proves to be a relatively straight-backed guy, even if he is a reporter. And no amount of shouting and finger-pointing will persuade Stan to divulge his source.

Mary Slevin, the *Standard's* editor, attempts to go to bat for Stan by pointing out that it is her paper's policy to guarantee anonymity to sources. But Blue Nose just reminds her that the Drumahoe Fundraisers have policies of their own – one of which Stan is very close to experiencing first-hand.

"The only way you can get out of this, Stan," says Blue Nose eventually, "is by getting your source to hand himself into us within forty-eight hours. Otherwise, you may start shopping for a wooden overcoat. Just for the record, I would like to point out that I myself would not dream of harming a member of the press. But unfortunately, there are those in my community over whom I have no control . . ."

And that, says Stan, is when you know you're in real bother.

But this particular storm cloud has no silver lining. And Blue Nose is barely out the door when Runaround Sue rings in demanding to speak to Stan.

"Runaround is even less subtle than Blue Nose," says Stan, "but I know her a bit better. Back in the bad old days, she often calls in with hush-hush statements about her outfit's misdemeanours and I would always treat her fairly.

"So after she blows off some steam, I put it to her that if I give her the name of my mole, she for one will never trust me again. Because she'll reckon that I would give her away just as quickly. So Runaround hos and hums for a minute, then says all right, she'll leave me in peace – just as long as my source hands himself into her within forty-eight hours. Otherwise, I'm for the short walk off a tall bridge. Though again, of course, she herself will have nothing to do with it."

"It goes without saying, however," continues Stammering Stan, "that my mole – who is, of course, Switchblade Vic that night we go out and get soused – has no intention of letting his minions know he can't hold his liquor. Vic is, moreover, extremely unimpressed with me for spilling the beans all over the paper. He refuses to take my calls, ignores all representations on my behalf and – twisted dog that he is – even presides at the two independent tribunals into my treachery. Things are looking blacker than a bookie's heart. That, however, is without reckoning on my good brother, Philip . . ."

There is little that goes on in Derry that escapes Chiselling Phil's keen eye. And so by the time Stan arrives up on Broadway to outline his predicament to his brother, Phil is already fully aware of the entire pickle. Unlike the Drumahoe and Caw units, Phil is cute enough to work out where Stan hears the story. For it is only three weeks since Stan is banging on his door at eleven o'clock one morning begging for a cure after his mother of all sessions with Switchblade Vic.

"Philip, bless him," explains Stan, "is a serious operator. And when Vic tries to duck his first call, Phil leaves a message on his machine telling him that he's got thirty minutes to ring back before he personally rings both Billy Blue Nose and Runaround Sue with the exclusive on the tout."

Vic duly agrees to meet Philip at a neutral lay-by on the Foyle Bridge to thrash out the problem and explains to him that there is no way he can hold his hands up as the rat. It is a matter of principle, a matter of pride in the regiment – and besides, Billy Blue Nose is unhinged enough to turn on him instead. There is also the matter of Stan's dubious ethics in writing down things he hears in public houses after the appointed hour.

But Chiselling Phil is ready for Switchblade Vic and tells him that there is no need for anyone to fall on their bayonet just yet.

"Supposing, for instance," suggests Phil, "you have on your desk some notes on the Spencer Road Post Office Inquiry, which are sitting close to a political speech you are due to give to the Limavady Civil Defence Association."

"Go on," says Vic, sensing a light.

Phil continues: "And supposing you ask one of your secretaries to fax the speech – which is on the left hand side of your desk as you sit at it – to the *Derry Standard*. But when she comes into the room, she lifts the little pile of paper to *her* left as she stands in front of the desk. And this pile, of course, contains all the notes on how Runaround Sue robs five big ones from Blue Nose's very own piggy bank."

"Aha!" grins Vic, "and my secretary, naturally, would never know the difference because they're not allowed to read my personal correspondence. And she leaves it back just where she finds it – so I never even realise it's away."

"Per-zackly!" laughs Phil. "And, of course, poor old Stan isn't to know he's publishing the wrong stuff. Indeed, he acts very honourably by protecting you, all things considered."

"Indeed and he does," laughs Vic.

So the two men shake hands, and Stan's life expectancy immediately soars back up from T-minus-zero.

*****

"So how come your face ends up with more lumps than last week's milk?" I ask Stan. "Does Runaround Sue still think you have a spy?"

"Not at all," says Stan with a wry smile. "Both units totally accept the explanation from Vic. I even get a phone call from Billy Blue Nose apologising for his ill-considered outburst.

"No. These lumps are down to sheer bloody-mindedness. Runaround Sue – who, incidentally, agrees to split her takings three to one with Blue Nose – is merely putting a marker down for the next time. Or to ensure there is no next time.

"In between swiping at me with her baseball bat, Sue does mention something about disrespectful wiseguys who poke fun at a woman's figure. Though the significance of this is lost on me. And I am far too careful to ask any more questions in her direction."

*****

Stan's injuries are quick to heal – even if he is left with a little two-tooth gap in his bottom set, exactly like Chiselling Phil's.

"Indeed," confides Letemout Lou the next week over a teatime gin and sausage, "Stanley is so happy not to be pushing up plastic wreaths that he never stops to fully find out why Runaround bops him with the bat."

"Well, he thinks she is just giving him a few warning shots," I reply.

"That is not exactly one hundred per cent accurate," grins Letemout. "Though the full SP is strictly not for repeating – and especially not to Stan."

"I'll take it with me to the grave," I promise.

"You just might," warns Letemout with no hint of irony.

"As you may be aware," she begins, "Runaround Sue is formerly a very pretty doll before she bloats away up on bottled ale. But she is still quite vain about her looks and very touchy about the way her jumpers are starting to sag in the belly. So when she hears that Stan is making smart remarks about her being a fatso, she has to get even."

"But Stan is far too careful for something like that," I counter.

"So you'd think," says Letemout. "But Stan is putting it about that the real reason Sue is called Runaround is not that the coppers can't catch her but that she's too fat to walk around."

"No way," I reply.

"Sure as apples," says Letemout. "Switchblade Vic apparently hears it himself and notifies Sue. And despite many pleas for clemency, there is nothing he can do to stop Sue dishing out the home runs."

I am altogether shocked at Stan being so loose tongued, particularly to a good friend of Sue's such as Vic. So I remark on this to Letemout.

"Well, no-one's claiming that Stan makes the crack directly to Vic," she explains. "In fact, it is Chiselling Phil who lets Stan's comments slip by mistake to Vic while they are in the throes of extracting Stan from his mess."

"But it is not at all like Phil to be so free with his mouth, either," I point out.

"My sentiments entirely," says Letemout. "So while Stan is over in casualty getting his bruises seen to, I call up to Phil's bar to find out what in hell is going on."

"So what does he say?" I ask her.

"Very little," replies Letemout, furrowing her brow.

"Initially, he figures he's going to tell me nothing at all. He just taps his nose like it's none of my business and walks off. So I call him back and advise him that I can personally spot four violations of his bar licence from where I am standing and will find another twenty, if so pushed, and shut him down.

"So he thinks for a minute and says, 'Alright – but for God's sake don't tell the brother. The bottom line is that Vic has to punish Stan in some way as an example to his troops – and to warn him for again. So he asks me to give him a way to make his point in return for not shooting Stan full of holes. A luck penny, if you will.'"

Letemout Lou pauses to drain her slimline gin and skewer up the last cocktail sausage from the basket.

"Phil then gives me this big wide smile," she continues. "But as he does, he points to this little two-tooth gap he has in his bottom deck, courtesy of yours truly, many moons ago. 'My dear departed father,' says Phil to me, 'is not a particularly rich man. Though in spite of that, he is often quite wise. And just after I lose these two teeth, he calls me into his little workshop to give me some counsel. Son, he says, there are three rules to ensuring a long and successful life. One, always learn from experience – that way you never get the same bat in the mouth twice. Two, never listen to anything your brother tells you, because, as you will work out before you are much older, he is a total featherhead. And three, if you ever feel inclined to make remarks about a lady's weight again, be sure and pass them off as someone else's.'

"Unfortunately for Stan, however," says Lou with a grin, "he misses that particular lecture."

OF DOGS AND MEN

"Never trust a guy who walks a dog," says Harry the Hurler to me one balmy, blue summer evening as we are dragged by his greyhounds out the old railway line along the Foyle.

"And why is that?" I inquire a little nervously, given that I am in the company of a man who spends his life walking dogs, now he has retired as Chief Executive of all the Boys in Derry.

"Because," he says, "such guys are dangerous. They have too much time to think.

"Of course, I would also advise you never to trust a guy who has no dog to walk either. Because it goes without saying that if a guy does not like animals, it is a fair-to-middling chance that he is not great on people either."

*****

Harry is a regular visitor to the old line – which runs from Derry's Craigavon Bridge right into Donegal – even long before he gets his dogs. The railway is gone now fifty years and the tracks, apart from a one-mile stretch kept open for the tourists, are much overgrown. But 'The Line' is nonetheless a very scenic walk, complete with views of the river, woodland, water birds and rich people's houses. Indeed, if there is a prettier walk in Derry, the odds are that you will be taking it with someone a lot more charming than Harry.

Before peace breaks out, the little road that runs alongside the old tracks is a favourite route for guys who do not like to go through the regular border checkpoints. The approved routes, as you know, tend to be staffed by armed soldiers, gendarmes and other guys with guns who have your picture on their sheet. But unapproved roads such as The Line, can, back then, be very useful for driving small vehicles carrying emergency supplies into the North. Indeed, you may remember, on one such occasion in the early nineties, Harry the H is captured by a posse of the occupying forces, who think they are about to seize a large consignment of such supplies. But the Hiace van he is driving is empty.

Harry is let off after maintaining his democratic right to silence for seven days in an eight-by-six cell. And the two hundred machine pistols, which the gendarmes are assured are in the van as it leaves Donegal, are never recovered.

Of course that is then and this is now, and there is no money in rehashing this sort of old history, especially with a guy like Harry the H, who, as we already know, is a guy who likes to walk a dog. So instead we talk about greyhound racing, which I figure is about as safe a subject as you can get with a man whose only other interest is one about which I want to know absolutely nothing.

"The problem with racing," says Harry, "is that the only person who really makes money out of it is the bookmaker. Personally, I believe that dogs are a lot smarter than people, because at least they have the sense not to throw money away betting on us.

"If you are involved in the betting industry on any level you have to have your eyes wide open, as everyone is always trying to get an edge. I myself am a very straightforward type of guy who generally despises any crookery, but even I would allow that it is a point of principle to stick one on the bookie."

Harry does not have to convince me. The only difference I see between bookies and loan sharks is that bookies get to wear better suits and charge higher interest rates.

"The only guy I ever know to clean out the bookies is this old fella from Cork by the name of Digger Collins," continues Harry.

"Digger is a tough little guy who, in his time, buries more people than the Boys and gendarmes put together. But that is okay, because he is a professional undertaker and grave-digger. Besides running his little funeral business, he also owns a few dogs on the side and makes a few pounds buying and selling them. Though he has the wit not to bet very much, at least not with his own money.

"Anyhow, Digger gets wind that this superfit Dublin bitch, name of Winks Like Twink, is about to whelp. So he hauls tail up from Cork to see if he can buy a pup. Winks Like Twink is of a very fine pedigree and a relation of Master McGrath who, you might remember, is the finest racer of all time.

"The Daddy of the new litter is the legendary Donegal Daniel who's owned by our old pal Sparkly Barkley. Indeed, Donegal Daniel is the fastest thing to come out of Dungloe since Mrs Barkley gets her first pair of hot pants."

I ha-ha nervously at this reference to Mrs Barkley, as Harry the Hurler's private friendship with Mrs B, aka Susie Short-Shorts, is another on the long list of things I wish to know nothing about.

"So what happens when Digger gets to Dublin?" I ask quickly, to move things on.

"Well, the haggling starts," says Harry, "and eventually Digger takes the pick of the litter. This costs him a cheque for ten thousand pounds and an equally large brown envelope stuffed with untraceable notes. The dog, as often happens, is named after the parents."

On his way back to Cork, Digger calls into Tipperary to see his cousins, who breed dogs but, to be frank, aren't any great shakes at it. The cousins are quite down at heel, so Digger – who is after laying down a small mortgage in Dublin – figures he'll do them a favour and buys a scrawny wretch of a greyhound pup off them for £100.

Back in Cork, Digger begins training the Dublin pup and, sure enough, he is a flier. Digger has never owned a quicker dog, and word begins to spread. Word, however, spreads a little too quickly for Digger's liking, and by the time Winks Like Daniel enters the Cork Novices Cup, the bookies are offering shorter odds on him winning than they are on the next cardinal being a practising Catholic.

There is so much money going on Winks Like Daniel that the bookies just laugh in Digger's face when he asks them will they take a bet of £100,000 at odds of five-to-one on. So it looks like he's not even going to be able to make back the price of the dog.

"There's a huge crowd at the stadium," says Harry, "to see Winks Like Daniel in the flesh. There's a buzz that he could be the next great thing, and everyone wants to be at his first big race. So when Digger leads him out into the enclosure, there's a big round of applause and some people are even stamping their feet. Of course, these people would not include the bookies, who are still attempting to lay off the thousands of ante-post betting they are stuck holding on Winks Like Daniel.

"The race gets underway, and Winks Like Daniel is away like a shot. But then, something very strange happens. He is about a third of the way around the track when another dog overtakes him – indeed, this other dog is so quick that he soon builds up a hundred-yard gap. And by the end of the race, to everyone's astonishment, he wins the Cup at a canter.

"The crowd cannot believe it. They are booing and slow-clapping Winks Like Daniel. But there is no doubt that there is nothing he or anyone else can do about the winner – who is by a mile the speediest thing ever seen at Turner's Cross Stadium.

"Indeed, the miracle dog's time is so quick that he is drug-tested twice. But of course, the officials find nothing."

Harry and myself are almost at the border now, and we take a minute to watch two falcons playfully dive-bombing the Foyle in the summer sun. The river is as still as glass in the evening sunlight, and the water is the lush green colour of the ancient Prehen woods which stand above it.

"So," I ask Harry eventually, "how exactly does Digger beat the bookies? I'm assuming he doesn't dope his dog to come second."

"You are dead right," says Harry. "Digger is far too clever to get caught at that sort of mischief. And besides, all the dogs are automatically tested now after big races like the Novices Cup. No, what Digger does is this. Five minutes before the big race, four of his Tipperary cousins go up to the bookies' windows and each places three grand on a rank outsider. They don't look for an each-way bet, so they get odds of ten-to-one – though that is cut down from twenty in honour of their large wallets. The rank outsider – who is named Sleight Of Hand – goes on to win the race. And the bookies are down one hundred and twenty grand.

"You see," continues Harry with a grin, "the dog that Digger leads into the ring – and the one that the whole world is attempting to get their mortgage on, Winks Like Daniel – is in fact nothing but the whelp from his cousins' Tipperary farm.

"And Digger gets a complete stranger to parade Sleight Of Hand – the genuine article from Dublin – into the enclosure and up to the starting blocks. In time, the bookies hear all about the decoy but there is nothing they can do about it. And Sleight Of Hand, as you will be aware, goes on to become Irish Champion."

Just then, we reach the marker denoting the border, and Harry's dogs about-face for home.

"Over here is where the Brits grip me in the Hiace van eight years ago," says Harry and points at the new tarmac on the ground. "Course, there's nothing in the van – as if I'm going to be hare-brained enough to try and smuggle in emergency supplies, now I'm such a major political figure and all."

"So the whole story about the two hundred automatic pistols is nonsense?" I laugh before I can stop my mouth.

"Well, not exactly," says Harry slowly, eyeballing me. "Though if you breathe a word of this, I will cut out your heart and feed it to those falcons on the Foyle. The guns part is true."

"I don't understand," I reply, "the van is empty."

"No," laughs Harry, "the van *I* am driving is empty. When we are moving stuff, particularly in recent years, we always assume there is a tout, so we keep the final game-plan very tight.

"On this occasion, too many people know that we're bringing across some boxes and too many people know I'll be supervising the process myself, as I'm worried about all the loose talk that's going on. So when the Guards see me getting into a Hiace van in Donegal Town, they reckon they have me. And they wire off the gendarmes here that I'll be home in Derry in about an hour.

"Fifty-eight minutes later, they arrest me just here on this road, just over from the dragon's teeth, where there's a little track connecting South and North, just wide enough for the van. But I, as you know now, am in the decoy van, which is empty.

"But, if you listen carefully, you can hear the traffic on the main Letterkenny Road up the hill above us. And half an hour before I am so rudely intercepted, the real van, chock full of our emergency boxes, is waved through the border checkpoint up above by a solitary copper who's raging that he can't be down at the river for when they bust Harry the Hurler."

"So who's the real driver?" I ask, again too quickly for my own liking.

"I suppose I can tell you now he's dead," says Harry, "but the usual rules apply. Digger Collins, God be good to him, is more than happy to drive the real van over. And sure he has to return the favour for me leading his dog round for him at Turner's Cross."

THE TRIAL OF TONY TWO TUTS

Dominic the Hurler's wake, despite being a relatively unscheduled affair, is a not-at-all solemn occasion – full of old guns regaling new hands with yarns of Dom's glory days at the helm.

Big Dom, as you know, runs the Boys in Derry in the fifties and is regarded as quite a heroic figure in certain quarters. Though not, I hasten to add, any quarters inhabited by peaceful-minded citizens such as yourself or myself. Likewise, Dom's patriotism never cuts much mustard with his own good wife, Old Ma Hurley. She disapproves roundly of his activities and chides him regularly about the need to get a real job.

"One day," Dom's youngest son, Gerry the Hurler, says as we slip out of the wakehouse for a breather from the Rosaries, "things come to a head. Ma is expecting son number one, Harold – later to become Harry the H – and is a martyr to the cravings. First it's ice-cream, then it's shellfish, then it starts getting worse.

"So this particular Saturday afternoon she tells Old Dom that she fancies some snails – and she wants them right this minute. You know how they are, yourself."

Well, personally speaking, I don't. But I hear on the mill that Gerry the Hurler's own wife is currently subject to the cravings herself and will bite through a muzzle for a spoonful of coal.

"Now, Dad is way too smart a guy to do battle with a lady's hormones – particularly Ma's," continues Gerry. "So right after she gives the word, he is up on his feet and straight down the town on the snail hunt. First of all, he tries all the pet shops but there's no joy there, though they can give him a few dead mice they have for feeding pythons. Next, he tries the butchers – and it's the same story. Indeed, the only reason they don't laugh him right out of the shop is because he's Dom the Hurler. So he's just about giving up and is planning to go home and dig up the garden on the off chance that Ma might settle for a few worms, when he meets one of his lieutenants, the late Bobby 'Dazzler' Deeney, and explains his situation.

"Dazzler, however, is about to set off on an errand which, as luck has it, Big Dom requests of him the previous day. Back then, you see, Dazzler is the leading light in the Boys' campaign to reopen the frontier. And he is in the throes of rounding up some crucial material to take to Strabane. This includes a dozen hand grenades and two kegs of explosives, which are to be discharged outside the front door of Strabane Police Barracks – thus reopening this particular section of the border.

"Anyhow, Dazzler agrees to help Dad find his snails – but in return, he insists that Dom must come on the outing to Strabane with him. The West Tyrone team, it appears, are without three of their players, who are hauled in earlier that very morning by the gendarmes. Strabane, even back then, is riddled with touts.

"Now, Dad always likes to keep his hands clean – given his profile. And he is not at all keen to run out on Ma's cravings. But he's not going to get his snails unless he signs on as sub, so after some badgering from Dazzler, he joins the squad. They shake hands on the deal and immediately Dazzler marches Dom into Ferguson's fish shop at the bottom of William Street where, sure enough, Dad is able to buy one hundred fresh snails for Ma. The fishmonger, apparently, has twelve children himself and makes quite a few clams out of this cravings' business. So there is nothing for it but Dom has to accompany Dazzler to Strabane.

"The border opening is to be conducted from the Southern side. So they get into Dazzler's old removal van and head out over the border and up the old Lifford road. They round up their team of six men at a pub outside Lifford shortly after teatime, then set off for the police barracks on the Northern side of the border bridge about two miles away. But, this being Strabane, every gendarme in Tyrone is lying in wait for them. And their van is ripped to shreds by a welcoming salute before they even get within two hundred yards of the station.

"The surviving Strabane men, true to form, dismount and throw their hands up straight away. But Dazzler shouts to Dom to try and run back along the bridge and into the safer confines of the Free State. Well, the two men hare back towards the frontier, bullets zipping past their ears, if you believe Dad. And when they come to the bridge, both of them dive headlong into the River Mourne, Dad still clutching onto his snails for dear life.

"The gendarmes fire a few rounds into the water after them. But by now, it's pretty dark and the cops aren't happy about hanging about so close to the frontier – particularly when they've already four men and a couple of bodies in the wagon. So Dad and Dazzler swim out onto the Free State bank of the river and eventually get back into Lifford, where they spend the next four hours looking to steal dry trousers from a clothesline.

"They then decide that their best bet for getting home is to commandeer a car. But the people of Lifford are all too aware of the rat-a-tat-tatting across the river and have no intentions of stopping for two raggedy-arsed hitchhikers this particular night. The two lads have no option but to walk the fifteen miles back to Derry, damp, exhausted and miserable. And Dad arrives in Creggan at about midnight – almost nine hours after he leaves for the snails.

"As he heads up the path to the house, Dom reckons he is in the worst pickle of his two-year-old marriage. Indeed, he would happily swap places with either of the two Strabane guys in the ice box. Ma, even on a good day, is as crabbed as two cats in a plastic bag. But ever the quick thinker, as Dad gets to the door, he lays out the hundred snails carefully in a long line back towards the gate. He then opens the front door with his key, tut tuts loudly and shouts back down at the snails: 'I've told you a thousand times, would you for Christ's sake hurry up!!'"

*****

Gerry the Hurler and I laugh heartily, though I'm sure you hear many variations of this story yourself about other people at their wakes.

Nonetheless, I ask Gerry if his Dad gets away with this excuse. "Well," pauses Gerry, "suffice it to say that it is a full eight years later before the second Hurley child, Little Donna, is born."

*****

Dominic the Hurler's demise is widely seen as a mercy in the end. As you'll remember, Dom is a man who can never let a good thirst go unslaked. And for the last year or so, the vodka and whites – or Volkswagens, as he likes to call them – are beginning to catch up on him.

His memory is the first thing to go – a sore loss indeed for a man who loves to bear grudges. His total recall is quite legendary and, as Harry the

H points out, in his entire working life, it only ever lets him down sixty-one times – coinciding identically with each of his sixty-one appearances in police custody. Dom, says Harry, can tell you the names, addresses and dates of birth of the four guys who steal his milk money seventy years ago. But now, in the last year, he can't remember if he has his teeth plugged in.

Eventually, Dom's speech starts to falter and slur, so much so that when he is finally forced to forswear the VWs, very few are able to tell the difference. And in the end, his mind goes entirely. So one cold night last week, wearing only his pyjamas and a pair of leather slippers, Dom jaywalks out of Clarendon Street Nursing Home into the middle of the street where he is mown down by a passing car.

It is quite a pain-free end, says Gerry – nowhere near as terrible as the one the doctor predicts is in the pipeline. And there are even some suggestions that Dom works this all out for himself in a moment of clarity.

*****

As ever with such accidents, there are many matters which need clearing up afterwards. Back in the not-too-distant past, a guy can wind up sailing down the Foyle in a sealed-up potato sack for so much as dinging a Hurley bumper. So dinging the Hurley patriarch to death, even in these civilised times, is bound to involve quite a bit of paperwork indeed.

And matters are further compounded when, the week after the funeral, it transpires that the driver of the car that hits Dom turns out to be an off-duty cop, a chap called Tony 'Two Tuts' Martin.

Indeed, from what Stammering Stan the Radio Man tells me, the new bilateral truce is seriously threatened for the first time.

"To settle the matter," explains Stan, "the Hurley brothers are forced to call a full-scale private investigation. And this will take place immediately after Dom's Month's Mind."

*****

Now, if you believe the papers, the Hurley family's private investigations never have more than one outcome. Over the years, more than twenty defendants are prosecuted for crimes such as talking out of school, selling recreational medicine without a permit, and stiffing guys without prior approval. But the one thing all the accused have in common is that each of them gets to exit the courtroom, toes up in a black sack.

The most notable trial, you'll remember, is that of the three plain-clothes cops who are caught making a movie outside the Starry Plough Bar and are never seen again. One of the trial's star witnesses later publicly admits his role at the behest of his conscience and a thirty-grand retainer from the gendarmes. Though by then, it is way too late.

Generally, however, the minutes of all such private investigations remain entirely confidential. And when word gets out that Tony Two Tuts is to go on trial, we can assume that nothing more will be heard about it until his dental records are checked against the next mouthful of teeth found in a Donegal bog.

But by blind chance, the very night after the Two Tuts Inquiry, I happen to run into Stammering Stan in The Jack Kennedy. And he is as drunk as a man with three sets of legs.

"It is quite an event altogether," he says, nodding me thanks for the brandy.

"Off the record, Harry the Hurler calls me up about a week ago and asks me if I would come along and take a full transcription of the proceedings in case there is a dispute about what's said later on. Strictly between you and me, I would sooner clear my throat out with broken glass. But then I hear Letemout Lou is being called in as judge – and when I put this together with the fact that I have really no option anyway, I agree to oblige."

The magistrate, 'Letemout' Lou Johnston, is a former legal advisor to the Hurley family – and, once or twice, even acts for the defence at such tribunals. Needless to say, she does this on a hush-hush basis in case someone might cite a conflict of interests with her day job. This will be her first opportunity to be the guy wearing the black hat in the middle – though like Stan, she has no real option anyway.

Now, says Stan, none of the Hurley boys want to be involved in putting the case against Tony Two Tuts in case it might be considered they are taking things too personally. So they call in a former Executive member from the seventies, the veteran hardliner Hate the World Herbie, to handle the prosecution. Hate the World, who now works in New York as a bookie and fundraiser, is back in Derry for a month on his annual Show The Yanks The Ghettos tour. And he is delighted to be entrusted with some real business. As a close pal of the late Dominic the Hurler, he resolves to give the chore the full nine yards. And Hate, as you know, is a man who could persecute for Ireland.

Tony Two Tuts, meantime, is to be defended by his shift sergeant, Jack 'the Black' Gilmore. Jack, as you'll recall, is husband to Donna

Hurley, Dom's eldest daughter – and, despite his obvious shortcoming, is now virtually part of the Hurley family and even allowed into some of their houses.

Given the circumstances, it would be no surprise if Tony Two Tuts refuses to show up at the Hurley household for the inquiry. Truth is, Tony, along with everyone else, knows that he's already deader than crispy bacon. But at least this way, he gets to see it coming.

*****

So a month to the night after Dom pops up his toes, as soon as the memorial Mass at St Mary's Chapel is over, the inquiry begins in the Hurley family home on Creggan Broadway.

Sitting in the big kitchen are the accused and his counsel, Hate the World as Director of Private Prosecutions, Lou in her judge's chair behind the breakfast bar, Stan in the reporting dock underneath the portrait of JFK, and all the immediate Hurley clan in the gallery on the sofa – except Old Ma, who refuses to take part in a three-ring circus. There are also, along the back wall in hard chairs, four long-standing members of the Boys' Executive, here to monitor that everything is fair and above board. Though there is no jury – just Letemout Lou's vote alone.

The accused, as is tradition, gets to wear a hood throughout the hearing so that he cannot identify who is who in the event of his acquittal. Though personally, says Stan, this is just to give him a straw to clutch at. The two sides toss up for who goes last, and the defence loses. So Black Jack has to kick-off.

Now, Jack, says Stan, is a very skilful ballplayer altogether. As you'll expect, he is well-used to the courts and comes prepared. The first thing he does is to produce all the cop diagrams of the accident scene. And the maps all prove that Dom steps out from behind a black Hiace van right into Tony Two Tuts's path. Next, Jack produces photos of the impact marks on the side of Two Tuts's car, which indicate that Dom is still in mid-stride when the car strikes him. Thus, he either keeps walking on purpose or he is so far through that he can't see a properly lit-up car on a properly lit-up street.

The reports further show that there are absolutely no skid marks before the scene of the collision, which means that Tony Two Tuts never sees what happens. Nor is there any suggestion of him going too hard, as Two Tuts knows that there is a hidden speed trap camera monitoring Clarendon Street.

Jack also points out that after the accident, his client volunteers for a breath test, which shows up clear. And a full check on his car proves that it is in excellent condition. Indeed, says Stan, I am thinking to myself that Letemout Lou could justifiably stop the trial right there. But with that, up jumps Hate the World onto his hind legs.

"Your Worship," he begins, "I think we should pay a little respect here to the interests of the late Dom the Hurler. In fact, I think if we go and check his new-dug grave we will probably find him gagging on his shroud at the thought that some cop could be cleared of stiffing him on the basis of what his best pals tell us.

"Just look at how the cops treat Dom before he passes on, God rest his soul. Not a week goes past when they don't try and drag him in on one thing or another, from spitting on the pavement to running Chastisement Squads. This is despite the fact that even the dogs on Creggan Street know that Dom retires way back in the late fifties – and that Gerry, Jimmy and, of course, the Honourable Harry the H are in charge this long time. No. Let us think hard on Dom's own motto: never trust a policeman until he's a year dead.

"So," continues Hate the World triumphantly, "given all of this, Your Honour, I move that all the testimony submitted by Jack the Black is thrown out."

"Some good points there, Hate," replies Her Honour Letemout Lou. And you can see her shifting uncomfortably in her seat, like she is choosing between a rock and a hard place. Lou is no dozer, and the impressed looks on the faces of the four vets at the back of the room are something she fully intends to take account of in her verdict. Hate is proving very persuasive indeed, so, judiciously, she kicks for touch.

"I'll reserve judgement on your application until the end of proceedings, Hate," she tells him.

It is now Hate the World's opportunity to put the case against Two Tuts, and it is apparent that his years in New York are mellowing him not one jot. In fact, like all returned yanks who only get to read about the war, he's of the mind that the Boys back home are becoming soft.

Hate starts off with the obligatory history lesson, which is mercifully cut short at the Battle of Clontarf in AD 1014, when Lou reminds him that he is not preaching to stupid Americans any more. So he then launches into this spiel about how the gendarmes are targeting Harry the Hurler for years, and when they can't get him, they eventually settle for his old man. He also cites many examples of so-called traffic fatalities, which the scumbags secretly arrange, and declares that Dominic is actually shoved out in front of Tony Two Tuts's car by appointment.

Hate then proposes that, like all enemy agents who come before this court, Two Tuts must be taken to a wooded place not far from here and shot through the head until he is dead. And may God have mercy upon his soul, Amen.

"Is there any such thing as a good cop?" interrupts Black Jack impatiently.

"Not in this world," snaps Hate. "It takes a particular type of lowlife to make the grade."

"So there are no grey areas? None are better or worse than others?" continues Jack.

"Well," says Hate hesitantly, "for some reason, Dom the Hurler finds you, Jack, a little less offensive than your colleagues – but that is probably only to keep his daughter, your wife Donna, happy."

"But other than me, there are no other acceptable cops at all, at all?" persists Jack.

"None at all," agrees Hate.

"What about the gendarme who snares Dom with his pockets full of home-made explosives and declines the opportunity to dispatch him to his maker once and for all?" asks Jack.

"I know nothing about that, Your Honour," says Hate, puzzled. "Can I have a minute with my corner?"

Letemout Lou assents.

"Okay," concedes Hate at last, "there is perhaps another instance of a good cop."

"Do tell," grins Black Jack.

"Well," says Hate the World, "it appears that Dom is very lucky not to be stiffed with his three best pals back in the late fifties. The four of them are in a house in Pennyburn, getting their gear ready for a border-opening at the Buncrana Road Customs house, when they are surprised by a team of gendarmes. The cops, who are specialists and not the local fatboys, kick down the door and smash their way through the house, shooting everything in sight. Dom's own brother, Jimmy Big Mouth Senior, is whacked, as are Getemup Gormley's old man, Teddy Badteeth, and Shakes Coyle's brother, Davey the Fuseman."

"But you say there is a good cop here as well?" says Black Jack.

"Well," replies Hate, "and I suppose this must be true – though it's news to me – Dom the Hurler manages to make it into the glory hole under the stairs just as the cops are smashing down the living-room door. So after the shooting, this one sergeant checks out the glory hole where he sees Dom curled up in the corner, saying his prayers.

"But the sergeant just looks at him, tut-tuts quietly, and calls back to the shooting party: 'Nope, it's all clear, there must only be three of them.' And the team then scram back to HQ, leaving the clean-up to the county mounties at the station."

"Now, Hate," says Black Jack, "you say there that this good cop tut-tuts when he sees Dom the Hurler. Now, does he tut once or twice?"

"How the hell would I know?" demands Hate. But after Lou catches his eye, he mutters: "Hold on and I'll find out."

So he checks with Harry and announces that the sergeant only tuts once.

"That," replies Black Jack solemnly "is a family trademark of the Two Tut clan – and particularly policemen of that ilk. If they tut once, they see nothing and are letting you go. But if they tut twice then they are forced to book you. This is a feature which I note many times when working with Tony Two Tuts Martin who stands before you here tonight. And a fairer man, more willing to give anyone a second chance, you will never meet. And I put it to you, Hate, that the sergeant who spares Dom the Hurler back in the fifties is actually Two Tuts's late uncle."

Well, the courtroom as a man gasps in shock. But before you can say order, Hate the World is back up on his hind feet objecting to this Hearsay, Nonsense and Downright Speculation.

"Do you have any idea of this old sergeant's number?" counters Black Jack quickly.

Hate the World again confers with Harry the Hurler, then announces: "LD one six nine. Old Dominic, not surprisingly, never forgets it."

Then, with deliberate slowness, Two Tuts Martin, who never speaks a word throughout the entire trial up till now, puts his hand in his jacket pocket and produces an old-fashioned shoulder badge, dotted with rust patches. The number on it, sure enough, is LD169.

"It is my good luck charm," says Two Tuts quietly through his hood. "I always aspire to follow my uncle's good example, and you can be certain I would never run down a civilian deliberately – and certainly not one whom my uncle rates so highly."

Hate knows he is beaten. And after brief discussions with his corner, he states he is withdrawing his prosecution.

"This court," announces a relieved-looking Lou, "finds the defendant, Tony Two Tuts Martin, not guilty on the grounds that the DPP – that's you, Hate – is throwing in the towel."

The move meets with general approval from the ranks and there is even some clapping from the veterans, who appreciate the way an old favour can be returned. Hate the World even has the grace to slap Black Jack on the back.

*****

It is perhaps another month after these events before I bump into Harry the Hurler again. He is hosting a Smash The Gendarmes picket on Waterloo Square and looking desperately around for a familiar face to drag him into a warm Waterloo Street snug.

"I am beginning to think I am there for the full hour," smiles Harry to me as he makes the Two Pints sign to the barman in the Four Green Fields. "Though it is important we have these protests to keep the pressure on the scumbags."

The stout is marvellous, if a little high, so we sup the head off it as we make our way up to the back snug.

"What is with this picket anyhow?" I ask Harry when we sit down. "There is me thinking that you are now ready to do business with the forces of law and order."

"Aha!" laughs Harry. "You're alluding to our own little private inquiry, which, of course, no-one knows anything about – except, perhaps, any dog in the street who feeds Stammering Stan brandy. Let me assure you that, despite that one-off result, our dispute with the gendarmes goes on.

"Off the record – and do not repeat this or I will flay you alive – my brothers and I accept all along that Dom's death is an accident. But we have to keep the old vets happy. And most of them believe that in keeping with Dom's memory, Tony Two Tuts must now be dispatched to meet his maker.

"This, however, would raise quite serious questions about the bilateral ceasefire. And speaking with my political hat on, it is much too delicate a time for such messing. Hate the World, naturally, is demanding his blood and guts. But he'll shortly be heading back to the safety of America, and it'll be left to all of us soft articles back home to clean the cake off the fan. So in the end, we have to fix the trial."

"So what about the story of the one tut and the double tut?" I ask Harry.

"Well, unofficially," he grins, "that is a big fat lie which myself and Black Jack Gilmore concoct between us."

I laugh and ask Harry if Letemout Lou is in on the scheme as well.

"God, no," grins Harry, "with so many big mouths in the one kitchen, Jack and I reckon it's best to keep the plan to ourselves. Truth is, we'd like to cut Lou in on it – but it is useful for her to remember how life operates at the sharp end of things.

"Tony Two Tuts, likewise, knows damn all. For the plan to work, he has to be fully certain he's for the off. But, just before the inquiry begins, Jack hands him his old shoulder badge from the nineteen sixties, which he says might come in useful as a good luck charm. And lucky he realises how to use it."

"So," I ask, "all that story about Dom in the glory hole is a big fat lie as well?"

"No, not exactly," says Harry. "Part of that story is true. Dom is in the glory hole all right. But so also is Jimmy Big Mouth Senior.

"They're found and surrender immediately – as does Teddy Badteeth. And they are all cuffed. Indeed, there is no shooting at all until Davey the Fuseman tries to bolt for it and is shot in the arm. Though it's nothing life-threatening and he's able to walk back into the room.

"But the gendarmes then line all four of the Boys up against the wall, and without any comment, the sergeant pulls out his revolver and shoots Jimmy, Teddy and Davey in the head. Dead as green meat. My father, Dom, who is fourth in line, is shaking and crying as he makes his Act of Contrition. But the sergeant, who, incidentally, is no connection whatsoever to Two Tuts, then re-holsters his gun and tells Dad to go home – and let that be a lesson to him.

"It is a move as old as war itself: always leave one alive to tell the tale."

"I'd say that is a lesson that Dom could do without learning," I suggest.

"You could say that," replies Harry. "Indeed, he never gets over it at all. His nerves are shot to pieces. He gives up campaigning immediately, and to his dying day will jump three feet at the sound of a balloon popping.

"But up until very recently, Dad is always a great man for giving advice. And as you know, I myself am a great man for listening. And for the last month or so, everywhere I go, I can hear Dom's voice in my head saying: remember, leave one alive to tell the tale.

"So you can gather that it is a real pleasure for me to pass on the benefit of my education to Tony Martin and all his colleagues in the cops, exactly one month after my father is laid to rest."

A Little House Off Broadway

Now, I don't know if you ever go to the Boys' Easter Commemorations in the City Cemetery, but from what I gather, they can be rather lengthy events. Indeed, back when Harry the Hurler is in charge of things, the ceremonies – and most notably his speeches – are so drawn out that it is often whispered in the snug afterwards that at least the fallen dead are warm in their beds.

So one year Harry's brother, Gerry the Hurler, decides to wrap things up a little earlier than normal by editing out the last half of Harry's contribution. Though needless to say, he doesn't tell Harry he's going to do this. Instead, what he does is convince Harry's bodyguard, Mike the Knife, to aid him in a bit of subterfuge.

As you'll know from the photos in the *Derry Standard*, Mike the Knife always stands right behind Harry on the platform during the ceremonies, standard-bearing a six-foot tricolour on a big iron pole. And the plan is that, given the signal from Gerry, Mike will pretend to slip, and, on his descent, strike Harry solidly on the noggin with the pole, so bringing Harry's oration to a quick and painless conclusion.

This particular year, Easter Sunday is earlier than normal and colder than a woman's heart. So cold that the cemetery is covered in a thin white shroud of frost and ice. So when Harry the Hurler is barely sixteen and a half typed sheets into his spiel, Gerry looks up at Mike the Knife and taps his watch twice – thus instructing him to do his bit for Ireland.

Mike, who is a guy you would never be afraid to send out to do a man's job, lifts the flag over his head to get a better swipe at Harry. But while he does, he loses his footing on the ice. And instead of falling forward and bopping Harry, he slips sideways and smacks Harry's youngest brother, Jimmy Fidget, who folds over like a broken stick, well and truly kiboshed.

But when Harry the Hurler leans down to check that Jimmy's okay, Jimmy, who is in on the plan, looks back at Mike the Knife and gasps: "Hit me again – I can still hear him."

*****

I am sitting in The Jack Kennedy this Easter Sunday night when in comes Stammering Stan the Radio Man at the end of his shift, looking very weather-draggled indeed. He is after covering the Easter Ceremonies and is clearly in great need of some defroster to get the pipes open again. So he stands beside me stamping his feet and baffing his gloves together until I duly oblige with some of The Jack Kennedy's in-house brandy – which is faster-acting than antifreeze and tastes only very slightly like it.

As I watch the blood return to Stan's cheeks, I am reminded of the Mike the Knife story and relate it to him to cheer him up.

"Tragically, that is only wishful thinking," says Stan, shaking his head. "I cover the Easter proceedings every year – and believe me, we are never that lucky.

"But I have an even better story for you – and one which I swear on my oath as an underpaid journalist is true. Though I may require you to furnish me with another large dose of lubricious pipe-opener to get me to remember it all – as it is quite an elaborate yarn indeed . . ."

*****

"The Boys," begins Stammering Stan suitably recharged, "hate reporters with a passion. We are possibly the only profession still allowed to ask them the hard questions and challenge them when they tell us lies. Though if truth be known, even we don't like to push too hard.

"Anyhow, for some reason, the Boys seem to tolerate me. I'm not saying they trust me, mind, because by the time you reach that stage, you're a fully paid-up member of the gang and tend to have no serious opinions – or clout – of your own. But they like me enough for us to work with each other. Indeed, Harry the Hurler is always telling me that my most redeeming feature is that, unlike most of my colleagues, I am smart enough to realise I'm really not that bright.

"So sometimes the Boys will grant me privileges that they wouldn't dream of handing to Charlie Cheapshot, Calamity Jean, or the rest of our

160

little sewing circle. Generally, this entails them handing you a speech to vet. Or, if they're testing a new political line, they'll want to know if it comes across forcefully enough, or whatever.

"They'll also ask you to check out the big words they use – particularly if Gerry the Hurler's writing the press statements, as they're worried he might be a bit too educated for his own good. But that is a whole other story . . ."

"But don't you also get first bite at the Boys' big exclusives whenever they break?" I interrupt.

"Very occasionally," says Stammering Stan. "Though nine times out of ten they are hushing stuff up and promising you the full SP on the never-never. Which is precisely what Harry the Hurler does when he eventually gives me the full gen on last year's highly controversial Easter Commemorations . . ."

*****

As you're aware, says Stammering Stan, Jimmy Fidget is now the Acting Chief Executive of the Boys since his brother Harry the Hurler hauls off into full-time politics about eighteen months ago. Back then, the Boys are slowly but surely inching their way towards the much-vaunted truce – though a worrying number of the veterans and ex-prisoners are resisting. And despite the fact he's not long past thirty, Jimmy is very much of the older school. And as the new Chief Executive, he effectively holds a veto over any plans to call off the war.

Jimmy, you see, never gets over winding up with a twelve-year stretch in Her Majesty's Country Clubs for not washing his hands properly as a teenager. Particularly since if the cops land only five minutes later, all traces of gelignite will be completely scrubbed off his fingers.

Anyhow, last Easter Jimmy Fidget has the privilege of doing MC at the Easter events for the first time. And he intends to stamp his authority on the faithful with an old-style blood and thunder speech. Now, Jimmy is also aware of the dropping numbers attending the ceremonies, which he rightly puts down to the fact that Harry is boring all but those already dead to death. So he decides to organise a bit of a floor show for the troops. And he arranges for a select band of entertainers to liven things up by discharging their AK47 rifles into the air above the Boys' plot.

Such entertainment, you'll realise, would normally require a special licence from the gendarmes. But, no surprise, Jimmy forgets to apply. Luckily for the gendarmes, however, one of Jimmy's more civic-minded camp-followers privately rings them up to advise them of his boss's plans. And the gendarmes – who, incidentally, are slipping this civic-minded chap a C note a week – are very keen to rectify the oversight.

They are so keen, in fact, that when Jimmy and the late Howard the Coward go up to Creggan to hoke their AK47s out of storage on the Good Friday morning before the ceremonies, the cops are there to welcome them with open arms. Indeed, they open up with around twenty arms in all, winging Jimmy twice on the shoulder and rendering the late Howard the Coward deader than an old joke.

The guns are being rested under the kitchen floor in a house just off Broadway. And with the cops firing in the back door at him, it doesn't take Jimmy long to work out that his only route home, without the option of a lengthy sabbatical, is through the front. So he quickly wraps a dishcloth around his shoulder to stop any tracks and scrambles out the front door towards Greenwalk Roundabout about four hundred yards away where his car is waiting.

But just at the last minute he hears the V8 engine of a plain-clothes cop car purring out from a secluded slip road just up from his taxi. So he stops briefly to refigure his options.

Suddenly, he hears a loud bang about twenty yards behind him – a wooden backyard gate clacking in the April wind. Nothing to lose, he doubles back and barges headlong into the open yard. He dives for the corner and crouches himself up behind a coal bunker, still as death.

Within seconds, he hears the gendarmes battering down towards the Greenwalk Roundabout. But they all pass by the gate. Then someone shouts that they see a guy running towards Malin Gardens and the cops all immediately clamber off after this innocent civilian.

You put away your chances in this game. And Jimmy Fidget rightly feels that now is the exact moment to get in out of the cold. So he tries the back door of the house, which, happily for him, is open.

*****

Inside, the kitchen exudes a grandmotherly air. It has a well-polished breakfast bar with matching stools, a picture of the Sacred Heart over the nearly-real fire, and a framed colour photo of a cherubic-looking black-haired girl of about seven or eight on the mantelpiece.

Jimmy can't help getting the feeling that he visits this little house sometime before. No doubt they once stash something in here back in the old days.

All the letters in the rack are addressed to a Mrs Rebecca Deeney. And in one of the presses are heart tablets, so Jimmy deduces that he's probably dealing with an old widow woman living on her own.

Sure enough, when he pulls open a drawer, he finds an Irish passport with a photo of a familiar-faced white-haired dame, who, according to the date of birth, is sixty-two. And in the plastic fly-leaf at the back of the passport there is a memoriam card for a Bobby 'Dazzler' Deeney, a chap of about fifty-five, who departs this turf about a dozen years ago. I know that guy, says Jimmy to himself, but dammit for the life of me, I can't think from where.

Jimmy relaxes a little and decides to perform a quick scout through the empty-sounding house. There's nothing much to report other than the usual religious bric-a-brac and more photos of Dazzler and the young girl. One of the upstairs rooms is locked – probably the old dear's spare room.

Then, on his way back into the kitchen, he notices a Saint Martin calendar on the hall wall and sees that the little boxes under Good Friday to Easter Sunday are filled in with the words Forty Hours in red pen. Aha! says Jimmy aloud, this could not be better. There are still a few of the old school who spend from Good Friday to Sunday morning on their knees in chapel to mark the Easter Passion. And he reckons it's odds-on that Mrs Deeney is enjoying the praying marathon up at St Mary's.

Still, he is in no mood for taking any chances. And he figures that it's probably best to lie low in the roof space in case some public-spirited neighbour might see him through the window – or indeed that Mrs D should come back.

But first, Jimmy needs something to kill the pain in his shoulder. Though his hostess is possibly the only non-practising hypochondriac in the city and there isn't anything in the drawers with more of a kick than digitalis.

A search for a drinks cupboard proves equally fruitless. But eventually, tucked behind a battery of baking trays, he unearths a large bottle of cooking brandy, which he stashes in his jacket pocket.

It's a slow process getting up the pull-down ladder and into the attic with only one good arm. But Jimmy takes it one step at a time. And after five minutes stopping and starting, he finally hauls himself up through the hatch-hole and collapses in a heap on an old rug.

There's no light in the little roof space and no room to stand up. But Jimmy is so exhausted now that he's content to lie where he is, sipping on the cooking brandy.

*****

An hour of brandy-sipping later and Jimmy Fidget feels no pain. Indeed, he passes out. When he wakes up some time later, he is aware that someone else is in the room, watching him. Though, unusually, he doesn't feel at all threatened.

"Who are you?" he calls out loud.

"I'm a friend," replies a girl's voice.

Jimmy is still groggy and a bit disorientated, and can't see too good because of the light.

"Come a bit closer," he says to the shadow.

The shadow, who is sitting in the corner, shuffles over on her knees to where Jimmy is lying beside the trap door. From the light coming up through the side of the hatch, he is able to make out that the shadow is, in fact, a beautiful young doll in her early twenties.

She has bright, flecked-brown eyes, a fringe of electric black hair, and teeth as white and even as a row of marble gravestones. Her blue-striped pyjamas are mostly covered by a red fleece dressing gown and she's wearing fluffy Mickey Mouse slippers on her feet. Despite the attire, Jimmy is transfixed. She is, without question, the most stunning vision he ever sees.

"What's your name?" he asks her.

"Angela," she smiles, "but my friends call me Angel Face."

"I recognise you," grins Jimmy. "You're the little fat-faced cutie in the picture downstairs?"

"I don't know how many times I tell Ma Becky to burn that picture," tuts Angel Face. "But yes, I give up, that is indeed me."

"No, no," protests Jimmy a bit shyly, "you are pretty as a picture . . . even then."

"That is what my old dad, Bobby Dazzler, always says, God rest him," says Angel Face quietly. "Just before he dies, he tells Ma Becky that it is his biggest regret that he will never see me as a young woman."

"Do you know who I am?" Jimmy asks her.

"Well," she grins, "you bear an alarming resemblance to this guy I sometimes read about in the papers – a certain James Hurley, alias Little Jimmy Fidget. Not that I am going to tell anyone, mind."

"Thank you," says Jimmy. "I'm in a bit of a pickle at the moment. But I'm sure you twig this for yourself from the two holes in my shoulder and the regiment of gendarmes out on Broadway."

Angel Face, who as a child has ideas of becoming a nurse, reaches over to Jimmy and puts her hand on his head to check for fever.

Her hand is ice cold, but he quite likes her gentle touch on his skin and he can smell the light musk of talc from her bath. He closes his eyes and breathes in and out deeply.

"Go to sleep and rest yourself, Jimmy," hushes Angel softly, brushing back his hair. "I will sit here and watch over you."

"Will you sing me a lullaby?" murmurs Jimmy.

So Angel Face smiles softly, and whispers to Jimmy how she gives her love a cherry that has no stone, all the while stroking his head. And within two ticks, he is out like a baby. And no crying.

*****

When he opens his eyes again, Angel Face is smoothing his cheek and telling him: There, there, don't panic, it's only a dream.

"Why are you thrashing about?" she asks him, when he realises where he is.

"A nightmare," he answers, "the same one as always. Every night of my life. Every single night of my life."

"Stop worrying," she replies, "the street is empty. The gendarmes are away since nightfall. They don't like to hang about here after dark."

"Then I better get going," says Jimmy Fidget, "let the guys know I'm all right. We have a big day on Sunday."

"You can't move yet, you're still too ill," says Angel Face, and she gives him these soft pleading eyes. "Besides, I like having you for company while Ma Becky is out. Stay a little longer or I'll poke my fingers in the holes in your arm."

Jimmy Fidget laughs. Truth is, he's still quite woozy and very sore. So he takes a belt from his bottle of painkiller and grins okay, he'll have another little rest.

"Maybe perhaps you have a date with some lucky lady – and that's why you're so anxious to get away?" asks Angel Face, brown eyes teasing him.

"No such luck," blinks Jimmy quickly. "What about you? Are you seeing your boyfriend tonight?"

"What boyfriend?" she counters, still smiling.

"Maybe when I get over this," says Jimmy quietly, "you might let me take you out to Tierney's new restaurant to thank you . . ."

"Believe me, you owe me more than a Tikka Surprise," replies Angel Face, pulling her red fleece dressing gown tightly about her, "but it's a lovely thought."

And again, she puts her ice-cold hand on his hot forehead. This time

Jimmy takes her wrist gently and thanks her for being so wonderful. And as he gazes into her eyes, he feels he's with a friend he knows all his life.

For the second time, the cooking brandy begins working its magic, and nothing will do but Angel Face has to sing Jimmy another lullaby. So he lies, staring up softly into her beautiful flecked-brown eyes, listening to her pure, sweet voice. And within two ticks, he is out like a baby. And no crying.

*****

When he wakes, Angel Face is sitting by his side, stroking the knot in the back of his neck and murmuring: Hush, hush, it's only a dream.

"It'll soon be daylight," she tells him, "Easter morning."

"I'll have to go," says Jimmy, "I have to speak at the events."

"Oh yes," replies Angel Face, "the Easter Ceremonies. I remember going with my father when I'm very little. He is quite a big wheel in the Boys back then – just like you are now."

"Of course," nods Jimmy. "Now I know his face. Though am I right in saying he isn't buried in our plot?"

"You're dead right," declares Angel Face. "He retires from all that a couple of years before he dies. Personal reasons – nothing political."

"What happens him?" inquires Jimmy quietly.

"It is a bit of a tragic tale," explains Angel Face. "Almost fifteen years ago, the Boys are carrying out a job on Greenwalk. They're trying to fire a mortar bomb into a police car, but it shoots way off course and crashes through the window of a nearby house. It kills a little child.

"Daddy himself isn't involved. But after that he loses heart."

Angel Face looks likes she's ready to cry. So Jimmy Fidget gently takes her wrist and tells how sorry he is for her sadness. Angel Face bends over him and hugs him tightly against her red fleece dressing gown.

"I love you, Angel Face," whispers Jimmy as he wipes a tear from her cheek. "I know this is quite sudden, but will you marry me?"

"I'd only try to reform you," sighs Angel Face with a sad smile.

"I might just like that," says Jimmy, returning the smile. "If only you would kiss me. It would be so special."

"You're a right charmer, Jimmy Hurley," murmurs Angel Face. And she pouts her head towards him, tightening her red fleece dressing gown chastely around her neck.

*****

The cool moistness on his mouth startles Jimmy awake. But when he looks up from the floor, he sees not Angel Face, but Old Ma Becky holding a damp facecloth to his lips.

"Where's Angel Face?" inquires Jimmy baffled.

"Ah, she is gone this long time," says Becky distractedly. "The doctor'll be here soon. He'll patch you up all right for your speech this afternoon. And don't worry. The medic is safe. I know the score from my husband."

The words are barely out of Ma's mouth when the doorbell rings and Doc Clancy shows himself in. Clancy and Jimmy are old associates, and there is no call for lame excuses. The Doc gives Jimmy a quick deadener to the upper arm, then uses a spatula to scoop two little lead balls out of his shoulder.

"You may feel some stiffness for a while," chuckles Doc Clancy unsympathetically. "Though that is nothing compared to the stiffness Howard the Coward is currently suffering."

Despite his pain, Jimmy laughs when it is put to him like this. And he starts to shuffle his way one-handed down the ladder onto the upstairs landing.

"Before I go," he says, "I must tell you, Mrs Deeney, that you have the most beautiful daughter in all of Creggan. Could you let Angel Face know I will call on her after the ceremonies this evening."

"Angela is indeed the most beautiful daughter on earth," agrees Ma Becky distractedly.

"So you'll tell her I'll call back later?" persists Jimmy.

Ma Becky just stares back at him, puzzled.

"But, Son," she says in a low hush, "that's not possible. I'm afraid you can't call on her tonight – or any other night. You see, Angela is gone almost fifteen years, God rest her. She is killed stone dead when the Boys try to blow up a cop car and a mortar shoots into our living room."

"But I am talking to Angel Face the whole time I am up in the roof space," protests Jimmy.

"Son," says Ma Becky quietly, "the only person you are talking to up there is yourself. When I find you about three hours ago, you are in terrible pain and hallucinating."

There is a long pause, then Ma Becky points to the locked door. "Ever since," she says, "I keep her room just as she leaves it. I only open it now to dust it."

The old dear motions him to come over, pulls out a bunch of keys from her blue apron and unlocks the bedroom door. Sure enough, it is a child's room with cartoon wallpaper, and teddies and rag dolls balanced carefully on the window sill, legs dangling.

On a little dresser beside the bed is the same school photo of the cherubic little girl with electric black hair. Jimmy shakes his head, puzzled. His gaze then falls onto the bed. And what he sees there leaves a hole the size of a mortar where his heart should be.

For sitting neatly on the bedspread are a pair of blue-striped pyjamas, a fluffy set of Mickey Mouse slippers to fit a child's feet and, on top of the pile, a little red fleece dressing gown.

Jimmy puts his head in his good hand and starts to weep.

"Strange you calling her Angel Face like that," says Ma Becky eventually. "That's her late father's pet name for her. Poor Bobby dies of a broken heart only two years after Angel goes. I think he blames himself. Still, I've many happy memories of the two of them."

*****

As Doc Clancy opens the front door to lead Jimmy out into the street, he catches sight of St Mary's Chapel just up the hill. And it is at that point Jimmy realises when he is in the house before.

So he turns to Old Ma Becky and says, "I am very sad for your loss. I'm so terribly, terribly sorry. If there is anything I can do, please tell me."

"It is a long time ago," replies Becky gently, "life goes on."

"Yes," replies Jimmy Fidget, "but I'm the guy who's to blame for your grief. And the worst thing is, I'm only after realising it."

"Sure I know, Son," says Becky kindly. "Do you think I don't remember you passing out on my kitchen floor in front of the coffin when Harry takes you up here to apologise for what happens? Am I not right in saying you're in the clinic for three months afterwards with shock?"

"I don't remember any of it," whispers Jimmy. "But you know, I dream about it every night of my life."

"My one regret," says Becky tenderly, "is that I'll never get to see Angel Face as a young woman."

"Please God, one day you will," replies Jimmy just as softly. "In the meantime, take it from me – there is nothing more beautiful on this earth."

*****

Stammering Stan looks at his watch and drains his brandy. He has to see Letemout Lou, and if he's late, she'll make him pay for his own dinner.

"Like myself," says Stan eventually, "you probably reckon that Jimmy's adventure off Broadway is quite an unlikely tale.

"But think back for a second on his Easter speech last year. You'll recall that it is very hands-across-the-water – particularly coming from a man of his reputation? Indeed, he virtually orders the Old Guard to back the new truce."

"Yes," I concede, "before that I always figure Jimmy for a Not One Bullet man. But then people say that this is just his big brother Harry the Hurler pulling him into line."

"And this is exactly what the Boys want them to believe," says Stan. "But I happen to know different."

"And how is that?" I ask him.

"Well," he grins, "at the tail-end of last year's ceremonies, I am just about to go back to the office and file my story, when Harry the Hurler sidles up behind me, grabs my arm and hustles me into his Merc. When they get me inside the car, he and Gerry rifle through my pockets and remove four neatly typed pages of A4 paper, which Harry stuffs into his jacket. Then Gerry takes out four new pages from his jacket and puts them into my coat."

"So what's that all about?" I inquire.

"Well," says Stan, "the Thursday before the ceremony, as is usual, Jimmy Fidget gives me his Easter speech to edit. And take it from me, it promises more war than the bible. And indeed, the only mention of the truce is to state, in no uncertain terms, that there won't be any – over Jimmy's own dead body.

"Now, like yourself, I have no absolute proof about what becomes of Jimmy since that Friday morning when he is shot off Broadway. But whatever takes place that weekend, by Sunday afternoon, both Jimmy and Harry feel it judicious to ensure that the only remaining copy of the original oration is called home . . ."

And with that, Stan looks at his watch again and announces he has just time for another quick one. If I'm on my way to the bar anyway.

GETEMUP RUNS
AWAY FROM HOME

It is a long time since I hear anything from Getemup Gormley, the retired bank robber. But this is always a good thing, as Getemup is a guy who only ever gets in touch when the world is collapsing around his ears. So this particular day when I am sitting in The Jack Kennedy and the phone goes and it is Getemup for me, well, you can gather I am going to be a little furrowed-of-brow.

Now, Getemup, you'll recall, is far too sideways a guy to come out and say what is troubling his sleep – for, in his mind, such behaviour is very presumptuous indeed. No, what Getemup does is make you guess, which goes something like this:

"I hear a good story the other day – will I tell it to you?" he asks.

"If you must," I reply, anxious to get back to my stout and cocktail sausages.

"Okay," he says. "This guy goes into the doctor to get some tests. And the Doc says to him, 'Well, Mr Gormley (or some other name, says Getemup), I have some good news and some bad news for you.'

"'Give me the bad news first, Doc,' says the guy, 'so I can take it like a man.'

"'Terribly sorry and all that,' replies the quack, 'but you've only three months to live.'

"'Lord, that's terrible,' says the patient. 'But hang on a minute, you've some good news as well . . .'

"'Yes indeed,' says the Doc. 'Do you see that tidy-looking blonde behind the front desk? The one wearing the pointy uniform? Well, I can have her out of it in seven seconds flat . . .'"

I ha-ha appropriately at Getemup's tale, not, of course, because it is particularly good – or even relatively funny – but because it's his way of telling me he's up to his neck in woman trouble.

*****

According to church records, Getemup Gormley is married to the former Miss Sally Gardiner from Foyle Road – though you and I would know her better as Moustache Sally. And to say that she is an argumentative woman is like saying the mayor likes to get his picture in the paper. For Moustache Sally could start a fight at the Blessing of the Graves.

But worse again, a few years back, Sal gets onto one of these late learners' courses at the university – and all of a sudden, she has certificates as well. So whatever chance you have of discussing things reasonably with her before, these are shot to pieces now that she is armed with a BA Hons in Women's Trauma Studies.

Getemup, however, is a patient guy – a habit he learns from spending five years on his own in a twelve-foot by eight-foot room with no visible means of escape. And he stoutly supports his wife in her new career as an authority on any topic you would care to bring up.

So when the electric is cut off in the middle of winter after Sal refuses to pay bills addressed to 'Mrs' Gormley, Getemup is quite happy to light up candles rather than curse the darkness. And when the headmaster refuses to change the Morning Prayers from 'Our Father' to 'Our Creator', Getemup agrees that Sally is quite right to withdraw the children from school. And when Sally reads that Valium is only the opium of the Oppressed Female Masses, Getemup says she is dead right to tell the doctor to stick his prescription up his oppressive male pill-box.

Getemup is a model husband, all things considered. He doesn't smoke, drinks a lot less than previous, and rarely looks at other women – indeed, as he often says himself, one woman is enough for any man, particularly when it's Sally.

But even the most loving of hearts and the strongest of loyalties can flag. And one day, a new (and very pretty) cheap cigarette supplier rolls into town and pulls up at Getemup's market stall. The pair get chatting, and 'Filter Tip' Philly, who has a lovely smile and lovely blonde hair, starts giving Getemup the big eyes and tells him what a hard life he is having.

Getemup, of course, agrees and from what he tells me, it is more than he can do to stop returning the lovely smile and making a few big eyes himself. Indeed, he is smitten. So much so that the very next day he decides to run away from Sally and move in with Filter Tip. So he sneaks home while Sally is out at her advice centre, packs his bags and leaves a little note telling her it's for the best.

But what he forgets from the note – and indeed what I am omitting to tell you up to this point – is that Filter Tip, the new (and very pretty) cigarette supplier . . . is a boy.

*****

"But that's not possible," says Harry the Hurler, former Chief Executive of all the Boys in Derry, when I break him the good news.

Harry is Getemup's brother-in-law, or rather the pair are married to two sisters, so Getemup feels that Harry should get to hear the SP before it hits the jungle drums. Getemup, who's still hiding out in the Waterside, figures that Harry might take it better from me.

"He's a boy," I repeat, "Well, at least Getemup says he's still officially a boy until he gets this operation next year . . . as soon as he's twenty-one."

"Does he look like a boy?" asks Harry. "Or is this all a big trap that Getemup falls into?"

"No, no," I reply, "Getemup knows all along that Filter Tip is a guy."

"But he has no inclinations whatsoever in this direction before now," pleads Harry the H. "Indeed, as I recall, he frequently makes smart remarks under his breath when pretty young totty walks past."

"A point I raise with him when I'm trying to talk him round," I retort. "But Getemup says that this is just a defence mechanism he adopts a long time ago to protect his true inner self."

"It'll take more than smart remarks to protect his true inner self by the time I'm through with him," says Harry, draining his pint and heading ominously for the door.

*****

Harry the Hurler, if you are to believe what you read in the papers, is responsible for more sudden death than ice on the roads.

Indeed, he is a guy that you and I would shun at the best of times, and whose name you would certainly not bring up in polite company. Unlucky for me, however, a couple of years ago, after I play a minor and involuntary role in mending his kid brother's nuptials, he adopts me as his good luck charm.

Now, despite his gut reaction to Getemup's conversion, Harry soon realises this is not an issue he can deal with using old familiar methods. Particularly since the Boys' official line is that it's now perfectly permissible to lead with whatever foot you wish – and indeed there should be more of it in the workplace. Though that end bit is only included to wind up the Planters.

So instead of tracking down Filter Tip's flat and performing the operation on him personally, Harry heads up to Moustache Sally's gaff on Circular Road to console his sister-in-law.

"Sal is putting a brave face on it all," Harry explains later in the snug. "She tells me it is very honest of Getemup to unleash his hidden child like this and reveal himself to the world for what he is. She says it takes strong character to overcome social conditioning and champion your true sexuality.

"Indeed, for a while there, I'm thinking she's quite proud that her husband is now a gay fellow. So I ask her if it's all right for me to give the okay for Getemup and Filter Tip to step out together in public.

"But all of a sudden, she starts crying and saying she can't live without him, and what is she doing wrong to make him run off like that, and how can he bring such shame on her. Before long, she is yowling so hard that I have to phone my own good lady, Red Light Lorna, to come over and settle her.

"If I say it once, I'll say it fifty times: whatever I know about the workings of a man's mind, I know nothing about women's."

*****

So judgement is reserved on Getemup and Filter Tip's official status – to give Moustache Sally some time to adjust to the shock.

Harry the Hurler has other concerns as well. His sister-in-law might be upset – but even still, she's not liable to pull an Uzi pistol out of cold storage and shoot her straying spouse dead, unlike others Harry could name. The Boys, you see, for all their talk, are quite embarrassed that one of their lieutenants is after leaving his wife for a twenty-year-old boy. Indeed, ordinary civilians are beginning to call after them in the street.

So after a confidential conference at the office on Chamberlain Street, the Executive agrees to give Harry the Hurler one last chance to put Getemup on the straight and narrow. Harry figures there's no alternative but to visit Filter Tip's *pied-à-terre* in Newbuildings. Though this, of course, takes place at night, as even in these peaceful times, the villagers still burn an effigy of Harry on top of their annual Eleventh-Night bonfire.

Filter Tip answers the door, wearing a little skirt you couldn't wash your face in. He smiles sweetly at his visitor, but rapidly works out that Harry isn't here for pretty smiles. So he disappears rapidly into the kitchen, to be replaced by his new lodger.

"I'm not going back," Getemup tells Harry. "The youngsters are half-reared, the dogs are dead, and I'm happy where I am. Besides, the woman is a dervish."

"What about the stalls?" asks Harry.

"Sal can have them in lieu of a settlement," says Getemup. "But for God's sake warn her about all the language at the market. Tell her she'll have to mind her tongue or people'll take offence."

"She really misses you," continues Harry, laughing, "and it would really upset her never to see you again."

"But sure she can see me about the town anytime," replies Getemup.

"Not if she's a widow, she can't," says Harry pointedly.

"Aha!" replies Getemup, catching on.

"Besides," presses Harry, "she'll do anything to get you back."

"Anything?" asks Getemup.

"Anything," repeats Harry.

"All righty," says Getemup. "Let's get serious. We'll start with the Valium . . ."

*****

"He has about forty demands, most of which Moustache Sally agrees to immediately and the rest after a bit of to-ing and fro-ing," says Harry, shucking the head off a fresh stout in the snug the next day.

"Not only does she have to go back on the calm-me-downs, but Getemup also feels she could use a couple of anger-management cours-es. The youngsters are to go straight back to school, and if Getemup Junior wants to play football, there's none of this crack that at least forty per cent of the team must be girls.

"She's also to write apology letters to Father Drownem for staging the Slaves in Chains demo at the Men's Retreat – and to Sparkly Barkley for pelting his strippers with old tea bags. She's even going to leave the advice centre, sell off her megaphone – and give up drinking pints of cider from the bottle.

"Indeed, if only I could strike half such a deal with my own wife I would be a happy man."

*****

It's about a month or so before I hear again from Getemup, though this time I am happy to see him, as he is buying me beer to compensate for my inconveniences.

"Are you back on terms yet with the Boys?" I ask quietly.

"Oh yes," says Getemup, "Harry lets them know that it's all just a bit of a brainstorm and that I'm right as rain again. It might be a while before they entrust me with more delicate matters. But to be honest, such matters are becoming fewer and further between. So I'm not too troubled."

"What about Sally?" I ask.

"Oh, she is never better," he grins. "In fact, I am happier now than when we are first married. She even allows me to watch Kung Fu movies when she is out at her relaxation classes. She's also letting her hair grow back and assembling quite a collection of pretty little dresses, if I say so myself."

"So is she still comfortable with this notion of you exploring the boundaries of your sexuality?" I ask, shifting a little in my chair.

"Exploring the boundaries of my sexuality?" laughs Getemup. "For Pete's sake, man, the whole thing is a cod to get Sally to loosen up a little. I'm not gay at all. Fact is, I'm not much of anything. The only time I ever get excited these days is if I get my first three numbers up.

"I've nothing against gay fellows myself, mind, it's just the way they are. One or two of our comrades will even admit, if you put them to the wall, that it's the only thing that gets them through a long stretch in the chokey. But I know that the backwoodsmen in the Boys will go buck crazy when they hear about this and demand that Harry step in."

"So what about Filter Tip?" I ask, stunned.

"The whole thing is his idea," laughs Getemup. "I'm bunging him a hundred quid for the room for the few weeks. And everybody's happy.

"Though for God's sake, don't be letting on to Harry, or it could put notions in his head. And sure as shooting, we'll wind up picking his teeth out of Red Light Lorna's kitchen wall. Inner child or no inner child."

KNOWING YOUR MARK

There is nothing that can get Stammering Stan the Radio Man off on a crusade quicker than a guy putting money on horses. So this particular day, when I am minding my own business in Charlie's Bar on Clarendon Street, leafing through the racing pages, I am, of course, fair game for sharp comment.

"Punters like you are mugs, pure and simple," snorts Stan as he busts in the door and sits down beside me without even a hullo. "And okay, so I am not the brightest bulb in the box. And yes, I am more at home with join-the-dots than with your fancy crossword. But even I know that the bookie is the guy who drives the Mercedes Benz, while you are the guys who get to wash it, wax it, buff it – and then hand the bookie back their pay cheque."

He is right, of course. Bookies, when you strip away their classy veneer – their smoky offices, dirty toilets and yellow-toothed collectors – are cynics of the lowest class. Their victims believe that God, Fate or The Man is going to step in and hand them a big payday. So the bookie plays on these superstitions by offering them odds on a future that is never going to come.

"Bottom line," says Stan, "is that bookies know their mark. And the guy with the real sense is the horse. Because at least you will never catch him putting money on people."

Stan is clearly about to go off on one, so I attempt to distract him by turning to the Astrology page and asking him what star sign he is. But again, he just snorts.

"It's back to the same scam – trying to tell the future," he says. "My old Dad, as you know, is an extremely smart fish – aside from the drink and good-looking women. He always says that the day the Lord wants to tell us the future, it will be way too late for us to argue about it.

"Pop also tells this story about an old French king who wakes up one morning and realises he is paying a soothsayer two grand a month and the returns aren't that great. So he decides to give the guillotine a work-out. But before he lops the guy's head off, he thinks he'll have a bit of fun with him first. So he calls the prophet into the court and asks him in front of the whole palace, who, of course, are wired off: 'When, my soothsayer, is the exact date of your death?' And the soothsayer, cool as a breeze, replies, 'Three days before that of Your Majesty . . .'

"Needless to say, the axeman gets the rest of the day off."

*****

Stan, aside from his occasional lunatic monologues, which I am assured are common among his profession, is good company and has the inside track on many issues about which I know nothing. So we sit drinking Charlie's fine stout and chatting for about an hour. And despite Charlie's attempts to fatten us up on free cocktail sausages, we eventually repair to O'Brien's fine grill across the Strand for a couple of well-done 10oz steaks and some Miller Ice by the neck.

It is payday at the *Derry Standard*, which Stan now edits since he leaves the Northern Broadcasting Corporation. And as he owes me more drink than would float Sparkly Barkley's yacht from the days when he has no arse in his pants, I allow him to catch the bill.

Letemout Lou, Stan's other half and the undisputed brains of the Stammering family, is now a High Court judge and stays over in Belfast three nights a week, so allowing us mice to play. Though only a little, as this is Derry and Lou hears every blade of grass that breaks.

After some of Mrs O'Brien's home-made banoffee pie and Baileys ice cream, we're forced to go for a walk along the river to free up a little more space for a couple of nightcaps which we might grab later at the City Hotel. And as we pass the new bookies on the riverfront, we get talking about its owner, the mostly legitimate businessman, Dessie 'Sparkly' Barkley.

Sparkly, as you may remember, purchases Barry the Bookie's turf-accountant licence the time that a bad debtor winds up toes-up in Barry's back lane and Barry and family vote to head for New York. The bookies is just the latest in a long line of businesses collected by Sparkly, who also owns a clatter of pubs, a supermarket, a score of market stalls and a share of two of the biggest shopping malls in the Six Counties. Not forgetting, of course, his little undertaker's shop – where it all starts – with its neat local motto: "You stab 'em, we'll slab 'em."

Despite his hard-headed reputation, Stan tells me, Sparkly is the most superstitious man in the city. He phones the Tarot lines on a daily basis, and checks four different Astrology columns before his wife serves him coffee in the morning. Though in fairness to Sparkly, if it is me, I would also be sending the Nescafe to a forensic lab – especially if it is Mrs Barkley who is filling the kettle.

And ever since his near-death experience in a car crash a couple of years back, Sparkly also goes to Mass every week as an additional insurance policy. Besides wanting to be seen as a good Catholic.

"Sparkly is scared to death that his good luck is going to run out," explains Stan as we lean on the railings at the city council pontoon, watching a bunch of well-fed Dubliners drink Chablis on their boat. "He knows he is due a good kicking from life – after all, he's handed out so many himself. So he always tries to stay one step ahead.

"One day, however, he is well and truly caught. This particular lunchtime, a bunch of gypsies – who the Press Complaints people tell me I must now call Travellers – arrive in De Valera's Bar and demand a drink. The barman, as you'll expect, shakes his head no. He recognises a few of the faces and has no desire to witness a riot in his own living room. The gypsies, however, refuse to move, so the barman rings Sparkly, who appears a few minutes later in that big Freelander jeep of his.

"'Five hundred quid and we'll never come back,' says one of the gypsies to Sparkly. "'Your arse,' laughs Sparkly, 'I'm going to get the gendarmes and have them jail the lot of you.'

"'Do that and I'll put our family's curse on you,' says one scary-looking guy who seems to be in charge. 'I promise you now that you or someone you love will be dead within a month . . .'"

Well, says Stan, Sparkly goes white as a winter morning at this. As you might gather, his 'You or someone you love' list has only one valid member.

So before you blink, he empties the De Valera's till and hands the head gypsy its entire contents – just short of two hundred quid. He then takes another three big notes from his wallet and passes them over. The barman can't believe it, but Sparkly just gives him the don't-argue look, gets back in his jeep and drives away.

Well, before long, laughs Stan, the head gypsy, whose name is Johnny

'Shovel Hands' Shovlin, is dining out – well, on roadsides at least – on the story of how he outguns the biggest gangster in the big city.

And Sparkly, when he hears this, is not one bit amused.

*****

"Sparkly's not the type of guy who's going to take this in the teeth," I suggest to Stan as we amble down past the new luxury apartment blocks that overhang the Foyle. Dozens of people are dotted about the verandas, drinking American beer from the bottle and gazing out at St Columb's Park across the water. It is perhaps the greatest view the city has to offer, with the possible exception of the sweep from the top of Creggan Southway – and, of course, Orange Jill Gillespie in the Delacroix Bar on Salsa night.

"You're right, of course," says Stan, "Sparkly is snapping to get revenge – hot or cold, he doesn't care. He even manages to overcome his superstitious fear of gypsies and sends a team out to find Shovel Hands and get his money back or the equivalent out of his hide. But there's absolutely no sign of him. He's gone quicker than a giro on dole day.

"But then one day, almost a year later, one of Shovel Hands's sidekicks comes into Sparkly's bookies and asks can he wager a grand on a two-to-one shot that's running in Thurles. Now, this particular character does not know two things: one, that the shop is now owned by Sparkly – because his name isn't yet over the door – and two, that Sparkly is watching him over the in-house CCTV system with his mouth full of drool.

"Sparkly buzzes out to the guy on the counter to take the bet. And as soon as the money's paid over, he rings the Turf Accountants' Professional Society to alert them to what is obviously a gypsy betting scam. He also, of course, wants to clear it with them that he can keep the stake money for himself, as the same guys are after stealing five hundred quid from him before and also owe him compensation for hurt pride.

"The gypsies' horse winds up disqualified from the race. And when Shovel Hands personally comes into the bookies to demand his stake back, who is standing there but Sparkly Barkley, grinning all over his face and fanning himself with Shovel Hands's fifty twenty-pound notes.

"Sparkly then gets four leading lights from his Collections' Department to escort Mr Shovlin to the door and advise him that if he returns to this shop, he or someone he loves will be dead before the month is out. And then, for good measure, they break both of Mr Shovlin's little fingers to ensure he understands them."

*****

Stan and I continue heading north along the Foyle, passing late-evening joggers, cyclists, the occasional sunburnt drunk and a few smiling couples joined at the hip. Just twenty years ago, the riverside was a filthy mess of dark and dangerous warehouses, street-walkers, army patrols and other skinhead glue-sniffers. Tonight, it could be Boston Harbour, only prettier.

We stop at the old Fort George army base to admire a few sailboats gliding by. The base contains about twelve acres of prime land right on the river, which is slowly being returned to the city by the old, departing enemy. But the Brits, setting new standards in cheek, are still looking for half-a-million for knocking down their barracks and clearing up the site.

Instead of heading back the long mile to the City Hotel, we opt for the nearer confines of Da Vinci's Hotel for our last shout. And we are able to sit outside on picnic benches in the warm air, away from the smokers, and admire some of the shortest summer dresses this side of Sparkly's new lap-dancing emporium.

"The gypsies, as you'll expect, leave Sparkly well alone after that," continues Stan as we shuck the heads off Coldflow Guinness and sigh at the tables full of long brown legs. "Then one day, Shovel Hands's father, Old Johnny, keels over dead after a heroic battle with the drink. And no funeral director in Derry will handle the arrangements, as they know Shovel Hands is a complete rapscallion and a crooked weasel, besides. And it looks for a long time like Old Johnny is going under in a big plastic bin-liner.

"So, cap in hand, Young Johnny calls into Sparkly's little mortuary and asks if he can see the boss. The scared little chap in the shop knows he's no option and rings Sparkly in his car who, surprisingly, says he'll be there in five minutes.

Sparkly is very scrupulous about the death business, says Stan, as are most men who worry they could be next. And his superstition means he can never turn anyone away. That's not to say he doesn't want to make a profit, however.

The full cost of packaging off your loved one – from death notices to removals to Masses – runs to about two grand. But as Old Johnny is such a huge size of a man, he's going to need a deluxe coffin and a couple extra of Sparkly's men to lug his body through the different rites. So this will probably set Shovel Hands back another £500.

"I don't have that sort of dough," Shovel Hands tells Sparkly, with big sad eyes. "And besides, it's our tradition to sort our own ceremonies. So you're no help at all to us, really."

Sparkly, however, doesn't want to let the entire deal go, even if it is with a gypsy, and suggests that Shovel Hands just buys a coffin.

But that won't do either. "You haven't one that would fit him here, and you'll only screw us royally for building one," says Young Johnny.

"Well," says Sparkly, "we've a pretty big one out in the back store, if you want a look."

So the pair go out for a view – and it is indeed ginormous – but Shovel Hands still says it's way too small.

"Tell you what," says Sparkly, "take the coffin with you in the van – and try it out."

Shovel Hands appreciates the gesture and nods his thanks to Sparkly. He tells him, "I know we don't always see eye to eye in the past, but I give you my word I will either return it or pay for it."

Sparkly is, of course, certain the gypsy isn't going to try and steal the coffin after the lesson he got the last time, so he helps him put it in the van and wishes him luck. True enough, about two hours later, Shovel Hands and two of his brothers drive back into the yard, call out the sales manager and tell him that the coffin doesn't fit.

"Just throw it into the back store," says the manager, highly impressed at his boss's knowledge of character.

*****

We drain our pints and make ready for the road home. Though there is still just time for Stan to watch a spectacular pink vest and a pair of yellow shorts weave their way in towards the Ladies' and give another big sigh.

"So what happens with the gypsies after that?" I interrupt.

"No-one knows for sure," says Stan. "They are never seen in these parts again, from that day to this."

"So what about Old Johnny then?" I ask. "I take it someone else sees to his burial."

"No, actually," replies Stan. "Sparkly looks after all of that."

"But how can he do that," I argue, "if he's not getting paid?"

"Well," grins Stan, "in the end up, he has very little option. You see, three days after the gypsies return the big coffin to Sparkly, the sales manager goes into the back store and notices this really bad smell . . ."

182

Gone Feising

In parts of the Australian outback, so police sergeant Jack the Black tells me, the natives herd a dozen or so hungry dingoes into a pen, toss in a live chicken and the last man standing gets to eat the bird. In Derry they use children, toss in gold medals, and call it a Feis.

For those of you new to the city, the annual Feis is a week-long festival of Irish culture, where youngsters from the age of three up get to spend their Easter week singing, dancing, reciting and playing instruments until their fingers bleed. To say the competition is tough is an understatement. It is not the taking part that counts, it is the complete annihilation of the opposition. It is two thousand little Hannibal Lecters in ringlets and green velvet dresses.

Indeed, Jack the Black, who is forced to attend the Feis now his daughter Curly-Bop is of the age, swears the ghost of Charles Darwin can be seen backstage, shaking his head and saying, "Enough. Enough."

But bad and all as the children are, their parents are ten times worse. "Do you know how many Feis mothers it takes to change a light bulb?" asks Jack as we stand outside the Forum, where he is collecting Curly from her Speech and Drama class.

"How many?" I answer.

"None," he says. "They all carry about their own spotlights."

*****

The Millennium Forum is a massive arts complex squeezed in tight against the city's old East Wall. Costing £14 million, its main hall features a very clever system of rollaway seats and floors which let it cater for everything from a 1,000-strong Charlie Landsborough night for grannies to your more intimate 300-seater Kafka play. The four-floor building also houses a host of ante-rooms, bars, cafés and shops, so it is perfect for a 400-event Feis.

Curly-Bop Black is entering three different singing competitions this year and, according to her proud Da, is fancied to do well. Jack, as you know, is married to Harry the Hurler's little sister Donna and is a decent enough character despite his obvious handicap. Though like many who can't shake off old habits, I still prefer not to be seen talking to him in the street. Not that it stops him, mind.

"Curly gets her voice from my side of the family," he laughs. "None of the Hurlers approve of singing in public . . . But she is very strong, confident and powerful. I think she gets that from them.

"My only fear for her this year is if Patches Patterson is doing the judging again. He's very sore at me for booking him for drink-driving at Christmas. Jeez, he's lucky I don't put in the real reading, or he'll go to jail. But typical teacher – you can't talk to them; they know everything there is."

I tell Jack that I'm sure Curly'll do okay and begin to back away before he can start talking about his brother-in-law. The pair tend not to bump into each other much. But it is too late.

"Do you see much of Harry these days?" he asks me.

"Hardly at all," I say, sticking to the script. "Though he's definitely mellowing towards your lot. In fact, he's now admitting that when he's younger, he nearly joins up himself."

"So why not?" asks Jack. "The fitness requirement?"

"Oh no," I reply, "the IQ test. His scores are too high."

"Good one," grins Jack. "Tell him for me, in that case he should become a tout – like all the boys around him."

*****

A couple of weeks later, on Easter Tuesday, I am sitting at the corner bar in the City Hotel, enjoying an early evening glass of Hennessy with my coffee, when I see Harry the Hurler come in through the sliding vestibule doors about forty yards away. I hullo him politely with a discreet half-arm salute and wonder if I could scone my drinks and head him off in the lobby before he gets to the counter. Harry is more dangerous than ever at the moment, as he's after buying a flat in the Canaries and offering all his pals free holidays – as long as they return with four suitcases full of cheap cigarettes.

But Harry flaps his hand to signal that he doesn't want to join me and perches himself on a soft sofa out in the empty foyer.

A few minutes later, who then enters but Jack the Black and sits opposite Harry. And before long, it seems from my leather stool that they are pointing fingers at one another and having quite a thorough ding-dong.

The previous day, sixty suitcases full of cigarettes – worth about forty K in all – are seized during a surprise Customs raid at City of Derry airport. And I am surmising that Harry is remonstrating with Jack about why the hell no-one gives him a quick call to say get a later flight.

After about five minutes of this, Harry storms out the door, stopping only long enough to turn back and point his finger directly at me to remind me that he is never here. Not that it's ever necessary.

Jack the Black then looks around, sees me and strolls over, looking pretty pleased with himself.

"Any cigs?" I ask him, patting my pockets.

"No – but I know where to get some," he chuckles and makes a same-again motion to the barman for me.

"So how are things going at the Feis?" I ask, seeing as I now have another drink.

"Not good at all," replies Jack, "which, believe it or not, is why I'm meeting Harry. Little Curly is zero for two in her competitions so far. No medal, no certificate, no nothing. It's all because of that little runt Patches Patterson, who, of course, has his name down to judge everything that Curly is in for.

"At the end of her first recital, Irish Folk Ballad Under-Eleven, there are people standing clapping in the audience – and not just me and Donna. But she doesn't even get a mention. So when Donna – who doesn't know the score – asks Patches what's his problem, he says he doesn't like competitors wearing hair extensions. Donna tells him that Curly is all natural, but he just waves her away with the back of his hand.

"Then today at the Under-Twelves, Curly brings the house down with the old love song *Neansaí Mhíle Ghrá*. Honest to God, there are people crying in the front row – and it's not because they want to get out. But again, not even a poxy commendation. And when Donna confronts Patches, he just says, 'Ask your husband, Mrs Black.' But I just play dumb and tell her he must be some sort of old bigot."

But Jack's problem doesn't stop with his wife, he concedes. His daughter, like many people who are very talented, is an extremely bad loser. And after two slap-downs in two days, she is heartbroken and talking about quitting the singing business altogether.

"So," he explains, "I call Harry, who is Curly's godfather, and arrange to meet him here. I ask him to talk to her. Tell her to get a sense of perspective. Tell her that winning isn't the most important thing in the world.

"Harry, of course, won't brook it at all and accuses me of raising my daughter to be a failure. And instead, he suggests letting Patches in on the extended family connection. You see, although Patches would remember Harry the Hurler from school, he would have no idea that Harry and Curly are connected.

"But I won't hear of that and remind Harry that he is supposed to be finished with threatening judges. Which is when Harry spits the dummy and walks out. But that's the type of him; he'll come round."

Jack, who sometimes can't help himself, then asks me if I see much of Harry these days.

"Now and again," I laugh.

"So what's he saying about me?" presses Jack.

"He says with all this peace breaking out, you can't sleep in your car all day any more. You have to go into an office and sleep in front of a desk, where they can see you."

"That's rich, coming from him," sniffs Jack. "Way I hear it, the only time he sees any action himself these days is when he winds up hiding under Sparkly Barkley's bed."

*****

Curly's final recital is the Irish Lament Under-Eleven, which is being held at the Tower Hotel on Butcher Street. The Tower, like the Forum, is squeezed against another of the city's old Walls and again is a torture for parking. But the dinner menu is well worth the walk – and the head chef gets more offers to shift than Orange Jill the barmaid.

Personally, I decide to skip the Feis today, as all my nephews and nieces are by now safely ensconced in college and other young offenders' centres. And my appearance at such functions, besides no longer being compulsory, could be construed as questionable.

But at teatime, back in Charlie's Bar, I look up and see the smiling faces of Harry the Hurler, Jack the Black and his daughter Curly. And I quickly work out that the reason for all the smiles is that Curly is hugging a big silver cup.

"At long last," says Jack, making a three sign to the bar. "And it's all down to her talk with Harry last night. He tells her there is no shame in losing – and that it's important to accept defeat with dignity. So she loosens up, stops worrying and gives the best performance of her life. Even that . . . b-a-s-t-a-r-d . . . of a judge can't mark her down this time."

Harry just blushes modestly and thanks his in-law. We toast Curly's success with our drink, after which Jack announces he's taking her home and they head off down the Claudy road.

I start to pack my kit to follow, but Harry motions his head no, and two more pints of black appear from behind the counter.

"Ask your question," he instructs me.

"What question is that?" I lie.

"Ask it," he warns.

"Okay," I reply, "what does Patches Patterson say when you tell him you are Curly's uncle and doting godfather?"

"Good question," laughs Harry. "But the answer is simple: he already knows."

"How's that?" I ask.

"Aha!" says Harry. "That is your second question – but seeing as it is an even better one, I will answer it anyway.

"After me and Jack talk yesterday, I call up Curly and chat to her for about an hour on the phone. I tell her it is important to lose as graciously as you win – and that no matter what walk of life you're in, you're going to have disappointments.

"I tell her about my own little import and distribution business, and how sometimes I get major setbacks – like that one at the airport earlier this week. Though, of course, I don't divulge any specifics to her. So she thanks me very much for the advice – this is a very good youngster. And then she asks me how to avoid losing. So I tell her, there's no way really. And that the best you can do is always be resourceful and try to have a fallback position – a contingency plan, if you like.

"So she thanks me again, and promises me she will sing her heart out for me tomorrow."

Now, you and I both know that Harry has no intentions of leaving things at that. And in the lunch-break before Curly's last competition, when Patches is having a couple of swift sharpeners in the Tower Bar, Harry sits down beside him for a natter.

The pair go way back – so far back that Harry is one of the few who remembers that the judge gets his name not from the leather patches on his jacket but because of the eczema underneath.

"I tell Patches, straight up," says Harry, "to stop busting Curly's chops because of her old fella. And then I lay it on him that I'm her uncle and that it would mean a lot to me if she gets her name read out today.

"Well, Patches, who is a very nervy sort of individual, says he is only just after learning this very morning that Curly's my niece and that he's so sorry he's picking on her, and it won't happen again.

"So then I ask Patches if it's Jack the Black who drops the connection – but he just closes his eyes slowly. 'No,' says Patches, 'Curly herself. She comes right up to me first thing to apologise for being such a bad loser the last two days. She says her Uncle Harry the Hurler tells her it is important to be gracious in defeat, and she asks me to forgive her for running out crying.'"

So, says Harry, Patches then asks Curly if her uncle gives her any more advice.

"'Yes,' she says, 'Harry the Hurler says you should always be resourceful and have a contingency plan.'

"'So what's your contingency plan?' asks Patches, a little too smartly.

"'I'm using it now,' says Curly and looks directly at Patches with ice-cold eyes that bore right through his head. 'You just aren't listening properly. But you'll be listening properly when I'm up there this afternoon. Or else I'll be looking for some more advice from big Uncle H.'"

*****

We sit sipping our pints for a while, chatting about very little, as I am far too long in the game to ask Harry if Jack the Black knows anything of this at all.

"I am not sure if I approve entirely of my niece's methods," says Harry at last. "But I suppose you can only play the cards you have in your hand. That's what being resourceful is all about.

"Incidentally – you hear the news this teatime? A couple of guys are after walking into Strand Road police station and helping themselves to the sixty suitcases of cigarettes they're storing from the Tenerife flight. Some dumb cleaner, apparently, is always forgetting to lock the door.

"By the way, you don't fancy a free holiday, do you?"

First To Score

The five-a-side indoor football game at Brooke Park Leisure Centre is running every Wednesday night for more than ten years now. And although Stammering Stan the Newspaper Man is practising hard, he is still no better at all.

So this evening after a particular stinker of a game, Stan is sitting in the changing room, thinking maybe he should give it all up and concentrate on his drinking, when Danny Boy Gillespie comes over to commiserate.

"Never mind," grins Danny Boy, who is no great shakes either. "It could be worse. 'Stead of just having no left foot, you could have no legs at all."

This raises the expected hair.

"You're some man to talk about legs," snaps Stan. "If you could keep your eyes off Orange Jilly's legs on a Tuesday night, you'd run a lot faster in here on a Wednesday."

"Guilty," chuckles Danny happily. Then, after a pause, he adds: "Am I right in saying, Stan, that you're originally from Donegal?"

"That's right," says Stan.

"So you can play for the Republic," continues Danny. "And your father's people are from England, so you can play for them, too. What about your mother?"

"They are originally from Scotland," says Stan, "so I suppose I'm eligible for them as well."

"Yeah," replies Danny, "and, of course, you can always play for the North."

"How's that?" asks Stan, "I've no relations here."

"Aye," laughs Danny, "but you're crap."

*****

Danny Boy tells this yarn about Stan so often that I know it by heart. Stan, of course, swears it is really the other way about. But you and I both know that the story is as old as the hills.

Despite the after-match to-ing and fro-ing, the Wednesday game is the high point of the guys' week. It's more or less the same personnel who are playing since the early nineties – apart from a few unavoidable departures due to retirements, cruciate ligaments and extradition laws.

The ten regulars are as thick as thieves, which is hardly surprising, as that is precisely what most of them work at. Dumpy Doherty and Getemup Gormley operate the market on the Foyle Embankment for Sparkly Barkley, who also plays; Tommy Bowtie the lawyer is, of course, the greatest stick-up man never to use a gun; Gerry the Hurler runs his brother Harry the Hurler's video and DVD department while the youngest Hurley, Jimmy Fidget, looks after their cigarette depot. The numbers are made up by the city council's head of engineering, Mickey 'Bangers' Johnston, who is previously an unpaid demolition expert for the revolution, and the hospital pathologist Sean 'Doctor Death' McGoldrick – a handy man in the bandaging department when Gerry the Hurler lets loose with his slide tackles.

Harry himself retires from playing about three years back, in his mid-forties, when he discovers he can no longer cut it using just fear alone. But like all those who never quite hit the top ranks, he has a hankering to go into management. Only problem is, who would have him?

*****

Harry still likes to hook up with his old team-mates after their Wednesday game for a pint. And despite their best efforts this night, he finds them anyway, upstairs in the Celtic Bar on Stanley's Walk.

"To be a good boss, you need to know what makes players tick," Harry tells them as they squeeze over to accommodate his size forty-six jacket and pants.

"Football is just like politics. They are games for professionals, played by greedy little amateurs. And while players and politicians pretend to be in it for the good of the team, it is all about grabbing the glory and the headlines for number one. There isn't one of them, when they get a brown envelope, won't tell you that they'll be looking for a bigger one next time.

"There's not one of them who will do their job for the love of it – there has to be an angle. Which is why it takes a guy like me – who understands these things and can deal with them – to run a team. All of which brings me to my point . . ."

Everyone freezes, aware that something big, stupid or crazy – and probably all three – is coming.

"I think," says Harry, "we should set up our own football club and enter it in the Irish Cup."

*****

Everybody cracks up; everybody, that is, except Harry – and Tommy Bowtie, who is a lawyer and thus completely devoid of humour.

But when the merriment subsides, in deference to Harry's well-known reluctance to be laughed at, he looks round the table slowly from face to face and says, "There is a lot of money in this – a hell of a lot. Hear me out.

"Earlier today, myself, Tommy Bowtie there, and Mike the Knife are over with Switchblade Vic McCormack in his pub in the Waterside sorting out a bit of business. A few young Planters in Nelson Drive are taking potshots at our taxis every time they go past – and our lads are starting to return the compliment as soon as they see the Planters' plates coming across the bridge.

"Anyhow, we're sorting out a protocol that we'll each kick our own lot's arses. But afterwards, we get chatting about football – 'cause, as you know, Vic's daughter Gigi is now in charge of Londonderry Legion's first team. And Gigi, it seems, is currently in a bit of a pickle . . ."

*****

Switchblade Vic's only child Gigi is as pretty as a poem. Her mother Maria, who's originally Catalan, is once a famous catwalk model in London, and Gigi is her double – only better built.

Her name isn't Gigi at all; it's Gráinne Gael, in honour of a famous sixteenth-century Irish buccaneer. As you'll expect, Vic hates the name, but Maria insists the full version goes on the birth certificate. "The father thinks he's a damn Irish pirate," she says, "so the daughter can be one as well."

Gigi, however, is a good and gifted child and turns out to be a clean-living sports nut. In particular, she shows a great aptitude for shooting, fencing and cross-country running – just like her father. Though, unlike Daddy, she never actually uses any of these in her day job.

She's also happy to avoid the other track sports, which pleases Vic no end. Up to this point, she's showing no real interest in boys, and he doesn't want her trying out for the wrestling team.

A couple of years back, after she gets her physio degree, Gigi takes some football coaching badges and is put in charge of the Londonderry Legion Under-14s. She works her way up the ranks and proves such a dab hand at it that earlier this season, at the age of twenty-four, she becomes the first ever lady manager of the full team. In fact, Gigi is the first ever lady manager of any Irish men's team – even if the Legion are languishing in the nether regions of Division Three.

Not surprisingly, the appointment of a new lady boss – and particularly such a tasty one as Gigi – makes a number of the senior players forget their manners. But the new chief tackles the mischief-makers quickly by demonstrating that not only does she have her mother's looks, she also has her black Spanish temper.

The message is relayed in no uncertain terms after the first training session, when the Legion captain, Red Roger Rogan, a remarkably ugly man-mountain with the manners to match, remarks that maybe Gigi should join the team in the shower. Without blinking an eye, Gigi kicks him so hard and so quick that not even his jockstrap can save him. And poor Red wakes up with a large crowd around him and a seven-stitch cut on the back of his head.

"Another crack like that," warns Gigi as she pulls Red to his feet, "and you'll be lining out with the ladies' squad. As a fully paid-up member."

From that day on, Red and the others just dote on Gigi. They fight among themselves to carry her physio kit, time the laps and cut the half-time oranges. They even swipe flowers from the neighbouring gardens for her little office. But she refuses to take them on at all. She has the players where she wants them – scared and eager, and most importantly, starting to get results. Within two months of her arrival, the Legion are top of their division and knocking all comers for four or five goals a game.

But last week, after the Legion hit Ballykelly for nine – including a Red Rogan hat-trick – Gigi lets her guard down a little and tells her captain, well played.

"Okay so, " he asks her, "what will it take to make you go out with me?"

"A loaded gun and no visible means of escape," replies Gigi, deadpan.

"What if I score the first goal against Glentoran in the Irish Cup next week?" suggests Red. "The Glens are second in the Premier Division, and the smart money is on them hitting us for double figures."

"No way," says Gigi, "you're far too lucky. That third goal today just bounces in right off your knee."

"What if I get a hat-trick against the Glens?" persists Red.

"Nah," says Gigi after a long pause, "their bus could crash on the way down here and kill half of them. Besides, Red, no offence or anything, but ginger-headed muscle-men just don't do it for me."

"Okay so," concedes Red. "One last go. What if I'm the first to score in this year's Irish Cup Final?"

"Do that," laughs Gigi, "and I'll marry you."

Well, the words are barely out of Gigi's mouth when she's trying to bite her tongue off.

Red just stands there, shocked. The odds of the Legion even reaching the final are exactly two-hundred-to-one, but all Red can see is himself standing at the altar with Gigi in a white satin dress.

"It's just a figure of speech," she protests.

"No backing out now," retorts Red, "you have to let a guy live in hope."

"Okay, okay," snaps Gigi, calming down a little, "but you so much as look at me sideways from now to the end of the season, and remember what I'm telling you about the ladies' squad . . ."

*****

Harry the Hurler laughs as he fills us in on Gigi's dilemma and Vic's complete lack of sympathy for his unmarried daughter.

"But that still doesn't explain how we can make serious money forming a football club," says Mickey Bangers.

"I'll take this one," says Tommy Bowtie on Harry's nod. "Switchblade Vic is actually quite a fan of Red Rogan and would be more than happy to see Gigi hook up with him. As we all know, being big and brainless is no crime in Vic's book.

"So we're chatting on for a while, when Harry asks Vic what odds he'll give on Red being first to score in the final. Vic thinks for a minute, then says about a thousand-to-one. So Harry then says, 'What odds will you give me getting the first goal in the final?' To which Vic, who's enjoying the fun, says, 'I'll give you ten thousands.' But Vic gets the shock of his life when Harry steps forward, shakes his hand and announces, 'Right,

I'll have a grand on the nose – and Tommy Bowtie and Mike the Knife here are my witnesses.'"

Harry eventually lets Vic whittle the size of his bet down to £50, which will still give him a cool half-mill' if he does the business. Though as part of the deal, Vic specifically bans Harry from buying his way into any team in the top three divisions.

If you ask me, Harry might as well throw his £50 away in the street. But ten other men sitting upstairs in the Celtic Bar see possibilities. And that very night, Derry Fianna FC is formed.

*****

The planning goes on well into the wee hours, with Tommy Bowtie appointed chairman so he can sort out all the paperwork with the Irish Soccer Association. Harry the Hurler is, of course, manager. None of the five-a-side indoor squad are signed to any club – nor indeed is Harry – so there'll be no difficulty registering them.

"We've only one real problem now," says Stammering Stan.

"And what's that?" asks Tommy Bowtie.

"We're a bunch of fat drunks who couldn't beat a team of little girls," answers Stan.

"That's where good management comes into it," explains Harry, nodding. "My young nephew Dee Dee will be joining the ranks tomorrow on a free transfer from Derry City. They won't let him play Gaelic on Sundays any more, so he's itching to move. He's coming in as head coach."

This is impressive news. Diarmuid 'Dee Dee' Dunne owns what is widely believed to be the best right leg on this island – only slightly bettering his left. He is the first centre-forward ever to average a goal a game in the League of Ireland premiership, and is also a GAA all-star – all at the age of just twenty-five.

If that isn't enough, he is as handsome as a prince – though some might say a little too swarthy and dark haired. In fact, he's so hairy that opposing fans sometimes throw bananas at him during games to wind him up. But he never bats an eye. And from what Harry tells us, his quiet, gentlemanly nature could charm the chickens down from the trees. But he's generally way too shy ever to switch it on.

Dee Dee's day job is managing an out-of-town meat plant and, says Harry, he is very pally with a squad of Chechen refugees who fix the machines there. Apparently half of them are full-time pro footballers before falling out with Old Mother Russia. And they're eager for some action.

"So does this mean we're all dropped?" asks Danny Boy.

"Yes," says Harry. "All except Stammering Stan."

"No way," protests Gerry the Hurler.

"You're joking," pleads Danny.

"That's right," grins Harry. "I am joking. Stan's dropped as well. Let's face it, you're a bunch of fat drunks who couldn't beat a team of little girls. But on the bright side, you'll all get turns on the subs' bench.

"Look, this is going to require a lot of organising. So help me pull this off, and each and every one of you gets two per cent. That's ten grand a man to you, Stanley."

*****

There is considerable crying and roaring from the ISA about Derry Fianna's decision to enter the Irish Cup – particularly when they find out Harry himself is registering as a player. But as he has no previous convictions that are relevant, and is not the subject of any specific banning order from any league ground, there is very little they can do.

They do raise the issue of a possible clash against the RUC Old Boys, but Tommy Bowtie argues that, in that unlikely event, the two balls will go back in the bag, and no-one will see nothing.

The ISA are also still reluctant to allow games on Derry's west bank since the unfortunate incident of the Ballymena team bus – an incident, which four independent witnesses can tell you, has absolutely nothing to do with Harry the Hurler. But Mickey Bangers pulls some strings at the council and manages to get the Swilly Stadium, in the safe and leafy confines of the Buncrana Road, registered as Derry Fianna's home ground. And the ISA – who already allow Oxford Stars to play from here – have no choice but to accept this.

Stammering Stan, who now edits the *Derry Standard*, sponsors a set of rigs and organises a glowing write-up about the new team for the back page. This will ensure a big crowd for the first game – which will be against the Division Two side, Stranocum.

Gerry the Hurler and Jimmy Fidget, meantime, are helping Dee Dee with the coaching – a sensible arrangement, given that both men exude a natural authority and have extensive experience of running training camps. And also in the dugout is Dr Death McGoldrick, who is very excited to have live specimens to play with. He is busy designing diet sheets and psych tests for the Chechens, who are overjoyed to be doing anything other than fixing stinking machines and drinking cleaning spirits.

Danny Boy Gillespie is put in charge of hospitality, while Getemup Gormley and Dumpy Doherty will take care of the gate receipts.

Sparkly Barkley, of course, is bankrolling the whole operation.

*****

Derry Fianna's first match is a total disappointment. Although the team are making great progress, Dee Dee is worried that they still aren't at full pace. So he warns them not to try anything too clever. As it turns out, it's his backroom staff he should be talking to.

More than a thousand fans are gathered at the Swilly Stadium for the game when a call comes to the Sports Complex to say that that the Stranocum squad are pulling out. It seems that a cardboard box containing lots of protruding wires is left under their team minibus the previous night.

There is nothing else remotely inside the box, other than a gift card signed 'A present from Derry Fianna FC'. But, as Tommy Bowtie argues at the hearing three days later, there is no proof whatsoever that his clients are involved – and both witnesses, who put Jimmy Fidget at the scene, are now withdrawing their statements.

Stranocum are ultimately disqualified for failing to field a team. And Derry Fianna, on the chairman's casting vote, are through to the next round – though in line with tradition, they are forever banned from playing matches at their home ground.

By the time the second round comes around, the Chechens are raring to go. The six weeks off the juice, eating pasta and fresh fruit, is starting to show. And Dee Dee's tireless training sessions, along with Doc Death's instructions to remember that every opponent is a filthy Russian Para, have them all ready to jump through fire.

This time the Fianna are drawn away to First Division Drumcree United in a tie the *Irish News* say will have more blood than The Alamo. Harry himself reckons that they could possibly parachute the team into Portadown for the kick-off, but he's damned if he can figure a way back out again that doesn't end up with him starring as Davy Crockett.

Even the ISA, however, recognise the potential of this one and step up to demand that the game is played behind closed doors at Windsor Park at eight o'clock on a Sunday morning. Windsor Park, of course, being a Neutral Venue.

A few Concerned South Belfast Residents stay up late to throw lighted bottles at the arriving Fianna bus, but it matters little. The Derrymen are too focused and rout Drumcree five-nil, with a hat-trick for Dee Dee Dunne and two goals for one of the Igors.

The bad news is that Dee Dee breaks his wrist when a big Armagh man with no teeth and an exceptional collection of misspelt tattoos, smacks him from behind at a corner. But while Dee Dee will miss the next game or two, the Drumcree centre-half is out for the rest of the season when two of the Igors snap his dirty Muscovite knees in the car park after the game.

Derry Fianna, thus, are into the last sixteen, and their next tie is away to Third Division strugglers Swatragh Farm.

This proves to be even more of a cakewalk for the Chechens, even without Dee Dee who's on the bench. And it's also a lot more fun. The territory is much less hostile, so around five hundred Fianna fans make the trip up to North Derry in buses rented out by Sparkly. Indeed, the only incident of note, other than the visitors' nine goals, is when the Swatragh and Fianna supporters join together to give Harry the Hurler a standing ovation after he comes on as sub with two minutes to go.

*****

Across the city in Nelson Drive, Gigi McCormack's Londonderry Legion are also fighting their way through the early stages.

In the shock result of the first round, they put out top-flight Glentoran one-nil, courtesy of a Red Rogan penalty. The referee's decision to award the spot kick to the home side, given that Red falls over eight yards outside the box, is curious to say the least. And he shows commendable bravery by sending off two Glens defenders for swearing at him in the aftermath.

A riot is averted, however, when Switchblade Vic announces through the PA that there will be free beer at the Sash & Drum for all Glens fans after the game. And the ref drives home with a bulge exactly the size of two grand in his pocket.

The Legion's second-round game, against Division Two front-runners Bangor, goes to a replay. But when Gigi promises her lads she'll give them each a dance at the post-match party, they dig in their heels and win by the odd goal in three. Gigi keeps her side of the bargain too and cuts a rug with each and every one of her fourteen-man squad, even if she does insist that the DJ plays nothing but *The Birdie Song* all night.

The Legion's third game, however, proves a little more contentious. A week before the match, their opponents, Lisburn Rangers, are thrown out for fielding an ineligible player in an earlier round. And it looks as though the Legion are going to get a bye direct into the quarter-finals. But then, all of a sudden, Stranocum are back in the Cup, after winning a High Court challenge against their earlier eviction. And they get to make the trip to Derry instead of Rangers.

On a very good day, Legion might fancy themselves to get a draw against Stranocum. But a new fish factory is after opening in the County Antrim town, and it is staffed almost entirely by Brazilian immigrants. And Stranocum are boasting that they'll be lining out three former stablemates of Ronaldo.

About an hour before kick-off on match day, however, a call comes through to Legion's ground at Nelson Drive to say that a cardboard box is sitting under the Stranocum team minibus and they'll not be coming.

One witness reports seeing a remarkably ugly, ginger-headed bodybuilder in the area just before the box is discovered. But coincidentally, Red Rogan has thirteen men putting him at a training session fifty miles away in Derry at the exact same moment.

*****

Gigi is pleased to avoid the Fianna in the quarters. Both sides pull home ties – the Legion getting a fighting chance against Cliftonville, who're doing no business at the bottom of the Premiership, while Harry's men are to face the league's real giants, Linfield.

The Fianna, of course, aren't allowed to host any more games on the west bank, and since the second Stranocum débâcle, it appears that the Legion can't play on the east bank.

So Gigi, being a practical sort decides to call up Harry the Hurler and propose a temporary ground swap. She rings the Celtic Bar, gets the number for Derry Fianna and who answers the phone but Dee Dee Dunne.

"Hiya, Monkey Boy," chirps Gigi, who is well used to abusing the hirsute Dee Dee from the line at university matches. "Is your uncle, the organ grinder, about?"

"'Fraid not," answers Dee Dee. "Though I'll tell him the charming Gráinne Gael McCormack is looking for him."

"How do you know my voice?" she demands, a little surprised.

"You're on the wireless after every game now," replies Dee Dee. "Surely you're never as stupid as your old man as well?"

"You know yourself – you can't escape the genes," laughs Gigi.

"Though at least my family marry inside their species."

"The jury's still out there, Sister," shoots back Dee Dee. "The way I hear it, you're hoping to mate with the world's only red-haired yeti."

"At least they let him shower with all the other boys, Sweetheart," sniffs Gigi. "I hear that they won't let you back into the changing room until you get yourself a lady friend. Indeed, the story in these parts is that the GAA is not the only other team you're batting for."

"Just saving myself for the right girl, Gigi," says Dee Dee. "'Fraid those wannabe models and football groupies do nothing for me. In fact, word over here is they might be more in your line, Sister . . ."

"My, aren't we bitchy today?" teases Gigi. "With a mouth like that, Monkey Boy, you're never going to land a girl. Unless maybe she runs out of legs to wax and fancies a challenge."

"This from a doll who hides the finest pair of legs in Derry under a pair of baggy tracksuit bottoms," retorts Dee Dee. "What's wrong – are you scared you might turn some nice boy's head?"

"It'll take more than that to turn you," sniffs Gigi. "Anyway, how do you know what my legs look like?"

"Sure they're the jewels in the crown of the Queen's Cross-Country team," pipes back Dee Dee. "I remember many a Saturday morning standing at the finish line to watch you break the tape. It's Coach's way of firing up the GAA squad before their afternoon match. Nothing better, he says, for stirring the blood than the sight of McCormack's legs, damp and dirty. The number of nights, even yet, I go to bed and thank the Lord for the man who invented bikini shorts for women runners. Your jogging bottoms, Gigi, are a sin against God."

"Enough," giggles Gigi, "any more of your charm, and I might forget I'm a football manager. Look, we were thinking. Do you want to trade home grounds for the quarter-finals? Vic reckons the ISA will okay it, if only to stop Linfield getting a bye into the semis."

"Per-zackly what we're thinking too," says Dee Dee.

*****

The ISA, predictably, try to insist that both quarter-finals are held in Belfast. But Tommy Bowtie then ties them in knots in the courts, and Stammering Stan makes them look so bad in the press that eventually they allow the ground swap.

Legion get to play their game first at Swilly Stadium on Friday night. The ground is only half-full as there are still quite a few Legion fans who won't travel west of the river. But Gigi's charges quickly hit top form regardless. It helps that Cliftonville are so bad that their own supporters are throwing chips at them by half-time. And there are no complaints when Legion run out two-nil winners.

The following afternoon at Nelson Drive, Cup-holders Linfield arrive in big numbers. At least nine-tenths of the two-thousand-strong crowd are Blues fans from Belfast – and they are expecting no less than a shootie-in. The other two hundred are Legion fans hoping to see the Fianna get a tanking.

As a gesture of respect, the home team vote not to wear their green and white hoops in the Waterside. And Harry the Hurler agrees to remain in the Celtic Bar and patch in his advice via mobile phone.

No-one is giving the Fianna a prayer. Indeed, Gigi McCormack – who for once is wearing a pair of shorts – and Switchblade Vic are holding a big banner which reads, 'See you in the final, Blues!' No-one, however, is reckoning on Dee Dee Dunne's determination to prove his host and hostess wrong.

Dee Dee's team talk before the game is short and sweet. "When you get the ball," he tells the Chechens, "give it to me. And anyone who goes to hurt me, stop them. Anyone who does hurt me – well, you know the drill.

"Now, let's go and teach these dirty Russian bastards a lesson they'll not forget."

Linfield, however, are a very different prospect to all the Fianna's other opponents so far – they're full-time professionals and are a lot fitter than the Chechens. The Belfast men start with all guns blazing and within five minutes they are a goal to the good. Seamus Coyle, the traitor, rattles in a volley from twenty-five yards, which hits the net before Big Vlad the keeper can even move.

Indeed, for the first forty minutes, it's all Linfield pressure and the Fianna are quite happy not to concede another. They have ten men behind the ball, and only Dee Dee up the field.

Just before half-time, however, Dee Dee gets on the end of one of Big Vlad's kick-outs and is so badly fouled in the box that even the ref can't ignore it. Dee Dee gets up and tucks away the penalty, while the two Igors quietly tell the Linfield centre-half that they will be speaking to him in the tunnel after the game.

The second half is all Linfield, apart from the centre-back, who doesn't re-appear. Big Vlad is busier than last orders on Christmas Eve, but nothing gets past him.

Then, two minutes before the end, Derry Fianna break on the right. Little Igor the Winger gets to the byeline and crosses to Dee Dee in the box, who feigns to shoot and takes the full weight of a Linfield defender in his ribs. But just as the defender crashes into him, Dee Dee dummies the ball through to Igor the Striker who wallops it past the keeper from fifteen yards.

Two-one, the game finishes, and the Fianna are in the last four.

As the final whistle goes, Dee Dee is carried off on a stretcher, to cat-calls from sulking Blues fans. Though at least this way, he has a chance of getting out the gate alive. As the stretcher passes by Gigi, still resplendent in her Bermuda shorts, Dee Dee props himself up on his good side and points over at her discarded Linfield banner.

"Guess you'll be needing a new one – for when you meet real men," he quips with a wince.

"A real man would get up and walk, Monkey Boy," she chuckles back.

"Walk," he laughs, "I can barely breathe . . ."

"Maybe if you ask one of your nice Chechen boys," she grins, "they'll give you the kiss of life."

"Well, it looks as if it's the only offer I'm getting round here," retorts Dee Dee. "If you don't start being a bit nicer to me, Gigi, I just might let that big yeti of yours score in the final."

"Do that," retorts Gigi with a wink, "and I'll never wear shorts for you again . . ."

And with that, Gigi and her lovely, long Spanish legs turn on their heels and head for the clubhouse.

*****

The draw for the last four is made that night and the romance of the Cup strikes again. The Fianna are away to Omagh Town, while the Legion travel to Institute for an all-Derry derby at Riverside Stadium, Drumahoe.

Institute are the clear favourites to win their leg – but Roddy McGinn's injury-wracked squad are further weakened by the fact that two of his midfielders are next-door neighbours of Switchblade Vic and are reluctant to line-out. Stute and Legion opt to play their match on the Friday night, while Omagh and the Fianna will go the following day.

The night-time kick-off, however is to prove another nightmare for Stute. All three of McGinn's first-team strikers have day jobs in Belfast and are travelling down the M2 for the game together, when an oil tanker jack-knifes about a quarter-mile down the motorway in front of them.

The spill causes one of the biggest ever traffic snarl-ups in the North. And the three players – along with hundreds of others motorists – are trapped in their car for the night.

Police reports say that, just after the crash, a remarkably ugly, red-haired body-builder is seen sprinting out of the offending truck and into a red sports car a hundred yards the right side of the mêlée. But they later concede that Red Rogan is playing cards fifty miles away at the Sash & Drum in Derry at the exact same moment. Oh, and the barman is certain that Switchblade Vic's new Porsche never leaves the car park.

So back at the Riverside Stadium in Derry, Stute are forced to start the semi with five reserves and, in truth, they never get going. McGinn's men are resolute in defence, but have no creativity in midfield, and with three 16-year-olds for forwards, they eventually come unstuck. Red Rogan gets the winner for the Legion with a few minutes to go, heading in from a corner kick.

Quite a party breaks out in the Legion's changing room after the game – it's the first time in forty years a Derry team is in the Irish Cup Final. And a crate of champagne quickly appears, courtesy of the Sash & Drum.

Gigi, however, is madder than hell and leaves the celebrations to hunt down her father in his office. "You'd damn well better not be planning any stunts like that against Dee Dee and the Fianna tomorrow," she yells.

"Well, I can hardly have Harry the H walking off with your inheritance now, can I?" laughs Switchblade Vic.

"Right, so," replies Gigi through gritted teeth. "I'm dropping Red Rogan from the team for the final . . ."

"Chrissake, Pet," protests Vic. "I have a thousand pounds of my own on Legion to win the Cup – at a hundred to one. I'm on since the first round."

"Tell you what then," says Gigi, "in that case, I'm going to drop the entire squad and field the ladies instead."

"Okay, okay," says Vic, recognising his wife's flashing eyes. So he picks up the phone and dials a number. "Hello, is that Mr X?" he asks. "I need you to remove Object A from under Location B immediately – no arguments. That's right, immediately . . .

"I don't know . . . Toss it into the river."

"Thank you, Daddy," nods Gigi as he puts the phone down. "Now, I'm going down to the Omagh game myself tomorrow to make sure there are no surprises."

Vic quickly picks up the phone again: "Mr X? Better call off Sniper C as well . . ."

*****

Dee Dee, with his four broken ribs, is quite understandably banjaxed for the semi-final. But Omagh are less of a threat than Linfield, and he is quite confident that the Chechens can handle them on their own. He's even planning to give Harry the Hurler and Sparkly Barkley a run-out for a bit of comic relief, if all goes well.

And sure enough, it turns out to be very easy – with the Fianna running out five-one winners. But the headlines are reserved for Harry the H, who becomes the oldest and undoubtedly most unfit man ever to score in a Cup match. And you'd think his bet is up, the way he celebrates his last-minute tap-in.

The only other point of interest is that Gigi McCormack turns up at the St Julian's Road ground for the game, and this time she has her civil tongue with her. She even comes over to congratulate Dee Dee as his side disappear into the changing rooms.

"So are you nervous about the final?" Dee Dee asks her.

"Only about one particular part of it," she laughs, "as you know very well. Vic is already writing his Father of the Bride speech, and Red is getting a special tattoo done as a surprise for me."

"Well, if it's any consolation," says Dee Dee, "we'll do all we can to kick your big ugly yeti out of the game."

"He's not my big ugly yeti yet, he's still my father's," retorts Gigi. "Your Soviet hitmen don't do private contracts by any chance, do they?"

"Wouldn't know," laughs Dee Dee. "But on the other hand, if Harry scores first it'll cost Vic five hundred K."

"Cheap at twice the price," declares Gigi, "if it'll stop him meddling in my life for a while."

"Maybe that'll leave a bit more room for the rest of us," says Dee Dee shyly. And he is rewarded by a smile that Gigi's saving up for him all day.

Both managers are suddenly out of small talk, so they amble silently across the byeline and head towards the tunnel. Dee Dee then points towards the dressing room and says he must go.

"Anyone sees me talking to a pretty face like you," he says, "and it'll ruin my reputation with the left-footers. Besides, I'm sure the lads will all be waiting for their after-match rub-downs."

"I give a pretty mean rubdown of my own," says Gigi, fixing Dee Dee with a look that shoots a thrill right through him. "And I'll tell you what, Soldier, when you join my team, the rest will have to wait in line."

"Ah, but I'll still have to share my card with fourteen other dancers," laughs Dee Dee.

"Who worries about dancing," asks Gigi, "when you have your own private key to the steam room?"

"I hate to repeat myself," grins Dee Dee, "but you still have a captain of your own."

"But," counters Gigi, flicking him two impish eyebrows, "a good manager knows exactly when it's time to hit the transfer market."

"To be honest, Gigi," replies Dee Dee softly, "you can have me on a free, any time."

*****

The Cup Final is to be played in Derry's Brandywell Stadium as a one-off, instead of Windsor Park, after Tommy Bowtie drags the ISA back into court. The Fianna tell the judge that the Concerned Residents in South Belfast will only torch their bus again, while the Legion argue that some of Vic's old Shankill associates could use the occasion to repay him a few favours. Via a long-distance viewfinder.

A ten-thousand-strong crowd pack into the Brandywell for the game – a full half of them from the Waterside, after Gerry the Hurler and Jimmy Fidget agree a security protocol with Switchblade Vic. The entire Foyle Road from the lower deck of the bridge, right up to the ground, is cordoned off and marshalled by stewards to let the Legion fans in and out.

Noel 'No Friends' Flynn, meanwhile, is the agreed ref on the grounds that he is the finest bouncer and late-night negotiator in the city. And also because both Harry and Vic are afraid of him.

The anthems are both played, the final gets underway and the Fianna immediately lay siege to the Legion goal. It is clear from the off that the Chechens are much fitter and more experienced than Gigi's crew. The Fianna are badly hampered, however, by the fact that Harry must start the game at centre-forward. And Harry is slower than his mother – and a lot less deadly around goal. No-one else on the Fianna side is allowed to shoot, of course, so at half-time it's still all square, and Harry is having about as much luck as Johnny the Dwarf in a police line-up.

Harry is also exhausted, as nineteen stones is a considerable amount to haul about for forty-five minutes. Indeed, the last time he runs for real is way back in the bad old days, when someone sets the wrong time on a home-wrapped alarm clock.

About forty yards behind him, Dee Dee Dunne is still feeling the rib damage and so is playing in defence, where up till now things are pretty quiet.

Then just after half-time, disaster.

204

Right from the restart, Igor the Winger puts Harry the Hurler clean through. But he blarges a sitter wide of an open goal from five yards, and Legion get a kick-out. Their goalie lamps the ball hard into the Fianna half. Red Rogan leaps high to head the ball down to his younger brother, Black Angus, who's about thirty yards from goal. Angus looks up and sees the Fianna keeper, Vlad, off his line and lobs the ball over the Chechen's head.

It looks a goal all the way, and the perfectly weighted chip is just dipping under the crossbar, when in rushes Dee Dee Dunne and punches the ball out over the byeline.

There is uproar. First from the Fianna when No Friends the ref gives a penalty, and then from Gigi on the touchline when she sees who's taking it. Despite protests from the bench, No Friends refuses to allow Gigi to substitute Red before he takes the penalty, which, of course, he drives home.

Red immediately rushes over to the celebrating Legion's fans and pulls off his shirt, to reveal a vest announcing: I love my Gigi. But he is quickly knocked unconscious by a tyre-iron marked Porsche, which appears to come out of the Legion dugout.

Dee Dee, meanwhile, is sitting on the pitch with his head in his hands wondering if his uncle or Gigi is going to be first to skin his stupid, hairy hide. He is so distraught that he doesn't even see Harry, who taps him on the shoulder and tells him to get his chin up.

"Come on," says Harry, "we can take these boys, easy. Besides, we can't let Vic lift another hundred K. But first things first, I'm going off."

And then all of a sudden, it is men versus boys. Dee Dee slots himself up front with Big Igor and starts banging in goals like there's no tomorrow.

At the end, it's so one-sided, they even bring on Stammering Stan for the last three minutes – and he has the unique honour of scoring in a Cup Final he's reporting on. Seven-one, it ends, to the Fianna, with Dee Dee Dunne becoming the first man ever to net five goals in a final.

Of course, no-one is really happy, except maybe Red Rogan – and, naturally enough, the Chechens, who don't know a curse what's going on.

*****

The Fianna are holding their post-match party at The Jack Kennedy Inn and invite the Legion along for a consolation drink – and to celebrate Red Rogan's engagement to Gigi. Despite losing the game, Switchblade

Vic is beaming and walking about with his arm around the new son-in-law. The lucky bride-to-be, meanwhile, is in the corner numbing the pain with a tumbler full of neat gin.

Dee Dee's future looks similarly bleak. Jimmy Fidget, Gerry the Hurler, Getemup Gormley and Dumpy Doherty, all of whom are businessmen and none of whom are particularly sympathetic individuals, are all blaming him for conceding the penalty. They claim that Black Angus's effort is set to go over the bar – and are insisting that Dee Dee pays them the ten K each they are due when Harry the Hurler scores first. Worse again, Dee Dee has no idea how much the seriously interested parties – Harry the H, Tommy Bowtie and Sparkly – are going to try and recover from his lousy £400 a week pay cheque.

Doctor Death, however, who is a good soul, assures Dee Dee he'll not be looking for his cut, before going over to console Gigi McCormack in turn. Indeed, the Doc spends quite a while chatting to Gigi, and even presents her with a little gift box which he says is on behalf of the Fianna.

As is tradition, the losers pay to fill the trophy with drink. So Gigi takes it upon herself to arrange this, and the Irish Cup is passed round the room. Gigi even manages to make a speech toasting the victors and – after swallowing hard – her husband-to-be.

Gigi is almost on her ear with all the gin, so gives the cup a miss, as does Dee Dee in the corner who doesn't feel much like drinking. Instead, they toast one another sombrely across the room with coffee cups.

But then, a very strange thing happens. All of a sudden, the Derry Fianna players start cowping over at their table. Mid-sentence. Heads are whacking off tables, and bodies are slipping off chairs.

As Dee Dee looks round, stupefied, the Legion squad starts to follow suit – then the top table of Vic, Red Rogan, Harry, Sparkly and the rest of the Fianna board members. Within the space of a minute, the only people left standing in the room are Dee Dee, Gigi, Doc Death and the waiter. Everyone else is slumped in a heap.

"This is where we make our exit," says an all-of-a-sudden alert Gigi skipping across to take Dee Dee by the hand.

"We've four hours' head start before the little tablets the Doc prescribes wear off them. Though I think for Red, it'll be a bit longer – as he's after pinning a double-dose."

"So what makes you think I'll run away with you?" quips Dee Dee. "Unless maybe you're going to drug me too."

"Because," answers Gigi, steering them towards the door, "the only thing hotter than me is the Porsche you'll be driving to Dublin. I don't know if you can handle the powerful engine, though. It's got one hell of a charge – and it needs just the lightest of touches."

"I love it already," says Dee Dee.

"I'm not talking about the car, Monkey Boy," grins Gigi.

"Neither am I," replies Dee Dee as they scuttle out through the little wicket gate to the garage.

*****

Now, both you and I would be certain there are going to be ructions following the disappearance of Dee Dee and Gigi – but then again, we would both be wrong.

The first inkling I get that things mightn't be as bad as they're painted is when I see Stammering Stan driving a brand new Volvo S80 into the Brooke Park car park about a month later. He is late for his Wednesday night indoor game at the centre, so I catch up with him over a pint of Coldflow in Da Vinci's after the match and ask him for the latest.

"Strictly off the record," he explains, "we are just after getting very substantial win bonuses – courtesy of Switchblade Vic.

"Vic, as you might imagine, is sweating the night before the final, and rings Harry with a proposal. He offers to buy Harry out of the bet for a hundred K. But Harry hangs tough for a while, and eventually they agree on double that. Way Vic looks at it, he's still saving quite a bit of dough."

"Why then is Harry playing in the final like his life depends on it?" I ask.

"Simple," answers Stan, "he's having the time of his life. And he doesn't want anyone to know the bet's off in case they won't let him start. He also really wants to be the first to score – it's a matter of pride."

"So they're not angry at Dee Dee?" I ask.

"Not at all," says Stan, "apart maybe from Jimmy Fidget who's allergic to the night-night drops, and is just out of intensive care. But even he'll be okay when he gets his cut."

"And what about Red Rogan?" I suggest.

"Well," replies Stan, "he's still very angry, and Dee Dee and Gigi may be forced to extend their honeymoon in Dublin for a couple more weeks till he cools down. But they're more than happy as Harry the H is after sending them on twenty thou of an elopement present.

"In truth, though, Red's stock is running pretty low at the moment. And I don't think he'll be playing for Legion much longer. Switchblade Vic is most distressed when we show him the CCTV footage of a ginger-haired yeti putting a metal box underneath Harry the Hurler's car. Strange thing is, though, Red comes back and removes the same box about an hour later. Anyhow, any thoughts that Vic would have him for a son-in-law are now well and truly kiboshed.

"I mean, you can't be inviting criminals into your family, now. Can you?"

A Resigning Matter

To say that Stammering Stan would love to see the current mayor, Dr Rex 'Lucky' Tucker, come crashing from a height is like saying Jackie Kennedy doesn't go a bundle on open-top convertibles.

Mayor Lucky, you see, is as crooked as a country mile – but worse again, he hauls Stan into court every time he tries to prove it. And today Stan, who now edits the *Derry Standard,* and Lucky are in chambers with their barristers and the High Court judge, Letemout Lou, trying to sort out the latest aspersions cast on Lucky's character.

The chambers are actually the back lounge of The Jack Kennedy Inn, to save all parties the travel costs to Belfast and give the lawyers something else to bitch about.

"I accept that much of what you write about Mayor Tucker last week is one hundred per cent correct," says Letemout to Stan over the coffee table.

"For instance," she continues, reading from a sheet, "there is no slander whatsoever in the claim, Lucky, that you own a bandit taxi firm. That is a fact. You're operating it since the nineteen-seventies, your drivers are never insured, and the whole town knows it.

"As for the allegation that you're only on the council to line your coat, well, again I have to go with the facts. You'll remember that five years ago, when I myself am a solicitor looking for late-liquor licences, you yourself tell me that you'll sort them out for one large note per club. And I am still waiting for a receipt for that brown envelope containing Sparkly Barkley's two grand. So again, I'm going to find for Stan there.

"The claim that you don't deserve your honorary degree for services to the city is a little more complicated, I concede. Stan states in his report that it is a black day for the university. But you're right, Lucky, in saying he has no evidence for this. So I am after ringing the Vice Chancellor who tells me privately, that while it is not a completely black day, it is certainly a dark grey one – but what can you do when someone hands you a hundred thousand of city money to buy yourself a suite of brand new computers?

"So no dice on that one, Lucky. And I'm also going to allow Stan his cheap shot that you now have one more doctorate than you do 'O' Levels. And yes, I know you have certificates in woodwork and geography."

Lou pauses for a sip of coffee and to let Stan sweat a little, as he knows by the way of these things that he is also about to get a good kicking.

"I do, however, take serious issue with Stammering Stan's failure to employ a full-time copyreader at the *Derry Standard*," she declares. "I do not for one minute believe that the, open quote, computer spellchecker, close quote, is at fault for changing last Thursday's front-page headline, 'What a twisted Tucker!', to what currently lies before us. Nor do I accept Stan's contention that the spellchecker is entirely to blame for accidentally correcting Mayor Tucker's name three out of fourteen times in the subsequent article.

"So I'm upholding this particular claim against Stan and the *Derry Standard* for injury to your feelings, Lucky, and am ordering them to publish a correctly spelt apology and to pay you damages."

Stan is immediately on his feet and objecting.

"No way," he protests. "You're breaking my heart here, Letemout."

"And I will break other soft parts of you if you interrupt me again," shoots back Letemout. "You will apologise to Lucky, Stan – on the front page. You will apologise to the reading public, you will pay damages to Mayor Tucker, and you will hire yourself a proofreader."

Tucker flashes a smirk at Stan, then looks round solemnly at Letemout.

"So, Your Worship," he says, "how much do I get?"

"Given you have little or no character worth defaming, Lucky, why don't we say two grand," sighs Letemout.

"Bit on the low side," sniffs Lucky, "but I suppose it'll get me a decent bottle of wine."

"Actually it won't," declares Letemout. "Because you're going to put it now in a brown envelope, give it to me, and I'm going to give it back to Sparkly Barkley."

And with that, Letemout tells Lucky's barrister to take that twisted little Tucker out of her chambers. Except, like Stan, she doesn't call him Tucker.

*****

After the hearing, Letemout Lou and Stammering Stan stay on for Stella and nachos – with her lordship footing the bill, now that Stan is all cleaned out.

It is a mystery to most people that a delicious doll like Letemout wants to waste her youth and pretty face on a guy like Stan, who cannot open his own milk. But she and Stan are as tight as skin on a stick since she's a little fat thing at primary school and he's the guy in the corner with the smart mouth. And, truth is, Letemout is starting to brood a little now she's over thirty.

Stan, however, is not a man for brooding at all – except perhaps over how he'll get his insurance company to cough up the two Gs to pay for this case on top of the seven hundred quid for his thieving lawyers.

"Come on, Stan," says Letemout. "It's worth every penny. Your paper is front-page news right across the country because of you and your dodgy spellchecker. Anyone but Lucky Tucker and you're paying out half a million – minimum.

"You've no friends in a courtroom, Stan. Remember that. From the court clerk to the usher, it's every scheming dog for himself. Though I hear if someone is married to a judge, they tend to get things a bit easier . . ."

"How could I ever marry someone who would break off my soft parts?" sniffs Stan. "There's me thinking that they're very dear to you."

This debate is going nowhere and Stan, for once, is delighted to see Harry the Hurler walk in, even if he does look like someone's after stealing his First Communion money.

Indeed, Stan may be thanking divine intervention a bit early.

"Where do you get off writing these lies about me?" shouts Harry at Stan, throwing today's paper at him.

Stan and Harry do regular business and are generally on the same page, if not exactly friends. But Harry's voice is as cold as a March grave – and the only thing going in Stan's favour is that he has a High Court judge as a witness in the next chair.

"What's the problem, Harry?" asks Stan, as casually as his nerves will allow him.

"Ten-Gun Tex, the American president, is refusing to meet me in Derry next month, because of these hurtful slurs in your paper," spits Harry. "You are saying that I am – and I quote – an unreconstructed gunman with more blood on his hands than the transfusion service."

"No, Harry," counters Stan swiftly. "It is Tex himself who says this. It

211

is an exact transcript from a press statement he puts out last night. You'll see the same remarks in every paper in the newsagents today. And if you check your mobile phone, which is probably still on the back seat of Mrs Sparkly Barkley's car, you'll find four messages from me attempting to warn you to get all your ducks in a row."

"You don't have to put it on the front page," grumbles Harry, calming a little. "My mother reads your paper."

"More than mine does," laughs Stan, "she never believes a word that comes out of my mouth."

"Okay, okay," says Harry, "we'll park it for a minute. But tell me now, how the hell am I going to get to meet Tex when he's here?"

"Why's it so important, Harry?" interrupts Letemout Lou. "You're not a man for the public arena."

"I need a visa to visit New York again," explains Harry with a heavy sigh. "We're low on funds since the Assembly elections. And now that Option B is closed to us, I have to hit the dinner circuit."

"Okay," says Lou to Harry. "First of all, can I remind you, as your lawyer, that your next trip to America will in fact be your very first. And do not forget that, particularly with the Customs. And secondly, can I remind you that protocol dictates that Tex will have to meet all political leaders in the city when he visits – even you."

"Not quite," says Harry. "Tex is only meeting guys democratically voted in at the ballot box. And this is an area I scrupulously avoid – on your very advice, Lou."

"What about the fact that you're Chief Executive of the Boys' political wing?" inquires Stan.

"That and sixty-nine pence will buy you a loaf of bread," moans Harry. "It carries no weight with Tex whatsoever."

Letemout Lou strokes her chin and thinks for a moment. "In that case, Harry" she says slowly, "you have one month to get yourself elected to office.

"What you need is for someone to leave the council – almost immediately – and for you to win the by-election to replace them. But, Harry, I strongly suggest you then resign your office after a very short time. No more than a week. Otherwise, you'll get creased. You've too many skeletons rattling around in the closet – and in your case I'm talking literally. Make your point, meet Ten-Gun Tex, then resign before the cake hits the fan."

"Okay, so," nods Harry. "Now, who can we run off the council?"

"I know just the man," grins Stan.

You never see the bus that runs over the top of you. And Lucky Tucker is drummed out of the Guildhall chamber before the week is out. Stan, it seems, is all the while storing a surprise up his sleeve in case Tucker should take him to the fair during the settlement negotiations.

Initially, Letemout Lou doesn't want him breaking the story on the grounds that these things can badly rebound on you, but when Harry okays it, there is little she can do.

And so, instead of an apology, the front page of the *Derry Standard* reports how Dr Rex Tucker is now using his council computer to arrange personal escorts. And these are not the type of escorts he brings to mayoral functions. More interestingly again, Lucky is paying for their services with his council-funded credit card.

Indeed, the whole dodge is undiscovered for months. It seems the name of the firm is Corporate Hospitality Ireland Key Services, and the auditor only cottons on when he finds an invoice from them for a torn schoolgirl's uniform.

Stan, of course, writes a stinking editorial, railing about the hypocrisy of the mayor – and calls on him to resign immediately. But there is a special council meeting to sack him anyway and he is out by the end of the day.

*****

"Part one of the evil genius's plan to take over the world," says Stan to Lou that night over spaghetti amatriciana and Chianti in Danano's.

"Don't joke," replies Lou, "it's way too close to the mark. Do you realise that if Harry wins the seat, it gives the balance of power to his lot and he could even be elected mayor?"

"But Harry's no interest in the council," says Stan. "Sure he's running the town already."

"No he's not," counters Lou, "he's only chewing on the gristle – taxis, bars, bookies and cigarettes. Imagine what he'll do if he gets his hands on the likes of the airport, the harbour, the new theatre and all the leisure centres. He'll make Rex Tucker look like the Virgin Mary."

"This is good crack coming from you," grins Stan, "seeing as you're the girl that keeps Harry out of jail."

"Well, I suppose I need something to keep my mind occupied," retorts Lou a little snippily, "seeing as there's damn all else happening in my life."

"Maybe we'll have to change that," says Stan, smiling gently at her. "I hear the bridal shop on Carlisle Road is opening a new department."

"Oh," declares Lou. "Now, that is interesting."

"Yeah," continues Stan, slurping back a forkful of pasta, "they might give you a Saturday job."

*****

The first thing that Harry has to do, now he is a candidate, is find himself an election agent. Indeed, that loud clang you hear is the sound of a hundred of his friends bolting the door as they run for cover.

In the end, Tommy Bowtie, Harry's other lawyer, agrees to do it on the grounds that it would be too much of a conflict for Letemout Lou, and it's much too useful to have her on the inside. Harry then appoints his brothers Gerry the Hurler and Jimmy Fidget as Campaign Managers.

Gerry and his late-learner's degree will be in charge of policy issues and PR. Though at Harry's request, Stammering Stan will keep a close eye on the press stuff, as Gerry is by no means as smart as he is qualified.

Jimmy, meanwhile, who is much less educated, is taking care of what are termed the Contra Campaign and the War On The Ground – two areas in which he has extensive experience. And not only in election terms.

Mayor Tucker is formerly a councillor in Waterside Rural, a ward in which his Voice of Ireland Party holds a slight majority. Normally when a council member resigns, dies or is sacked, his party gets to adopt another member in his place. But these are not normal circumstances, and Harry the Hurler's colleagues quickly jam any possible co-option.

The VIPs quickly select Rex Tucker's former agent, Tim 'Thomo' Thompson, to run for them on the grounds that he's under forty, has a face that will appeal to women voters and lives far enough away from Harry the Hurler not to be too frightened by him. The Planters agree not to run any candidate and issue a statement instructing their voters to back Thomo this one time only, to keep Harry out.

The papers are lodged one fortnight to the day after Tucker resigns, and the contest gets underway in earnest, with the two hopefuls pounding the rounds from Eglinton to Ardmore to Claudy. Thomo is a great presence on the doorstep – good-looking, articulate and funny. But he is no match for Jimmy Fidget.

"When you come to a house," Jimmy tells his pool of sixty-odd canvassers, "check from your registration sheets what sort of reception you're going to get.

"If the name is marked with a green pen – it's ours already. Go up to the house, say a quick hello, make sure they have some form of voter ID and a lift to the polling station, and move on quickly.

"If it's marked in black, it's a Planter house. You can put a leaflet in the letterbox. But I wouldn't go up any long paths, as you're going to get a dog set on you.

"If it's marked in blue – it's almost certainly a Thomo vote, so again, get away quickly. They'll all be under instructions to keep you chatting there for an hour to waste your time.

"But if it's marked in red – and these are the most important houses – it's a floating vote. And it's here that you really have to earn your money."

Floating votes, says Jimmy, will decide the election, and there are ways to ensure that Harry gets every single one of them. He explains: "If, for example, the householders are middle-aged or elderly, tell them that your candidate is a loving family man with a wife and two lovely daughters. Then mention that Thomo is still a bachelor, and just raise your eyebrows slightly. Don't overdo it. Though if you have to, you can bring up the fact that Thomo's degree is in drama.

"If you get a mother alone in the house, don't forget to tell them about Thomo's drink problem. Thomo, of course, doesn't drink at all – but if they should know this, just answer, 'Not *publicly*, he doesn't,' and nod your head knowingly.

"If you get the impression – as you will often – that people are saying they'll vote for Harry just to get rid of you, be sure and thank them very much. Then tell them the funny story about how at the last election, Harry's poor mother accidentally votes for a Planter instead of her son's party – and that the reason we know this is because somebody is able to match the serial number off the clerk's electoral record with her voting paper. This is a nice way of telling the punter we see right through you – and by the way, there is no such thing as a secret ballot.

"Finally, and this is important, if a couple come to the door, always talk to the woman. Married men – and I mean no disrespect to all of you who are now house-whipped – have no minds of their own. Also, a man is less inclined to vote – we're lazier. But if you make an impression on the wife, she will hound the husband out the door all the way to the polling booth."

Gerry the Hurler, meanwhile, is busy getting statements from Harry into the papers on everything from water charges to the dangers of slurry pits. And he's also taking charge of defence, now that Thomo's supporters are raising a few issues of their own on the hustings.

"For God's sake," he warns the troops, "don't get drawn on the closure of the rural post offices. Just play dumb, or you're going to get it in the teeth about how the Feeny office is forced to shut because Harry keeps cleaning it out like his own personal piggy bank.

"If you get anything about Harry's time indoors for extortion, directing terrorism and trying to whack those three cops twenty years back, just point out that he's appealing his convictions and that they stem from a non-jury Diplock court. Don't, for your own sake, get caught up in a debate over whether he's actually innocent or not, or you're going to hear about how the whole gun battle on the bridge is on film – and Harry's big belly can be seen bounding up Abercorn Road ahead of a posse of masked-up coppers.

"If the punters want to discuss family values, concentrate on Harry's lovely daughters. If they mention Red Light Lorna running around with half the town, just pull a big sad sympathetic face, shrug the shoulders and say, 'What can the poor man do?'

"And one final point. If they should bring up Harry and Mrs Sparkly Barkley, deny, deny, deny – and then disclose that Harry is actually in the throes of suing Thomo for repeating that very claim to a party supporter."

Gerry then hands the floor back to Jimmy who asks a very select group to stay after school for some additional duties. It appears that Thomo's posters are out all over the ward, and they're presenting an opportunity too good to miss.

The picture has the candidate in full thespian mode, hand determinedly wrapped around a cordless radio mike. Underneath, the slogan reads: VOTE THOMO, THE MAN FOR THE HARD JOB.

"Just two little alterations," says Jimmy, passing round a box of markers, "I don't have to tell you what to do . . ."

*****

Election day dawns, and the *Derry Standard* poll is giving Harry a slight advantage. The *Irish News* has it neck and neck, while the MI5 man in the ITN election unit is still calling it for Thomo.

Just before the booths open, Jimmy Fidget calls aside his select group again and passes around two hundred new driving licences donated by the Boys' Graphic Design department. The IDs bear the names and addresses of two hundred VIP supporters who work the 7.00am to 7.00pm stint at Seagate and won't be able to vote until late that night. Incidentally, the photos on the licences are altered so that the shift-workers' own mothers wouldn't recognise them – which, of course, is the entire point.

"If anyone challenges you at the polling station," Jimmy tells the twenty volunteers, who are going to do ten booths each, "give them the middle name and date of birth.

"If they challenge you a second time, then they know you're not the real McCoy, so leave the polling booth immediately. Don't attempt to brazen it out, or you'll wind up in front of Letemout."

Voting is steady throughout the day, with the good weather giving Thomo a slight boost. Harry's supporters, it's assumed, are a lot less fair-weathered.

But come 10.00pm and the traditional close-of-poll riot, it's clear that, while the scoring will be tight, there is no stopping the machine, and Harry the Hurler will be returned to the Guildhall.

The count, unusually, starts at the Templemore Sports Complex that night, as soon as the last of the ballot boxes arrives under armed guard. And the only event of real controversy is the allocation of the spoilt votes. About a dozen or so of these make very smart remarks about Thomo, and Harry also gets a bit of a touch.

Three papers in particular irk him: the first reads, 'Harry the Hurler is a tout'; the second, 'Harry steals money from the Boys'; and the last one, 'Hurley plays away from home'.

"Big mistake to let Lorna vote that third time," Harry tells Jimmy.

*****

Well, as you know from the papers, Harry winds up elected with fifty-two per cent of the poll – despite the protests from Seagate, who are now demanding their own on-site polling station for all future elections. And things get better and better for Harry after that. On his first day as a councillor, his party meet at the Guildhall and, now they have the majority, duly appoint him mayor.

Immediately, Harry introduces an emergency motion stipulating that the mayor should get a five-year term. And this is passed convincingly after the VIPs are promised five-year stints as deputy-mayor and Chairman of the Tourism and Trips Abroad Committee.

A second proposal from Harry calling for the annexation of the west bank of the city is narrowly defeated by his own party when Dublin announce they will not pay out on Northern dole cheques.

And finally, right on schedule, Ten-Gun Tex arrives, slaps Harry's back and tells him he is a great guy. He even gets his visa.

"Tex and I have a lot in common," explains Harry to the table in the Monico Bar on the night he resigns as mayor. "Both of us have fathers who run our outfits before us, and both have daughters with a high regard for cheap cider and falling over. And apparently his brother knows a thing or two about how to swing a tight election as well. Though I, of course, have a majority."

"So why are you stepping down?" inquires Stammering Stan.

"Out of respect for Letemout Lou there," says Harry. "I am a man of my word. And I know how important that is to a lady – unlike some."

"So you're giving up office for good, solely on her advice?" asks Stan.

"You have it in one," replies Harry. "Some of us are happy to honour and obey. Isn't that right, Lou?"

"Yeah, yeah," responds Stan. "Find your phone yet, Harry?"

Though he only says this last part after Harry goes to the jacks.

*****

After the retirement party breaks up, Stan and Letemout head up the riverbank to Charlie's on Clarendon Street for a late one. It's a balmy summer evening, and dozens of couples are dotted about staring at the boats and the night sky. The pair rest their elbows on the embankment railings for a better look at a departing Oyster Catcher, with Letemout shouldering her way in close to Stan to escape an imaginary breeze.

"Very gracious of Harry to withdraw like that after only a week in office," says Stan. "There's me thinking he'll stay for the full five years."

"Never let the truth get in the way of a good story, Stan," sighs Letemout. "Harry would give his right arm to stay and is winding himself up for that full five-year term. He loves the limelight, he loves the notoriety and he loves the thought of playing with a much bigger train set.

"His mother even has the photo of him and Ten-Gun Tex up on the wall. And Lorna's dining out on stories of how she's going out to Florida to play golf with that dumpy little First Lady later in the year. No, Harry doesn't want to go at all. He's even talking about running as an MP. But happily for society, myself and Tommy Bowtie have him by the wee short hairs."

"How's that?" demands Stan.

"I can't tell you," replies Lou, aware that she's talking out of school. "Court stuff – suffice it to say, it's over."

"You have to tell," laughs Stan. "I'm a journalist. I can't help it. You know where the bodies are stashed? Isn't that it?"

"Hate to tell you this, Stan," says Lou, "but half the town already knows where the bodies are, and the other half don't care."

"Must be the cigarette importing then?" presses Stan. "Are you worried that he'll get caught with a smoking suitcase while he's in office?"

"Not in the least," snaps Lou. "Now, leave it."

"Help me out here," protests Stan, "you can't keep me on ice like this."

"The irony of that remark, if only you knew, Stan," quips Lou with a sharp glint. "Okay, I'll tell you. But if this gets out, I'll batter you to within an inch of your life. And not in a good way either."

"On my honour as a journalist," grins Stan.

"Well," continues Lou, "you know that escort service that Rex Tucker gets himself hooked up to? You'll never guess who owns it . . ."

"You're joking," gasps Stan, absent-mindedly taking Letemout's hand.

"Afraid not," says Lou. "The council auditor – on the High Court's instructions – is just after finishing his report on the money trail. And eight hundred pounds of the city's money – which comes via the credit card of the last First Citizen – is currently resting in a bank account belonging to the replacement mayor."

"Hard to believe," whistles Stan. "But even so, I'm sure Harry has enough smoke in the air to give himself plausible deniability."

"To the council, yes," replies Lou, "and to the court, definitely. But to Lorna and the Boys – no way. And when they hear what's paying for Harry's private pension, they'll be performing a few personal services on Harry himself – none of which are in the brochure.

"But Mr Hurley, as you know, is a pragmatic sort. So when all this is put to him, he wisely decides to make a virtue out of it and opts out at the top. Course, Stan, this is all totally on the q.t. If you repeat any of this, I will be in so much trouble they'll strike me off."

Unusually, Lou does look a little worried. So Stan muses over this for a minute, puts his hand in his pocket and produces a small box. He looks dead centre into Letemout Lou's eyes, hands her the little packet and smiles, "But isn't it in the rules somewhere that a husband can't testify against his wife?"

And Letemout Lou, all of a sudden, realises that perhaps for the first time in twenty-five years, Stan is after outsmarting her.

"Gotcha!" he laughs, putting his arm round her waist.

"You have indeed," she replies, kissing his cheek with a mouth that won't stop grinning. "And there's me thinking no-one is ever going to make an honest woman of me."

"Let's not get carried away altogether," says Stan, looking softly into her eyes. "After all, you're still going to be a lawyer, aren't you . . ."

THE CURTAIN FALLS ON SPARKLY

There is a very dark side to Susie 'Short-Shorts' Barkley, which, fortunately for her, remains mostly concealed by her blonde bobbed hair, adorable smiling face and long, lovely legs.

The High Court judge, Letemout Lou, knows her fiancé, Stammering Stan, has a soft spot for Susie and is also conscious that he's a good-looking boy who will sometimes bark a little too close to the buses. So now and again, Lou likes to throw him a subtle reminder to quit before he's run over.

"You ever see Fatal Attraction, Stan?" she asks him one night over two nicely burnt T-bones at the new Mange 2 steakhouse on Clarendon Street. "First thing that Glenn Close does when she gets the part is ring Susie Short-Shorts and ask for tips . . ."

"Hmm," says Stan carefully.

"Susie has a temper that you wouldn't believe," continues Lou. "Plates, knives, pencils, any sharp objects – when her blood's up, hide them. Though even Glenn doesn't believe the pet-rabbit story. As we speak, Sparkly has four separate protection orders out barring Susie from coming within five hundred yards of him or any of his many businesses. He only has to put his neb in the courtroom and the magistrate gives them to him right away.

"That's not saying Sparkly doesn't deserve what he gets. He goes through more fresh meat than Doherty's Butchers."

Stan is, of course, aware of the point of this story and nods soberly like a good groom-to-be.

"But aren't they back together again?" he asks Lou, pouring her a soothing glass of Morellini di Scansano.

"Temporarily at least," concedes Letemout, sipping the fine Chianti. "Thank God they've no children. Though from what I hear from Red Light Lorna, Sparkly's in the punishment block again. Apparently, he's doing more than window-shopping on his trip to London last weekend, and Susie is just after finding out."

"So who's the tout?" asks Stan a little nervously as he watches Lou expertly bite the flesh from her T-bone.

"The tout's actually a desk clerk at the London Hilton," laughs Letemout. "But it's entirely accidental.

"Sparkly's there for a vintners' conference. So Susie rings the hotel looking for him. Of course, the receptionist tells her that 'Mr and Mrs' Barkley are just after checking out . . ."

"Whoops," chuckles Stan.

"Whoops is right," grins Letemout. "Word is, it's going to cost Sparkly a brand new Mercedes Coupé for Susie and a whole lot more besides."

*****

From what Stan tells me later, Sparkly will pay for his London *faux pas* for a very long time. Originally, Susie is intending to re-stage the shower scene in Psycho, with her as Norman Bates. But happily, her mother calms her down and persuades her to serve the dish cold.

So instead, as part of his atonement, Sparkly must arrange and pay for a charity concert to put a new roof on Clooney Presbyterian Church, where Susie's Ma is organist.

Sparkly is not a man who travels to the Waterside too often during business hours ever since he first appears on Harry the Hurler's Well-Known Associates' list. And despite marrying Susie, Sparkly would normally rather cut his own throat than give money to the Planters. But given that these are precisely his options, he thinks again and agrees to organise the do.

First thing he needs is a compère. So he rings the Northern Broadcasting Corporation's Derry office and asks to be put through to the new morning presenter, Ruth Ball. Ruth lives just beside the church, and like any good radio wannabe, is only too delighted to oblige. And this suits Sparkly big time, since he's getting her for about a tenth of what he'd have to pay somebody decent like Gerry Anderson.

*****

Rule Number One of being a radio presenter is always assume that every mike is live – so never say anything that you wouldn't say in open court. Rule Number Two is never get anyone better than you to fill in for you when you're going off on a holiday. And Rule Number Three – and the most important rule of all – is trust nobody.

Fortunately for Ruth Ball, her predecessor in the mid-morning show at NBC, 'Clean' Jean Quigg, momentarily forgets rules number one and three, so leaving the morning slot open for her understudy on a full-time basis.

Up until now, Ruth is a DJ with the pirate station Cityside FM, which, although it doesn't pay very well, gives her a good grounding in the technical side of things. So when the opportunity comes up to stand in for Clean Jean for a couple of weeks with NBC, Ruth grabs it with both hands.

Clean Jean jets off to Lanzarote happy in the knowledge that Ruth couldn't tie her broadcasting shoes. Ruth, of course, can't present a programme worth a damn. She has a grating voice, reads like a robot, asks stupid questions of her guests and never listens to their answers. Oh, and her choice in music is pure North Antrim – if it's not country, it's western.

What Clean Jean doesn't appreciate, however, is that Ruth has other talents ready to deploy as soon as she gets her sheer silk stockings in the door. For one thing, Ruth knows exactly how to wear a tight blouse and high heels. For another, she's still in her mid-twenties and single, and for another, she has yet to meet a man with a pulse that she can't twist around her little finger.

Ruth's also aware that because there are way too few Planters in the local media, if she gets a foothold with NBC, she's going to be damn hard to shift. If only to keep the monthly quota of on-air Londonderrys out of single figures.

On the plus side, however, every woman who ever comes across Ruth hates her.

*****

On her first day back from sunning herself, Clean Jean is surprised and not entirely pleased to see that Ruth Ball is still in the building – as a locum producer on the mid-morning show. Jean, who has a cabinet full of trophies and likes things done a particular way, prefers to self-produce, so she pages the editor Ivan 'the Terrible' Coltroun for an explanation.

But Ivan simply informs her that Ruth is working on an entirely voluntary basis to get the experience – and at no cost to the station. Oh, and the bosses in Belfast are keen to do anything to help curtail the Fenian ratio, so suck it up.

Ivan fails to mention, however, how Ruth also brings him tea and croissants every morning that Clean Jean's off – and regularly uses the opportunity to tell him that he has the most masculine name in the dictionary. And do you know that Ivan means 'virile' in Russian?

He is also impressed by how clever Ruth finds him – particularly when the tape machine jams or the CD player sticks, and he knows just what button to push. Sadly, Ivan is completely unaware that it is Ruth who is pushing the buttons.

Now, part of a producer's job in a small station is to 'drive' the radio desk while the presenter concentrates on interviews and the like. And for the first week, Ruth has a few disasters – opening the wrong faders and mikes, and playing in the wrong clips and CD tracks. But she's a quick learner and by the end of the second week, she's an old hand.

More importantly for Ruth, she is breaking the habit of a lifetime and deploying her charm on Clean Jean – so much so that the two are now total gal-pals. They write scripts together, pick the music for the show together and lunch together, with Ruth only too happy to learn at the master's knee.

One morning, however, Jean comes into the studio, just before the sig tune is played, in the foulest of moods.

"I'm after going at it hammer and tongs with Ivan up the stairs," she says to Ruth. "Let's get this damn show over, and I'll tell you all about it at lunch."

The first hour goes off well enough – with Jean doing a professional job of containing her rage. But just after the ten o'clock break, Ruth has a pre-recorded interview to play, which lasts about fifteen minutes, so the two use the inter-studio talkback to dish out – and lap up – the gossip.

"Ivan's such a desperate sleaze," complains Ruth. "He's always getting me to practise on the new panel in the centre studio so he can watch me bending and stretching over the big desk."

"He knows better than to try it on with me again," retorts Jean. "About five years ago, back when he's drinking, he sticks his tongue in my mouth at the Christmas Party. But let me tell you, this girl has teeth. And Mr Coltroun gets to spend his holidays sucking milkshakes through a straw. No, the row's not about that. I'll tell you after the show."

"There's twelve minutes left of this tape," says Ruth. "Sure fire ahead."

"Strictly between ourselves," requests Jean, getting a reassuring nod, "I think that Ivan's supplying information to police intelligence.

"It's not unheard of in the media. Conservatively, I reckon that five per cent of journalists here in the North are working for one branch of the British Government or another. Bottom line, the Brits are always going to plant agents in news organisations. It only makes sense, given the sort of information we're privy to. It's happening here since the start of the Troubles and long before. But I don't think they try it so much in Derry as they do in Belfast – as we all tend to know one another and don't trust outsiders."

"So why do you think Ivan?" asks Ruth.

"Different reasons," replies Jean. "For example, some of the stories that appear on our programmes – and some of the ones that don't. Some of the people who are on air regularly, and some of the people who aren't. Nothing concrete really. Just a suspicion. Until today, that is . . ."

"What's so special about today?" presses Ruth.

"I'm after telling Ivan that I want to interview Jimmy 'Fidget' Hurley on his new book," explains Jean. "As you know, Jimmy's the man in charge now that Harry is retired as the horse's mouth, and he has quite a story to tell. Of course, the interview will have to be a 'phoner', because Jimmy's not really a guy who likes to appear in public view.

"But when I say this to Ivan, the sneaky toe-rag, he says there's a few guys who would be very keen to talk to Jimmy Fidget about a number of outstanding matters. And he suggests that I persuade Jimmy to come to the studio, do the interview, and he'll then be arrested outside as he comes off air. Great kudos for the station – as a liberal broadcaster prepared to talk to Jimmy Hurley – then a big furore as the bad guys swoop in and snatch him."

But before Jean can tell Ruth how she responds to Ivan's offer, all of a sudden Ivan himself is standing in front of her at the door of the studio, his face black with anger. He viciously snaps up the central power switch in the studio – putting the station completely off air – and then sacks Jean on the spot.

Ruth, it seems, is after accidentally leaving Jean's mike on pre-fade since the ten o'clock news, and Ivan the Terrible is now outed as a spy to the 15,000 or so morning listeners.

Fortunately for Ruth, however, her own mike is off during all this time. And after making the appropriate sympathetic noises to Ivan, and assuring him she never believes a word of Jean's terrible smear, she is appointed new full-time presenter for the morning slot.

The following day, the new host then attempts to show her sense of fun by re-christening herself Ruth 'Havana' Ball.

But the rest of the station are wise to her by now and simply call her Buster.

*****

Sparkly spends the next three weeks putting his heart, soul and cheque-book into the charity concert, which is to be held at the new state-of-the-art Waterside Theatre on Glendermott Road.

He even phones Switchblade Vic to ensure that his presence across the bridge won't cause undue offence. And, of course, he plays up the cross-community nature of the event in the local press.

"Want us to say that you're doing all this to atone for your sins against your wife and all other Planters?" Stammering Stan asks him when he visits the *Derry Standard* offices to place an ad.

"Something a bit more subtle," laughs Sparkly. "Hype up the fact Buster is hosting it, and that the Ulster-Scots mob will be doing wonderful things with bagpipes."

*****

The night itself is magical. Sparkly persuades Derry's Greatest Living Export, the raunchy rapper Missy Gelignite, to cancel a gig in London and travel home for three songs – which turns into six. As it's a church function, Missy is warned to wear a pair of trousers, so breaking the hearts of the first six or seven rows. But thankfully, her strapless top is more than enough to send the Young Farmers' deputation home with a few plans.

The Riverside Showband cruise through a medley of upbeat fifties' hits, and pull off the coup of the night when Country star Shugo Kirwin, who's after sneaking in the back door, takes to the stage for a song with them.

The East Bank Accordion and Pipe Band keep their contribution mercifully short – but just long enough to ensure the bar does a roaring trade.

And the comedian Knock-Knock Noel, who's on his way across town for a late gig at the PO Club, stops in long enough to insult every district in the Waterside.

"Woman at the Top of the Hill," says Noel, "calls all six of her youngsters the one name – Seamus. So I says to her, what if you're calling them in for their tea, what do you shout?"

"I just shout Seamus," says she, "and they all come."

"But what if you want to talk to one of them individually?" says I.

"Easy," says she, "in that case I just call them by their surname."

Even Buster Ball rises to the occasion, and she carries off her MC duties with something approaching panache. She is helped enormously by the fact that Sparkly pays for an elocution expert to come in and put her through her lines. And as an insurance policy, she is also wearing a killer red mini-dress, which ensures that exactly one half of the audience won't notice her stumbles.

Then, just after 10.30pm, a helicopter touches down in the theatre car park and out hops the tenor Pretty Jim Jameson, fresh from the Waterfront stage in Belfast, to perform a series of numbers from his new musical *My Caledonia Home*. It is the cap on a very special evening.

After the finale, Sparkly himself takes to the stage to pay a stirring vote of thanks to all the participants and to his wife Susie for her commitment to the church.

"I see Switchblade Vic in here at the back," he tells the cheering audience. "Well, Vic, if this is what it means to be loyal, then I'm signing up tonight . . .

"Sincerely, it's great that people from all over the city and both communities can get together for such a good cause. I'm leaving here tonight with hundreds of new friends. It's magnificent. And it's all down to my wife, the very beautiful Susan Barkley, the most wonderful wife any man could wish for. I don't deserve her – and am so glad and so proud she's mine and no-one else's. I'd just like to say in front of everyone in here tonight, I love you more than life itself, Susie. You are the only woman in the world for me."

Well, Susie's eyes are full of tears at this mush, and she blows a kiss at Sparkly who then winds things up, sending everyone home happy.

Yes, the night itself is magical and, indeed, would be entirely perfect – but for one small detail. Our genial host, Sparkly Barkley, is waiting at the traffic lights at Craigavon Bridge on his way home, when someone steps out of a doorway and shoots him dead.

Two bullets are lodged in his rotten little heart and a small white card, bearing just one word – Hypocrite – is found under the wiper of his BMW.

*****

The whole town, as you can imagine, is gripped by panic at the whacking of such a high-profile name. Harry the Hurler and his seconds convene an immediate meeting at their Chamberlain Street offices that night, while across the river in Drumahoe, Switchblade Vic closes the Sash & Drum to all but a select group of very serious men.

The police sergeant, Jack 'the Black' Gilmore, is put in temporary charge of the investigation – a shrewd move by his commander, who is well aware that Jack, as Harry's brother-in-law, is possibly the only man in the city who can negotiate between the two camps.

Understandably, however, Harry is in little form for accepting Vic's assurances that bumping off Sparkly is not his idea. By no means and not at all.

"It's his turf – it's his doing," says Harry to Jack. "At the very least, he knows all about it and is keeping a lid on it."

"We're ruling out nothing, and ruling in nothing," says Jack. "And let's not forget that Susie Short-Shorts is still very much in the running. She already has two different Actual Bodily Harm charges on her sheet against Sparkly. But Doc Clancy says she's in severe shock and we can't talk to her until the jag wears off in about twelve hours time. In the meantime, hold your fire, Harry."

"Jack's right," says Tommy Bowtie. "And if the cops decide to start questioning jealous husbands, we'll be waiting a whole lot longer again. They'll have to recruit an entire new night shift."

Harry smiles – knowing full well that three years ago, he himself is top of that jealous husbands list.

"Okay, Jack," he says, "tell Vic we'll do nothing till the dust settles. But if we find out it's him, he won't see us coming."

*****

For a while, speculation about Sparkly's murder takes up acres of space in the local and national press. But by the time the week's out, the headlines are smaller and interest dimmer, as people get on with their lives.

Conventional wisdom agrees with Tommy Bowtie's assessment – that Sparkly is probably plugged by an angry spouse. And there's a growing consensus that Switchblade Vic is way too smart to knock out Harry the Hurler's number one financier.

Susie Short-Shorts, meanwhile, is largely discounted on the grounds that she is so teary-eyed and loving after Sparkly's declarations on the night of the shooting. Though with the gunman at large, doubts still remain about her. Her grief appears genuine enough, however. Indeed, she spends the entire three days of the wake sobbing over Sparkly's casket and crying how she wants to go with him. Though she perks up a little, however, when she hears that NBC intend to broadcast the entire charity concert as a tribute to Sparkly – including his last great speech to her.

*****

Ten years ago, all programmes at NBC are recorded on, and broadcast from, quarter-inch reels. Today everything is edited digitally – a process that is clean, quick and very simple to learn. It also allows you to enhance your recording with little difficulty, either by making dialogue clearer and crisper, adding on additional tracks, or by removing extraneous sounds. Unfortunately, if anything goes wrong with the digital machinery, it can lead to disaster. And you can be left with nothing but fresh air to broadcast if someone unintentionally hits the Delete key instead of the Save.

All of which is why the designers now install gizmos in all the new machines, which automatically save the producer's edits every ninety seconds or so. And it is thanks precisely to this gizmo that NBC are able to air their three-hour Sparkly tribute last Saturday night, despite a power outage earlier in the day.

And it is also why Buster Ball is handed her cards by the station in the small hours of Sunday morning.

To be honest, there are maybe only one hundred people in the city who are listening to the concert along with Susie Shorts on Saturday night. So, like myself, you probably only know about it from hearing Stammering Stan's tape of it, or from reading about it in the *Derry Standard*.

Anyhow, because of the technical glitch, when the 180 minutes of song, comedy, speeches and bagpipes are coming to an end, instead of tailing off into the finale as planned, the next-to-last saved version of the concert is played rather than the last.

And unfortunately, some behind-the-scenes chit-chat from the dressing-rooms inadvertently goes out on air. Indeed, it appears that this chit-chat takes place in Buster's room – with Buster enjoying the starring role, as she is the only one whose radio mike is on.

"You're looking very well in that tux, my one true love," she says. "Very manly. Do you know that you have the most virile of all names?"

Another voice can be heard laughing and saying something back, but even after listening to it three times, I have to say it's too muffled to make out.

A door can then be heard being closed and a bolt is slid into place.

"So why don't you step out of that smoking jacket and see if you can find anything else that's smoking instead?" giggles Buster flirtatiously. "Do you see Susie Short-Shorts out there prancing about like she's Lady Patron Of The Arts? The only reason she's not number one slag in Derry is 'cause her husband already holds down the job. Ha! Ha!

"You like this garter? I'm only wearing it to wind up the Presbyterians. Po-faced bunch of do-gooders – almost as bad as the Fenians . . .

"Nice boxers – silk. Mmm. I like silk on you – almost as much as I like skin . . .

"If those donkeys up at NBC could see us now they'd die. Not that I'll have to look at them much longer – after I knock them dead at that audition you're getting for me in London. TV is definitely my medium – there's no point wasting this face on the thick Derry public . . . Oh thank you so much . . ."

This dialogue is then followed by a long series of assorted pants and grunting noises not publishable in a family newspaper, before being rudely interrupted by Ivan the Terrible rushing into the studio and knocking the programme – and the station – off the air.

*****

Ivan himself is lucky to hold onto his job – on two counts if you ask me. First, he's ultimately responsible for what goes out on NBC's airwaves. And secondly, although his voice isn't audible, he's clearly the other player in the dressing-room drama.

"Not so," says Stammering Stan, as he brings me up to speed on the drama in Charlie's Bar. "Indeed it is Ivan the Terrible who himself gives the full unedited version of the recording to Harry the Hurler."

"Why would he do that?" I inquire.

"Well," replies Stan, "Ivan owes Harry for trying to set up Jimmy Fidget for the gendarmes. Everyone knows Ivan's not a spy – he's just trying to put his radio station centre stage and get people excited. And let's face it, if Jimmy is stupid enough to go into a studio and start talking all about the good old days, he deserves to be hauled off to the chokey.

"But by bringing the full tape of the concert to Harry, Ivan is able to show him who exactly is to blame for whacking Sparkly."

230

"What do you mean?" I ask. "Is there more on the tape that we don't know about?"

"Totally off the record," says Stanley, "Ivan himself is the guy who produces the Sparkly tribute show for the wireless. And, of course, when he gets the recordings back from the theatre, he realises that Buster Ball is starring in Last Tango in Paris, the radio version. But Ivan is very peeved that it is not him who is playing the Marlon Brando role. So he decides to fade out the other star performer's voice – and then take the tape to the NBC Board of Governors and have Buster fired.

"Now, the shenanigans backstage are actually taking place before the concert. But Ivan's a bit of a novice at the digital technology. And when he's attempting to separate all the huffing and puffing into a different file from the concert, he inadvertently manages to attach them to the end of the programme instead. Though maybe that's just what he's saying now. We will never know.

"Harry, however, now has the full director's cut. And on it you can hear, clear as day, Buster instructing her companion – who I'm sure you know by now is Sparkly Barkley – that he better make good on his promise to leave his wife and move to London with her. And when Sparkly says no, you can hear all manner of threats which are not very ladylike and in language not at all suitable for the radio."

"Such as 'I'll shoot you dead'," I venture.

"You know, yourself," says Stan, "women say all sorts of things in temper. Though most of them do not have gun licences, thank God.

"What I do know is this – Harry is now completely satisfied that Vic isn't involved in Sparkly's demise, and is prepared to put round a yarn that it is all down to some renegade outfit, who Vic is going to deal with. This will also spare Mrs Barkley's feelings a lot more than a show trial. And you never know who could be dragged into something like that."

"So what about Buster?" I ask.

"Oh," says Stan, "she's out of the country. Gone for good.

"But from what I'm hearing, she's after playing a blinder at the audition in London – and will be starting as a Children's TV presenter next month."

LOST AT SEA

The new car-ferry across Lough Swilly to Rathmullan is after opening this particular summer, and half of Derry are heading the thirteen miles down to Buncrana Pier to use it.

Among those persons are Harry the Hurler, who is keen to revisit some boyhood memories, and Stammering Stan the Radio Man, whose people are buried in Rathmullan graveyard.

"Back when my old Da is still with us," says Harry to Stan as they roll the dark blue Mercedes down the slipway, "there's this passenger ferry from just down the road there at Fahan. And for Dominic, there's no better way to spend a summer day than cruising along Lough Swilly, past the Inch Island beaches and along the south Fanad shoreline on your way to a pint of the black stuff at Rathmullan House Hotel.

"Anyway, this day we're going across and in this cove just off Inch there is a little boat fishing the dead body of a swimmer out of the water. And Old Dom, who knows everything, uses the scene to explain to me the meaning of irony.

"There is this lifeguard, he tells me, who for years and years warns everyone against trying to swim the four miles or so from Fahan to Rathmullan. 'There are too many channels – and they are far too strong,' says the lifeguard. 'You would need to be a crazy fool to try and swim across. Don't ever do it.'

"'That lifeguard is a very smart man,' I say to Dad. 'And I would imagine that the guy lying with the blue lips on the deck of that row-boat would be thinking the same.'

"'I doubt that,' Dom says to me, a big grin on his face. 'The captain here is after telling me that the lifeguard is missing for eight days now, and the corpse in the dinghy is a dead ringer for him.'

"'It is a good reminder,' says Dom, 'that no matter who you are, you are never as clever as you think you are.'"

*****

As the Foyle Rambler hauls anchor for the twenty-five-minute trip, Harry and Stan get out of the Merc and into the sun for a better look at the stunning views of the Inishowen peninsula behind them.

The departing shoreline has a series of long sandy beaches, bordered by dozens of chalets, most of which started life as little more than tin huts for Derry tourists but which now change hands for 200,000 euros and up. Also dotting the landscape you have hotels, factories and Lisfannon Golf Club, still waging a valiant war against the encroaching Swilly tide. All sitting under forested green mountains. And to the far right as they look back – hard starboard, stresses Harry – there's Inch Island and the finest colony of wild birds anywhere in Donegal.

"Somewhere underneath there," says Stan, leaning over the rail and pointing at a buoy out in the middle of the lough, "is the wreck of the *SS Laurentic* – this World War One British Navy vessel. Apparently it's carrying this big cargo of gold over to Canada to buy munitions when it gets caught up in this storm. So it comes into Lough Swilly to shelter – but winds up sinking anyway. From what I remember, most of the gold is long recovered – but according to the records, there's still a few bars on the seabed."

"Yeah," says Harry, eyeing Stan dead centre, "twenty-two of them to be precise."

"It's interesting you knowing that," grins Stan back at Harry.

"Don't play cute with me, Stan," retorts Harry. "The whole town and half the country reckon those twenty-two bars are lying in the bottom of my wardrobe. But sure I get the blame for everything from the crucifixion to Abe Lincoln."

Stan knows better than to press a man like Harry the Hurler when he doesn't want to be pressed – but equally he knows how to appeal to his vanity.

"They say those missing bars are worth almost five million quid now . . ." mutters Stan to no-one in particular.

"Try fourteen million – or six hundred and forty thousand a bar," snaps Harry impatiently. "The whole consignment is worth about two billion in today's money. Okay, and yes, I know I little about it. And yes, at one stage, there's an attempt to locate the missing bars – quietly. But sadly, there's no Tuscan ranch on my horizon – unless Sparkly Barkley, God rest him, leaves me one in his will.

"Bottom line is, the Guards down here are too damn crafty and see us coming a mile off."

Stan, of course, knows all this but is busy chipping away for a gold nugget of his own.

"Yeah," he says to Harry, "and sure you could never find anything down there anyway. It's too dark, for one – and the seabed is so churned up over the years that any gold bars are probably lying under eight feet of muck and silt. The way I hear it, the wreck is spread over about a square mile. It'd be like looking for a holy medal in an Orange graveyard."

"Good point," replies Harry. "But again totally wrong."

He then sighs a big sigh and grins at his travelling companion. "Okay, Stan, you can stop busting my chops," he says. "I will tell you the story. But you know the rules. If I hear it back to me in any guise, I will personally row you back to this very spot, attach rocks to your legs and throw you in. Okey-dokey?"

"Fire ahead," laughs Stan, wondering if he'll be allowed a set of armbands.

A grand total of 3,200 ingots are lost from the *Laurentic* when it goes down in 1917, explains Harry, but most of them are located by navy divers within a few weeks. Later, in the 1960s, another couple of bars are found – within a few metres of the original wreck site. But then that whole patch of the seabed is bought over by a professional salvage team, so no-one is allowed to dive there without express permission.

Anyone diving on the site since then is subject to strict conditions, foremost of which is – you find something, you give it to the salvage people and they alert the authorities. But this is strictly not what Eamonn 'Clarence' Mallon has in mind eight years ago when he asks Harry if he fancies a midnight dip in Lough Swilly.

"Truth is, I'm never a particular fan of Clarence," says Harry. "I am a long-time believer that his eyes are not the only thing about him that's crooked. Growing up, he's always tortured about being ugly. But because of his eyesight, he doesn't like to fight. Then, as he gets older, and people work out that he has no particular interest in girls, his life becomes pretty intolerable altogether.

"So I suppose what I'm saying is that he's all too easy for us to reel in. He's desperate to be accepted by anyone. So one day when we need a driver and he's sitting doing nothing, we tap him up.

"After a few months, he graduates to one of the Chastisement Committees, which is where I first become aware of his nasty streak. This young cub, who is due a visit for stealing cars, is a demon for shouting abuse after Clarence in the street. So while this wee fella is getting his knees seen to – bats only, the guns are long gone – Clarence takes out a home-made knuckle-duster and knocks four teeth out of the guy's top jaw. He then hits him another thump that knocks three teeth from the bottom jaw. 'Don't believe what they say 'bout names never hurting you,' says Clarence – and the boy eventually needs a coupla operations to put things right."

When Clarence first bounces Harry with his proposal for an underwater bank robbery, he is laughed right out of court. But then Harry happens to mention the scheme to Mickey 'Bangers' Johnston – a former demolition expert for the revolution who is now a senior engineer with the city council. And Mickey, who is a very serious individual, says the plan might have merit.

"So after seeing a plan of the ship and getting the co-ordinates of where it goes down," explains Harry, "Mickey Bangers reckons he has a fair idea of where the gold might be. At least he thinks he can narrow the search area down to a one-hundred-metre-square area of seabed, which isn't altogether unreasonable, given that there's fourteen million clams at stake. So I talk to my brother Gerry, who does a bit of sub-aqua diving when he's on holiday, and he says, 'Why not? It'll hardly cost much.' So we decide to put a squad together.

"Mickey Bangers, of course, is in as team leader. He also has a little motor boat and, like Gerry the Hurler, he knows a bit about scuba diving. Jimmy Fidget, who spends all his spare time fishing in his little boat at Fullerton Dam, volunteers as pilot. And our final man is Getemup Gormley, who's a champion swimmer when he's at school – and very knowledgeable about water pressures, scuba gear and generally how to avoid floating up with next week's fish.

"I myself don't fancy the idea of playing hunt-the-thimble forty metres under the sea – I'm a little claustrophobic. So I volunteer to secure the boat with Jimmy and scout out for spectators, while the others are down below."

Obviously Harry has no intentions of including Clarence in the team. But about a week before the kick-off, Clarence sees Gerry the Hurler leaving JJB Sports with three pairs of flippers under his arm – and some serious finger-pointing ensues. So after some haggling, Harry admits

Clarence to the squad. But it turns out that Clarence is no liability – and is quite a hand at this scuba lark.

"Apparently he goes out quite a bit with the Muff Sub-Aqua Club," says Harry. "That's how he comes up with the plan. They go all the time to the Armada wrecks on Kinnego Bay – though, needless to say, the likes of the *Laurentic* is off limits. In fact, Clarence knows a lot more about diving than all the others, so he'll take the lead under the water.

"So this dark summer night we set off for Lough Swilly in two vans. Clarence and Mickey Bangers make sure the gear is okay – suits, tanks, underwater spotlights, metal detectors, metallurgy kits, and so on. The whole shooting match costs just under fifty big notes.

"We're all also carrying fishing gear, of course, to keep the local snoops off our back, and there's even a harpoon gun in case we run into any warm water sharks, though personally, I think Jimmy Fidget's being way too cautious."

Stammering Stan is privately of the opinion that the harpoon gun is not the only weapon in the armoury but is, of course, much too discreet to say so. So instead, he asks Harry what happens next.

"We launch the boat from Fahan, and when we get to the dive site they all drop off the side – leaving myself and Jimmy sitting in the complete pitch dark," he explains. "There's absolutely no moon in the sky and obviously we have no lights on – though we can see the odd house lit up and the odd car moving on the Lisfannon shore there. There's also a bit of light from the seabed where the underwater spotlight is shining, but nothing you'd see from land.

"Anyhow, the whole thing takes hours and hours. And we're just sitting there – not talking. Jimmy can't even smoke. Now and again, one of the four divers will come up for a break and a change of oxygen tank. But it's all done in the quiet.

"Then shortly before dawn, Clarence and Mickey surface together, silently punching the air. They have something. Mickey signals 'four' with his fingers, and he and Clarence between them hoist this bulging dive pouch onto the deck. And sure enough, there are four bars inside.

"The four of us are smiling till our faces hurt. It is like the Brits pulling out of Ireland on Christmas Day, and Orange Jilly taking off all her clothes to celebrate. Jimmy jokes that we could maybe drive off and leave Gerry and Getemup under the water where they are – to keep the cut at one bar each. But he is overruled on the grounds that Getemup would only hunt us down and kill us. So we haul them up, and within minutes, all six of us are lying on the boat kicking up our feet.

"We point the boat back to Fahan – but then someone notices some strange lights at the pier there, so we decide to head on into Rathmullan, where there's an old pal of Dom's who can put us up for the night."

*****

The Foyle Rambler is by now just about a half-mile out from Rathmullan Harbour, and the engines are getting noisier as the captain manoeuvres the boat into the home channel. Stan is dying to ask the question about what happens to Clarence, but knows that this is not an area where Harry can be rushed.

"Sadly," sighs Harry at last, "if you have six Derrymen in a boat, you can be pretty sure that one of them is in the process of selling out the other five. And as Mickey's little boat is cruising quietly into Rathmullan, all of a sudden these blue and white lights start flashing just under the pier, and a spotlight begins searching the sea in front of us.

"We're a little further out than we are now – but have no chance of outrunning the Guards. On the prow of their boat is this massive machine gun, which, by the look of it, could fill us with more holes than the city cemetery. So we cut the motor and wait for the inevitable.

"It is obvious to all of us that Clarence is the plant. Me and the brothers are all ex-lifers – as is Getemup, and Mickey Bangers has way too much to lose. So I look right into his face and ask him just one word, 'Why?'

"Tragically, I will never know the answer. Because, before you can blink, Clarence snatches the pouch from the deck, sticks it inside his wet-suit, and dives over the side. He starts trying to swim towards Rathmullan. But he's no chance with that bag on him – so we shout to him to come back. It's not worth dying for.

"And to be honest, we're not going to harm him. These things happen – and the worst the Guards can do is hold us for a few months before Tommy Bowtie proves entrapment. But as you know, Stan, poor Clarence is found floating toes up just off Rathmullan beach ten days later, God rest him. His body is pretty mashed up because of the rocks and the scavengers, but there's no doubting it's him."

"So what about the bars?" asks Stan, after a decent pause.

"I presume they're still down there somewhere," replies Harry. "We certainly can't take the chance of going back. And anyway, we'd never find where Clarence goes down.

"The Garda, of course, trawl the seabed for weeks afterwards – all on the q.t. But it's far too widespread an area. And as luck would have it, they never find any of our scuba gear either, which means that for all they can prove, we are indeed late-night poachers out looking for some wild salmon. Even the autopsy finds that, in the absence of any other available evidence, we must accept that Clarence is drowned in a fishing accident.

"Still, it was a great dream. And for five whole minutes, the six of us are millionaires. And let me tell you, I'll not swap those five minutes for the rest of my life."

The Rambler docks slowly at Rathmullan Pier, and the two men get back into the Merc and drive up in silence to the main road, where Stammering Stan gets out. He plans to visit the Flight of the Earls centre at the quayside and also intends to take a look at the old castle graveyard where a couple of ancestors are sleeping.

Harry is meeting his brothers at the Rathmullan House Hotel for a pint – though can't invite Stan to join them, as they have a bit of business to sort out. And Stan is happy to be party to as little Hurley family business as possible. Anyhow, the boys intend to stay overnight at a pal's chalet. But Stan is expected back promptly on the 5.40pm ferry, and his fiancée, Letemout Lou, is not a girl to keep waiting.

"Not a word about any of this, of course," says Harry to Stan as he zips up the passenger window.

"You know me," grins Stan. "Too scared to open my mouth."

Harry the Hurler smiles back, then disappears up the road towards the hotel.

*****

A few hours later, Stan finds himself a little early for the ferry home, so he opts for a pint of stout in the Beachcomber Bar, just round the corner from the pier. And he is sitting in the picture window, admiring the magnificent panorama of the bay, when who plonks himself in the seat opposite but Jack 'the Black' Gilmore, Strand Road desk sergeant and reluctant brother-in-law of Harry the Hurler.

"Your health," says Jack, clinking his Smithwicks off Stan's glass.

"My, but it's a small world," replies Stan, remembering that it's now okay for him to be seen talking to cops.

"Wouldn't want to paint it," quips Jack. "You shouldn't be surprised, but. We holiday here quite a bit, now I'm allowed to visit. Donna, like the rest of the Hurleys, is a regular here ever since she's a baby.

"Unfortunately, I have to go back tonight – half the shift are out on the sick as per usual. And the other half are so wet behind the ears they couldn't find their zipper with both hands and a metal detector."

Stan laughs at how the transition to normal policing is playing out at the coalface – and then points out the window at a child skimming stones down on the rocks.

"Isn't that where Clarence Mallon washes up?" he asks Jack, casually.

"Roughly," answers Jack carefully.

"Pretty crazy to be out poaching like that on so dark a night," persists Stan, curious.

"He is not the only one fishing about here," laughs Jack, wagging his finger at Stan. "I fancy, maybe, that you know a little more than you are letting on, Stanley. Though that is nothing new. But it's a bit public here. Maybe we'll have a natter on the boat on the way home."

Both Stan and Jack have their cars at Buncrana pier, so they can embark as foot passengers at three euros a head. It's quiet, so they easily find themselves an empty two-man railing at the back left corner of the ferry, which is also a bit of a suntrap.

"Is Clarence really one of yours, then?" asks Stan as the Foyle Rambler pulls out past the little oyster farm, just off the beach.

"Strictly between ourselves," concedes Jack, "yes, Clarence is our guy. Though to this day, I am ashamed of the whole mess.

"There is a very dirty side to our job, Stan, which I'm sure you know all about. Policing is all about control. Cops are basically glorified bouncers who keep order using threats, extortion and retribution. What it boils down to is that we are professional blackmailers – and to do the job properly, we must always have the edge. It is never about me dropping a drink-driving case against you for you to tell me who is throwing litter. I want to know who has guns in their kitchen. If I catch you with an ounce of dope in your pocket, I'm not interested in who has an eighth – you have to give me the guy who's dealing in kilos and tonnes. And, once I have you, you are always small fry which I will use as bait to catch bigger and bigger sharks.

"But the bottom line is I don't want to prosecute you, I'm much happier owning you. If you're a publican who's serving late, then perhaps I'll let you keep your licence if you keep me up to speed on the loose talk around the bar. If you are a headmaster stealing from the building fund, I'll turn the other way if you tell me who's selling tablets in your sixth form – and who's buying. And, say, if you're a newspaper man who, for example, gets a guy to burn his old car for the insurance, I might give you a bye-ball if you agree not to write lies about my colleagues for a while, or even perhaps the truth."

Stan has a flashback to the fire that engulfs his old wreck of a Datsun Stanza five years back, and a chill passes through him.

Jack grins like a wolf then shrugs at Stan not to worry.

"Never trust a policeman who's still warm," chuckles Jack with a wink. "The point is, Stan, there's virtually no-one we can't own if we put our heads to it. Take your straight up-and-down neighbourhood do-gooder. Taxes his car a month in advance and never walks on the cracks in the pavement. So you get this customer to feed you a few pieces about petty crime in his area. But when the really hard men are up to something, he doesn't want to know you. So you point out to him that if he doesn't give it up, the whole street's going to know he's a tout. And all of a sudden, he's nowhere to go.

"But the real parties take place in our office when we catch ourselves a lawyer. There's nothing worse than going into court and being made a reel of by some smart-arse shiny-suited solicitor. So when we find one maybe peeing in an alley, he's looking at five counts of indecent exposure unless he learns some serious manners very quickly. And take it from me, they all learn.

"Recruiting Clarence Mallon is like shooting a fish in the freezer. His attic is full of boys-only magazines, so during a raid we look at one closely and inform him that two of these lads in the photos are under sixteen. Another guy is serving two years for this self-same picture book. We're winging it, of course, but as far as Clarence is concerned, it's the end of the world. So when we ask him to help us out in other matters, in return for our complete silence, he signs up on the spot."

Clarence, to be honest, is a pretty poor informer as his access to good information is limited. Sure enough, he can drive some big sneezes to meetings – and he can see who else is going inside, but he is always left sitting out in the car. And the Boys tend not to talk at all in their cars, after they discover that a number of impounded taxis are returned complete with listening devices installed in their roofs.

But this particular day, when the owners of the *Laurentic* are in the paper explaining how they are trying to get an old safe out of the wreck, Clarence mentions to his Special Branch handlers how he himself enjoys a bit of diving. But the cops' ears really prick up when he also tells them that there is more than just a safe lying in the *Laurentic*. Indeed, Clarence reckons there's still more than £10 million in gold bars lying in the sand.

The Derry Special Branch see the potential for a sting, so they get Clarence to drop the idea into Harry's ear. The Branch's plan is to link up with their colleagues in Donegal and together net a few top characters – and maybe a bucket of gold besides. So they wire off their good pal, Garda Inspector Dennis 'Goosey' Lucey, and Goosey counts himself in.

Both police forces are pretty sure that even if Harry and Co find nothing, they will be able to hang a swathe of piracy charges on the conspirators, which will knock a few holes in the Boys' political hide.

Harry the Hurler's problem is, of course, that he has now too much time on his hands since things are so quiet, and he can't turn down a bit of rakery. So the plan gets the go-ahead, and everything goes swimmingly. Indeed, the cops even make sure their man gets on the diving team by keeping tabs on Jimmy Fidget so Clarence can catch him coming out of the sports shop.

"Course, Goosey then goes and blows the whole set-up by launching the patrol boat before the guys hit Rathmullan Harbour," says Jack. "The timing couldn't be worse. By the time they pick up Harry's boat, Clarence is gone, and all the diving gear is lying on the bottom of the sea. Ourselves and Harry do a private deal to write off Clarence as a fishing accident – they don't want to appear like suckers, and we don't want to admit our guy is caught."

"So what about the gold?" asks Stan.

"Far as we know, there is no gold," laughs Jack.

"So why are the Guards so keen to sweep the Swilly bed for weeks afterwards?" persists Stan.

"Interesting you knowing that – given that it's a totally secret operation," laughs Jack. "Well, very much off the record, yes, we know there has to be gold on Mickey Bangers' boat as soon as we see it heading for Rathmullan. Clarence is under strict instructions to divert the team there if, by some miracle, they're successful.

"If they find nothing, they'll continue back to Fahan, where they'll get done with attempted piracy. But if they actually strike gold, it'll mean all manner of other robbery and conspiracy charges, so we'll lift them at Rathmullan. It's a bit more private and further from the border – Fahan has too many boats coming in and out, and there's a chance someone will see us and wire the Boys off.

"But by the time we hit the boat at Rathmullan, it's empty – not so much as a diving belt. Harry and the others are saying absolutely nothing, and within ten minutes, Tommy Bowtie is on the blower, screaming false arrest. So we've no option but to let them go."

*****

The channel into Buncrana Pier is a lot narrower than the one into Rathmullan, so the Rambler begins its docking manoeuvres from about a mile out.

Stammering Stan and Jack the Black look over the rail at the shadows of the Swilly and remark on the hundreds of jellyfish swimming past, which Jack reckons is a sign of a good summer.

"In the end, I suppose poor Clarence has only himself to blame," suggests Stan as the ferry straightens up for its last run in.

"What?" asks Jack. "For talking to us?"

"No," replies Stan, taking the bait, "for trying to swim to shore."

"Come off it," says Jack, "you really think Harry and his brothers are going to let a guy like Clarence grab three million pounds and jump into the sea with it?"

"But where is the gold, so?" presses Stan. "It's not on the boat."

"Well, I don't know for sure," continues Jack. "But I would imagine the four bars – and I know there are four from a fence we have in Belfast – are securely fixed into Clarence's pockets when the Boys chuck him off the boat about a mile out from Rathmullan pier."

"So how come the body is able to float up – and without the bars?" asks Stan.

"I have no idea," replies Jack. "Nor have I any idea why no questions are asked about the harpoon marks that go in one side of Clarence's neck and out the other. But what I do know is that, by a happy coincidence, exactly three months after all this excitement, a brother of Old Dom Hurley dies in America and leaves the three Hurley brothers enough money to build a luxury holiday home each outside Rathmullan.

"Indeed, I myself am after enjoying one hell of a week drinking from Harry's private bar and lounging in his jacuzzi."

"So where exactly are these palaces?" asks Stan, shaking his head, not for the first time, at how little he knows.

"Just off the main road to Ramelton," replies Jack. "Goosey Lucey has one up behind them – also courtesy of an American uncle – though his has an indoor swimming pool as well . . ."

HOSTILE TAKEOVER

It is a sunny August day in Derry, and all is right with the world, now the marching season is over. Well, mostly right, that is – unless you happen to be Stammering Stan the Newspaper Man, who is pining pathetically after his former bride-to-be, the High Court judge, Letemout Lou.

Lou, you may know, is after dumping Stan like snot off a nail to hook up with ex-jockey Barry 'King Size' Barkley. And while King Size may be just four foot three in his lifts, he is now the richest man in the city since his late Uncle Sparkly leaves him the farm. He's also five years younger than Stan – and as flash with the cash as Stan is cheap. Both attributes which impress Lou no end.

In time-honoured fashion, Stan is now filling the void with pints of the Oscar Wilde Bar's finest painkiller and bitching to the pub's new owner, Danny Boy Gillespie, about his midget rival.

"As my old man always says," sighs Stan, "never trust a jockey with bad breath. Nor indeed any other sort of breath."

Danny Boy laughs, but mainly out of politeness for his customer's money. Though he is entirely in agreement with the sentiment. Indeed, his own experience of King Size is that he is indeed a twisted little dwarf, who has no business cosying up to Letemout. And Danny – like most of the newspaper-buying public – also knows that the nephew is very much from the same bloodstock as the late, unlamented Sparkly when it comes to shady business.

"Do you know," Stan tells Danny, "that when King Size is a jockey down in Kildare, he's at the centre of this big investigation into race fixing?

"Apparently, he has this wonder horse, Star Face – named on account of this big white diamond on its snout. On its first year out, the horse wins everything, but then, just before the new season kicks off, it dies tragically in a training accident. No-one's really sure what happens – but there's general devastation in the stable.

"The day the new season opens, however, King Size gets a new mount for the Novices Cup at Thurles – a horse called Blackout. Couple of people come to watch it training – but no-one fancies it much, and it goes into the race at fifteens. Then, just before the off, Sparkly Barkley, God rest him, goes into Paddy Power's Bookies in Grafton Street in Dublin and manages to get ten grand on Blackout on the nose. And the horse, of course, wins at a canter.

"But the questions start when they get back into the weighing room and a couple of other jockeys remark that Blackout is the spitting image of Star Face – except for the diamond on the nose, which is missing."

"Aha!" interrupts Danny, laughing. "Star Face is not dead at all – and King Size is applying the boot polish."

"Nothing so crude," smiles Stan, shaking his head. "But that is exactly what the stewards are thinking. Indeed, they spend a full hour rubbing down the horse's snout with soap, shampoo and paraffin oil. But the hair stays blacker than coal.

"So they decide to quarantine Blackout for a month, to check that the roots of the hair don't come up white. But four weeks later, everything grows out black. So they're forced to give Blackout the race – and the bookies have to hand over a hundred and fifty big notes to Sparkly."

"So the whole thing's on the level?" asks Danny Boy, puzzled.

"On the level, my eye," sniffs Stammering Stan. "King Size is after spending the entire previous year painting on the white star . . ."

*****

King Size's treachery in the Novices Cup is small beer, however, compared to what he does to Stan over the past few weeks.

"Tell you what," says Danny Boy to Stan, who is slumping like a dead man over his empty glass, "you can give me the whole story if you come with me on a lap around the Walls to get some air into you."

Stan, who knows he isn't getting another one anyway, nods okay and the pair head for the door.

*****

The Oscar Wilde Bar is situated just inside Ferryquay Gate, one of seven portals in the city's seventeenth-century Walls. And Danny Boy will frequently ask regulars to prove they are really fit for another drink by consigning them to a one-mile circuit of the ramparts. Though this, of course, is a particularly unpopular tour in the dark of winter, and when the Orangemen are making camp outside the Memorial Hall on the Twelfth.

Today, however, the only dangers are the heat and the hordes of tanned and long-legged Italian tourists upsetting the pale and dumpy native women.

Danny and Stan clamber up the steps onto the Walls opposite the Linenhall Bar and start making their way down the ramparts towards the Forum theatre.

"The whole thing is down to some troubles we're having at the *Derry Standard*," explains Stan, who now edits the paper. "King Size fancies himself as a bit of a media tycoon and wants to buy out my Uncle Hugo, who owns just over seventy per cent of the shares. Myself and my mother have the rest.

"Now, the *Standard*'s making a little money, and Hugo enjoys running it, so he has no interest in selling. But King Size has this foolish notion that owning a paper will buy him even more influence than his money. So he keeps pushing and pushing. And, to cut to the chase, he eventually goes and gets himself a silver bullet – and unless we can do something very quick, the *Derry Standard* is going to be the latest addition to the Barkley empire."

*****

There is nothing, says Stammering Stan, that can cure trapped gas quicker than a writ in the mail – except perhaps two writs. Which is precisely what lands on his desk at the *Standard* one morning about four weeks ago.

An envelope containing a writ is easy to spot, as it has a very distinct, long and narrow shape – quite unlike the A4 envelopes, which hold photos and sample packs, or the smaller A5 ones, which bear press releases and hate mail from crazies.

And this particular morning, there are two unhappy-looking envelopes in the postbag – both of them from Stan's old lawyer pal, Tommy Bowtie. And Tommy is taking great exception, on behalf of two different clients, about a piece written by Cheapshot Charlie Camberwell on the sale of some land on the riverbank.

Cheapshot, unfortunately, is back working for the *Standard* for the past three months, following an extended absence from journalism due to libel suits, incarceration and chronic drinking. The former *Londonderry Leader* columnist has the rep of being a rotten little scumbag, and Stan is quite happy to leave him tapping odds on the street. But Uncle Hugo is a kindly soul and brings him back in, despite the protests.

Cheapshot's work for the *Standard* up to now, however, is quite sound. He is still One Day At A Timing, pulling down ten-hour days and producing some first-class news stories.

So instead of marching down to Cheapshot's desk and fecking him out the door, Stan hokes out the article that Tommy Bowtie doesn't like and calls the old hack into his office.

"You say here," says Stan, reading the piece, "that our old friend Councilman Seamus 'the Saint' Timoney is selling his ten-acre timber yard along the Foyle."

"Yes," says Cheapshot, "the Saint tells me this himself on the record. He also says that King Size wants to buy it, but that a nucleo-chemical company is making a higher offer. Again on the record."

"The problem," replies Stan, "well the problem, according to Tommy Bowtie at least, is that the Saint denies ever talking to you at all. He also denies knowing anything about a nucleo-chemical company. In fact, he says here, in his letter on the Saint's behalf, that you are ruining his reputation by making these implications. And he wants an immediate apology and a small bagful of money in compensation."

"Chrissake, Stan," exclaims Cheapshot in a panic, "I have notes of the whole damn interview."

"The second letter," continues Stan, without looking up, "is also from Tommy Bowtie on behalf of his client Mr Bartholomew 'King Size' Barkley.

"King Size is very unhappy that his private negotiations with the Saint are now public. He says the price of the timber yard is liable to shoot up by hundreds of thousands of pounds because your story's going to kick-off a bidding war.

"And get this. King Size wants an apology – and for the *Derry Standard* to pay any difference between the original price he and the Saint are discussing and the cost of the final sale. This could be anything up to a million pounds."

"They're screwing us, the pair of them," yells Cheapshot.

"Yes, indeed they are," says Stan calmly. "Now, I know, Cheapshot, that you have a history with the Saint – as you do with many people. And I also can see why he might want to wreck you. But if it comes to court, it's his word against yours – and as you'll recall from your last experience before a judge, your word counts for squat.

"Lucky for us, the Saint is a mostly decent individual and may just back off. Particularly when he remembers that I still have the goods on him regarding another matter. No, the Saint will settle for an apology and a small donation to charity.

"Our real problem is King Size. I think I'm going to have to talk with Letemout Lou."

*****

Letemout Lou, as Stan's long-suffering intended, is an unpaid consultant to the *Standard* on legal matters. Though when they have to go to court, they generally use Tommy Bowtie as long as he's not the one suing them.

But when Stan arrives at Letemout's Derry office in Bishop Street courthouse, he is in for a rude surprise. His fiancée is already acting as an advisor to King Size on the building deal – and on a salaried basis.

"King Size is totally right to sue you," snaps Lou before Stan opens his mouth. "From what he tells me, he's getting that land for a song, until you go and blow the entire meeting. I'm only sorry I can't act for him in the lawsuit as well. I'd love nothing better than to get a seven-figure pay-out for a client."

"What if King Size doesn't buy the yard?" argues Stan. "I can hardly be expected to pay out then?"

"He's going to buy that land for certain," replies Letemout. "He wants it to build an outdoor market colonnade alongside a big memorial garden for his uncle. He's even in line for a couple of European grants. I'm sorry, Stan, but you have no option but to alert your insurance company and give King Size his cheque."

"Except for one thing," says Stan quietly.

"What's that?" inquires Lou.

"We're not insured," replies Stan. "It's too dear. After last year's hit, we just can't afford it."

"You can't afford not to be insured," counters Letemout with a very hard edge to her voice. "King Size could wind up taking the paper off you."

"You can't be serious," says Stan.

"Yes I am," declares Letemout. "You were just too damn mean to pay your policy, Stan, and sometimes these things catch up on you."

"I'm not mean," he protests.

"Stan, the only time you ever take me out any more is when you're getting in free to review the films," says Lou. "I'm the only girl I know, whose 'something borrowed' on her wedding day will be her dress and her going-away outfit."

"Sure you'll hardly be wearing those again," laughs Stan nervously. "And anyway, what about your engagement ring?"

"My engagement ring!" cries Lou. "There's bigger diamonds on a dentist's drill."

"In which case," sniffs Stan, "give it back to me – and I might just find someone who appreciates it."

"Some hope," yells Lou, "and I'm sure they'll also appreciate the blue mark the band leaves round your finger. Take your ring, you cheap little runt, and go to hell."

"At least it's warm there," retorts Stan, snatching the little ring from Lou and stomping out the door.

*****

Sure enough, the price of Timoney's timber yard goes shooting way up in value as bidders start coming in from all parts. And this puts the Saint in good enough form to drop his claim for damages against Stan.

King Size, meantime, isn't too worried at the additional interest in the land, as he knows he's getting it anyway – with the newspaper footing the bill. Though as the soon-to-be owner of the *Derry Standard*, King Size hopes the price doesn't get too high.

And it is the proposed takeover he raises with Letemout Lou when he calls to her office for advice on the sale.

"I'm afraid I can't help you there," says Lou, "as I still act for them in other areas – even if the editor is a tight little blowhard."

"Yes," grins King Size, "I see you're not wearing your ring. Is it true he needs it back to fix his kitchen tap?"

"At least it comes from honest money," sniffs Lou. "Way I hear it, King Size, you're so crooked, your own mother sleeps with a gun under her pillow in case you come after the fillings in her teeth."

"Don't believe all you hear," counters King Size. "But next time, I'll be sure and use more chloroform."

"I don't doubt it," laughs Lou. "But is it true you make your mother taste all your food first in case someone poisons it?"

"No," shoots back King Size. "That I categorically deny. It is in case *she* poisons it."

King Size, like his late uncle, has that peculiar charisma which comes from no sense of self-awareness and too much money. And he continues pouring it on.

"But if you let me take you out to dinner, Letemout," he says, "I promise I'll taste everything for you first. I'll even eat right out of your hand."

"I'm not so sure about that," answers Letemout. "You're a bit on the short-arse side for me. The girls in the office say you like to buy your underwear at Junior Next to give yourself a sense of achievement."

"Yes," grins King Size, "that part is true. But I also have an account at Toys 'R' Us – and sometimes they let me go into their adult section."

"Okay, okay," chuckles Lou, "one dinner so. But you have to bring your ID. I don't want you getting turned away at the door for being too young."

"Fair enough," retorts King Size. "Though I could always just tell them you're my mother . . ."

*****

Danny Boy sizes up the problem in front of him as outlined by Stan and sighs a big sad sigh.

The pair are about halfway round their lap, looking down at the outdoor market at Castle Gate. Below them, if you look carefully enough, a stallholder is selling Celtic T-shirts from a table, and pirate DVDs that are taped on the underside. He will also do you a deal on cheap cigarettes, which he stores in a binbag in a nearby drain. And, of course, ten cents on the dollar from each of these transactions is now going to King Size.

"Only one thing for it," says Danny, getting back to the matter at hand, "time to get your brother involved."

"Chiselling Phil doesn't want to be messed up in this nonsense," says Stan. "And besides, he's always bailing me out."

Chiselling Phil is without question the city's top private mediator. A former lawyer and kickboxing champion, what he can't negotiate by dint of good argument, he tends to solicit by more old-fashioned methods. Indeed, the incident with the chisel is one of the reasons he is asked to leave the legal profession in the first place.

These days, Phil has his own pub on Waterloo Street and acts as occasional advisor to both Harry the Hurler and Switchblade Vic. He's the man called on when Vic's mob want to march through Harry's front garden on the Twelfth of August – or when Harry's lot on the council vote to change Vic's home address into Irish. But mostly now, he just enjoys running his bar and pulling his elder brother the newspaper man out of occasional scrapes, particularly when Letemout Lou and Tommy Bowtie won't get their hands dirty.

But Stan doesn't want Phil to know how bad things are with Letemout, nor indeed that the paper is about to hit the wall, so he tells Danny Boy that he will figure another way out of the hole and asks him to drop the subject.

Thankfully, however, Danny Boy doesn't hear too well and by the time the pair finish their circuit and are back at the Oscar Wilde Bar, he is already of the firm mind to ring Phil. And when Stan goes home to cry into his pillow, this is exactly what Danny does.

*****

King Size Barkley has his new suite of offices on the penthouse floor of the Colmcille Heritage Centre, just three hundred yards away from the Oscar Wilde Bar.

It is a perfect location – exactly one hundred feet above the Butcher Street pavement, with big picture windows giving panoramic views of the city both inside and outside the Walls. And more importantly for King Size, there is also a parking yard round the back for his big purple Lexus.

And it is here in this office, just twenty-four hours after getting his phone call from Danny Boy, that Chiselling Phil goes to meet King Size to discuss the matter of his dispute with Stan. King Size isn't too keen on seeing Phil at first, but given that both security guards wave Phil right through and then refuse to answer the emergency buzzer, there is little he can do.

"You are going to drop your law suit against my idiot brother and his equally stupid uncle," says Phil, sitting down on the edge of King Size's desk.

"I don't think I am," mumbles King Size a little nervously.

Clearly King Size isn't hearing Phil properly, so he crosses the floor and with one giant hand lifts him out of his soft leather recliner, all the better to explain.

"I have in my pocket here," continues Phil, smiling at King Size, "a signed affidavit – that's a sworn statement to you – from Charles Camberwell – aka Cheapshot Charlie of the *Derry Standard*.

"In it he concedes that it is you, Bartholomew Barkley, aka King Size, who gives him all the wrong gen about Timoney's yard. He says you know that word is going to break about your talks with the Saint – so you make up this scheme to stick Stanley with the additional bill. You even make it look like the story's coming from the Saint so that your fingerprints are nowhere near it.

"Cheapshot further states that you give him twenty grand to publish this wrong information – which he knows will allow you to sue Stan for a packet and take the *Derry Standard* off my uncle. I also have here Cheapshot's bank balance showing the payment of twenty thousand pounds.

"And here is a bonus, King Size – I also have records of your own private bank account, that's your second account, showing that twenty grand is removed that self-same day."

"You're bluffing," yells King Size. "That's impossible."

"No," grins Phil, "nothing is impossible. Not when you are old school buddies with a High Court judge – who, by the way, says that even as a rebound boyfriend, you are a complete loss. Oh, and despite what you hear, size *is* very important."

"So what are you going to do – hand me over to the cops?" sneers King Size, knowing he's far too well in for that.

"No, actually," laughs Phil, "We're giving you to Harry and the Boys first, as it appears they are very sore at your plans to seize the paper from Stan without allowing them in on the deal.

"They also allege that you owe them seventy-five grand as a return on a wasted investment in last year's Novices Cup in Thurles. They're only after hearing that the whole thing is fixed for Blackout, while their bundle is on a whole different horse. And while personally I figure they might be trying it on, what can you do?

"Harry is also asking me to conduct an audit of your market stalls – as he is very impressed that you can afford to build a new emporium down at the river. Indeed, he is wondering why your contributions to him are no better than Sparkly's are five years ago – and thinks maybe it's time for a cost-of-living rise.

"Okay, okay," says King Size. "Tell Stan I'll leave his paper alone. But for Chrissake drop the audit."

"We're starting to understand one another," grins Phil. "One more thing, King Size. Cheapshot is going to return your twenty big notes to me, which I am putting in trust for my idiot brother in case that poor wretch Letemout Lou ever loses the run of herself again and they get married.

"Agreed?"

"Agreed," concedes King Size, who knows when he's done.

And that, as I gather, is the bones of the conversation between Chiselling Phil and King Size. Though what Phil omits to make public, but what the security man later discloses to Stan, is that the bulk of this chat takes place with Phil suspending King Size by one ankle out a picture window, exactly one hundred feet above the Butcher Street pavement.

*****

That night, Letemout Lou is working late and avoiding life in her chambers at Bishop Street courthouse when her clerk comes in looking worried.

"The police need an emergency order and need it right away," she tells Lou. "Sergeant Jack Gilmore wants a search warrant to trawl through the *Derry Standard*'s computers. They have photographs of a major brawl at the weekend and are refusing to hand them over.

"Stammering Stan is refusing to budge. They think he might be on the sauce. He's telling Jack to go to hell – on the grounds, quote unquote, that he doesn't work for the cops, the whole legal system's crooked, and judges are the worst of the whole damn lot."

"We'll see about that," snaps Letemout. "Show Sergeant Gilmore in, please."

So the clerk disappears and about ten seconds later a knock comes to the door.

"Come in," barks Letemout, ready for war.

But who is standing there, only Stammering Stan.

"Hey, Letemout," says Stan with a half-smile. "This guy I know – any chance you'll let him out of jail?"

"I don't know," replies Letemout slowly, "he has a pretty poor case by all accounts.

The last day he's in here, he walks off with some pretty valuable jewellery. Well, valuable to me, at least . . ."

"I think he'll be more than happy to return the items," answers Stan. "After all, he's missing a jewel of his own – and I have to say that this particular jewel is priceless to him."

"If he gets this jewel back," inquires Lou, "how's your client going to ensure he never loses it again?"

"Good question," grins Stan. "He promises to put it on a pedestal where it can rest for ever. Apart perhaps, for when he takes it off for a quick rubdown."

"Or maybe not such a quick rubdown . . ." suggests Lou, flicking two eyebrows.

"Oh, I assure you he'll be very thorough," laughs Stan. "He is also proposing to get himself established as the jewel's one true keeper as soon as possible. If, indeed, the jewel will still have him . . ."

"All very interesting," says Lou. "Maybe if your client would like to put his case to me, say, over dinner . . ."

"Certainly," smiles Stan. "I think you'll find his appeal hard to resist."

"That's the problem – I always do," says Lou, face starting to crack.

"So where do you want to eat?" asks Stan.

"How about McDonald's?" says Lou. "It's right up your client's budget."

"No way," protests Stan. "Cheapshot Charlie is back doling out the Happy Meals. And he'll only sneeze into our food."

"How about Italian – Danano's so?"

"Good idea. One thing, though, Lou."

"What's that, Stan?" says Letemout, taking his arm.

"I'm after paying my libel insurance and am all cleaned out – if you lend me a tenner we can have garlic bread . . ."

Praise for *Private Diary of a Suspended MLA*

"The best Northern Ireland political novel of the century"
Sunday Times

"If there is anything good that came out of the suspension of the Assembly, it has to be the idea which inspired Garbhan Downey to write *Private Diary of a Suspended MLA*"
Irish News

"A hilarious romp"
Sunday Tribune

"A gem . . . this new author is eagle-eyed and as sharp as a lance"
Belfast Telegraph

"Rude'n'racy . . . gleefully sends up the Northern political process"
Hot Press

"The first book about the Troubles which made me laugh . . . the dialogue is slick and the one-liners terrific"
Sunday World

"Poking fun at politicians has become a national sport but to write well on the subject requires talent. I thoroughly recommend *Private Diary of a Suspended MLA* as a must for all those interested in taking the mickey out of our politicians"
Derry Journal

"Viciously funny"
Eamonn McCann, *Londonderry Sentinel*

"An irreverent look at the crazy world of Northern politics. Genuinely amusing . . . with laugh-out-loud lines"
Ireland on Sunday

"By the time I had read the second paragraph I knew it was going to be a tour de force . . . I can imagine a time in the not-too-distant future when you will be nobody in Derry if you cannot talk knowledgeably about this book"
Sunday Journal

Private Diary of a Suspended MLA by Garbhan Downey is published by Guildhall Press under its Stormount Books imprint.